S0-AXI-701

BLACKMAIL EARTH

ALSO BY BILL EVANS FROM TOM DOHERTY ASSOCIATES

Category 7 (with Marianna Jameson)
Frozen Fire (with Marianna Jameson)
Dry Ice (with Marianna Jameson)

BLACKMAIL EARTH

BILL EVANS

TOR®

A TOM DOHERTY ASSOCIATES BOOK | NEW YORK

This is a work of fiction. All of the characters, organizations, and events portrayed in this novel are either products of the author's imagination or are used fictitiously.

BLACKMAIL EARTH

Copyright © 2012 by Bill Evans

All rights reserved.

A Tor Book
Published by Tom Doherty Associates, LLC
175 Fifth Avenue
New York, NY 10010

www.tor-forge.com

Tor® is a registered trademark of Tom Doherty Associates, LLC.

ISBN 978-0-7653-2783-3

First Edition: June 2012

Printed in the United States of America

0 9 8 7 6 5 4 3 2 1

To my children, Maggie, William, Julia, and Sarah.
You have brought me more joy and love than anything else in life!

—DAD

ACKNOWLEDGMENTS

I am a firm believer in work hard, keep your head down, stay above the fray, work as a team, and then good things will happen. I have a wonderful team to work with that has made me a great success. "Thank you" is just not enough for the outstanding work you have done to make *Blackmail Earth* come to life.

I want to first thank the wonderful people at Tor/Forge Books for having the confidence in me once again! You guys apparently love the punishment of producing a book with me!

Thanks to Tom Doherty, Linda Quinton, and Melissa Singer at Tor/Forge for believing in me and for your extremely hard work. Melissa, you are the best editor on the planet. Let's keep that our secret. Thanks to the world's greatest book agent and friend, Coleen O'Shea of the Allen O'Shea Literary Agency. Thanks for all the great guidance and white wine. Thanks to Mark Nykanen for your love of weather and geoengineering.

I want to thank my "extended family" at WABC-TV for their love and support all these years. Lori Stokes, Ken Rosato, Susan Greenstein, Eddie Arsis, Sandy Kenyon, Andy Savas, Vanessa Botelho, David Bloch, you make it a pleasure to go to work every weekday at 2:00 A.M.! Sorry for all those times I came in a little grumpy. You really find out who your friends are when you work the harsh hours that we do. Thanks so much for your love, kindness, and friendship.

Thanks to my wonderful wife, Dana. I know I'm often away on book tours, and I thank you for your advice and support! You are the greatest.

BLACKMAIL EARTH

PROLOGUE

There's no need for retreat but he steps back anyway. For a better view. A body lies spread-eagled on the floor: once a woman, now a bloodied, disfigured form. Red smears on rough planks.

The smells of salt and sweat and blood rise like the crackling madness of cicadas, millions of them beating their belly membranes in the surrounding fields and forests.

A taper burns in his hand, flickering light that dares the shadows to dance, the reckless darkness to come to life.

Carefully, with a true aim, steady hand, he dribbles wax on the five points of a pentacle that he's carved into her chest, then stares at the smaller stars that he's gouged into each of her perfect cheeks and her lightly lined brow.

Her empty eyes are open, but even in death—so ravenous and raw— they hold his gaze. Not for long. He will grant them special attention.

He retrieves two white votive candles from his pocket and lights them. The scents of anise, cinnamon, cloves, and rose hips fill his nostrils. Like cookies.

He doesn't touch her. Not directly. Not anymore. He tilts the taper till it spills hot wax on her fallen eyes, patiently sealing their glum surfaces. The rest of her face, though lit with an orange glow, proves no less opaque, its features drowned in a crimson flood, as if she's been flayed in a furious rage. Purely unidentifiable at a glance, and that's all he allows himself, for a calm has come; and his attention to the macabre details of murder is spent. For now.

He smiles. He didn't choose her. She chose herself. The laws of night coming alive in veils of sudden wonder.

He stares at the red length of her, then places the taper on her bloody belly, where babies might have nested. The candle falls over, sticks to her richly scored skin, and sputters in the silence. As she did. Quickly snuffed. As she was.

Straightening, he runs his index finger and thumb down the slippery sides of a beveled blade, his eyes on the drips that spatter the floor.

Like the rain that never comes.

CHAPTER 1

Jenna Withers could see more than fifty miles from the shotgun seat of *The Morning Show* helicopter. None of it looked pretty. The farms and forests north of New York City had turned to tinder. Mid-October was as hot as mid-August had been, the third scorching year in a row. Lakes and reservoirs were drying up and the rivers looked like they'd slunk away from their banks, thieves in the night.

It was just as dry—or drier—on the West Coast and across the Sun Belt. The hottest growing season on record. Much of the Midwest had been singed, too, with farmers in Iowa and Nebraska losing 80 percent of their corn crop. Food and fuel prices were rising as fast as the mercury.

Minutes ago Jenna; her producer, Nicole Parsons; and their crew had choppered out of New York City, the heart of a drought emergency that had been declared two months ago. That was the second highest level of official panic, right below drought disaster—conditions so dire that they were bluntly unthinkable in a metro area of twenty million people.

No one in the Big Apple had escaped the vicious grip of the Northeast drought. Water for parks, golf courses, and fountains? Fahgeddaboutit. Let 'em brown, where they hadn't burned. Car washes? You gotta be kiddin'. Pools? You're still jokin'.

Not even sprinklers to cool off the kiddies, and fire hydrants were locked up tighter than Tiffany's. Most of the water for everything but drinking now came from the Hudson River, where crews worked 24/7 to pump out tens of millions of gallons. The water level had dropped to historic lows. Sailors had to take extra steps to climb down from docks to their decks, but this was a minor inconvenience to a city in survival mode. A city that looked like it was on chemo.

Jenna, a meteorologist, didn't need the Ph.D. after her name to tally up the terror that could come from a cigarette tossed into the brittle brush down below, where a single spark could turn the region crisp as Southern California when the Santa Ana winds wicked all the life from the land, before burning the mountainsides black. Merely looking down at the devastation from the front passenger seat brought to mind the scores of scientific studies linking high temperatures and high-pressure systems to homicide and the full spectrum of urban violence.

The current condition was a classic summertime high. It had originated just east of Bermuda. For most of the past two months, it had driven the polar jet stream north, into Canada, and the subtropical jet stream south, below the Gulf of Mexico. That left the "Bermuda high," as it was aptly known, hunkered down like a big old bear at a beehive, far too content to move.

"You finding our reservoir? I'm getting nervous back here." Nicole's voice came through Jenna's headphones. In the seat right behind her, "Nicci" to those who knew her well, was the off-camera part of the weather team. She was as short and dark-haired as Jenna was tall and blond. They were the best of friends—real friends, not frenemies—which was good because they were virtually joined at the hip, "married" in the parlance of network television.

"I don't see it yet."

Nicci shot back, "We've got to land somewhere and go live in *nine* minutes."

The countdown, thought Jenna. *There's always a frickin' countdown.* Her stomach tightened as seconds flew by, softening only slightly when their pilot, Harry "Bird" Stephenson, pointed to a huge empty bowl in the earth that was their destination, a reservoir wrung dry of every last ounce, as if a plug had been pulled on the whole works, but not a drop had drained: All the water had burned into the sky.

Dust was rising now, engulfing the copter, swirling wildly as if they were in Iraq or Afghanistan. Bird flew by instruments—eyes locked on the panel, pudgy hands on the controls—and landed on the edge of the dry lake bed with the softest bump.

With the engine shut down and the AC off, the glass bubble heated up faster than a cheap lightbulb. Jenna started to sweat immediately. Her blouse and panty hose felt like warm, wet leaves plastered to her skin. Even the dust still eddying outside looked more appealing than sitting in this sauna. But the instant she reached for the door, Bird took her arm.

"I don't want that goddamn grit getting in here. It's hell on the instruments. Give it a sec to settle down."

"Bird," Nicci said in her most urgent voice, "we've got about five minutes to get out, get set up, and get on the air. *Five minutes,* Bird. Let's go."

Nicci shouldered open her door, rousing Andi, the camerawoman, from her open-eyed torpor. Andi cradled the high-definition digital camera in her arms as she started to climb out the left side of the chopper.

Jenna sucked in one more breath before heading into the chest-choking air. Ducking, she hustled out from under the still whirling rotors, and spotted a man and his border collie in the drifting dust. Not a happy pair. The guy stood stiffly, rifle by his side. That made Jenna uneasy. She found little relief in glancing at Bowser. The dog was poised next to his master, staring at Jenna from a pair of unblinking blue marbles. Eerie freakin' eyes. *Doesn't the dust get in them?* Jenna's own eyes were closed to slits.

Squinting, she looked from beast to man. They looked like attitude squared, an opinion only confirmed when he roared, "You didn't even see us, did you?"

"I'm not the pilot," she said calmly, hoping to soothe him. He did have that rifle. *How* did *we manage to miss them?* she thought.

"You almost killed us."

"I'm really sorry."

"Everywhere we ran, that helicopter kept coming at us, and then we couldn't see a damn thing with all the dust. Four miles of open reservoir, and you just about planted that thing right on our heads. How stupid is that?"

Jenna glanced at Bird, still sitting at the controls, staring straight ahead. Leaving her to own up.

"Pretty damn stupid," Jenna agreed. "Look, really, I'm sorry. I'm Jenna Withers. I do weather for *The Morning Show*."

"I know who you are."

Now she noticed a pistol hung from his hip.

"Law enforcement?" she asked softly. Hoping. She'd grown up with guns—her dear departed father had been a hunter and marksman all his life—but years of city living had made her more wary of firearms.

But you're not in *the city,* she told herself.

Before he could answer, Nicci snapped, "Weather girl"—only she could get away with that moniker—"three minutes. *Three.* Ready?"

Jenna nodded, still hoping that the gunslinger was a cop because presumably they possessed a strong measure of self-control with their weapons. On the other hand, there had to be some really nasty FAA regulations about almost landing a chopper on an officer and his four-legged friend.

"Dairy farmer," she heard him say in the next breath.

"Dairy farmer," she repeated. That sounded friendly enough: *Elsie the cow, right?* Reassuring. So was the lowered volume of his voice. Which was good because she needed to focus on the live update, now less than ninety seconds away. She pulled weather data up on her laptop screen, then checked temperatures for the region; this was a story on the Northeast drought, so she didn't need to worry about the entire country on this go-round.

Pulling a tissue from her pocket, Jenna patted her face; sweat and dust stained the tissue when she was done. Or was that tan stuff makeup? She'd applied it during the flight, after all. Opening her purse, she drew out a small mirror in a sleek black leather case that looked like a notebook, and gazed at her face. The little case was a discreet way to check her appearance without reinforcing the narcissistic TV talent stereotype. The headphones had messed with her hair, but she straightened and fluffed it, then noticed that her eyes were red from the dust. Murine emergency.

Andi peered through her viewfinder, then snapped together a wireless microphone and clipped it to the inside of Jenna's blouse. The camerawoman kept eyeing the farmer and his border collie. Jenna understood the concern: Loonies were known to mess with live shots in the city. *But you're not in the city,* she reminded herself a second time. And the dairyman didn't look like a loony. Actually, he looked kind of handsome, but she had to put aside his presence and turn her thoughts to the work at hand, though in truth she figured that she could do an update in her sleep. And given the schedule of a meteorologist on *The Morning Show*—up at 2:00 A.M., on at 7:00 A.M.—she probably already had on numerous occasions.

Besides, what she would say would play second fiddle to the split screen that the show planned to use as her backdrop: empty, dusty reservoir cheek by jowl with old footage of the lake brimming with cool water. The sweet "then," the sour—and *scary*—"now."

Cued, Jenna chattered to the camera, alternately smiling and turning serious as she boiled down the update to "hot and dry," the daily mantra since a high-pressure system had settled over the region five weeks earlier. The stagnant weather had shown no more inclination to move on than a two-ton boulder plopped on a trail.

She engaged in snappy closing patter with Andrea Hanson, *The Morning Show*'s visibly pregnant host, a darling of viewers and a mainstay of morning television for the past five years.

The dairy farmer and his furry pal watched Jenna sign off. She felt a familiar sense of relief when the camera went dark, then noticed that Andi was back to keeping a wary eye on the guy with the guns.

"Is the drought making dairy farming tougher?" she asked in her most empathetic "the weather really sucks" voice, hoping to charm away the tension. She unclipped the mike and handed it to Andi, who pocketed it before heading back to the helicopter. Nicci had already boarded.

"We don't need a drought to make dairying tougher, but the cows are okay. They're just moving a little slower."

"They free range?"

"That's chickens around here. Only thing free range these days are the roaches. They love the heat. Ever been to Puerto Rico? Cockroaches big as your fist. They're getting that way around here."

Who did he remind her of? Somebody appealing. Tall as she was, wiry, with smooth skin and sharp features. "What's your name?"

"Dafoe. Dafoe Tillian."

"Good to meet you, Dafoe." He shook her hand, and she knew that she had, indeed, charmed him, but try as she might, she could not place his face.

The rotors whirled faster. Jenna climbed aboard and belted herself in. Dafoe hurried away from the dust storm whipping up from the lake bed, then turned around so quickly that even through a hurricane of dust and heat he caught her staring at his retreat. She wanted to look down, peel her eyes from his; but her body wouldn't obey, and a smile betrayed her even more.

As Bird flew them over the barren bowl, Jenna felt herself sink back to earth: *He's a farmer, for chrissakes. You left that life.*

She closed her eyes, catnapping till Nicci asked her to join a call to *The Morning Show*'s executive producer, Marv Balen, or "the twit," as the two women called him in private. "He texted us a few seconds ago."

Up ahead, the city's skyline poked through the low-lying smog like quills through a dirty old quilt. Jenna turned on her headset.

"We're here, Marv," Nicci said. "Go ahead."

"We had three murders in the Bronx last night. Cops found the victims about an hour ago. They think they've got the shooter. Word is he snapped and started shooting his poker buddies when the air conditioner went on the fritz. So that makes three more heat-related homicides this week."

"So you want us to do the story?" Jenna said, hope as irrepressible as ever.

"Noooo. One of our correspondents will. But don't get ahead of me. There's more of the gore out on the West Coast. Fresno's had a week of one-hundred-ten-degree weather . . ."

Like we need you to tell us that.

". . . and last night *they* had their fourth murder during that heat wave. So you're going to be our resident expert on how weather affects behavior, Jenna."

"It's not really my area of expertise, Marv, but—"

"Yeah, I know," he interrupted, "but you can say that heat and high pressure systems are linked to higher murder rates."

The 101s of weather, Jenna thought.

"It's a lot cheaper than flying a crew up to MIT to get some professor to spew," Marv went on, "and you're an author. You can spout off."

He was referring, in his typically ham-handed way, to a book Jenna had published seven years ago on geoengineering—how technology could be used to combat climate change. There had been little interest back then, but the publisher had reissued her volume three months ago to great interest in both the academic and mainstream press.

"So talk about heat and murder, and don't go throwing in a lot of other stuff. Don't complicate it. And Nicci, make sure she doesn't go yammering on about global fucking warming. We're keeping it supertight."

All stories had to be supertight these days: reports, live shots, updates, even the banter with Andrea Hanson. It was a presidential election year, and the news hole for everything but polls, politicians, and pundits had shrunk faster than a Greenland glacier.

Minutes after they'd landed in Manhattan and raced back to the Weather Command Center, a crew hurried over from the Northeast Bureau. The correspondent was an up-and-comer who put together reports for *The Morning Show* as well as the evening news. He was all smiles and good cheer, which Jenna appreciated. Life was too short for sneakiness and sarcasm—for people like Marv, in other words.

A cameraman set up quickly, positioning Jenna in front of *The Morning Show* logo. Product placement. As she finished answering the correspondent's question about heat and homicide, Jenna spotted Cassie Carter, the Weather Command Center's frizzy-haired assistant, waving frantically for her attention. "It's the White House," Cassie said breathlessly.

"The White House?" Jenna asked. Nicci looked up from her laptop. "Is this a joke?" Jenna asked her. "Did you put Cassie up to this?"

"No, I didn't."

And she hadn't, Jenna learned an instant later when she heard "Please hold for Ralph Ebbing." The White House chief of staff. In seconds he came on the line.

"Good morning, Ms. Withers."

"Good morning." Her voice sounded as bright as one of her weather maps. Still, she shot Nicci a final questioning look. Nicci gave an immediate shake of her head, but even without that, Jenna had heard Ebbing on the Sunday morning talk shows often enough to know that the voice on the phone really did belong to him.

"I'm sure you're busy," he said, "so I'll get right to the point: We'd like you to serve on the Presidential Task Force on Climate Change."

"I'm very honored. Very. But I'll have to check to see whether that's permitted. The network has rules about this. As you probably know," she hurried to add. Her heart was pounding.

"Absolutely. But I want you to know that we'd really like you to serve."

Serve? The word had such an honorable ring to it. Jenna thought about asking about per diem costs and transportation, but decided those pesky questions were best left to one of Ebbing's underlings—and after she made sure that the network had no objections to her . . . serving. "I should be able to get back to you in a day or two," she said.

"We'd appreciate that greatly. We believe your expertise could be helpful to our nation," Ebbing said. "The vice president will chair the task force, and if you could communicate with his chief of staff, that would be best." Ebbing gave her a phone number for his counterpart.

"On behalf of the president, I want to thank you for considering this appointment, Ms. Withers. I hope you'll serve."

"Thank you. And I will if I may. I'll let the vice president's people know."

And then the conversation was over. Jenna kept the phone to her ear after Ebbing hung up, savoring the request in silence for a few seconds because she was all but certain that as a member of the news division, she would be barred from taking any appointment to a governmental body. Those were the network's rules.

After a breath, she cradled the receiver and passed the bulletin to Nicci and Cassie.

"Wow," Cassie said. "Big, big wow."

"The suits are never going to let me take it," Jenna said to both women, shaking her head. "They don't want us doing that kind of stuff."

"Maybe you're right," Nicci said, "but you're a meteorologist, and that's a little different."

"I doubt they'll see it that way." Jenna shrugged. But she could take solace, scant as it was, that someone had seen her as more than the morning weather bimbo. Not many years ago, the joke in male-dominated newsrooms was that a woman's sole qualification for a weather job was whether her breasts reached from New York to Kansas when she stood next to the map.

The phones started ringing and Nicci went to work. Cassie took a message, hung up, and handed it to Jenna. "Just a guy who wanted to talk to you—"

Another one. It seemed to Jenna that half a dozen guys called after every show, most of them vowing to make her happy. Their means for accomplishing this were notably unmentionable.

"He said you almost landed on him this morning," Cassie finished.

"Really?" A lilt colored her voice. "What did he want?"

"He said just to talk." Cassie rolled her eyes.

Jenna stared at the name: Dafoe Tillian. Before she could do more than remember his rugged, pleasing appearance, Nicci cupped the receiver on her phone and said, "It's Rafan on line two."

"Rafan?" Jenna sat up. He was an old boyfriend, one of the few real loves of her life. "Where is he?"

"The Maldives, I guess. He says it's pretty important."

Jenna got on the line right away.

"I saw you on *The Morning Show*," Rafan said in his accented English. "You do weather now."

Had it been that long since they'd spoken? She'd been doing the show for three years. She told him this gently, as if she might break his heart all over again. They used to talk all the time: in bed, first thing in the morning, at the beach, the market—

"Here, the weather gets hotter. The islands, they will disappear."

"I know, Rafan. It's so sad." She'd been aware of the threat to his country's archipelago of twelve hundred islands since she'd started on her doctoral work ten years ago. The Maldives had been her home for several months of research. She'd look out and see nothing but islands and Indian Ocean all the way to the horizon. Now the Maldives was destined to become the first country to fall victim to global warming. Seas rising much faster than the U.N.'s predictions had already claimed coastline, and now had started claiming thatched houses. *To see your homeland washing away must be heartbreaking,* she thought.

In recent years, the Maldivian president and his ministers had strapped on scuba gear for an annual underwater cabinet meeting to dramatize the plight faced by his country's three hundred thousand people. To no avail. Most Americans, Jenna had found, still hadn't heard of the Islamic nation, much less of its highly endangered status.

She listened closely to her old lover, but knew that if he was pitching a climate story, he'd picked the wrong person. Especially in a political year. But no, he was pushing a story that *always* had traction.

"Muslims here, they are angry. It's not like before. Remember? We would go to parties, have a good time. Here, it's changing, Jenna. It's changing very fast. People say the West, your country, is doing this to us. They say the decadence is killing us. Come see for yourself. I think they will strike back. Soon."

"What do you mean, 'strike back'? How?"

"How do you think? How do you think?"

Jenna looked out her window and saw another warm summer day not so many years ago.

"You should come. I can show you." Rafan said good-bye.

She walked to the window and looked as far as she could see to the right. She didn't do this often. It hurt too much. But she let herself stare at the smoggy sky where the Twin Towers once stood.

How do you think? How do you think?

CHAPTER 2

I am now Minister of Dirt.

Rafan was actually a civil engineer in the Maldivian Ministry of Home Affairs and Environment, but at the moment he couldn't get that strange title—*Minister of Dirt*—out of his head.

With that absurd burden, he stepped into the throng hurrying down the narrow winding street of the Maldivian capital of Malé, where government officials huddled behind white walls and hatched crazy plans to pile dirt on an island to try to save it from the hungry sea.

That's if Rafan could find dirt. Millions of cubic meters of it. Not easy in the middle of the Indian Ocean. And these days that wasn't the only absurd plan afloat (though perhaps that was the wrong word for the circumstances). A real government minister—of development—had proposed building a towering skyscraper to house his country's people. Kind of a modern-day castle with the whole ocean as a moat. Rafan whistled at the madness. *Cuckoo.*

A crazy country. Crazy. The president was even more ambitious, if equally deluded: He was looking for an entirely new land where he could move everyone, as if a Xanadu were waiting just for them—the cursed Maldivians. And last night Rafan had heard a rumor that some of his government colleagues were already feeling out Sri Lanka, India, and China to see if they wanted to buy the country's fishing rights. Testing the waters, so to speak. Or, perhaps more to the point, cashing in while they could. Maybe he should, too. Buy land in Asia or Australia and move, like other Maldivians were doing. Every man for himself on a sinking ship.

But Rafan would never abandon his country, so he'd hunt for barges, and try to pile dirt on an island faster than the waves could wash it away. Sisyphus in the age of global warming. Truth be known, even the gossip about selling fishing rights was easier to bear than other rumors that he'd heard, rumors that teemed with memories of smoke and death and screams.

In his white ball cap and dark glasses, white pants and white shirt, Rafan looked too impeccable to be Minister of Dirt. He looked better suited, in the most literal sense, to working behind a desk while a Casablanca fan stirred the sweet tropical air above his salt-and-pepper pate. He was distinguished looking, in the manner of some government officials schooled abroad, and a good head taller than most of his countrymen, who jostled one another in the tight confines of the narrow street.

He maneuvered toward an alley as a muezzin's call to prayer—adhan—quickened the crowd's pace. Five times a day the call rose from loudspeakers to remind the faithful of their Islamic beliefs and obligations. It reminded Rafan how much his country had changed in the past decade.

People peeled away to go to mosque, leaving men like him with the uneasy eyes of those who don't want to be seen ignoring the call. Ten years ago there had been no muezzin and no need to worry about snubbing the faith. Now, more and more Maldivians prayed with the fervor of men and women facing the loss of their homeland, a diaspora like the Jews and Palestinians and so many others had known.

The fever of faith had spread across the archipelago, along with anger hot as cook stones. Even the president and his ministers had made a show of praying underwater at their annual meeting in masks and flippers and oxygen tanks, all of them exhaling perfect bubbles of carbon dioxide and uttering *"Allah akbar"* before they signed hopeless proclamations with waterproof pens. But if God is so great, why do the pandanus trees bow to the sea, their roots eaten by salt, trunks by waves, until they lie facedown, limbs flattened and extended like worshippers heeding the muezzin? If God's so great, why does He let the lesser deity Neptune swallow us alive?

When Jenna had been with him, Rafan might have shared these inflammatory thoughts with her and his other friends. Not anymore. Better to let the believers loudly implore the heavens while he quietly moved the earth, taking dirt from one island to another. Robbing Peter to pay Paul. *That's what Jenna used to say. We could make that the official slogan of the Maldives—if we weren't Muslim. We rob Peter to pay Paul all the time.* Rafan thought immediately of the country's biggest money-maker: the half-million vacationers lured to the Maldives every year by the Ministry of Tourism. Europeans, Asians, and North and South Americans flew thousands of miles to stay in isolated island resorts; each traveler churned out as much greenhouse gas in an average ten-hour flight as a Maldivian produced in a month. But Rafan's country needed money, so it welcomed the wealth of the developed world, and robbed the future—and the world's children—while wearing the smiley face of tourism.

The aroma of curried tuna drew Rafan's eye to a food cart by the entrance to the alley. He hadn't eaten in hours, though he hadn't thought about food till now. It had been like that when he'd fallen in love with Jenna at the start of the new century. He'd walked hand-in-hand with her on this very street on New Year's Eve 1999; and as the clock struck twelve he pulled her close and kissed her for the first time, hungry only for her, his other appetites as still as the concrete beneath his feet.

Now he relaxed with his meal and leaned against a building, taking a bite of tuna. He was thinking of how to arrange a rendezvous with Senada when a bomb exploded a hundred and fifty feet away. He looked up, stunned by a horrifying ball of flame as wide as the street. An oily cloud rose to the sky.

He dropped his plate and ran toward the screams, dodging survivors reeling past him and glimpsing bodies lying in the ruins of a storefront. He rushed closer, and through the pall saw men, women, and children riddled with nails, scrap metal, and razor-sharp coral chips, their limbs twisted, charred, and melted like the bicycles incinerated by the blast. His eyes raced over the dead and injured, three of them trying to crawl away; he shouted in anguish at the sight of Basheera. She lay in a crater, smoke rising around her where minutes ago the muezzin's call had turned Rafan's thoughts to questions of devotion and diaspora.

His sister reached a hand to him, and he ran to her knowing with his first panicky step that a second bomb might await the rescuers.

Khulood walked a sandy path that separated her thatched home from a seawall on the small island of Dhiggaru. The concrete chunks and coconut shells rose as high as her chest, but could hold back only the refuse the sea tossed to shore, not the warm salty water that spilled through the wall. A week ago the ocean touched her house for the first time, soaking the floorboards by the front door. The wood stayed damp for a full day, and a stubborn stain remained even now, as if the future had cast an inescapable spell.

Khulood had lived on Dhiggaru all her life, as her ancestors had. Her skin was as brown as the voyagers who'd migrated to the Maldives: Ethiopians, Arabs, Indians—people of color and sweat and the sea. But she had traveled only to Malé. Her son, Adnan, had sailed the world and returned with pictures of wondrous places. He worked on ships bigger than many of the islands she could see from her house. But he hadn't left Dhiggaru for five months. The world, he'd said, was slowing down and didn't need so much oil. Maybe next year.

She spied him at prayer, eyes filled with Mecca. So much more devout than she.

He turned when he heard her steps, smiled, and rolled up his prayer rug and tucked it under his arm. He'd begun to pray earlier this year when Parvez, his closest friend since childhood, had returned from four years of foreign study of Islam to become a cleric.

Parvez had chided her to pray like her son, but Khulood had declined. She did wear a headscarf, not as a concession but to keep the sun off her scalp.

She and Adnan spoke Dhivehi to each other, although her son's English had surprised her. Parvez had sent him English language CDs and urged him to study them. No one but Parvez and her son spoke English on the island.

"I will cook fish and cassava," she said to Adnan.

He walked into the house with her and put away his prayer rug. "I'm not hungry, Mother. You eat. I must see Parvez."

He spoke his friend's name shyly, then kissed her cheek. She watched him walk away down the path, which narrowed to a single set of footprints when it passed through a palm grove. Out there, in the gathering darkness, Parvez had made his home.

Rafan cupped the back of Basheera's head, easing it inches from the smoking earth. Acrid fumes rose all around them, as if hell itself had exploded. Basheera's eyes were stark with shock. Blood poured from her mouth.

"They're coming," he said to her. *Doctors? Or the ones with more bombs?* he wondered.

He looked around frantically for help, nose burning from the smoke. Waves of heat drifted over his back, and he turned to a flaming cavern that had been a tea shop. The dead and dying spilled at odd angles all around him, bodies lifted by force and dropped with fury. An old woman struggled to stand. A much younger man with sopping red pants tried to help her, agony in his eyes. They staggered away slowly, clutching each other.

Another bomb. Rafan's constant fear. He slid his arms under Basheera's back and legs and climbed to his feet. She was the last of his family, a young woman so slight that he couldn't feel her weight through his waves of terror. He held her so close that her heart beat against his chest; he remembered her as a curly-haired toddler whom he carried to bed, and as a pretty young girl who splashed in the surf.

Rafan ran toward the hospital, spotting two physicians in white jackets racing to the bombing. "Help her," he screamed, holding Basheera higher, like an offering.

The woman doctor stopped and opened Basheera's eyes; Rafan hadn't noticed that they'd closed. She checked his sister's pulse. The heart that Rafan had felt seconds ago had failed.

"No," he pleaded. He shook his head, and his refusal came loudly and without relief.

The doctor held his face in her warm hands and whispered, *"Ma-aafu kurey."* I'm sorry. An instant later a second bomb tore apart everyone near the original explosion, and claimed the lives of those who'd tried to rescue the dying, including the doctor's colleague.

Rafan turned slowly, aware now of Basheera's enduring weight. His tears fell to her burned and sodden dress, and he cursed the earth and all it held sacred. Then he looked up, shaken by the sight of the doctor, whose life had been spared by his sister's death, running fearlessly into a curtain of black smoke.

Tenderly, as if he could bruise her still, Rafan laid Basheera on the ground. *"Ma-aafu kurey,"* he cried to her before he, too, ran into the blackness.

Adnan lowered his gaze from Parvez. The cleric stared at him from across his prayer rug in the single room of his small house. Then Parvez shifted forward, speaking of an attack by Islamists in Malé. Twelve people killed. Three children.

"This is cruel," Parvez said. "The radio said they used an IED on our own people. Muhammad, peace and blessings of Allah be upon him, said this is always wrong."

"Is that what they taught you at school?" Adnan asked.

The cleric nodded without taking his eyes from Adnan, whose skin felt frighteningly alive in the presence of a man so steeped in the highest realms of Islamic thought. And to think Parvez had been his closest childhood friend. That seemed like another life, Parvez another person.

"We must not shed the blood of our own, unless it is our supreme sacrifice." Parvez leaned closer in the dusky light. "Do you know what I mean?"

Adnan answered with a nod. Parvez rose, his robes swaying. Adnan followed him to a bamboo wardrobe. The cleric opened both doors. Adnan stared at the single item draped on a hanger. Parvez turned it so Adnan could view all of the vest.

"It can end the world as we know it."

Adnan looked at the heavily stitched pockets—so many of them, and each so empty. Like him. Barely breath in his lungs. It stunned him to know that he had so little of Parvez's faith, when he wanted to be as true to Islam as his friend.

Parvez placed his hand on Adnan's shoulder and drew him closer. They stood side by side. "The man who wears this will know Allah's love. It can end the world as we know it," he repeated.

"How?"

Parvez whispered his answer, shivery words that spoke of flame.

CHAPTER 3

Jenna boarded a train at Penn Station, joining an early Friday afternoon crush of commuters eager to flee the compressing heat and burgeoning violence of New York City. Two more murders had made the news in the past forty-eight hours, including the savage knifing of a twenty-two-year-old woman whose terrifying screams had been heard by hundreds of West Side residents. Photos of her wholesome, hopeful face were still splashed across the Web, TV, and newspapers; and a sad shrine of flowers, pictures, handwritten notes, and teddy bears now rose inches from the doorstep where she'd been slain.

The summer and fall were living up to the macabre moniker the *Daily News* had headlined back in July, SUMMER OF SAM 2, in recognition of the grisly parallels to the searing months of 1977 when David Berkowitz went berserk and every imaginable strain of violence escaped the city's soul like the foul steamy funk that slipped out of the sewers and tunnels lurking beneath the broiling blacktop of the Big Apple. As Jenna had said in an interview with the up-and-coming correspondent from the Northeast Bureau only two days ago, "Everybody's got to take a deep breath and try to stay calm because heat and horror sometimes go together."

Simple as sunshine and dark as death, she reminded herself as she made her way to the club car.

Not that the dairy country she was heading to was any paradise: crops dying, water rationing, ugly struggles over state and federal disaster aid. Upstate New York looked as crispy as California's Central Valley, which looked as parched as Illinois, Iowa, Alabama, and Georgia. Drought, distress, and despair across the country. The Four Horsemen of the Apocalypse saddling up.

At least it was cool on the train. She lucked out with a stool at the bar, and ordered white wine. She needed a cold drink, preferably cold enough for condensation. Few things felt better in the swelter than pressing chilly dampness to her brow, even if she were passing through Hades—her eyes alighted on the blighted South Bronx—in air-conditioned comfort.

She'd be riding plenty of trains over the next few days. This afternoon, she was off to meet Dafoe—and stay at a B&B after politely declining his offer of a spare bedroom. They'd talked twice on the phone in the past two days, and she'd sensed very quickly that she wanted to see him under more agreeable circumstances. Then, on Sunday, she would return to Penn Station, where she'd promptly board another train to Washington.

The network would have paid for a flight to the capital but the carbon footprint of train travel was a fraction of flying the same distance. And the hassles of struggling through airports and cramming herself into a shuttle bus made a train trip seem like a vacation. She would have to do some cramming on the train—as in study hard for the first meeting of the Presidential Task Force on Climate Change. She had received word just that morning that the network had no objection to her taking the appointment, further underscoring her nonstatus in the news division. But she'd taken great delight in calling Vice President Andrew Percy's office to say that she'd be coming aboard. Percy himself got on the phone to tell her how much he appreciated her willingness to serve. There was that word again—"serve"—that made her feel so good about joining the task force.

In her heart of hearts, Jenna knew she wasn't a dispassionate ob-server of the Earth's steady demise, but an advocate of responsible envi-ronmental policies. And, in all honesty, she was excited to take an appointment from President Reynolds, who looked likely to be around long enough for the task force to have some effect: He'd increased his lead to a five-point margin in the latest *New York Times*/CBS News poll, a boost fueled by the racy revelation that his opponent, Roger Lilton, had indulged in an affair in graduate school with a woman who was now a leader of the nation's Pagan community.

Give the guy a break, had been Jenna's initial reaction. *It was forty years ago.* But even Jenna had become fascinated by the growing scan-dal. Not by the sex, though from published accounts it was boldly outré, even by the loose standards of that rabidly libidinal era, but by the woman's alleged influence on Lilton in the here and now. If he wasn't careful, his old paramour, a strikingly tall, self-described witch who went by the name GreenSpirit, would become the Jeremiah Wright of his campaign.

Even after the scandal broke, Jenna had been leaning toward Lil-ton, but then he called the task force "a dog-and-pony show by a presi-dent who's shown a callous disregard for the environment."

President Reynolds, about to board a helicopter for Camp David, was asked about the dog-and-pony comment. He responded, "Is that what the candidate said? Aren't those the words that his old girlfriend used just last week?"

Which, to the Lilton campaign's profound embarrassment, was true.

President Reynolds had continued: "At least we know the name of somebody in his kitchen cabinet." Then the president offered his hand-in-the-cookie-jar smile, waved, and climbed aboard.

A low blow, but Lilton had it coming, Jenna thought. *Don't his people vet what he says?* To further hammer the "candidate as puppet" charge, the president's supporters immediately debuted a YouTube video of Lilton and GreenSpirit, their statements roughly synced so that the audio track echoed "dog-and-pony show" as the words WHO'S THE LEADER HERE? crawled across the bottom of the screen.

One point three million views . . . and counting. Washington did love a wild and woolly sex scandal, and this one looked to have legs. *Four of them,* Jenna quipped to herself.

She waved off the bartender's offer of more wine, wanting her wits about her when she saw Dafoe. *She* would have been scandalized if, in the wake of that run-in at the reservoir, anyone, especially Nicci, had suggested that Jenna would have ended up accepting a date from the armed and agitated stranger. On his turf, no less.

Yet, she had returned his call, on the theory—or so she had assured herself—that a few conciliatory words might save the network from a lawsuit and herself from endless depositions. *Won't take more than a minute or two.* The call had turned into a two-and-a-half-hour conversation. What struck her most was the fluid ease of their give-and-take and the genuine interest that he'd shown in her, as opposed to the paint-by-number questions that so many guys felt obliged to ask before indulging in their favorite subject: themselves.

So it all came out: Jenna's family-farm childhood in Vermont, which had included a Guernsey cow called Hoppy; two acres of vegetable garden; chickens; turkeys; rabbits; and two pigs, whose names and shapes changed, but whose number remained constant.

She'd talked so much about herself that she'd experienced a weird role reversal when she finally thought to offer her own queries.

Toward the end of the call, Dafoe revealed that he'd spent his boyhood summers on his grandparents' farm in southern Illinois, and his early adulthood as a notorious computer hacker. Right then she remembered whom he looked like: Hugh Jackman in *Australia,* minus the star's facial scruff.

Perhaps the memory of Jackman's lean, alluring face prompted her to say yes, with nary a pause, when Dafoe asked if she'd like to go out. Almost as swiftly, he began to explain why it was tough for him to get down to the city this time of year. He needn't have, not to a woman who'd grown up with the incessant demands of roots and leaves and livestock.

"So I'll come up there," she'd said, speaking quickly again.

Now she looked at the passing terrain—*his* turf, indeed—and wondered if she'd been a little rash. The answer came with the force of a heat wave: *You sure were. What do you really know about him? Not much. No, not true: You know that he carries a frickin' rifle and pistol when he goes for a hike. And your best friend had huge misgivings.* "Are you crazy?" Nicci had blurted out. But her producer didn't trust men on principle. *Hey, you Googled him, right?* Jenna insisted to herself. *And he's the president of the Organic Dairymen's Association. That sounds reasonable, so chill.*

She glanced at her watch. If the train was on time, he'd be meeting her at the station in less than five minutes.

Jenna took out her black leather case, the one that resembled a notebook, and used the small mirror to carefully reapply her lipstick; her wineglass bore mute testimony to the need. *If you're going to see this through, by God, see it through.*

She wore little makeup away from the set of *The Morning Show,* and had kept her clothes to weekend getaway casual: jeans, powder blue top, and cream-colored ostrich leather cowboy boots. Modest. Nothing flashy. She'd had her more elegant outfits shipped to the hotel in Washington where she'd be staying.

But Jenna knew she would have looked striking in rags. With her white-blond hair and blue-eyed Icelandic heritage, she'd come up a winner at the genetic roulette wheel. And she was grateful. She had no illusions about the reason she'd succeeded so quickly in television, and it wasn't spelled "P-h-D." But she wouldn't have minded an end to those phone calls from male viewers—*With the possible exception of present company,* she thought as the train slowed and she spied Dafoe on the waiting platform.

Please don't let him be crazy.

He looked more relaxed than he had on their first encounter. A good sign. Then again, she realized with a start, Hannibal the Cannibal at his hungriest would have appeared more relaxed than Dafoe Tillian in those first few moments after the chopper almost hit him. Still, she was looking for normalcy and was reassured: clean khaki cargo pants, crisp white tee, sunglasses that weren't duct-taped together. Handsome enough that if she'd seen him in fine threads in the city, she would have been more inclined to wonder if he was gay than whether he was a horror. Not that he'd said anything that had registered on her gaydar, just that he was, in fact, good-looking, clean, and shaved. *And let's face it,* she told herself, *the benchmark for straight guys isn't real high these days. Clean and shaved? Come on.*

Jenna was grateful for her gay friends, including Nicci, but she knew without question that she wanted a husband and children. Now, at thirty-seven, she'd become focused on this. Not panicked about her prospects, but clear of mind and motive.

She shut off her BlackBerry before she stepped from the train. No calls this weekend; Nicci could handle anything that came up. Dafoe took her hand, letting go after they hugged gently. Not *too* awkward, as such things went. Then he took her bag. He did not attempt further contact while they made their way to his dusty old pickup, which sat right by the station, completely charming in its lack of pretense.

"What's your preference?" he asked once he closed the door for her, resting his arms on the open window. "I can take you to the B&B, or I could take you to my farm, give you an icy beer, and show you around."

Decisions, decisions. If she went with him now, they'd have daylight for their first hours together.

"I'm not one to turn down a cold beer on a hot day."

"You're a wise woman," he shouted as he rounded the front of the truck, moving with ease. *Like an athlete,* she thought.

He drove with the same confidence; and despite the drought, the countryside looked pretty. Dafoe's twenty-two acres could have been a photo in *Sunset* magazine, the golden hues of the pastures so enticing that they almost obscured the tindery conditions.

He turned onto a dirt and gravel driveway, and they rolled down the two-track for a quarter mile, cattle fencing on both sides of them. She oohed and ahhed at appropriate moments, knowing enough about farm life to appreciate a tidy and well-maintained operation—and hoping that it wasn't evidence of obsessive-compulsive disorder.

His home sat on a slight rise, a classic square farmhouse with a veranda on the main floor, and two dormers and a balcony on the upper level. Celery green with white trim and a white roof.

"Hey, that's smart. I was just reading about white roofs but I don't think I've ever actually seen one."

"I had to replace the old one," he said as they climbed out of the cab, "so I figured why not? Send some of that sunlight back up where it belongs. I should warn you that I don't have air-conditioning, so even with that roof the house might be a mite warmer than you're used to."

If so, she wouldn't find out till later; he stepped up onto the veranda and grabbed two pilsners from a green minifridge that blended artfully into the wall. "Saves me from having to take my boots off every time I want something to eat."

Then he led her on a leisurely stroll to a nearby pasture, reduced by the drought to dead grass and dust. His herd had congregated near the barn under the sparse shade of two withered maples.

Bowser, as she'd dubbed his border collie at the reservoir, kept his vigil by the cows, eyeing the two-legged intruder warily.

"I had those fields in hay," Dafoe pointed past the barn, "till the crop burned up two years running. Seedlings never got higher than half a foot."

"What are you doing for feed?"

"I'm buying hay by the truckload, and this year I started supplementing with alfalfa and flaxseed, which kind of mimics the wild grasses they used to get in the spring, before everything dried up. Their methane's down seventeen percent."

"You're putting me on."

"Not a bit, and they like it. They're hungry right now. That's why they're hanging around near the barn. Bayou." He whistled to the dog and gave him a hand signal. "Watch this," he said to her.

Bayou darted through the cows to the gate, clearing a view. Jenna watched him rise on his hind legs and use his long narrow snout to flip open a latch. Then the dog scrambled aside and the cows finished the job by pushing the gate open and filing toward the barn. Only a calf failed to move. Bayou worked her toward the opening.

"You just get the one this year?" Jenna nodded at the reluctant calf.

"Two, but I almost lost that one. You see the way I've got her back leg all wrapped up over the hock?"

"What happened?"

"Damn coyotes almost dragged him off. Bayou about went nuts with the pack of them, but he did a good job saving her. I'm just lucky that little guy there didn't get torn up any worse. We were tracking those creatures"—he referred to the coyotes like a curse—"when your idiot pilot damn near killed us."

The force of his words startled Jenna, but then he smiled and raised his hands as if to quell his own outburst.

"I'm not complaining, not anymore. People have met under stranger circumstances. I meant to tell you when we were on the phone that I don't usually carry around a rifle and handgun, in case you were wondering. It was for the coyotes."

The news came as a relief. "You get any of them?"

"Nope. A big bird put a stop to that." He was still smiling.

When they turned back to the house, their hands brushed. A second later their fingers knitted a pleasing pattern. She wasn't aware of her role in this, and could scarcely believe that she'd let it happen; but the simple act of holding hands with him felt better than a lot of kisses she'd known.

Trust your instincts, she said to herself, putting off any consideration of an early check-in at the B&B.

He took off his boots in the mudroom and helped with hers. She was struck anew by the oddly intimate act of letting a man take hold of your leg so he can tug on the heel.

The house felt cooler than he'd suggested, a pleasure after the hard rays of late afternoon. She eyed an airy bathroom and slipped inside to wash up. Clean towels, floor, commode, and a newly enameled claw-foot tub. *Not bad.*

"In here," he called when she stepped out.

She followed his voice to a dining room filled with natural light, and eyed blueberry earthenware and a white tablecloth. "This is so nice. You do like your light colors."

"It's the farming," he replied. "You can go either of two ways, it seems to me. You can do what a buddy of mine did, which was take a sample of mud from his farm to the carpet store so he could match up the colors perfectly; or you can try to have a nice clean place to come home to at the end of the day."

"Option number two for me," she laughed.

He gave her a thumbs-up on his way into the kitchen, returning with a smoked turkey salad. "Sorry, but it's too hot for turning on the range. Hope you like Gorgonzola. I traded a couple of gallons of milk to a cheese maker in town. Everything else," he filled her plate, "used to come from my kitchen garden; but there's no sparing water for that now. Another beer? Wine?"

"I'll stick with this." She was still nursing the pilsner. "So it's off to Safeway these days?"

"That's way too big city for us. We've got the Alverson Natural Food Coop. But the turkey's mine. I've got a smoke shack back there." He glanced out a wide window but all she noticed was the strong line of his chin.

"The turkey's really good. So's everything. Thank you."

By the time they finished dinner, Jenna felt fully at ease. They cleared the dishes, and at his suggestion moved to the veranda to watch the sunset, an idyllic notion that lasted about thirty seconds before Bayou stood up next to Dafoe's deck chair and barked as sharply as a car alarm.

Dafoe hurried around the corner of the house, Jenna trailing at a slower pace. Two attractive young women—early twenties, Jenna guessed—were climbing out of a salt-eaten Subaru wagon. Jenna hoped this wasn't about to turn weird; she'd experienced more than one jealous girlfriend in her time.

"Come on, join us," Dafoe called to the pair as he walked toward them. The taller one, sporting black braids and a brilliant sunflower tattoo that sprouted from under the shoulder strap of her fully filled tank top, called to Bayou and rubbed his ruff.

Jenna drifted over, and Dafoe introduced Forensia as his "number-one farmhand."

"Your only one," she quipped.

"And Sang-mi is her friend," Dafoe added.

Forensia looked up from Bayou. "Hey, you really are Jenna Withers. You do the weather in the mornings."

"That's right," Sang-mi said with a Korean accent.

"Guilty as charged," Jenna said.

"Well, you're good at it." Forensia shook her hand. "I mean, even before you almost landed on my boss, we always caught your first weather report of the day. Working on a farm and all you kind of have to."

"Forensia's my chief troublemaker," Dafoe said.

"More like your chief slop hauler," the young woman replied.

"What's up?" Dafoe asked her.

"I left my pack by your computer and I'm going to need it for the weekend."

"And you wanted to meet Jenna?"

"Could be that, too," Forensia said good-naturedly.

"Go on, grab your pack. You're probably running off to a midnight meeting of your coven."

"It's not a coven," Forensia harrumphed playfully. Jenna sensed that this wasn't the first time they'd had this exchange. "It's a gathering, and we're not officially witches."

"Not yet," said Sang-mi in all seriousness.

"Pagans," Dafoe explained after the young women drove off and he and Jenna settled back on the veranda.

"Really? They've been in the news enough lately. Do they know anything about that GreenSpirit woman, the one who's landed Lilton in all that hot water?"

"I asked them but they wouldn't say much. I got the feeling that they like all the cloak-and-dagger stuff of having people think that Green-Spirit might be around here, but I really doubt it. Here?" He shrugged. "Reminds me of the Dylan rumors from twenty years ago: 'Hey, Dylan's renting a place up the Deben Valley.' That sort of thing. Now it's Paganism."

"Not your everyday belief system, at least not where I come from."

"Vermont? Are you kidding? There are lots of Pagans up there."

"Not when I was growing up."

"World's changing, but I'm fine with them. They care about the land as much as I do. And despite the rumors in this little burg, they're not sacrificing babies and goats."

"There's actually talk like that?"

"Oh, yeah, Forensia and Sang-mi aren't the only Pagans around. There's a bunch of others in their twenties, late teens, and new ones checking it out all the time. You take in a twenty-mile radius around here, and you'll find quite a few of them living on small farms or in town. Some are even younger and still at home with their folks—who are freaking out, if the letters to the paper and what you hear around town mean anything."

"We're not that far from the city; it's hard to believe that people are getting so riled up about it."

"We've got more churches per capita in this county than anywhere else in the state, so this Pagan stuff is really stirring up the pot. There have been some harsh words thrown around. The sheriff even held a town hall meeting to try to calm everybody down. Which is amazing because I would have pegged him as somewhere to the right of Attila the Hun. He's got two teenage girls himself, and Forensia says they've been slipping away at night to go to their gatherings."

"What a place of intrigue. Who'd have thunk?" Jenna joked.

"The thing is, I get a little worried about those two, especially Forensia. Religion can bring out the crazies, and I've tried to warn them to be careful, but Forensia's attitude is 'Screw them. I'm Pagan and I'm proud.'"

"You're not a Pagan, are you?" She could accept Paganism, even admire aspects of it; but she didn't think she was ready for a Pagan boyfriend.

He laughed heartily. "Me? God no."

"So you won't be running off to some gathering on Sunday morning?"

"I'll be running to the cows, like I do every day, to worship at the *udder* altar."

"That was *bad,*" she said, but she was laughing, too.

"I'm just not a joiner."

"Hold on there, you're president of the Organic Dairymen's Association."

"God bless Google." He laughed again. "But that's it. You won't find any pentacles hanging around my neck. What about you?"

"I'm a scientist. I believe in the betterment of the species through evolution," she said with feigned hauteur, then added more seriously, "although the species *Homo sapiens* has me a little worried of late."

"Here's to our betterment." He raised his glass, and Jenna followed suit.

She canceled her reservation at the B&B, taking Dafoe up on his offer of a spare room. The arrangement felt comfortable and safe, and she luxuriated in waking to find her new beau priming the espresso maker.

Before she left late on Sunday morning, they found themselves back in the kitchen, making out like a couple of teens. That's certainly how her passion felt: fresh and alive—a great unknown all over again.

She was tempted to go further, but told him that she wanted them both to get tested. Her words sounded breathless; and she held his hips firmly against hers, savoring the sweet pressure. When he started to speak, she put her finger on his lips and said, "No arguments, Mr. Dafoe Tillian."

"You worried?"

"About you or me?" she asked.

"Either."

"I'm not worried about me but fair is fair."

Still aroused, and still sorely tempted, she belted herself next to him in the pickup, feeling like a cowgirl as he drove her back to the train station with his arm wrapped around her shoulders.

"Look," she said, once she'd unbuckled to face him, "I don't have a lot of time for games. That's why I don't waste my time dating much. But I like you, Dafoe. If you're serious about getting to know me, call me again, or e-mail me"—she pecked his lips impulsively—"whatever you want, but be in touch. I'm putting it to you straight: I like you a lot. It's in your court."

With that last word—verb as much as noun—she put her finger on his nose. For what reason, she had no earthly idea, but in the next instant he kissed it, and she was back in his arms till the train rolled in.

She watched him on the platform, waving until he passed from view. She leaned back in her seat, sighing with delight. *Our first weekend together.* She told herself to hold on to these memories. *So I can tell our kids someday.*

Aghast at what she'd thought—that sneaky unbidden words could arise from such an unknown place—she started leafing through a discarded section of the Sunday *New York Times,* finding little to engage her until she saw a story datelined "the Maldives," covering the bombing two days earlier. When she skimmed down the column and spotted Rafan's name, she almost cried out, but he was described as a survivor whose sister had been killed by the first blast.

Basheera. Jenna had known her as a shy girl of thirteen, smart and funny in her quiet, mischievous way.

Jenna thought of other terrorist attacks over the years, and all the times she'd sat in sad wonder, shaking her head over the enveloping tragedies; but this was unfathomable because the Maldives had always been so special. Not just to her. Not just because of the precious months she'd spent with Rafan ten years ago. The Maldives were special because the Maldives were paradise. And paradise had been brutally, ruthlessly bombed.

The Times quoted Rafan: "My little sister died in my arms on the way to hospital. I heard the second bomb and saw the others dying, too."

Jenna pulled her BlackBerry from her bag. She'd kept it off all weekend, and now knew another regret.

Tons of calls, but there was the message she was hoping for: Rafan's on Saturday morning. In a desperate voice, he'd pleaded with her to come, "Or send someone to do this story, or we'll all drown in . . ." A pause, and she was sure he'd say "the sea," that they'd all drown in the rising, frightening, murderous sea.

But when he regained his voice, it was so heartbroken that his words could have been pitted with shrapnel: ". . . in blood."

We'll all drown in blood. She said this to herself, head still shaking. And then her eyes pooled, salty and swelling like the waters of the world.

Rafan turned from the row of fresh graves and the harsh glare of white headstones, and lowered his eyes to where Basheera lay buried. Yesterday, under the same strong sun, his little sister had been shrouded in a white cloth and placed on her right side to face Mecca. In accordance with Islamic practice, the other eleven victims of the bombing also rested with their eternal gaze on Islam's holiest city, while their killers—men of renegade faith—took noisy credit for the carnage, promising more blood with every breath, and claiming that God Himself had anointed their mission.

Muslims murdering Muslims. Rafan shook a fist at the burning sky.

They would have murdered him, too, if he'd been seconds slower walking down that crowded street. If he hadn't tried to carry his dying sister to hospital. If he hadn't hurried.

If . . . if . . . if . . . An army of ifs had marched him to the borderlands of life and death, and spared him the miserable instrument of their choosing.

He sank to his knees. The newly settled dirt received him softly, and he tried to pray, as he'd tried at the burial with seven men beside him, all of them staring into her open grave. None of them had known Basheera well. For her sake he'd cast prayers to heaven, trying to reel in grace, forgiveness, hope. But his eyes had returned unsoothed to this fresh wound in the earth.

Basheera's three dearest friends, fellow teachers at the English Language School in Malé, were not permitted at her gravesite, for "Allah has cursed women who frequent graves for visitation," a quote attributed to the Prophet Muhammad. It gave rise in many locales to the rule barring women, made and enforced by men, to spare them the emotions of wives, sisters, daughters.

Basheera would have hated the ceremony, so male and mannerly, though she might have laughed, as she had many times, at the irony of her life as a Muslim woman: torn by her faith, troubled yet true—and scorned by extremists whose anger stifled debate and silenced dissent.

Do you know you killed one of your enemies? Rafan had wanted to scream yesterday as dirt darkened the shroud that covered Basheera. *She hated what you do. What you say.* But to shout would have granted them a greater victory, and he never would have done that.

Instead, he would defy them—and honor his sister—under the quiet cover of darkness. He would usher Fatima, Musnah, and Senada—the dark-eyed, dark-haired married woman whom he loved dearly—to Basheera's grave. The three women, all friends of his sister's, planned to scatter petals of the pink rose, her favorite flower.

No one guarded the cemetery. No one would stop them when night came. Even prying stubborn eyes had to sleep.

Hours away, on the small island of Dhiggaru, Adnan took his first clumsy steps in a pair of black flippers. *Like a seal on a beach,* he thought. He turned to look at his impressions in the sand, so big he could have been a giant. *Or a monster?*

Just nine steps to the water. That's all. The strip of sand had narrowed and trees had fallen. They'd washed away, or languished in the gentle surf, shifting side to side with the thrust and parry of the sea.

Parvez had loaned him the mask, snorkel, and fins. "You must see for yourself," he'd said.

"But I know about it."

"*See* it," the religious leader had insisted. "*Touch* it. It is not only sand that disappears. The reef is dying."

The warm water swirled around Adnan's legs; but in the distance the ocean appeared flat and still, reflecting the sun's blinding rays like a mirror.

He rinsed the mask before he put it on, and swam with his eyes on the ocean bottom, watching the scalloped sand slowly recede as the water deepened. He'd swum with sea turtles as a boy, when his fears of sharks had lessened and he'd chanced the dark blue waters far from shore, once shadowing a turtle as large as himself. The creature had glided fathoms below him, fins lifting and falling in unison, effortless as palm fronds in a breeze. For many minutes he'd trailed the turtle, mesmerized by a hard shell so alive in the soft embrace of sea. He'd felt buoyant and free, unfettered by land or air or need.

The turtle swam away, and the spell was broken. Adnan had treaded water and looked to shore, so distant that it had been almost impossible to see. Yet he'd been filled not with the immensity of the ocean—his speck of life on the blank face of water—but with the vastness of the universe itself, for that's what he'd known in his absolute isolation: the endless unraveling hand of God.

Only the memory remained—not the overriding sense of the divine—as he swam the last few meters to the coral reef, white and lifeless as sand, killed by an invisible gas that spilled from the sky and formed a deadly ocean acid.

"They have played God with our world," Parvez had said when he'd handed Adnan the snorkeling gear. "They took all of creation in their hands and squeezed it like a lime until no more juice ran into their bowls."

Adnan had listened. Now he placed his hand on the coral. *Dead.* He'd never known that a reef could feel so devoid of life, but this one did. The silent heartbeat of the ocean's hardest growth had vanished. He remembered an admonition of his youth—"Don't touch the reef"—because human contact killed it, but Parvez had told him that you can't kill the dead, and Parvez was right. Adnan could touch this reef for hours and he'd never harm it because . . . *you can't kill the dead.* Parvez had pointed to the resort islands, where tourists stayed in sprawling beach bungalows. "You can only give them rest. Let them dream. Let them sleep. We are coming."

Starlit, Rafan crept alongside Fatima, Musnah, and Senada to within whispering distance of the cemetery.

"Wait behind there." He pointed to two towering palms that rose inches from each other.

The three women in headscarves crouched down. Rafan took a steadying breath and walked to the entrance. An Islamic inscription had been chiseled into the arch centuries ago: ALLAH GIVES LIFE, AND ALLAH TAKES IT AWAY.

He headed directly to where Basheera's body salted the earth with minerals and blood. He did not sink down, as he had earlier that day. Instead, he listened with the ears of a sentry as his eyes studied the commanding stillness, looking for those who would condemn him and the three women by the palms.

Slowly, he walked back to the gate, hanging his head as a bereaved man. But he was still searching for what he did not want to find.

Adnan had stopped snorkeling more than a decade ago, when the reefs began to die. He'd been sickened by the disappearance of batfish, with their bold stripes and wing-shaped bodies; and the loss of speckled green puffer fish with their long, snoutlike faces, bulgy eyes, and professorial airs. So many whimsical species—angelfish and triggerfish and the grumpy-looking grouper—had vanished as quickly, it seemed, as the tiny tessellated schools that had darted away in flashes of yellow, pink, blue, and orange.

Only this whiteness remained. This blankness. Adnan touched the coral again. White was the color of death. Not black.

Swimming over the reef, he peered down into the small caverns where moray eels once lurked, evil-looking and sly, and nattily attired parrot fish had nibbled contentedly on algae. The emptiness shocked him.

He circled back over the reef to swim to shore. He would tell Parvez what he had seen: nothing. The blank white face of nothing.

A shadow passed so swiftly on his left that it didn't register fully. Then he turned and saw that the shadow had a body fifteen feet long and a mouth that could crush his skull.

Fatima, Musnah, and Senada stepped away from the palms. None of them spoke, but Rafan saw light in Senada's moist eyes, and thankfulness. Basheera had been at Senada's side when she gave birth to a stillborn son; and his little sister, who had always been the quiet one, had stood up to Senada's husband when he had screamed at his grieving wife, "Murderer. Murderer."

To be out at night with Rafan and two women was dangerous for Senada. Not so much for Fatima and Musnah: As single women, they did not have threats to fear in their homes. Only threats from those who might be spying on the cemetery.

"You are sure no one is there?" asked Senada, half a head taller than the other two.

"I am sure," Rafan said, though certainty was never possible with so many followers of Allah searching for the sins of others.

They did not pass under the arch. Rafan walked them along the perimeter, four hunched, hurrying figures moving through starlight and shadows until he turned and led them to Basheera's grave. The women gathered side by side. Rafan stepped back to keep watch.

A murmur of prayer arose. Rafan's surveillance revealed not a trace of movement in the cemetery. A stillness as absolute as death.

Fatima, Musnah, and Senada reached into a woven bag and released handfuls of lush pink petals. They glittered and floated to Basheera's grave like the snow the women had never seen. A blanket, luminous and pure, covered the freshly dug earth.

* * *

Adnan stared at the massive tiger shark and tried to tread water with the slightest movement possible, torso and legs dangling in the water like bait from the great hook of heaven. Dozens of shark species lived in the seas around the Maldives, most no more threatening than a squid, but tiger sharks attacked swimmers, divers, even boats.

This one swam so close that Adnan felt water shift against his stomach. Then the shark moved on.

No, it was turning back for another pass. Hunting. Adnan looked wildly for a fisherman, sailor—anyone—to haul him aboard, but saw only a fin cutting the glassy surface of the sea.

The shark circled him, a lazy, rippling whirlpool. Any second it might bump him, see if he was a living creature.

Adnan prayed, guilelessly and true for Allah to save him, and imagined his God saying, "For what? What shall I save a such a sinner for?"

Adnan gave Allah the first answer that came to mind, repeating what Parvez had whispered in his ear: A life for a life.

Rafan led the three women from the cemetery, forsaking care for a hasty retreat. He saw no gain in staying a moment longer, for now it was essential to escort Senada home before her fisherman husband returned from days at sea.

When they stepped back on the street, Musnah, dark hair cascading from under her headscarf, breathed loudly in relief. Rafan smiled to himself, for he felt the same freedom. They moved a few more steps before a voice ordered them to stop.

Imam Reza walked up to them. He'd conducted Basheera's funeral and burial, always keeping his back to the young woman's body, his eyes on the faithful, though Rafan knew he would question their faithfulness now. *If he knows.*

"You have been to the cemetery," Imam Reza said. His beard was a dark bush that brushed his chest, and in the sparse light his turban could be glimpsed only in outline.

"Yes," Rafan said. "I took a message from Basheera's friends to her."

"We watched him go," Fatima said.

"You have no faith that your prayers can be heard in paradise?"

"Yes, Imam Reza, I'm sure they can." Musnah spoke without looking up. "But we miss her so."

Rafan noticed that all three women kept their heads bowed. Senada stood behind her friends, almost cowering. Imam Reza would like that.

"What prayer did you take to your sister?" Imam Reza asked him.

This was a test. Rafan refrained from glancing at Senada; as a married woman, she would not wish to be noticed under such compromising circumstances.

"The prayer of forgiveness for all my sister's sins," Rafan answered. "The prayer of hope for all the faithful. The prayer of memory, that she would never be forgotten."

Imam Reza's eyes moved over the headscarves that faced him. "Did you enter the cemetery?"

"No, they did not," Rafan said "Only I—"

"I asked them."

"No," answered the women, keeping their heads low.

He doesn't believe us, Rafan thought. *But he doesn't have to. This isn't Iran or Waziristan. Not yet.*

Imam Reza walked toward the cemetery, leaving Rafan chilled by the man's sudden silence, by what it promised for the future. By flower petals resting on a grave, and footprints in the dust.

"Did he believe us?" Musnah whispered after they'd walked on.

"I do not know what he believed or what he saw." Rafan looked over his shoulder. "I know only that these imams never forget."

Senada stepped lightly toward the back door of her home, sticking close to the wall, away from the starlight. What would she say if Mehdi was waiting in their bedroom? She would tell him the truth.

That you lied to Imam Reza? That you were with Rafan?

Mehdi hated Rafan. A man who consorts with women. A man who doesn't go to mosque. A man who doesn't pray. A man too proud for his faith.

Senada touched the door handle, wondering if her husband had left a trace of his heat, if he'd gripped it so hard in anger, twisted it so violently—as he had her—that she could sense him even now.

But the metal was cool in the night air, and when she opened the door the room was black. Silent. She struck a match and held it out like a frightened child, peering into the pitch. Her bed was empty. She did not smell fish.

She climbed under the covers and said a prayer of gratitude: for safety, for friends, for Rafan.

"Allah saved me," Adnan told Parvez, who stood in the door of his one-room house on the north end of Dhiggaru. A lantern burned behind him, lighting a simple desk and an open Koran. "He drove the shark out to sea after I made a vow."

Parvez nodded knowingly, but then asked which vow. Adnan spoke without moving: "The vow of paradise."

Parvez took the lantern and walked him along the path through the palm grove still teeming with their secrets. He didn't stop until he brought Adnan to the end of the seawall, where he placed the lantern before putting his arm around his friend's shoulder.

"If you could see through the darkness for many miles," Parvez said, "you would see diamond island."

Not its real name—what the Maldivians called the richest resort island. Adnan's mother took a boat there every weekday to make sure that the rooms were cleaned and that every toilet was scrubbed till it shined. Then, on Saturdays, a small supply ship picked her up on its way back from Malé. She usually added a big bag of locally grown limes to the hold, already heavy with cases of champagne, caviar, chocolates, and the other everyday luxuries of diamond island. Her job, though she wasn't paid for the crossing, was to watch the seamen for pilferage. Not a lime, not a single dark chocolate truffle could be missing when they docked. Bags and cases had to be sealed tighter than a hatch in a storm.

His mother had been astonished the first time that she'd seen the resort. The "bungalows" were larger than any house she'd ever known, almost as big as the presidential palace, but roofed with ornamental thatch to look native. Each was lavishly appointed with silver, gold plate, marble, and exotic hardwoods, and came with a staff of three, a private pool, and a yacht for $10,000 a night. More than his mother earned in four years of hard work on diamond island.

"Your mother could put the dead to rest," Parvez said in the quiet that had fallen.

"No." Adnan shook his head. "You said I would do this. I would put the dead to rest."

"So you will. But your mother can do what you cannot: She can go to the heart of diamond island and stop their sins forever. Every hour of every day they slap Allah in the face."

Liquor, sex, drugs, parties with unmarried girls. *Muslim* girls corrupted by the West. *Muslim* men corrupted by the West. *And she worries about their truffles and toilets.* That thought—and Parvez's words about Allah—stung more sharply than the memory of his mother's hand when he was nine years old. All his young life he'd waited for his father to come home. "Mother," he'd said one afternoon when he realized that the sandy path to their house had never borne any footprints but their own, "he's not coming home."

She'd slapped him. Just the once. Told him that his father was a jihadist fighting the Russians in Afghanistan. "Maybe a martyr, and you say such things."

But then she'd wrapped him in her arms, weeping as she wiped away his tears.

It is so much worse for Allah to witness the sins of diamond island, Adnan thought, *than for a boy to feel even his mother's deepest grief.*

"You can bury the gift of paradise in a bag of limes," Parvez said. "She'll carry it to them. She'll never know. We can time the arrival."

"But this is what they did in Malé. They made a bomb." *And you said it was wrong.*

"No, they killed many brother and sister Muslims in Malé. Out there," Parvez turned his gaze seaward again, "the dead still wait for their rest."

"But what about me? The vest?" So much more willing to take his own life than his mother's.

"The vest will still be filled, and when the time is right and Allah speaks, you will wear it. You will see your mother in paradise. Someday, you will see me, too."

Parvez turned away, leaving Adnan trembling in the sultry tropical night.

CHAPTER 5

President Victor Reynolds gripped Jenna's hand in both of his, looked directly into her bright blue eyes, and thanked her profusely: "Your president and your nation deeply appreciate your service."

She was impressed. He was the *president,* after all, even if he was afflicted with that annoying, self-important tic of referring to himself in the third person. Indeed, his warm welcome might have overwhelmed Jenna, if she hadn't already heard him repeat the very same words to nine other members of the newly assembled task force. And there were still a half dozen in line behind her.

Little matter, she was proud to shake the chief executive's hand and enter the Oval Office. They'd been herded here by Vice President Andrew Percy, who was well positioned to succeed his boss in four years. The press corps had dubbed him "Hair Apparent," hardly a unique sobriquet, but aptly applied to Percy with his wavy black locks; at sixty-three, they remained suspiciously unstreaked by gray, à la Reagan, and rose like a crown above his handsomely weathered face. It was as if every hair were straining to reach the nation's highest office, openly betraying the man's scantily clad ambition.

For Jenna, walking up to the White House gate this morning had come as a welcome distraction. Last night's arrival at Washington's historic Union Station had capped a trip horribly tainted by the terrible news from the Maldives. Bidding good-bye to Dafoe had been sweet, but the weekend's pleasure had dimmed the moment Jenna had read about Basheera's death. She'd made her way to the venerable Hay-Adams Hotel still stunned by the news—and grateful for the capital's edifices of white marble with their reassuring displays of permanence and resilience. Even in Washington's most frenetic periods, the city offered a mellower mood than New York. And the District, though hot and muggy, hadn't endured the grisly murders that had made New York so bleak and edgy of late, perhaps because the high temperatures didn't feel like an order of magnitude beyond what this Southern town had always known.

Jenna glanced around the Oval Office. *How great is this?* she asked herself. *Very great.* By joining the task force, she'd plunged right into the fiercely unpredictable currents of history.

As her eyes settled on the carpet's presidential seal, she realized, with a bolt of sadness, how dearly she wished that her parents could have known about this event: Their lives had been swept away by black ice just outside Burlington three years ago, a mere month after their only child had joined *The Morning Show*.

The *click-click-click* of the White House photographer's camera snagged Jenna's attention as easily as the young woman behind the lens had caught her smiling minutes ago at President Reynolds, who didn't possess all of Hair Apparent's polish, but the president did have that uncanny, hand-in-the-cookie-jar smile, which had charmed tens of millions of voters. Another *click* made Jenna think that the photo of her with the president would be great for her scrapbook, if she ever got around to making one. *Show it to the kids someday.*

There you go again with the kid thing. That's no biological clock you've got ticking, she thought. *That's a biological storm trooper beating down a door, determined to have his way with you.*

Maybe you should focus on this, she scolded herself, now that the president had cleared his throat—so noisily that she worried he'd use the historic brass spittoon inches to her left. Thankfully, he did not.

"All of you are about to embark on a task critical to our nation's future, and to the future of our children and our children's children . . ."

She tried to focus—she really did—but clichés always sent her thoughts reeling, making even the most sincere sentiments sound as limp and disposable as a wet paper towel. Reynolds concluded his mercifully brief remarks with "And may God bless each of you and guide you on this momentous journey. Now, I have to go down to the Situation Room, and you've got your own duties to attend to." Pausing only to grip the vice president's shoulder for a moment, Reynolds headed out the door with that mischievous and—Jenna had to admit—appealing smile of his.

A White House aide ushered the task force out of the Oval Office—though it was likely the group would have followed Vice President Percy down the hall without the aide's help. As she left the room, Jenna took a final look around, noting the portrait of George Washington above the fireplace. And Abraham Lincoln, just to her left as she headed out the door. She adored Lincoln and had read several biographies of him.

Jenna trailed the other task force members to a conference room where carafes of coffee awaited them. She didn't need caffeine to get jazzed, not this morning.

The vice president, in his role as task force chair, moved to the head of the long mahogany table. As he perused his notes, another aide, as clean-cut as a pine plank, handed out confidentiality agreements that each member signed.

Though Jenna recognized a number of scientists on the task force, the person grabbing her immediate attention was Senator Gayle Higgens, who'd represented Texas until two years ago. "Tossed out with the other rascals," was how she'd described her defeat to *The Washington Post.* In that interview, Higgens did not mention how deeply she'd been bankrolled by the petroleum interests so dominant in her home state, or her controversial six-figure "speaking fees." They had become such a scandal that in the end, most voters in Texas went for the other guy . . . a landslide defeat that made Higgens even more memorable.

Two environmentalists of note sat to Jenna's right. She nodded and smiled, and had to look away when the one with a white goatee—old enough, and then some, to be her father—stared too intently into her eyes. *No, I'm not trolling for a date. Jesus.* She was reminded, once again, of Washington's strange sexual charge, where power—and access to power—was the dominant aphrodisiac.

Across the table she spotted two scientists who wrote immensely popular blogs on climate change. One of them, Ben Norris—balding, freckled, jowly—had been an outcast at NASA during George W.'s regime, forced to abide a callow press aide who'd monitored his every public utterance. Jenna was glad to see that Norris had finally been granted a seat at the table, literally and figuratively. She gave him a quick smile, pleased that the panel was dominated by men and women of his caliber.

"It has become painfully clear," the vice president began, looking over the assembly of men and women from across the racial and religious spectra, "that we are nowhere near the level of reductions in greenhouse gases necessary to prevent disastrous consequences from climate change. That's the overwhelming scientific consensus, which is no longer in serious dispute . . ."

Jenna sat up, astonished to hear such direct and—yes, *dire*—language from the VP, who was speaking far more frankly about global warming than any administration official in history.

Of course, all of us just swore to keep our mouths shut.

"Even if we had managed to convince the American people of the need to make dramatic changes in the way we live," Percy went on, "which we've utterly failed to do, the developing world—especially China, India, and Brazil—has shown a tragic unwillingness to make more than nominal attempts to cut back." Percy shook his head sadly; it didn't look like an act to Jenna.

She shot a glance at Gayle Higgens, wondering what "Senator Fossil Fuels," as the greenies called her, made of the vice president's shocking admission. Higgens—Jenna could scarcely believe this—was smiling and nodding.

Have I just walked through the looking glass, she wondered, *where nothing is as it appears?*

The vice president paused, looked meaningfully around the room, and said, "We have to see what science and technology can do to lower the Earth's thermostat. We have to move forward aggressively with geoengineering. I want you to consider everything that's feasible, from CCS"—carbon capture and storage, usually underground—"to launching sulfates into space to reflect sunlight. We want to hear about whatever you think will work."

Whoa. Jenna had assumed that geoengineering would be on the agenda—why else would they have invited her?—but not that it would *be* the agenda. And to talk so causally about using sulfates, in particular, was sobering to her. She'd actually had a nightmare about sulfates being blasted into the atmosphere, which she was willing to bet was one of the very few dreams about that odd subject ever to afflict humankind. Desperate to awaken, she dreamed she was standing at a window watching a beautiful sunny day turn bitter cold. Her reflection in the glass showed frost coating her face, and she felt her heartbeat slowing. Worse, in the dream she *heard* it stop, which awakened her, ironically enough, in a sweltering pool of perspiration.

"That's what all of you have in common," Percy said. "You're acknowledged experts in your fields, and you've all expressed deep skepticism about our country's willingness to take the steps required to reduce GHGs." Greenhouse gases. Percy nodded at Norris, the prodigal son from NASA, who sat grimacing with his arms crossed. "You need to understand that we basically agree with those of you who have been most critical of your government's efforts in this regard."

"Hold on, Mr. Vice President," NASA's own said. "What you're telling us—let's cut to the quick here—is that there's no real commitment to reduce GHGs, so now we're going to tinker with the planet's incredibly fragile heating and cooling system, something our forebears did a couple of hundred years ago, which some of us are now calling the 'Industrial Rotisserie.'"

Percy ignored the play on words. "They increased temperatures by burning carbon-based fuels, and we intend to lower them."

"Unbelievable. Do you have any understanding of the risks? This could kill all of us. Miserably."

"We do, of course. But we think that doing nothing will be much worse."

"But you won't address the risks publicly?"

"No, we won't. We recognize that this is the most serious crisis ever faced by any administration, but talking publicly would only set off panic."

"If you'd spoken openly five years ago when you were running for—"

"That was then, this is now. Ben, let's not squabble over what's done. There's no time. Look," Percy pushed aside his notes and leaned forward, "we've tried complicated international agreements, and no one, including us, has ever lived up to them. And it's not just climate change by itself that has us worried: The CIA has just completed a two-year research project investigating the impact of what's happening with the planet on national security. The conclusions are dreadful: In Africa alone, warming is expected to make civil war as common as drought."

No coincidence there, thought Jenna.

"Some Agency models predict four hundred thousand *extra* deaths from those extra wars in just the next twenty years. And none of us should think that we'll be able to write those wars off as 'just another African tragedy' because the carnage will happen in the world's most critical oil- and mineral-rich regions. Think of it: civil wars waged around the world's biggest oil spigots. It's happened before, and it's going to happen a lot more in the future."

The vice president held up a document from the stack in front of him. "This is the actual CIA report. It says we'll risk being buried by defense spending because countries all over the world will be in open conflict." He read from the report, "'Nations will engage in armed conflicts over rapidly diminishing arable land, because of drought, floods, windstorms, and rising oceans; rapidly diminishing fresh water; rapidly diminishing food; and rapidly diminishing oil supplies.'" Percy looked up. "The Agency says we're in for an unprecedented period of what it calls 'social and climate chaos.' So we must consider *all* our options."

Jenna put down her pen. She'd planned to take notes but she'd already written the book from which the vice president could have been quoting.

"Most of you have highly specialized knowledge. A few of you, like our well-known colleague, Ms. Jenna Withers, are highly educated generalists, if I do you no disfavor by saying so, Ms. Withers."

"No, not at all."

"Hey, me, too," Senator Higgens chimed in. "I'm all about generalities," she added with a self-deprecating laugh that drew smiles from most of the people at the table.

Senator Higgens was a big woman with an incongruously lean, pretty face. A "table date," the network's Pentagon correspondent once called her. Jenna had asked what he meant. "Back in the day, she'd look great in a restaurant, as long as you couldn't see her from the waist down."

Jenna had bristled at his remark and turned away. Remembering the exchange softened her to Senator Fossil Fuels.

Since losing the Senate seat that she'd held for twenty-four years, Higgens had become executive director of the United States Energy Institute (USEI), the oil and coal industry's powerhouse lobbying group. She'd reportedly written more than three dozen energy bills in the last session alone, and found plenty of former colleagues—beneficiaries of USEI largesse—to introduce them under their own names. A boisterous, robust presence, Higgens had long been a favorite of Sunday morning interview shows: a plain-talking Texan whose twang-tinged homilies belied a superior intellect and political savvy widely respected inside the Beltway, where cunning counted as a virtue, not a vice.

"The esteemed senator," Vice President Percy said with a smile, "is not giving herself proper credit, but I'm sure she'll agree that it's vital for us to come up with a plan that will really deal with global warming. If we don't, we're . . ." And here Percy paused, maybe for dramatic effect. If so, Senator Higgens usurped the tension entirely:

"Toast, Andy. We're toast, baked, bar-bee-cued." The senator guffawed, spurring surprised laughter around the room.

But Jenna sat in startled silence, shocked by what the senator appeared to endorse: wholesale acceptance by the oil and coal industry of the impending peril posed by climate change. Amazing. Momentous. Even bigger than when some of the oil industry giants finally stopped funding institutes that denied climate change with pretend science.

"We *are* warming," the vice president agreed wryly with the senator. "Evan Stubb," Percy's chief of staff, "will coordinate your efforts to come up with the cheapest, most efficient means of sharply reducing temperatures and GHGs. In other words, the president wants a short list of the most promising geoengineering options, and he'd like it in the next sixty days, along with your recommendations on how to proceed."

"Planning on being reelected?" asked the goateed environmentalist who'd leered at Jenna. The election was only ten days away.

The vice president just grinned and directed one of his aides to pass out the memo his office had prepared on geoengineering. Jenna skimmed the first page quickly. Under "Most Feasible" she saw a short section on increasing cloud cover, which noted tersely: "Will cool Earth by reflecting sunlight back into space. Will not remove greenhouse gases."

Sure won't, she thought. Increasing cloud cover would only make it possible to live with higher levels of the gases . . . in the short run. Carbon dioxide would still be absorbed the by oceans, generating ever more carbonic acid, which killed sea life. This was no theoretical threat: In just the past nine years, vast stretches of ocean in which algae had died and disappeared had grown by 15 percent. *Nine years.* And every scientist, including Jenna, knew that algae was overwhelmingly important: It was the source of much of the Earth's oxygen and was the beginning of the food chain for many animals. Far more visible than the loss of algae was the destruction of half the world's major reef systems, dying from carbonic acid overload. The human species was not likely to survive if life vanished from three-quarters of the planet.

Under a separate "Feasible" category, the vice president's memo included "underground sequestration of carbon dioxide." *Might work,* Jenna agreed, but she knew that it would lower temperatures only *slowly.* Geologic sequestration, or GS as it was called, entailed injecting huge amounts of CO_2 from manufacturing or power plants into rock formations deep within the Earth. Over time, the rock would eventually "wash out" the carbon. But "eventually" meant centuries, and the amount of CO_2 being produced even in just the United States was overwhelming. Plus, if this was to work, there would have to be a sea change in attitudes at the EPA because the agency had approved only a few rock formations for sequestration. Meantime, glaciers would continue to melt at record rates. Already, the lives of a hundred million people in South America were threatened by the loss of their chief source of drinking water: low-lying Andean glaciers.

As the author of the most celebrated book on geoengineering, Jenna might have been expected to have been in a celebratory mood as she left the White House: Her time had come, along with a great deal of attention. Clearly, the executive branch had given up on making any additional efforts to try to get people to change how they lived, ate, traveled, and worked. But she felt deeply ambivalent about this surrender. She wondered what would happen if people were given the real, painful reasons—or real incentives—to modify their patterns of production and consumption. Geoengineering, even at this late stage, felt like giving a heart patient quadruple bypass surgery instead of putting him on a low-fat diet. It *might* save the patient, but it could just as easily kill him.

Jenna no longer wondered why USEI was on board: As long as geoengineering muscled its way to the forefront of climate change efforts, the fossil fuel industry could argue that it was okay to burn every last barrel of crude and bucket of coal.

Exiting the White House, she was escorted to one of a fleet of electric cars that would ferry away the task force. As Jenna climbed into the backseat, she was unable to think of a viable geoengineering technique that did not threaten lethal consequences for humanity. But as the car eased past a regiment of reporters hurling questions that nobody on the task force rolled down their windows to answer, she also knew that political impotence—and widespread public skepticism of global warming—had sent the Earth cartwheeling down a precipitous slope.

The car had no sooner turned onto Pennsylvania Avenue, the White

House looming in the background, than she realized with a start that geoengineering truly posed the most daunting question ever faced by humankind: Do you embrace a dangerous technique that could save the planet—or, with a single miscalculation, plunge it into a final frozen collapse? Or do you soldier on with potentially safer solutions that lacked political support and had failed to arrest the devastating climate changes taking place on land, in the sea, and, most crucially, in the tender skin of sky that protected us all?

Quadruple bypass surgery, or low-fat diet?

After one meeting of the task force, Jenna knew the White House answer: Welcome to the operating room for planet Earth.

CHAPTER 6

On Capitol Hill, the Senate Select Committee on Intelligence was holding an emergency meeting with James Crossett, the director of the CIA. His tense visage was matched by the lockjaw expressions on the faces of two assistant directors who flanked him in the highly secure hearing room. Laptops sat open before all three men. Crossett snapped his screen shut before resuming his testimony:

"When we talk about the bombing in the Maldives, what's most important, from our standpoint, is that it's a stark example of the impact of climate change on national security. Yes, it was a tragic terrorist attack; but it was also the most powerful warning yet that even a stable Muslim nation can experience brutal national security effects from global warming." In a softer voice that caused several senators to lean forward, Crossett added, "And don't forget that the Maldives isn't far from Diego Garcia." The United States' closest naval base to Afghanistan.

"These Maldivians, they aren't screaming about global warming," insisted the rotund, bespectacled chair of the committee. "It's a simple power struggle. They want what they don't have."

Crossett rubbed his chin. "Mr. Chairman, there's a power struggle because the country is in a growing state of panic over the ocean rising all around them—much faster than the U.N. said. We're hearing from our agents in situ that Muslims are loudly blaming our 'decadent' lifestyle for the impending loss of their country. They're building on stilts, senators. Stilts." The CIA chief eyed them all. "They're raising seawalls, and now they're announcing plans to barge dirt from one island to another to try to save themselves. Climate change is not theory to them. It is day-to-day reality throughout the archipelago. We've got to get our heads straight on this: Climate change is an increasingly serious national security issue for all nations. We will not be spared."

"The Muslims sell most of the oil." With a histrionic flourish, the committee chair whipped off his tortoiseshell glasses. "*They're* the ones emptying our pockets. It's the height of hypocrisy for them to blame us for whatever lifestyle we choose to have. I'm not going to apologize to those buggers for anything."

"The leaders of the oil-rich nations are draining our treasury, that's true," the director rubbed his chin for the second time in a minute, "but let's acknowledge what we also all know to be true: The people of the Mideast petro states view their leaders as corrupt despots—and for good reason. The ferment in Islamic nations is as much about corruption, and the poverty it produces, as it is about radical reinterpretations of the Koran. Those factors are all linked. I'm sure I don't need to add that the Maldives doesn't produce a single drop of petroleum."

"No, just panicky reactions from your analysts." The octogenarian chair sat back, twirled his glasses, and tried unsuccessfully to stifle a grin. "So you're saying that you want to take analysts away from hunting for Al Qaeda and put them on *The March of the Penguins*?" His barely suppressed smile exploded into laughter. Most of the committee joined in. Freshman Senator Jess Becker of Vermont waited for the mood to settle before glancing at the CIA chief.

"The Agency's assessment is backed up by military intelligence." The Senate's youngest and newest member turned to his colleagues.

"They're reporting that Al Qaeda operatives in the Maldives are doing everything they can to drum up resentment by claiming that the U.S. is trying to drive them into the sea. This is no laughing matter."

The CIA director offered the brush-cut Becker the slightest nod. The chair responded by saying, "Calm down, 'cause we got bigger fish to fry with the Pakis and Afghans."

Senator Gayle Higgens had perfected the Texas swagger, no easy task for a gimp-kneed, sixty-six-year-old woman who carried more extra poundage than the purveyors of red ink in congressional budget committees. She used a tightly wrapped pink umbrella with a titanium tip as a walking stick, and carried herself with such aplomb that constituents had been known to burst into applause when she paraded past. Might have been the hat, too: big, broad-brimmed, and every bit as colorful as its wearer.

She entered United States Energy Institute headquarters on K Street, a thoroughfare long home to lobbyists, think tanks, and advocacy groups of all stripes. None had a more prestigious address—or reigned as powerfully—as USEI with its oil- and coal-money muscle. Higgens swept into the lobby like she owned the place, pointed her umbrella walking stick at a spry woman with an armful of reports and said, "Round 'em up, Edie, we've got to powwow in teepee number one. Giddyap."

Higgens had become a parody of herself, but she didn't give a damn what the Washington mandarins thought. Part of her appeal was her complete indifference to decorum. It had worked with Texas voters for more than two decades, and it had landed her a high, seven-figure "appreciation" from the very industry that she'd represented so ably in the Senate. The revolving door of government and politics had landed her in this unapologetically opulent, marble-floored building designed entirely along classical Greek lines: symmetrical and perfectly proportional right down to the Ionic columns that graced both sides of the vaulted lobby. It reeked of riches, the enduring power of fossil fuels.

"And you," she pointed the gleaming titanium tip at a male intern who could have moonlighted as a model, "a club sandwich *with* mayo. Some joker got me one last week that was drier than a Texas pee pot."

This is going to be fun, Higgens mused to herself. Even though she'd always said—often very loudly—that patience was a "vastly overrated virtue," persistence had now paid off: Geoengineering would give oil and coal a new lease on life. *Many new leases,* she thought merrily.

The senator took her place at the head of a conference table, club sandwich in easy reach, wholly unselfconscious about eating while her staff settled into their seats and she chatted up an aide about his new-born son. Higgens had a superb politician's gifts of empathy and curiosity; in her case, both were genuine. People liked her, even people who abhorred her politics. The perfect voice for USEI.

She smiled at the staffers assembled around the table. Twelve of them. *My disciples,* she thought without a smidgeon of seriousness or sanctimony.

"Okay, boys and girls, life's going to change around here. Y'all are fired."

She relished their shocked silence, but only for a moment. "Ease up, for chrissakes. Can't y'all tell when an old cowgirl's ringin' your bell? We are in bidness, folks, like never before. The White House has signed on to ge-o-en-gin-eer-ing, all six lu-cra-tive syllables. No leaks about this to the media. You hear me? *No* leaks." She broke into laughter. "'Cept to the usual suspects. Now, I want updated reports on all of the following. Ready?"

She took another bite of her sandwich, loving the smooth mayo spreading over her tongue. *That cute little intern's got a future.* Then she wheeled on a young man directly to her left, rangy as a fence post on her Abilene ranch, which she hadn't seen in two years. "You've been looking at sequestration of CO_2." Pumping carbon dioxide into oil reservoirs, coal mines, saline aquifers, and the like to prevent it from entering the atmosphere. "Keep at it. Give me the latest costs, which—" She put up her hand to shush the fellow. "I *know* they're enormous. The risks?" Raising a question no one at the table was now foolish enough to try to answer. "*Comme ci, comme ça.* But probably on the safer side. Give me footnotes, too, to show we did our homework. I want it by Friday. You may leave," she said to the rangy one. All of them knew that meant: "Get to work."

"You two." She waved the turkey-stuffed sandwich at a middle-aged man and a younger woman rumored to have posted a video of them-selves on the Net having blindfolded sex in the office. "I want you to give me the postmortem on filtering CO_2 from air. That's DOA but I want to be able to say 'Big bucks and big problems,' so dot the i's and cross the t's. Go." They left. To work, she hoped.

Higgens gave a sigh that might have been rooted in longing or nos-talgia, then tapped the table with a fingernail as pink as her umbrella. Her gaze had landed on another edible youngster, as she thought of the twenty-somethings. "Charles," spoken as another, more maternal woman might offer the name of a long-lost son, "you get mineral carbonation." Turning CO_2 to stone. "List the advantages, say that it's not too risky for the faint of heart, but make sure that you point out that the engi-neering challenges are a killer. And Charles," she mewed again, "make this sink like a . . . stone. It's a time waster, and what's time?"

"Money," he answered to her beaming approval.

"Scoot. Now you, Prince Harry," she said, smiling, to a junior re-searcher who shared the royal's first name, cherubic well-scrubbed looks, and upswept ginger hair. "You get to tackle clouds and space mirrors. I *know*, Prince Harry," as if he actually had the cojones to ob-ject, "it's another defensive move, but if we don't line up all our duck-ies, how can we possibly gun them down? So explain how we *could* increase the number of clouds to reflect sunlight back into space using those automated boats that fire mist into the air, or whatever the devil they shoot up there, and then explain why it'll cost a fortune. Be creative. Also, knock down that kook's ideas for sending thousands of mirrors into space to reflect the sun. That really will cost billions and basically hand China the keys to the treasury." They nodded. "Oh, wait, we've *already* done that, haven't we?" She hee-hawed.

"You, you, and you." Higgens polished off the last of her sandwich and licked her fingertips before turning to three Ph.D.s in chemical engineering. "I want y'all to get an update on that report you did six months ago on blowing up sulfates in the stratosphere." She liked this idea a lot. Kind of like setting off volcanoes in the sky to cloud the Earth, block the sun, and reduce temperatures in a hurry. *Raindrops keep fallin' on my head* . . .

Sulfates were salts that contained a charged group of sulfur and oxygen atoms, SO_4, the basic constituent of sulfuric acid. Using sulfates as aerosols could cool the climate in two basic ways: by having the sulfates attach to particles of solid matter, such as dust, or by having them attach to existing aerosol particles, such as clouds. However, this cooling would not neatly cancel out the effects of greenhouse warming. As Higgens knew, it could actually make the situation more complex, because the cooling and greenhouse effects would likely occur in different—and not always desirable—places. For instance, the aerosol impacts would be focused mostly over industrialized areas of the Northern Hemisphere, while the warming impacts would be greatest over the subtropical oceans and deserts—where island nations like the Maldives were facing complete submersion into the ocean. That would mean the loss of all the life-forms and ecosystems that made those lands their home. The result? The world would see dramatic changes in regional weather patterns in the future, not just increases in temperature. *Ouch!*

And if sulfates cooled the planet too much or too fast, there might be an ice age. *Big* ouch.

On the plus side, firing up sulfates would mean partnering with the Department of Defense to put thousands of rockets to good use, instead of letting them molder in their silos. USEI and DOD always made a powerful one-two punch. But much as Higgens relished the prospect of calling her friends at missile maker Lockheed Martin, her enthusiasm for turning sulfur particles into fireworks was purely provisional: She knew better than to expect a White House buy-in for bombs in any first-stage effort.

"Now, Turtles," Higgens's moniker for an unfortunate-looking older Pakistani man whose elongated head appeared ready to dip into his torso at the slightest hint of danger, "here's *your* chance to move up the food chain. Show me *how sweet it is*." A credible Jackie Gleason that meant nothing to Turtles, who'd grown up in Lahore, or to most of the people left at the table, who were too young to have ever bothered with *The Honeymooners*. "You get to present the option of fertilizing the ocean with iron oxide." Iron oxide in seawater helped absorb CO_2 by facilitating the growth of algae. "Go hard on cost, which is low, and light on risk, which some of our critics might claim is high. Besides, plankton everywhere will thank us. When do I want this report, Turtles?"

"Friday."

"The rest of you," Higgens threw them a wicked grin, "are going to keep working on that special project on the Maldives. Is the tanker on the move?"

"Yes, right on schedule," answered a red-haired sprite who looked sixteen, but was on her third year of working toward a doctorate in international relations and, surprisingly, had taken leadership on this issue from her two older male compatriots.

Higgens hadn't mentioned to the White House task force that USEI already had launched a private geoengineering project with the cooperation of the highest echelons of the Maldivian government: What was the point in appearing presumptuous? But with the White House now moving forward, it was hard to see how anyone could raise objections that might have been hurled at the institute even a week ago. Hell's bells, there wasn't even a single international law preventing a nation from dumping half a million tons of iron oxide into the sea. They could make an algae bloom big as Australia, if they wanted to. Scary, when Higgens considered how irresponsible parties could make a unilateral decision to fundamentally alter the Earth's climate. It was enough to make even her shiver.

"How many days away from the Maldives is our tanker?"

"Three days," the sprite said.

"You guys are good. Now, do you have Maldivians ready to put a local face on the project once that tanker sails into their waters?"

"They're recruiting in Malé even as we speak."

This kid's a gem. "I know I'm about as subtle as my grandpappy's old hickory stick, but I love this iron oxide option. It's cheap and it's *so* visual, and it'll make us look as green as Gore. We'll cool the planet and the glaciers will stop melting, the seas will stop swelling, and we'll be heroes with a solution as environmentally pure as the Natural Resources Defense Council."

"Which hates geoengineering," the institute's media strategist said, lean as the tie he stroked nervously.

"Let them be the haters," Senator Higgens said. "Remember our new slogan? 'On the side of life. Naturally.' Live it."

"There's a problem with terrorism there," the media strategist said, abandoning his tie.

"They call *that* terrorism? Pikers. Besides, we won't be *there,* strictly speaking. We'll be at sea, working to make the world a better place. And I'll bet you enchiladas to empanadas that the government keeps doing exactly what we want it to. They're holding cabinet meetings underwater, for crying out loud. They're desperate, poor. Perfect. We're bringing them a pilot project to solve their ills. They'll probably canonize us."

"I just want to make absolutely sure," the media strategist said, "that they're not going to get skittish about the video: We're going to get it from start to finish, right?"

"Does a horse poop? Is Billy Graham still dead? 'Course we're going to get the video. Otherwise, what's the point? Hey, I can already hear the string section we'll use in the ads that we'll get out of this. We'll use that new guy the ad agency found, the one with that really sweet voice. I love the way he says 'USEI: On the side of life. Naturally.' I swear, I get excited every time I hear it. Don't you? Come on, y'all say it to me, right now. Get over here and whisper it in my ears: 'On the side of life. Naturally.'" The pink fingernail beckoned them.

Her staff, including the upstart sprite, stared at her, panic plastered all over their frozen features; then Higgens laughed harder than ever. "You young 'uns," she managed to say between guffaws, "y'all are *so* serious."

Dafoe called Jenna as she deplaned at New York's LaGuardia Airport. Seconds earlier, Jenna had received a text from Nicci: The network's investigative reporter had been dispatched to the Maldives and wanted Jenna to call him ASAP. When the phone rang, for a moment Jenna thought it was the reporter. Then she spotted Dafoe's number and her breath caught. Smiling to herself, she pushed the button to accept the call.

"How was Washington?" Dafoe asked.

"Hold on." Jenna waved to attract the attention of a network driver she recognized. He rushed up, took her overnight bag, and led her to a black Ford Fusion, a hybrid that she'd had stipulated in her last contract. She thanked him with a nod, settled into the backseat, and fastened the safety belt. "There, I'm set," she said to Dafoe. "I met the president, but that wasn't the high point of my day."

"Really? What was the high point?"

"Are you kidding? This call."

"You don't have to say that."

"Well, maybe it's a *slight* exaggeration, but it's mostly true. How are you?"

"Crazy day. I'm just coming up for—"

"Crazy? How can you have a crazy day on an organic dairy farm?"

"Forensia didn't show up for work. First time in six years. She's never been sick, and she didn't even call."

"Is she okay?"

"I'm not sure. She got in touch about twenty minutes ago, full of apologies, but when I asked what happened, she wouldn't say. I didn't want to press her—she sounded a little shaky to me—but everybody's entitled to a day off without having to explain themselves."

"Sounds mysterious."

"It *is* mysterious. And it's totally unlike her."

"Maybe the rumors are true, then," Jenna said.

"What rumors?"

"About that GreenSpirit woman being in your 'hood. Half the reporters in the country are trying to track her down. Maybe that's why Forensia's getting all mysterious on you."

"Nah," Dafoe said, and Jenna could picture him shaking his head. "I think it's a personal crisis of some kind. She's got a crazy mom. Or Sang-mi might be having problems with her parents. She's five months pregnant."

"She must be barely showing; I sure didn't notice." The cab was entering the Queens-Midtown Tunnel. Garbagey air, smog everywhere.

"Me, neither. Anyway, Sang-mi's pregnancy is the reason her family defected. If you're a single Korean woman, you do *not* get pregnant and have a child."

"They defected? From the North?"

"I thought I'd told you that. Her father was a member of the North Korean mission to the U.N., which means, basically, he was a spy. Then Sang-mi got pregnant by—get this—her *white, Pagan* boyfriend. There was no way her father's career could have survived that. It might even have cost him his life." He took an audible breath. "Please don't mention *any* of this to your colleagues. Forensia says Sang-mi's father has been getting debriefed by the CIA for three months."

"This can't have been easy on any of the family."

"Yeah. About a week ago she moved in with Forensia."

"Who's getting all secretive on you now," Jenna said.

Approaching Midtown. Still hot and sticky in the city, even though the ten-day countdown to the November fourth election had begun. Jenna found it strange to see leaves of all colors still clinging to the trees. Nature going visibly wacko.

"Can you make it up this weekend?" Dafoe asked.

"Can you see me smiling? I'd love to."

"I made an appointment," he added softly.

"For what?"

"To get tested."

"We're pulling up to the building. How about if I call you later to-night?"

"Not too late: I'm a farmer."

"I'm on *The Morning Show,* remember? Late is seven o'clock."

"I miss you," he said.

Jenna was still smiling. She thanked the driver and hopped out, then unloaded her bag and headed into the building. As she dialed the network's investigative reporter, her smile disappeared. And though sworn to silence, she planned on Googling Sang-mi's father as soon as she could.

Rafan eyed the island from the barge's pilothouse, which stood about fifteen feet above the wide, flat-bottomed vessel, giving him one of the higher perches enjoyed by anyone for a thousand square miles. He thought it proper, as the self-ordained Minister of Dirt, to oversee the arrival of the barge and front loader on the bedraggled island of Dhiggaru. According to a real minister—of the Environment—there was plenty of dirt on its northern end and few residents to object to its removal.

"Binoculars?" he asked the captain, a short man with a staved-in face. Rafan wanted to survey his new territory.

Wordlessly, the captain handed over a chipped, dented pair that looked like they'd survived hand-to-hand combat in the South Pacific during World War II. But they focused well enough to reveal two people, one in the robes of a religious leader, standing in the shade of the palm trees. They must have caught some glare from the field glasses because they looked up in alarm. That seemed odd—given the distance, Rafan could see nothing amiss, and hearing them wasn't possible. *Guilt? Over what,* he wondered, then chuckled softly because it reminded him of the guilt he felt over the kiss that he'd shared with Senada yesterday.

They'd been talking about Basheera, about the way his quiet sister used to suddenly burst into loud laughter over some absurdity of modern Muslim life. Then Senada touched him, as she had so sweetly in the past. Her fingertips had drifted down his shirt so slowly, revealing her desire. He'd caught her hand and pulled her close, once more committing himself to a kiss and all that it might mean for a single man and a married, religious woman, whose fisherman husband often arrived home unannounced.

Rafan raised the binoculars for another lazy look at Dhiggaru and saw the man who was not in robes retreating into a palm grove that bordered the beach. *And here I am,* Rafan thought, *coming to take their dirt, to present them with an order of confiscation.*

Up till now, he hadn't expected any serious resistance: They weren't demanding that anyone leave Dhiggaru. But maybe that's why those two were there, to watch for the barge. It was a small country, and word traveled fast. "Do not worry. They will not kidnap you and chop off your head," the Minister of the Environment laughed.

For taking their dirt? Rafan wasn't so sure, not after the bombing.

The captain nudged the barge's broad bow against the shoreline, raising a creak of protest from the snub-nosed hull and a rattle from the chains securing the front loader to the centerline. Three laborers began to unshackle the heavy earthmover.

Rafan eased around them and stepped down the ramp, smelling the sweet rot of dead fish washed up along the shoreline.

The robed man waited a few feet away. Rafan introduced himself, but the young, bearded cleric made no effort to take his hand. Instead, he spoke his own name slowly, as some men do when they believe they are worthy of note, while peering intensely at the visitor through rimless glasses. Rafan avoided the cleric's dark eyes by looking past him.

"Was there someone else here? I thought I saw two of you but it was hard to tell because of the sun." He lowered the brim of his white ball cap to emphasize the blinding light reflecting off the white sand.

Parvez Avila didn't reply. He looked at the barge and cumbersome front loader. "What are you doing here?"

Rafan told him.

"You do not think that you will get away with this, do you?"

Rafan spotted shadowy movement in the palm grove less than thirty feet away. For the first time, he felt afraid. Most likely the other man was back there—*Doing what?* Rafan wondered. He decided not to present the order of confiscation. He feared that Parvez Avila would tear it up, and that even a simple act of violence against paper could unleash much deeper anger and resentment.

"You should never have come here," Avila said. "Never."

The sun pounded on Rafan's cap, but all he felt was a coldness deeper than the sea.

"Rafan," the captain called, "are you ready?"

Rafan waved, signaling that the earthmover should come ashore.

The diesel engine belched a thick black pillow of smoke that enveloped the two men facing each other on the sand, stinging their eyes and filling their noses with the acrid smell of industrial waste.

Jenna whirled through the revolving door, keeping her cell to her ear, quickly shaking her head as she began to speak: "I can't give you his name without talking to him; and I doubt very much that I'll be able to give it to you even then."

Rick Birk, a codger in his mid-seventies—and the network's principal investigative reporter for five decades—had landed in Honolulu en route to Malé. He'd called Jenna to try to cajole Rafan's name and contact information from her. *How does he know I know Rafan?* was her first thought.

Birk now hardened his tone: "For fuck's sake, Jenna, you were sleeping with him."

How'd he know that? she wondered. The answer came right away: *He's an investigator.* "That's *my* business, and bringing up personal stuff is out of line."

"The terrorists could be planning to bomb the network next. Getting me in touch with him could save the lives of everyone we work with." *What a frickin' James Bond complex.* "I already know he works in government."

"What do the plans of some Islamists have to do with my giving you the name of an old friend? Even if he is in the government?"

"He might know someone who knows someone."

"I'm sure he knows someone who knows someone, but *you're* badgering me, Rick, and I don't appreciate it one bit."

"And I don't appreciate getting stonewalled by a fucking meteorologist over such a ridiculously simple—"

She hung up on him. Jenna could count on one hand the number of times that she'd hung up on someone. You just didn't do that when you'd been raised by parents like hers, who'd given her a strong sense of propriety. *"Fucking meteorologist"!* Even if he was old school, *very* old school, that was off the charts.

Christ, there he is, calling me back. Leave a message, creep.

As she stopped out of the elevator on the third floor, her friend and producer, Nicci, rushed toward her, short, dark hair flying. "Birk's in a tizzy. He's on line one and says he wants to apologize."

"He can stay on line one till his ear rots off. I've got work to do." In her office, Jenna tossed her overnight bag onto a chair, then turned to the pixie-size Nicci. "They should have sent us to the Maldives, not him. You know that, don't you? He'll make a hash of it. It'll be another one-dimensional story that begins 'This is the Maldives . . .'" Jenna offered a fair impersonation of Birk's typical basso profundo story opening. As creative as a paint-by-number kit.

"We may get a chance," Nicci said. "The *National Review* broke a story online half an hour ago: USEI is sending half a million tons of liquid iron oxide to the Maldives in a supertanker. It's part of some geoengineering project. Everyone's jumping on the story."

"USEI?"

"The ship's been underway for more than a week."

"They sure played that close to the vest," Jenna said. "Not a peep about it this morning at the White House."

"Remember our friend from the Northeast Bureau?"

"Sure." The up-and-comer.

Nicci smiled. "He wants a sound bite about USEI's plans, since you're on the task force that's considering whether to actually recommend *using* the technology."

"I can give him something, as long as it's just about the technology. I won't go into any of the task force's work."

Though she knew almost nothing about the USEI tanker, what Jenna would have most liked to say was that somebody should have stopped the ship before it set sail. She found it hard to believe that any good would come from this voyage.

She Googled Sang-mi's father. But after quickly scrolling past a spate of stories about his defection, she found little. No updates. No reaction from North Korea. No statements from U.S. officials. And certainly nothing about his wife and pregnant daughter. Jenna could conclude only that he was a small fish in a mighty big diplomatic pond. In other words, if he was a spy, as Dafoe had suggested, the North Korean had cast the perfect profile.

Parvez returned to the palm grove, where Adnan's footprints stood out in the shaded sand. As he stared at the outline of his friend's feet, he saw the astonishing shape of the immediate future. It was such a stunning vision that Parvez found himself holding his breath for several seconds. In those incendiary moments, he knew exactly how he would become the architect of the greatest martyrdom in modern history. Just an hour ago, he'd heard a shortwave radio report about a tanker heading to the Maldives, loaded with iron oxide for a year-long attempt to slowly lower the Earth's temperature. The BBC said that Maldivian sailors would be hired once the ship arrived in Malé. And Adnan was a fully licensed seaman.

The ground beneath Parvez's feet trembled, as if the Earth itself were waking to the weight of what would come to pass, but he saw that it was only the front loader taking another savage bite of the earth. More sooty smoke drifted over him, invading the island as surely as the salty water that had stained the floor of Adnan's house. The man in the white hat probably planned to take away all of Dhiggaru, load by load, till nothing was left. *Who can stop me?* he might have thought. The island was home to so few: Adnan and his mother, Khulood; and two old fishermen who'd always kept to themselves.

And me. Parvez added himself with a smile. He'd learned so much about resistance and jihad from the religious leaders of Waziristan. They'd fought the Russians, the Americans, the Afghan army, and the Pakistani military. The war against nonbelievers was spreading everywhere. Even in America, Muslim men heard the call for jihad and became true martyrs.

Parvez knew that Allah—who else could inspire such divine greatness?—had shown him what to do. Nothing that Parvez had planned for diamond island could match a martyrdom that would be watched by billions. But he would continue that plan even as he undertook this much greater calling, which would need the help of jihadists from Waziristan. Not many; a few could bring to life the vastness of the vision Allah had granted him. Soon, the religious leaders whom Parvez most admired would know that a humble cleric from the Maldives had proved worthy of their company.

Parvez quickly followed the trail of footprints to Adnan's house. He found his old friend eating cold rice and fish.

"What is it?" Adnan stood. "You look so happy."

"I am, my friend. Allah has blessed us with a vision." Squeezing

Adnan's hand, he told him about the tanker. "You are a seaman. Show them your papers and they will hire you. Then you can wear the vest on board."

"But they check everyone. I can't get on board without being searched."

"You will have help. Jihadists will get you onto the ship, and then you will hold the world's attention like no one ever has before."

"What about diamond island? My mother?"

"Yes, I will continue to plan for diamond island, but the tanker will be here soon; and it is coming for you and all that you can give Islam. Paradise truly awaits you."

Parvez explained that the Americans planned to dribble the liquid fertilizer into the sea over many months, "But you will blow up the tanker. It will fill the sky with flames, and the ocean will turn orange as far as the eye can see. The infidels will pay the highest price for drowning us. I have done research," he glanced at his iPhone, "and it is simple: If we release all the fertilizer at once, it will make temperatures drop till they freeze in their colder countries. Then they will stop stealing our island."

Adnan agreed to sign up for tanker duty without the hesitation that he'd shown about bombing diamond island. His eyes brightened when Parvez told him that they would make a video of him and post it on scores of Islamic Web sites. "You, Adnan, *you* will declare victory for Muslims everywhere."

Parvez stared at the open ocean, imagining flames and orange floodwaters—the surface of the sea reflecting the holocaust of sky—and knew that martyrdom would greet his friend, and that both of them would be honored the world over.

CHAPTER 7

Forensia sat "sky clad" on the crunchy meadow grass. The strikingly pretty twenty-three-year-old wore only the sunflower tattoo on her right shoulder and a red ankh—the oddly anthropomorphic-looking Egyptian cross—on her left breast. She resisted a powerful urge to brush aside one of her long black braids and look at the other naked bodies gathered behind her and Sang-mi.

The two young women were about to be initiated into a witches' coven. A few feet in front of them a "circle of power," formed of white stones, glowed under the full moon. Inside the circle, an altar of rough-hewn pine had been raised. A twig broomstick, known as a besom, rested against the altar's left side. Three candles burned at its center. Forensia worried that they'd set off a raging conflagration. Then she spotted a bucket of water just outside the circle and hoped that it would be enough to snuff the flames if the candles fell over.

At the end of the altar closest to Forensia, incense smoldered, giving off a sharp, spicy odor that she couldn't identify.

A thick iron cauldron squatted beside the candles; the tip of a boline—a black-handled knife with a foot-long blade—had been sunk into the wood beside the pot. Reflections of the red and orange candle flames danced on the blade's shiny silver surface.

Forensia worried about what would come next—the blindfold, the tethering of her hands behind her back, and the scourging with whips. She struggled to take solace in the reassurances from Heart Warrior, her spiritual adviser, that these practices were largely symbolic. "You will not be hurt," Heart Warrior had told her. Even so, Forensia's nakedness—her sense of vulnerability—made her squirm silently. But more than any other goal in her life, she wanted to become what she had always known she was: a witch. It made bearable all the anxiety swirling through her system.

Reminding herself of her aspiration steadied her nerves until she realized that seeing the boline had caused a tiny knot to tug at her gut. Even the most benign-looking butter knives had always unsettled her, and this weapon did not look kind or gentle or forgiving. *Made for murder,* her mind whispered. Her worst fear—by far—had always been that she'd be killed with the savage inefficiency of a blade. One of her earliest memories was of hearing a news report over the radio in her mother's old Ford Falcon about a twelve-year-old girl who'd been stabbed forty-seven times. Fear of such a fate never left her and she was somehow drawn to every bit of news that mentioned a knifing death. Just days ago, she'd read of a young woman who had been killed with a butcher knife in New York City.

It's just a symbol, she reminded herself, *of how you're cutting yourself off from your old life.*

Forensia forced her gaze to a large pentagram of woven animal skin that was hanging from a branch behind the altar, like a giant pendant from a neck chain. But this was no laser-cut diamond heart or sapphire oval. The ancient five-pointed star had been hacked from crudely tanned hide spotted with patches of dull fur and scattered shanks of coarse hair that hung unevenly, like roughly chopped fringe. A cattle horn, grayed by smoke and time, curled out of the twisted pelts, a forged fang in an errant grave.

The star's harsh appearance was not reassuring and Forensia quickly reminded herself that the five points symbolized the five appendages of her body. That it hung from a tree also was symbolic, for trees represented the five true elements: earth, air, fire, water, and spirit. And each element represented the five points of a compass: Air was east, fire was south, water was west, earth was north, and spirit was the center. Microcosm upon microcosm of creation. Real meaning in all that you did and thought, especially on this day.

Only hours ago, Forensia and Sang-mi had given themselves a ritual bath in a spring, though finding one that hadn't succumbed to the devastating drought hadn't been easy. They'd had to drive forty-three miles and then hike for an hour up into the Catskill Mountains to bathe outdoors. But on the day of their initiation they knew that their skin and spirits needed to feel nature's elements directly. A bathtub would never do.

Once a witch, always a witch. Even as a young girl, she'd been drawn to witchcraft. Not the dark side, but not Disney's commodified version, either. Or Harry Potter's, for that matter. Much as she'd loved the Potter series—yes, she'd been one of those kids lining up at midnight for each new book—the world of Hogwarts had never appeared as real to her as the world within herself.

For Forensia, witchcraft was all consuming: befriending the trinity of maiden, mother, and crone who lived inside her; learning about the spirits of the land, sea, and air; using natural herbs and balms for healing and to gain wholeness; and enjoying the companionship of like-minded women. Practicing spells, too. Yet despite several years of study, she felt that she had only begun to learn these ancient magics. She'd be studying enchantments and charms—and a few carefully selected curses—the rest of her life. Spells were so hard to perfect, yet so vital to her growth.

Her fears ebbed as she considered her long path to the circle of power. Then she noticed a distinct trace of giddiness blooming in her belly, sweetened by the knowledge that Richtor sat, also shamelessly sky clad, only feet away. Over the past two months she'd been drawn to his quiet overtures, lured by his shockingly abundant blond dreads and his densely blue eyes that reminded her of cornflowers. She tried mightily not to look at him, not to linger on his lovely nakedness, but her body wouldn't obey such an easily eluded command, and a smile parted her lips when his open gaze met hers.

The feelings that had drawn her to Richtor, to hold his hand and kiss him, felt strong as thunder. They'd spent many evenings reading by candlelight in his simple wooden cabin, imagining the rites and rituals that neither of them had yet performed. But she'd never shown him her private *Book of Shadows,* an intensely intimate journal filled with jottings about spells, and the results—still spotty—of her magic making. And he and the other nonwitches would not be permitted at the initiation ceremony itself.

She looked at him once again, caught his eye, and felt ever more naked, open, willing. Any thoughts of blood or blindfolds or blades had been eclipsed as totally as the brazen face of the moon in the willfully calibrated heavens.

"Let's go check 'em out. Naked. *No* fucking clothes." Jason Robb pumped his fist, felt his abs clench. Girls loved that shit; too bad none of them was around to see him.

But maybe mo' betta, mon, not havin' dem shorties wich you. Ever since his parents had taken him to Montego Bay, Jason had begun talking to himself in what he thought of as his "Jamaican voice." He might be white, but he didn't have to sound like it. Still, he kept his quarterback's bark alive for his teammates: "Come on, you assholes. They're gonna be dancing around gettin' all horny. Got to strike while the punani's hot."

"Sounds too good to be true," groused Carl Boon, his center. Jason had seen enough of Boon's fat butt to last a lifetime, and he'd about had it with all the fag jokes about reaching down between Carl's chunky fucking legs. "You jerking him off during audibles, QB?" *Like I'd juke him, mon, even if I was some batty boy.*

"Hey, you know the one with the tat on her shoulder?" Jason said. "Big fucking flower?"

"Big fucking tits?" Gabe, his halfback, smiled. Built like his father and uncles: square body, square head, stumpy legs. Tiny dick.

"Yeah, Forensia, the one my brother drilled." She'd never fucked Gareth again. Wouldn't even kiss him. Called him a "bad mistake." And then Gar ran off and signed up and got his ass shot to death in Baghdad. The bitch didn't even come to his goddamn funeral. She breaks his heart, gets him sent to fucking Baghdad, and then spits on his grave. *Time to defend de family honor, bredda.* "She's joining some kind of witches' thing along with that new chink chick. Christy told me." Christy Walker, the sheriff's younger daughter.

"Christy gonna be there?" Carl asked, sounding like he couldn't have cared less.

"She wasn't sure. Suze's going." The older sister, the one Jason had played grab ass with forever. *More like grab dem everything, mon.*

Jason and about half his team squeezed into two cars and tore down the old lake road, which led along rolling hills before they roared onto a dirt track and raised a huge cloud of dust that tailed them past the Empire Campgrounds. If not for the drought, the campsites would have been packed with every kind of suck-ass city shithead, but since the lake started looking like a burned-up biscuit the place had been practically deserted.

Jason slowed, turning off Shabba Ranks's reggae rap because now he had to focus. ("Make yuh choo-choo like a train . . .") *This is where it gets tricky as shit,* he thought. He pulled over; the second car followed closely. Jason kicked open his door and hopped out. "We're gonna hafta huff it for about a mile up to Pointer Ridge."

"Shit, man, I don't want to hike all that way," Carl complained.

"You know what?" Jason stuck his head back into the car and stared as Carl tried to crawl out of the Camaro's tiny backseat. "You really are a fucking faggot."

"Fuck you," Carl muttered for the millionth time. "I'm just tired's all."

"Get out so Bert can move. You're no faggot, are you, Bert?"

Bert was a lineman, a body crusher; and he'd be a lineman the rest of his life, near as Jason could tell. Always staring at girls like he was

Lurch from *The Addams Family*. Not that any girl would go near him. Jason figured Bert was storing up the sight of legs and tits for later use. A goddamn squirrel thinking only of his nuts. *Well, not only de nutbag, mon.*

"Everybody," Jason said after the guys emptied out of the two cars, "shut the fuck up when we get near the ridge. You want to see some fucking ass, you shut your fucking pie holes."

"I'm planning on a whole lot more than *seein'* some ass," Ryan Petress said. The team's split end.

"Yeah, Ryan, what're you thinkin'?"

"I'm thinkin' we're raidin' their hot witchy asses." That set off a cheer.

"Yeah, nobody ever recognize you."

"It's dark."

"Ain't that dark, bro. Full fucking moon. Let's just get up there, see what happens. Hey, they may be rapin' *us*."

They set off like they were possessed, except for Carl, dragging ass like always. *Got de moves of a potted plant.*

The team settled down, but the trees went off like .22s every time an arm or a shoulder caught a branch.

"Watch your goddamn step," Jason hissed. "You want them throwin' on their panties before we get there?"

"Long as we get to tear the fuckers off," Ryan said.

Carl laughed, but like he had to.

Jason scrabbled up to where the trail fed onto the ridge, and crept to the overlook.

Holy fucking boom dogs, mon. They were all starting to stand, turning this way and that, really showing off their snatches. Giving him a crotchful, thanks to Mr. Moon. Couldn't be more than a hundred, hundred fifty feet away down in the clearing. Twenty of 'em, at least.

Shit. Some were guys, including the one with the butt that had caught Jason's eyes.

"Hey, Carl, check it out," he whispered. "There's your boyfriend," he said, pointing to the dude Jason had wanted to ream till he figured out the owner of that firm round ass had a goddamn dick.

Now he could see the girl who'd fucked his brother, moonlight splashing all over her tits and tattoos. *Fucking whore.* Killer *whore.*

"We got to get closer," Jason said, drawn in by the raw excitement of so much willing pussy. Beside him, Ryan was panting and Bert was almost drooling, staring like a starving squirrel.

Forensia brushed bits of dry grass off her legs and bottom, more conscious of her nudity now that she was standing and could feel eyes on her. Richtor's, yes, but other Pagans, too, about half of them witches. She didn't blame any of them for looking—she would have, in their place. Still, all those eyes on her . . . it felt like a million. Not that she was self-conscious about her appearance. She worked hard on the farm. Her arms, legs, back, all showed her strength, and her belly was tight and narrow.

GreenSpirit stepped naked from the shadows and raised her arms before them.

Oh my God, Forensia almost exclaimed aloud. *It's* her. *It's really her.*

Heart Warrior had intimated that a high priestess would conduct the initiation, but GreenSpirit herself? The rumors about her being around had been true, after all. GreenSpirit had been known to suddenly appear at such ceremonies, but Forensia had refused to let herself hope that the Wiccan leader would show up at her own initiation.

The tall woman stepped into the circle of power, her back to the altar. Her eyes roamed the gathering: almost two dozen devoted followers. She was naked but for a beaded necklace with a wooden ankh, the same symbol Forensia had tattooed on her shoulder. And GreenSpirit's face glowed in the moonlight, lean as her long limbs, and as serious as the spiritual practice she had long embraced.

"Shall we begin?" With a brief wave of her hand, GreenSpirit drew Forensia and Sang-mi into the circle and made them kneel before her. With another gesture, she banished the Pagans who were not witches, including Richtor, to a natural amphitheater hidden in the trees beyond the far side of the clearing. Heart Warrior had instructed them to conduct a silent ritual in support of the two young initiates.

Forensia felt the lingering intensity of the woman's gaze even after GreenSpirit turned to study Sang-mi. She thought the witch had a handsome face, a commanding presence. GreenSpirit had reportedly spent her adult life moving from coven to coven, nation to nation, making mysterious visits to powerful men and women, and occasionally speaking in public of the threats to Gaia. "Gaia is an organism as alive as you or me," she'd often said, "and it has its own survival foremost in mind." Now she repeated those cautionary words as the ceremony began, adding, "Gaia is magic. And magic is the science of the control of nature. Someday, science will understand what we know in our hearts: that other worlds thrive within and without."

She looked back down to Forensia and Sang-mi. "Have you studied the Law of Threefold Return?"

"Whatever action a person takes, good or bad," the two answered in unison, "will return to them with three times as much force."

"Do you know this in your hearts?"

"Yes," they said.

"And the eight virtues?"

"Beauty and strength, power and compassion, honor and humility, mirth and reverence."

GreenSpirit turned from them, raised her eyes to the pentagram, whirled back around—arms reaching up to the night sky, as if imploring the moon. Then she lowered her hands so that she could cup Forensia's face and draw her close. The initiate closed her eyes in anticipation of a kiss.

"Open your eyes," GreenSpirit whispered.

Forensia complied, staring into the witch's large green irises, eyes that were wild with an exuberant, entrancing spirit. The Pagan leader remained only a sweet breath away, so close that Forensia could indeed have kissed her. *Wanted* to kiss the swooning seductive power of belief, not body. For the first time that night, Forensia fully sensed the lush world of mysticism and magic that awaited her.

The witch's hands warmed, quickly becoming as hot as stove pads.

GreenSpirit drew away so slowly that seconds passed before the tips of her fingers lost contact with Forensia's cheeks.

GreenSpirit repeated these actions with Sang-mi. She and the Korean woman were locked in an intense union when the night's silence was suddenly broken by the snapping and trampling of nearby branches.

CHAPTER  8

Jason and his teammates froze. They had crept down from the ridge and slipped behind a thin curtain of parched forest that encircled the clearing. They'd stood there in silence until Bert lost his balance while beating off and fell into some tinder-dry and *noisy* bushes. Now the boys stared through a wicket of branches at the eerily silent witches, who were staring back.

"Step out from behind those trees," the older witch called.

Jason wanted to kick Bert's horny ass for giving them all away. Green-Spirit started forward.

"Let's get the fuck out of here," Ryan said, no more raidin' on his mind. "They're doing some spooky shit, man, and I don't want any part of it."

"That shit's shit," Jason said. But he might as well have been talking to the trees—the whole team was scuttling off.

Hell with that. Jason watched the witch walk toward him, moonlight on her sweet spots.

Dem de full fuckin' Monty, mon. Jason smiled. Old, but doable. A real MILF.

He stepped out, met her green-eyed gaze full on. His boner wanted to rip open his pants . . . and a whole lot more.

"What are you doing here?" she said calmly.

Jason peered at her closely. "Hey, I *know* you. Everybody's looking for your ass." He'd seen her face so much on TV that he would have known her even if she'd whipped by on her goddamn broomstick at Mach 5. He laughed. This felt great. *Wait'll I tell dem fools.*

"What is it that you want?" she asked.

"Shit, I don't want anything. Just heard there was a party. Thought we'd check it out."

"Where are your friends?"

Jason shrugged. "They got a little freaked."

"But not you."

"Nah, not me." *Check dem jumbly fucking bumblies, mon.*

"I think you're curious. That's healthy, a good thing," GreenSpirit said.

"Not *that* kind of curious," Jason volleyed. He let his eyes wander all over the witch.

"You needn't be ashamed of your interest in witchcraft. People are called to it from all ways of life."

"I'm not called to this shit. I'm just checking out the party."

"Then join us."

She's bluffing. He'd call her on it: "Yeah, sure."

"But you must take off the rest of your clothes."

No shirt, and now she wants dem pants? "No can do." Not with his woody saluting the commander in chief.

"Don't worry about *that*." She eyed the bulge in his jeans. "Nobody cares."

Another naked group drifted out of the forest to his left, the younger ones whom he'd watched from the ridge, including Christy. She stared at him like she was worried that he'd give her away. Her sister, Suze, stood close by. Suze knew what he had in his pants.

The old witch put her hand on his shoulder. Before she could speak, he slapped it aside. "Don't you fuckin' touch me."

"Leave," the witch replied.

A guy with blond dreads hurried over—a hippie asshole Jason had seen around town. Standing next to her like a goddamn bouncer. "Leave," he said, but to Jason, he sounded like a jerk-off, and his dick looked smaller than a stinkbug.

"Yes, go," the witch said to Jason.

"Nah, I'm staying, see how you naked witches party. Then I'm selling your ass to the highest bidder. See this?" He pulled out a business card. "CBS News. I got one from all of them. They're all over the place looking for you. They want you to tell them all about your sex parties with your old boyfriend, Roger." As in Roger Lilton, the presidential candidate.

He could see her face clearly now and knew that he'd spooked *her*. She was so desperate she was trying to fix him with a stare. What was that supposed to do? Melt him like he was some goddamn Snow Queen?

"I'm going to cast a spell on you, if you don't leave."

Did he hear her right? A spell? "What? Turn me into a fucking frog? *Ribbit, ribbit.*" He grabbed his swollen crotch, gave it a nice tug. "I'll cast one on you, you're not careful. Hey," he tugged again, "you'd probably like that, wouldn't you?"

Much as he was loath to admit it, the witch's eyes were freaking him out. He turned away, thinking it was time to go, then spun back, refusing to admit his fear to himself or to her.

The fucking witch threw something in his face. So light, it could have been dust; but no, it felt moist, like she'd spritzed him. Hard to say what it was, except it was cold, *freezing fucking cold,* and his face turned numb. A goddamn fucking ice cream headache. He pressed the heels of his hands to his temples, wincing. Her green eyes were looking past him. No, they were staring *through* him, icier still. Scared him half to death. Nobody had ever looked at him like that. Her lips were moving, but he couldn't hear shit.

"What? What?" he shouted.

The icy cold drained from his head. He was so grateful, he whimpered. But it kept draining—down through his chest, belly, and in the next instant he knew with horror where it would stop. *You fucking bitch. You goddamn fucking, green-eyed—*

The frigid flow froze every imprecation, settling like a blizzard on his cock and balls. Draining all desire.

His boner was gone. Forever. That's all he kept thinking: *Forever.*

He ran off, moonlight still on his bare back.

Forensia stared at Jason's panicky departure, and vowed to herself to work even harder on spells. She had never seen one executed so effectively. Everything she'd ever heard about GreenSpirit was true. She had amazing power. Jason and his friends had violated the Pagans, a sacred ceremony, and GreenSpirit—and he had paid a high price.

Forensia was so mesmerized by what she had witnessed that she didn't notice GreenSpirit walking back to the circle of power. The witch startled her by touching Forensia's shoulder, then told her and Sang-mi to remain on their knees in the circle while everyone chanted.

Forensia turned her thoughts away from what had just happened and lost herself in the lulling rhythm of the Wiccan chants. Soon she felt herself lifted high above the forest, flying over the scorched, prickly canopy. The surge of sensation proved so intense, so intoxicating, that her feeling of flight—of swift, ethereal remove—superseded her other senses: The whole of her being was imbued with the spirit's own sway.

Now GreenSpirit blindfolded both Sang-mi and Forensia, and in the darkness behind the cloth Forensia heard a creak as the boline was drawn from the rough pine plank of the altar. The priestess pressed the flat of the blade down on Forensia's head, then against first one cheek and then the other, angling it just enough to give the younger woman a keen sense of the weapon's edge. But fear had lost the battle with trust high above the clearing, when Forensia had looked down from the depthless night sky and seen her vast unfurling future, a world bereft of blood and death.

When the tip of the knife touched her lips, she opened them wide as a mother giving birth. And like legions of women before her, Forensia's belly tightened and twitched in a harsh labor of longing. She accepted the symbolism of the harrowing blade, and tried mightily not to flinch or shake.

The boline withdrew slowly, touching her tongue with intention, leaving a metallic trail along her taste buds. Next the buds of her breasts felt the blade's insistent tip and, strangely, stirred in tender defiance.

Had she been cut? She couldn't tell, and the weapon traveled like a sharp shadow to the base of her spine before rising over every vertebrae—a peculiar if ancient blessing—before returning to her tongue, as if to sever Forensia from the chains of her own flesh. But she tasted no blood, and this surprised her.

Minutes passed. Forensia assumed GreenSpirit was blessing Sang-mi. At last, the young woman heard footfalls as the other witches gathered around them inside the circle of power. A knotted leather whip suddenly burned her back. She smelled risen dust, thought of Calvary and steel—old religion and new—and filled with the unwavering power of pain as the whip changed hands. But she did not bleed.

A new chant, dark and unfamiliar, raised the hair on her arms and neck: The animal in her heart unleashed torrents of terror in her retreating mind. Fear blackened her belly and she abruptly felt the claustrophobia of blindness, dense and graven as the black borders of the eternally shaken universe.

GreenSpirit drew close to Forensia and Sang-mi. "If it harms none?" she asked in an urgent voice.

"Do what ye will," the two young women said.

"And will you guard the Craft, the Secrets of the Craft, and all your brothers and sisters, no matter their age, no matter their state of grace?"

"I will," Forensia yelled, hearing Sang-mi's softer voice echo her response: a marriage vow to all of Gaia's creations.

GreenSpirit bade them stand. The blindfolds came off and the two new witches embraced their sisters of faith, who held them gently, avoiding the new welts on their backs.

Richtor and the other Pagans raced from the trees like moonlit sprites. All of them—initiated and uninitiated alike—joined hands. Forensia took Richtor's with a smile as full and rich as any she'd ever offered him or anyone, then reached for Suze Walker, the sheriff's oldest daughter. Sang-mi stood across from her, linking GreenSpirit and one of the older witches who'd driven down from Ithaca.

They danced, counterclockwise, never losing contact with one another. The candle flames flickered wildly in the draft of their movement. It threw shadows everywhere, licking color across the boline, back in place on the altar.

Forensia felt intensely aroused by Richtor's touch. She wanted to remember him always like this, with his hair flying, and his hand warm and soft and tightly grasped in hers. She squeezed her eyes shut in delight, then snapped them open as she heard someone crashing through the woods. A new light revealed a reporter and cameraman marching toward them with Jason close behind.

"Paul Kellison, CBS News. I'm looking for GreenSpirit. I have just a few questions for you, GreenSpirit," he added, as if he'd already spied her, but that wasn't possible because they'd closed their circle around the altar, concealing their leader, and their faces, from view. After a moment, as naturally as the circle had closed, it opened, unabashed as a flower.

GreenSpirit had vanished. It was as if they'd rehearsed, but what Forensia found inspiring and dauntingly mysterious was that they'd reacted instinctively, almost primordially, to protect her. *Guard the Craft, the Secrets of the Craft, and all your brothers and sisters.*

Then she realized that every second of her life had been preparation for these moments.

Her thoughts were interrupted by Suze whispering "Oh, shit" over and over, as if profanity were the only mantra that mattered. Forensia realized why—it was inevitable now that Suze's father would know that she and Christy had been here, naked and with other Pagans. Even if the news report blurred Suze's features, Jason Robb would tell everyone.

Kellison said, sharply, "Where's GreenSpirit?"

"What are you talking about?" Forensia quickly stepped in front of Suze, blocking the camera's view of her friend. "If you mean that woman on the news, she's not here."

The other Pagans agreed.

"You said she was here." Kellison turned to Jason.

"She was. I saw her. I *talked* to her. But that was," he glanced at his watch, "an hour ago."

"He's a liar," Forensia said. "A total bullshitter."

"Everyone knows that," Richtor said, "except you, I guess."

"He probably made you pay him to bring you down here," Sang-mi chimed in. "We're here once a month, and he's done this kind of thing before."

"Most of the time he just takes money from perverts," Forensia said. "We just wish he'd grow up."

Kellison and his cameraman hurried along the perimeter of the clearing, shining the strong camera light into the woods. Then they stormed off, taking their gear and their anger but not their discredited guide: Jason stared at Forensia.

"You fucking lying bitch. You fucked me royally."

"Just leave and *don't* come back," Forensia said.

"You're not gettin' away with this, you fucking bitch."

"You're an asshole just like . . ."

She stopped herself, but not soon enough to quash the memory of Jason's dead brother—or to hold on to the magic and mysticism she'd felt during her initiation.

Jason lunged for her neck, nearly seizing her. Richtor pushed him down and the other Pagans crowded the young man on three sides.

"Go," Richtor shouted. "Get out of here."

Jason scrambled to his feet, brushed himself off, and glared at them. After a moment, his gaze focused on Forensia. She felt the heat of his anger as if he were clawing at her skin; she had to force herself to stand boldly before him. Under his stare, her ankh, long revered as a symbol of life, felt like a target, teeming with the imminent dreadfulness of violent death.

Jenna's stomach started to swirl the second she spotted the black Ford Fusion waiting outside her building. She loved the silence of the day's awakening hour, when she'd rise at three thirty to a strangely subdued city, but that stillness vanished with synaptic speed when she spotted the shiny beast that signaled the beginning of the morning blur.

Before she made it to the curbside, the spry driver was holding open the rear door of the hybrid. She eased into the backseat, more intensely awake than usual because Dafoe had promised to meet her at five by the unobtrusive side entrance that everyone on *The Morning Show,* including visitors, was expected to use. In the spirit of reciprocity, Jenna had offered Dafoe her guest room. But he said he'd get up just a little earlier and drive down; Forensia, he'd explained, would be fresh from her initiation and wouldn't be able to take over for him until "the cocks crowed."

"Can she handle the whole operation?" Jenna had asked him on the phone.

"Forensia can handle anything," Dafoe had answered. "Plus, she'll have Bayou keeping his eye on the herd. She'll be good to go."

But would Jenna be "good to go" with Dafoe watching her race through all her primping and prep for *The Morning Show*? Not until this instant, driving toward the studio, had she realized that she'd never invited a love interest to the set.

Just be on time, Dafoe. It would be a huge hassle with security if he ran—

Ah, there he was, standing by the entrance, chatting to one of the black-suited security staff. About . . . *cows,* she overheard as the network's doorman helped her out of the Fusion. *That subject sure could get old fast,* she worried. A friend had married a prominent rock drummer, who'd talked about nothing but drumming for the first five years of their marriage. Jenna's friend had told her that when her husband had suggested bedroom spanking, she couldn't help wondering if he'd wanted to replace his tom-toms with her buttocks.

Dafoe saw her and smiled: toothy and ear to ear with the sweetest crinkles around his eyes. Jenna's doubts fled. His swift, head-to-toe glance made her happy that she'd chosen her outfit with him in mind: a white, crinkled poplin dress with a scoop neck. As summery as the weather, the dress flattered Jenna in all the right ways.

They approached metal doors two stories high. Stage hands used this entrance to roll equipment, including cranes and cherry pickers, into the building. Each door was reinforced with steel plates to stop bullets and bomb fragments. To the right stood two security officers by a standard-size metal door that had the same steel-plate reinforcement. Jenna told the men that Dafoe was a friend.

As soon as they entered the building, they came to the network's second line of defense, two security officers who worked behind four inches of bulletproof glass. The "two Joes"—Joe Santoro and Joe English—smiled broadly, which gave away their thoughts as readily as Jenna's blush revealed her own fizzy feelings.

She swiped her ID card and looked into a screen that read her eyes. Dafoe slid his driver's license through a narrow slot, then watched Santoro study the license, type on a keyboard, and stare at a computer's screen, waiting to see if a crime report started flashing. Seconds later he announced, "He's clean."

The other Joe handed Dafoe a clip-on badge, warning him not to take it off in a heavy, put-on New York accent. "Someone, he sees ya widout it, youse goin' down for a cavity check, and I don't mean youse teef." The two Joes laughed.

"Real jokers," Dafoe said to Jenna as they hurried to the elevator along with other new arrivals.

"I don't know about that. They've given me three cavity searches so far. They keep saying it's for security purposes, but I'm beginning to wonder."

Laughing quietly, they walked past the show's glassed-in, street-level studio, where fans could watch the proceedings from outside. The glass was deceptively thick—seven inches that could stop bullets *and* bomb fragments—and extended all the way up through the third-floor set. Television in the age of terror.

Jenna led Dafoe into an elevator with the same two-story metal doors. Massive, especially by the claustrophobic standards of the city. They stepped off on the third floor, bearing left to go through another standard-issue metal door that took them into a long hallway.

"We're entering the brain trust," Jenna joked.

"Meaning?" Dafoe still walked with a big smile.

"This is the floor with the greenroom and all the offices for every-one on the show."

"And there you are," Dafoe said, pointing to her photograph, one of the many familiar faces that lined both sides of the hallway.

"How was the drive down?"

"No problem. I even found a parking spot on the street for Bessie." His ridiculous name for his old International Harvester pickup. "I doubt anyone's going to want to steal her."

"You never know," she said cheerily, smitten not by the prospect of the truck's theft, of course, but by her own feelings for the vehicle: She liked the musty smell of old hay, and the memory of Dafoe's arm around her shoulders when she cuddled up to him on the bench seat.

They came to yet another set of metal doors that led them past the third-floor studio, even larger than the one below. Jenna's weather set was in view, but they hurried past the studio almost as quickly as the grips and stagehands and gaffers who raced to ready the sets. Four of them darted past the couple and ducked into the greenroom, where food for staff and guests was provided. The buffet was delicious and included something for every taste.

"You can help yourself whenever you want to," she told him as they moved on. "Your little badge gets you in there, too."

The really big names were never taken to that greenroom. VIPs, like Brad or Angelina, or the president, were hustled directly to a special, exclusive greenroom.

The Morning Show had more than fifty staffers, and the bustle at this hour equaled the energy of any other busy studio at midday. Jenna noticed the looks that she and Dafoe were garnering, even a few hellos from staffers generally more taciturn, and knew that she'd be prime gossip on the network grapevine. *Comes with the territory,* she reminded herself.

Her office was at the end of the hall. As they approached, Nicci called out, "It's a fatty," and thrust a thick packet of papers into Jenna's hands—a set of computer modeling data on worldwide weather. The report was generated by the show's assistant meteorologist, who worked the overnight shift and was often gone by the time Jenna came in. Years of experience let Jenna usually guess the report's length within a few pages. Seventy-two, she figured, then looked: seventy. *Not bad.*

"I remember you," Nicci said to Dafoe, offering him a smile that seemed to expand her size-two proportions. "Our helicopter almost hit you."

"Yes, that would be me, the helipad."

Nicci turned her barely bundled energy on Jenna: "Weather girl, I'm having problems getting video of a huge tornado down in Arkansas. I'm on my way to pound some heads and find out why."

"Anybody hurt?"

"No."

"Tell me it's not more trailer park footage."

"No, that's what's so great," Nicci exclaimed. "It's a gated community."

"Yes!"

The two women high-fived.

"We're *so* tired of seeing trailer park video," Jenna explained to Dafoe, "that sometimes it's nice to be reminded that weather is a great equalizer."

"Tell me about it," Dafoe said sympathetically.

"I talked to the affiliate," Nicci said. "Supposedly you can see the actual gate sticking out of the roof of a McMansion. Oh, and a flyaway mattress the size of Manhattan jammed into a bay window. Inquiring minds want to know."

"Any interviews?" Jenna asked, already flipping through the weather data.

"With the owner of that house, who—get this—is the conductor of the Little Rock Symphony. But the affiliate says she sounds like she's straight out of Bah-stuhn." Working the Kennedy accent.

"Why can't people fulfill their cultural stereotypes? Is that asking too much?" Jenna pleaded playfully. "It would make our jobs so much easier. Do we have anyone who actually sounds like they're from Little Rock?"

"I'll check on that, too." Nicci rushed off.

Jenna was about to get serious with the weather packet when she realized that an important and highly appealing task had yet to be undertaken. She closed the door, walked to Dafoe, and kissed him. "Good morning." She clasped her hands around his head. "You look great."

"You *really* do."

"Well, get a gander now because they'll be putting me through makeup in a little bit."

Another quick peck and she planted herself back at her desk, scrolling through a list of video on her three large computer screens—the two on the sides angled slightly, like a three-way dressing room mirror. As she shifted the cursor over each listing, weather video from around the world came to life on the screen to her right, just enough to give her a flavor of the disasters of the day. She had three minutes and fifty seconds to fill in each of her four *Morning Show* appearances, and each had to be packaged differently to keep viewers watching, even though they would contain the same key information.

She explained to Dafoe what she was doing. "If this is putting you to sleep, you can go hit the buffet. The food really is good."

"No worries. It's just good to see you."

"Back at you. I'm looking forward to the end of this show."

She returned her attention to the videos, then reviewed the rest of the world's weather. She checked the Maldives, as she did most days of late, thankful that there were no tsunamis or bulletins about anything turbulent—meteorologically speaking, anyway—taking place. Rick Birk, the network's crusty old investigative reporter, was nosing around the capital city, no doubt in search of Rafan or anyone else he thought could give him a lead on the Islamists terrorizing the country. At least Birk had given up badgering Jenna for contacts.

She heard a knock and looked up, instantly charmed by the appearance of Kato, a sable German shepherd bomb-sniffing dog, and his handler, Geoff Parks.

"May I?" Jenna always checked with Geoff, who nodded. "Kato, come," she called.

The dog walked over to Jenna and looked at her with what Jenna always felt was a smile. "Kato, sit," she said.

The shepherd snapped to and waited, ears rotating like radar dishes, always on alert. "Kato, shake." The dog extended his right paw. This was no sloppy stab at a handshake—Kato had a king's dignity.

She held his thickly padded paw. "You're a sweetie." Glancing at Geoff, she said, "Dafoe here has an amazing border collie on his dairy farm. Totally trained for herding."

"Really?" The two dog fanciers started talking. Jenna patted Kato's head—their daily ritual—and turned back to her work. Kato and his master exited moments later.

"You've got more security than the airports," Dafoe said.

"*Hmmm.* I wonder who's doing it right," Jenna answered over her shoulder. "Them or us? Nobody's blowing up our sets. Of course, we get a lot fewer people coming through here, and most of them aren't looking to hijack the network."

A stylishly coiffed dark-haired woman poked her head in the door. "Are you reh-dee?" she asked in a distinctively French accent.

"Be right there," Jenna said and the woman walked away. "Hair and makeup," she explained to Dafoe. "I'll look a little different when you see me next."

A quick stroll across the hall landed her in Chantal's hands. The woman exclaimed, as she did most days, "You 'ave zee most boo-tee-full 'air." Jenna sat in one of five chairs before a mirror that extended across the entire wall. She still had the packet of worldwide weather in her hands. Her attention was quickly captured by data about thunderstorms. *These could be real beauties,* she thought, spotting a temperature difference of almost one hundred twenty degrees from the minus forty degree top of the sixty-thousand-foot-high system to the ground. That could produce awesome T-storm activity.

She'd have to keep an eye on this one. The jet stream, cruising at 175 miles an hour, could help pull the budding storm right into the troposphere. Or, to put it another way, right smack into the face of every New Yorker. A funnel cloud—aka tornado—could follow. One of the interim signs she'd be looking for would be hail the size of baseballs. The Razorback State didn't have a monopoly on twisters.

Nicci popped into hair and makeup. "I've got Cindy"—as in Clark, chief of the National Weather Service—"for a quick Q and A on the storms."

"I was just reading about the biggie heading this way."

"Not to mention Florida, Texas, and California."

"Really? I hadn't gotten that far yet."

"You want to do a minute with Cindy?"

"Sure. Let's ask her to talk about protecting yourself from electrical storms. We haven't done that in a while."

"I'll prime her." Nicci pivoted to leave, then spun back. "Dafoe? He's a lot cuter without the gun."

Chantal finished Jenna's hair and makeup and stood back to admire her handiwork. "Boo-tee-full, boo-tee-full," trailed Jenna to wardrobe, where she donned an Anna Sui dress with a hint of red, a color that always looked stunning with her white-blond hair. This completed her transformation from an attractive businesswoman to a *Morning Show* superstar. A few moments later, in her office, she watched the makeover register on Dafoe's face—and wished she hadn't. His lips tightened, and he actually pulled his head back a couple of inches, as if he feared touching her now. She hated having that effect on people but it was a fact of television life: every hair in place; lips reddened; eyelashes curled; and her cheeks, chin, nose, and brow powdered precisely. A friend once said Jenna looked so perfect going on the air that she appeared untouchable and not quite real. "Like a porcelain doll."

"I'm still me," she said to Dafoe softly, "the woman who was kissing you just a little bit ago. It's just that you can't kiss this me because it would smudge my makeup."

"I know what you mean. I run into that every day with the cows."

She laughed, loving the fact that he could make a joke of it so quickly. She settled at her computer and saw a message from Nicci saying that she'd finally run down the tornado video.

Then Jenna realized that she could be sitting front and center for New York City's own tornado. *Better check the roof cam.*

It was hard to see much in the dim early daylight but she definitely spied clouds massing to the northeast.

Nicci buzzed her that the morning meeting was about to start.

Every day at 5:45 A.M., they convened in executive producer Marv Balen's office. The twit would offer a show overview that Jenna could listen to with one ear: Her role was so defined that on most days she could keep paging through updated weather summaries while he yammered. She'd been blessed with a photographic memory for weather charts, and had been studying them for so long that she could spot a troublesome trend in a nanosecond.

Jenna discreetly slipped her earpiece into place. Her long hair made its presence nearly undetectable. On set, Marv, Nicci, and James Kanter, the wiry director, used the earpiece system to talk to her and the other on-air staff. Marv just barked, a one-note dog; Kanter almost always remained collected; and Nicci said only what was necessary. During the morning meeting, the earpiece allowed Nicci to dart away to monitor weather news and relay anything important to Jenna.

Marv's big announcement was that they'd landed presidential candidate Roger Lilton as the show's first featured interview. "He's going to talk about his relationship with that GreenSpirit witch and his campaign manager told me a few minutes ago that Lilton's going to denounce her as a 'freak.' Quite a coup, folks."

No kidding, Jenna thought. The only thing better would be to have GreenSpirit walk onto the set in the middle of Lilton's interview.

While Marv briskly laid out the show's flow, periodically verifying details with the weary overnight staff, Geoff and Kato passed through the room, the shepherd sniffing everywhere. Jenna patted him as he passed; he gave her a wag.

After the meeting, Jenna found Dafoe sitting on the couch in her office, texting. He looked up, consternation spelled out on his wrinkled brow.

"I can't reach Forensia. We text all the time, even when I'm there. It's a big farm, and it beats shouting. But it's like she's disappeared."

"She's there. She's got to be. You said she's incredibly reliable."

"She is. Or *was,* till the other day. But she's not responding, and I'm worried. It's not just about her: Those cows *have* to be milked." He put away his phone. "Sorry, I know you've got your show to think about. You doing okay?"

"Great." Shorthand for nervous. She always felt nervous going on air, but more than usual this morning because Dafoe was there. *Don't start dwelling on that.* "Guess who's going to be on the show?" He raised his eyebrow. "Lilton. To denounce GreenSpirit."

"Forensia's going to be heartbroken. She actually sent him money."

"If he's going to have a prayer of winning, he's got to cut his losses," Jenna said, which was more generous than she felt: She hadn't gotten over Lilton's "dog-and-pony show" comment about the task force.

"I guess nobody loses with honor anymore."

"Not when you're within striking distance."

"So how's the weather doing?"

"Oh, *that,*" she joked. "Big thunderstorms. Wait. Hold on." Nicci's voice had come alive in her ear. "You hear what's going on outside?" her producer asked. Jenna paused, nodded to herself: the proverbial bricks tumbling in the sky, getting ready to stone the city.

Seconds later Nicci flew through the doorway. Before she could say a word, Jenna blurted out, "Do they want me on the roof?" She hated going up there. The only time Marv ever wanted her by the roof cam was in a storm. She strongly suspected that he found her instant transformation from staid perfection to total dishevelment—hair flying, hem, too—to be a ratings booster. One of these days, Jenna worried that a powerful gust would pluck her up and throw her down sixty stories, into the maw of Manhattan. Dying with her dainties on full display. And she'd be hard to miss in these red shoes—to highlight the red note in her dress. The guy in wardrobe loved to dress her; Jenna was his Barbie and her outfits were carefully color-coordinated.

"No, not the roof. Even Marv doesn't want you zapped live."

"I'm not sure of that."

Nicci leaned over Jenna's shoulder and clicked on the camera icon on her computer. *Big* thunderheads, but still on the horizon. "Time to go. They want you on set. And you, Helipad," Nicci waved Dafoe up from the couch, "come with us. I'll park you by Zack." Head of set security.

Nicci, you're so trusting, Jenna thought as she followed her producer. Dafoe trailed them down the hall.

Andrea Hanson was already ensconced on the main set, where she would spend the first hour of the broadcast. The chestnut-haired anchor deemphasized her pregnancy as much as she could in autumn's darker hues. Her face, a little fuller than it had been a few months ago, beamed as beautifully as ever. She had ideal features for morning television: not too sharp, not too bland. Easy on the eyes, in short. For the second hour—the lighter half of the show—Andrea would migrate downstairs to the public studio, where audiences smiled and waved for the cameras through the seven-inch-thick security glass.

Theme music thumped throughout the studio and Jenna watched Andrea come alive, giving the camera her most engaging smile. In minutes, Jenna was chortling with the host. Jenna kept it light, airy as an orchard, before turning to the camera to give an overview of the nation's weather, gesturing to a blank blue screen as she talked. Viewers at home saw Jenna's hand heading toward Arizona.

"And it's scorching in the desert Southwest where temperatures in

Phoenix set a new October record of one hundred fifteen degrees. The average high for them this month used to be eighty-eight."

She was determined not to say "hot and dry" one more time this year, but it slipped out as she spoke over video of the city's numerous—and long-drained—fountains. Though she cursed herself mentally, Jenna's voice never faltered as she took viewers on a snappy tour of the West, still moving her hand over the blue screen, before video of the tornado damage in Arkansas appeared, along with Nicci in her ear: "You've got Cindy Clark now."

Jenna chatted about the damage in Little Rock, noting the huge, ungainly looking gate protruding from a roof. As she talked, Nicci told her the mattress was coming up in "Five, four, three . . ." Jenna timed it perfectly: "And as you can see here, someone's boudoir is missing a Beautyrest; but as tornado damage goes, this wasn't too bad, was it, Cindy?"

"No, Jenna, it wasn't. Only a few minor cuts and bruises. I'd say that Little Rock rode this one out in style."

Jenna, still standing on the weather set, casually introduced the country's chief meteorologist, whose face filled the screen and whose practical advice about thunderstorms filled the air. Cindy Clark's perky visage was quickly replaced by the flat affect of Sondar Hammerson, the Little Rock Orchestra's conductor, who was so boring that Marv was immediately in Jenna's ear saying "Wrap it ASAP. I'm hearing crickets"—millions of viewers clicking their remotes to change channels. "Switch to the roof."

Jenna cut off Hammerson at the first opening and ushered viewers to the rooftop camera as if that had been planned all along, stifling her own surprise when she saw the sky filled with massively thick clouds. They'd moved into the city far faster than she'd ever seen before, although extreme weather events were beginning to feel routine.

"This is the view from our rooftop garden, and if you think those are thunder clouds that we're seeing, you're right. There's a whopper of a storm brewing out there. Here," she pointed to the right side of the screen, "you can see the classic anvil shapes of thunderheads. So, New

York, get ready, because this monster is marching right at us. We're already seeing rain on our Doppler. So far it's evaporating before it hits the ground, but that's not going to last long. Florida, Texas, California, we've got your back, too. Andrea?"

Hanson thanked her and teased Lilton's imminent appearance as the show's theme music signaled the first commercial break. Jenna hurried over to Dafoe. Catching his grimace as he looked up from his iPhone, she guessed that he still hadn't reached Forensia. She hoped the young woman was all right.

Dafoe managed a smile, though, and a whispered compliment: "You were great."

Viewers could not possibly have heard him—*TMS* was off the air— but she shushed him anyway: no unnecessary talk anywhere near the set. A moment later she violated her own dictum: "There he is," she said softly as Lilton loped toward Andrea. The lean sixty-two-year-old—a runner—always presented an effortlessly fit image, which in politico speak translated into "readiness." And he sported his never-changing attire: dark blue suit, white shirt, red tie. Nothing subtle about the underdog's campaign duds. Every candidate had a stump speech, but Lilton also had a stump suit.

"Twenty seconds," the floor director snapped. Andrea shook Lilton's hand and gave him her familiar smile. Boom mikes hovered over the two of them as they sat down.

"And in five, four, three . . ."

The commercials ended and the cameras went live. Andrea flipped aside her luscious mane of dark hair, warmly welcomed viewers back, and introduced Lilton. The candidate nodded genially as Hanson leaned forward, gesturing directly at him. Her manner reminded Jenna why Hanson's numbers had dominated morning television for five straight years: The host could switch from the sweetness of an ingénue to the toughness of a federal prosecutor faster than most people could exhale.

"That witch is haunting you, isn't she, Senator Lilton?"

"I'm glad you brought that up, Andrea, because the president has been trying to make it appear that someone I knew forty years ago—"

"In the biblical sense." Andrea conjured her most impish smile.

"I was involved with her forty years ago and—"

Andrea interrupted again: "How did you two end up so much in sync? That's what everyone wants to know. You called the Presidential Task Force on Climate Change a 'dog-and-pony show' two days *after* GreenSpirit used those exact words."

"I'd like your viewers to think about something, Andrea. *If* I'd been in touch with Linda Pareles, as the president suggests—"

"Linda Pareles? You won't even use her chosen name: GreenSpirit?"

"I knew her as Linda Pareles. As I was saying, if I'd actually been in touch with Pareles, why would I quote her and open myself up to the ridiculous accusation that I've got a witch as a consultant?"

"Nancy Reagan had an astrologist."

"I've never consulted with a witch or an astrologer, and I never will. More than three decades of public service informs my decisions, and my campaign has attracted first-rate foreign and domestic policy advisers because they know that in a few days voters will be making the most critical choice in our nation's history. The American people are not going to let themselves get sidetracked by this sideshow."

"Voters are sure paying attention to the YouTube video of you and GreenSpirit saying the same exact words. That's got a lot of traction."

"And if you were to do a simple Internet search, you'd find that dozens of bloggers also called the task force a dog-and-pony show. Look, in plain English, I consider GreenSpirit to be a wacko. I've had no contact with her in thirty-eight years." Now Lilton leaned forward. "Andrea, the real issue—"

"Is how you're going to get rid of your witch problem long enough to win this election? Your numbers are tanking."

"My numbers are strong. We're gaining momentum in all the swing states. As for Linda Pareles, I'm addressing that issue head-on. I think the American people are too smart to fall for any more of the president's cheap, diversionary tactics. Reynolds has failed to recognize, much less address, the very real danger that climate change presents to the vital national security of our great country. We need to have leadership that can assert itself on the world stage. There are real issues facing the American people . . ."

As Lilton launched into political boilerplate, Jenna guided Dafoe away from the set. Marv was no doubt barking at Hanson to end the interview as fast as she could: The "witch haunting" had been the "gotcha" question, and now it was history.

Jenna and Dafoe hurried to her office. She closed the door, turned to him, and put her arms around his neck.

"We have about sixty seconds," she told him. "Smudge me. Please."

Rain splatters the packed earth, pouring down so hard that the fat drops *ping* when they strike the brittle branches, muffling the panicky footfalls of a murderous chase. They strike her face. She tries to blink them away, but can't.

Ping, ping, ping.

The rain blurs her vision. Tree limbs tear her skin, rip her clothes. Shredded strips hang from prickly snags. Dense dead woods. She can't see ten feet. Doesn't dare look back. Not anymore. *Run,* she screams at herself. *Don't fucking stop.*

He checks his watch. Half an hour's gone by. She's getting tired, can't keep it up much longer. He can hear her horror, even from here. It's clawing at her throat. She wants to find a nice little hidey-hole, but he's not going to let that happen. And the crying sounds so *good,* like the kind of fear you can't stop.

A storm like this can wipe away her trail. Probably what she was hoping for when she started running. But she can't outrun him, and the rain's washing away his tracks, too. They'll be floating all the way down to the Hudson and halfway around the world, like ghost prints. You can't see them, but they'll be there. He's already fleeing the scene of the crime and the real fun's not even begun. The perfect murder.

What's she going to do? Get on a broomstick and fly away? This is easy. Every step's taking her right where he wants her.

Yippie-yi-yo-ki-yay. Herding time. Heading to a nice cozy cabin. She'll slam the door and lock it (he's been there, so he knows, he *knows*), and he'll laugh, 'cause there's no keeping him out. A door doesn't say, "Stay out." It says, "Come on in and take your fun. It's waiting right here for you, all roasty warm." Still, when she slams it, he'll take a breath. Long as there aren't any other witches around, he'll have all the time he needs for all the vengeance he wants. She doesn't have a phone. He's seen this before. If she had a phone, she'd have it out by now. Her hands are empty. But not her heart. It's filled with fear, and she's earned every bit of it. She just didn't know when to stop, did she? You *don't* do what she did to him.

He pulls a swatch of purple fabric off a branch. *Look at that, will you? There she goes again. She just can't keep 'em on.*

Now she's less than a hundred feet away. So tired she's bent over. Wet, torn clothes clinging to her, showing off lots of everything. She's trying to stand straight so she can look back this way. Hasn't done that in a while. Got herself all chesty now, sticking them out, rising up and down. Big breaths.

There's someone in the woods and he's coming after you. There's someone in the woods . . . Talking to himself as he steps out from behind a tree, waving both arms in the air. Her eyes go as big as pinecones. She starts to back away, falls, drags herself to her feet.

There's someone in the woods . . . He's running hard enough to pound the earth to death. . . . *And he's coming after you.*

CHAPTER 10

Jenna appeared on *The Morning Show* four more times in the next hour and a half as the thunderheads drenched the thirsty city, over-whelming storm drains and New York's beleaguered sewer system, which sent what was flushed out of toilets right into the Hudson and East rivers. Lots of "brown trout" this morning. All 840 miles of the subway system also shut down after water rushed over the third rail. And the downpour sent scores of kids into the flooded streets to play and splash. On Fifth Avenue the water rose so high that pedestrians had to take off their shoes and dodge rooster tails of water from passing taxis. But the real nightmare—a tornado—hadn't formed. They were rare in New York, but by no means unheard of.

When Jenna collapsed next to Dafoe on the couch in her office at a little after 9:00 A.M., she felt drained.

"You earn your money," he said.

"Some of it." Sometimes it was hard to believe she earned far more in a month than nurses, cops, and teachers earned in a year. Not to mention dairy farmers or her deceased parents on their hardscrabble family farm.

"Come on." Jenna stood and grabbed Dafoe's hand. "I want to see firsthand what I've been talking about."

She didn't let go of him as they hurried to the elevator, despite the openly curious glances of her coworkers. She didn't much care. His warm touch felt positively delicious.

They hurried out of the building's grand entrance—all brass and marble and crystal sconces—to find every seam in the sky still wide open; but the rain was warm, the air warmer still.

The two of them sprinted under a jewelry store awning—bearing one of New York's most notable names—and watched the world trudge by under umbrellas or with the collars of their slickers cinched to their chins. No one noticed the handsome couple huddling together; the weather, ironically enough, was granting her precious minutes of anonymity.

"See all that water." She pointed to the overflow now inching onto the sidewalk. "That's exciting. Not good," she added quickly, "but exciting: Nature's reclaiming the city for a few hours."

Buoyant over Dafoe, the rain on her skin, and the percolating thrill of these ebullient seconds, Jenna scooted to the curb and dipped the toe of one red shoe into the rippled rainwater rushing by. "I hate these shoes," she said, face beading with droplets. "They're so tight they make my toes ache. I told the Barbie Master that I'd never wear them again."

With that, she took them off and splashed into the water. She had a wild impulse to scoop up handfuls and drench Dafoe, but a crazier urge overtook her instead, and this one proved irresistible: She pinched his open collar, lured him even closer with a look, and kissed him lusciously, right there in the pouring rain.

Almost instantly she pulled away in alarm, realizing that one unflattering cell phone photo could land her on Page Six, the *New York Post*'s notorious gossip column. But in a city under siege, no one offered more than a glance at the romantic couple.

Jenna kissed him again and took his hand. "My apartment's a ten-minute walk from here."

"What about work? Your—"

"It's done for now. What about your cows?"

"A friend's getting them milked."

They ran through the rain, wetter with every step. By the time they reached her building, Jenna's dress clung to every curve, and she didn't mind a bit when Dafoe undressed her with his eyes.

You're getting closer, he thinks. He looks ahead through the Hansel and Gretel forest, bare branches drooling rain.

She's right in front of him. *Striking distance.* But his eyes race past her to the cabin. His first glimpse this morning. Same brown color as the woods but the roof line gives it away.

You're getting closer.

Asthma. She hasn't had an attack since she was a kid and would get frightened and anxious. She's having one now. Gulping for air, but getting nothing. It's been so long since this happened, yet it feels so familiar, like the body's memory is better than the brain's.

I can't . . . breathe.

Five more steps to the door.

Dear God, get me there.

She doesn't consider the strangeness of her plea, the wildly tangled prayer of panic to the patriarchal "God-the-Father" of her broken childhood. She beats on the door with her fist while her other hand tries the handle. The door opens. She barges in, looks back. The first time in minutes.

He's twenty feet away.

"Fuck," she gasps. Breathless, she slams the door. Flimsy lock in the handle.

Her gaze finds the window. Glass. So fragile.

Like you.

She looks around the room. For anything. It's small and empty.

BAM.

She jumps at the wicked sound of his fist on the door. She takes precious seconds to concentrate on breathing while he beats a bizarre rhythm on the wood. It *is* a rhythm. Like a rite. And strangely, this scares her more than anything that's happened so far. She catches a half breath. Enough to make her want more. Enough to make her think she might survive. Enough to let her look up.

He's staring at her through the glass.

So fragile.

Like you.

Jenna's doorman stepped aside with a smile that undercut his dignified façade. She possessed little more restraint, stepping into the lobby still holding her red shoes. They ran to the elevator, leaving behind wet footprints.

Alone, sweeping up through the building floor by floor, they kissed feverishly before she jerked away from him once more. With a quick glance, she indicated a security camera in the corner of the elevator. "It's not supposed to be on unless there's an emergency, but you never know." She wanted her appearances on YouTube to be on her terms.

But waiting for the privacy of her apartment was agonizing. With a lurch, the doors opened, and they raced down the hall. She stabbed a code into a keypad before pressing her thumb against a Plexiglas plate. The bolt slid open.

As soon as the door shut, they held each other like they were the first and last people on Earth. Her dress dropped to the floor, sopping wet, and she felt the warm caress of his eyes as keenly as his hand moving gently against her legs.

Jenna unbuttoned his shirt and kissed his chest, then luxuriated in the feel of his fingers slipping into her panties, touching her.

He kneeled, and she watched him peel off her panty hose. He nuzzled her hungrily, and her breath began to come in bursts. She felt a teasing release of lace on her hips and bottom as her panties came down, like he was peeling her open. His kisses never stopped. He removed her bra so smoothly he might have been a magician.

Shaking too much to stand, she lowered herself to the plush Persian carpet and moved her legs apart, accommodating his intentions without a word, trembling. He brought his lips to hers, though his hand remained faithful to her most intense pleasure. She wished he had five hands, and pressed herself so hard against his chest that she felt enveloped. In a frantic flurry, she yanked his pants all the way down, rolled him over, and pressed his back to the floor. His hands cupped her bottom and drew her forward to his tongue. In furiously fast moments he made her cry aloud.

Tiny cabin. Staring at her is like looking at someone in jail. *She's not going nowhere.*

She's chesty again, like she's still running hard. Those big breaths that make her big breasts come alive. He sees their outline clearly, like watching a wet T-shirt contest. He smiles 'cause he knows that kind of breathing doesn't come from running. It comes from being scared shitless. Nothing else does it like that. He's seen it before. Lots. They run and run and where do they end up? Cooped up just like this. Rats in a corner.

He taps the window. Gently. Catches her eyes. Still big as pinecones. This is working out *fine.*

He picks up a rock. Size of a cabbage. Heavy. *Real* heavy. He looks at her. Shrugs. Smashes the glass.

He pulls out his knife. A big bowie. Blade's ten inches long. *Overkill.* He smiles at the thought. Blade's silver. Shiny. Like you could blind a man—or a witch—with its reflection.

He uses the butt of the hilt to clear away pieces of glass still embedded in the frame. They pop out cleanly. Putty's so old it crumbles like stale cake. He reaches through with his knife, pointing it while he talks, as if he's giving voice to the gleaming weapon.

"Open the door."

She grabs a wooden candelabra. The only thing she can find. He laughs.

"Open the door. If I have to climb in there, you're going to pay."

I'm going to pay anyway. She slaps her sides, searching again for her phone, even though she knows better. Still, she pleads with it to appear.

She had it earlier, before she started running. *It's in your bag, where you always keep it.* But it doesn't matter: She's miles from nowhere, and he's taking apart the window pane by pane. Smashing it to pieces. Glass and wood chunks hit her. She can't get away. Can't breathe. Can't even move enough to smash his hand with the candelabra. The world's exploding, and she knows with shocking certitude that she's about to be murdered in their house of meditation.

She shakes her head. *A spell,* she tells herself. *Cast a spell.* But her breath still won't come. It feels like he's already choking her to death.

Air freezes in her chest every time he shatters more glass. She hopes she dies before he touches her.

She thinks that may be her life's final plea, that her body will choke her to death before his hands—and that knife—can touch her.

Jenna and Dafoe had eventually reached the bedroom and now looked as thoroughly disheveled as the covers. He propped himself on one elbow as she ran her fingertips across his chest. "I feel *so* ravished," she said.

Dafoe moved aside strands of her wet hair. "Me, too."

She shivered and grabbed the phone. "I should call Nicci and let her know I've ducked out. We always take a break right after the show, but this was a long one."

Moments later Jenna watched him read a text message. He mouthed, "I've got to go."

The candelabra rests by her side. It's her only hope but she can't lift it. She's almost paralyzed by panic. She tries to breathe, and hears air whistle weakly through her chest. She manages to lift the candelabra, and thinks that if she could get one good swing at him, she might stop this madness. But she needs one good breath and she can't get it. She keeps seeing the damage she knows the knife can do.

"You witches know about sacrifices, don't you? They can't be done too fast. You got to take your time. Get as much out of it as you can."

He pauses and fear washes over her again.

"Sacrifices don't happen every day. But I'm not telling you anything you don't know." He says this matter-of-factly and eases a leg through the window frame, casually, like he's got all the time in the world.

And he does. This is what sickens her most: recognizing that whatever time she has left belongs to him. She's gripped by rage and yearns to run at him while he's still, just staring at her like she's a disease.

But her breath forsakes her, chokes her.

Don't die this way, she tells herself. *Don't.*

He swings his other leg in so he's sitting and facing her, the knife at his side.

"Put that down."

She drops the candelabra. Not because she wants to obey him; because the lack of air has left her so weak that she falls to her knees.

He pushes himself off the windowsill. His feet pound the floor. She feels the cabin shake and prays for the strength to run through walls.

He stands in front of her, placing the tip of the long blade under the point of her chin. But she won't raise her head. Her eyes are closed.

"You messed with a lot of people, and you got away with it, but you don't mess with me. You went too far when you did that, and now you have to pay. Do you understand?"

She doesn't reply. Keeps her eyes closed. It's the only choice left to her: enter a darkness of her own volition. She feels the blade press harder into her chin.

"This takes time," he whispers. "It's never fast. The commandments are clear."

The first cut opens her chin all the way up through her lips, leaving her gums bare and bloody.

Dafoe raced his old green and white pickup north on the New York State Thruway: He couldn't get back to his farm fast enough. He'd called Forensia repeatedly, greeted only by "Please leave a message." He'd finally reached his old friend and fellow dairyman, Jasper Fricke, who'd promised to get the cows milked and pastured. Now, while Dafoe steered with one hand, he rang him again.

"She's not here," Jasper blurted out as soon as he picked up.

"What about Bayou?"

Long pause. "He's not here, either. I've been moving so fast that I didn't stop to think about him."

"*He* should be there. That doesn't make sense."

"Wait a second, Dafoe. I just walked up on your porch to get some shade and I don't like what I'm seeing. There's a blood smear right by the door. A good foot long."

"Jesus, call the sheriff. Forensia could be—"

"There's some muddy coyote tracks here, too, right near the blood."

"Coyotes?"

"No mistaking them. Four or five sets. Christ, one of them left a calling card."

"Jasper, go into my mudroom and see if my varmint rifle's in the closet."

"Okay."

It sounded like Jasper was rummaging in the closet.

"Your varmint gun's not here," the man reported. "Definitely gone."

"Forensia must have grabbed it." That's good. More than likely it wasn't her blood.

"I'm back outside," Jasper said. "I want to take a closer look at those tracks. I'm following them down the steps now. I can see Forensia's footprints, too. The rain's washed away a lot of them but it looks like she was taking big steps, moving fast." Jasper grew up hunting and tracking like Dafoe.

"How much blood did you see on the porch?"

"Just that one smear. Know what I'm thinking, Dafoe? That—"

"The coyotes got Bayou. He stopped them last week when those sons of bitches went after my calf; and now—first time my truck's gone for more than a few minutes—they tried to get him so it could be open season on the herd. Forensia would have been hell on wheels if they were tearing up Bayou. You see his tracks anywhere?"

"Nope."

"That figures if he got dragged off. You mind following Forensia's prints as best you can? If she went after them, she could be in a lot more trouble than she counted on."

"I'm on it."

"You got your gun?" asked Dafoe.

"Not with me."

"Take my pistol. Top shelf, kitchen cabinet by the stove."

"Hold on." Dafoe heard Jasper walk back in the house. "It's not there."

"Oh, shit."

"Look, I'm going anyway," Fricke said.

"I'm calling the sheriff."

Ninety minutes later, Dafoe pulled up to his farmhouse. His recent cell phone calls to Jasper had gone unanswered and the lack of news was driving him nuts. The sun beat down harder than ever, a big red blister boiling in the sky. The herd was the only sign of life. The sheriff's old Bronco was parked by the house, but the man was nowhere to be seen.

Dafoe ran inside, hoping to find everyone settled in his big country kitchen where he'd first kissed Jenna. But the room was empty and his shouts raised no response. He saw Forensia's capacious shoulder bag on the counter and hesitated briefly before poring through her stuff. He pulled her phone from the bag, confirming that she'd run off in a hurry. Or been dragged off. She always had that phone with her. A ring tone confused Dafoe until he realized that it came from his iPhone in his pocket, not Forensia's cell, still in his hand.

At a glance he saw that it was Jenna calling. He gave her an update, hung up, and ran out of the house. On the porch, he stared at the woods and brush where the coyotes skulked day and night, like barbarians on a border. He hated those sneaky four-legged thieves like only a farmer can.

To his shock, three figures staggered from a distant thicket—Jasper and Sheriff Walker with Forensia between them. Jasper also cradled Bayou; the border collie hung limp as a November leaf.

Dafoe raced across the parched land. Blood soaked Forensia's hand to her elbow, and the coyotes must have ripped up her leg just above the knee because her jeans were torn and sodden with dark stains.

"I'm sorry, Dafoe. I'm so sorry," she said.

"He's not dead yet." Jasper nodded at Bayou. The dog's eyes were shut—one of them was crusted in blood—and he didn't stir when Jasper handed him to his master.

"I got you, boy." Dafoe's soothing tone belied an inner rage.

"I just got here, but I'm sure he needs a vet, and this one needs an ER," Sheriff Walker said. "She killed three of them."

"I wish I'd killed *all* those fuckers," Forensia cried. "They were trying to murder Bayou. I was getting coffee in the kitchen when he started barking and growling, and then he screamed a second later—I mean *screamed*. I grabbed your gun and ran outside. A coyote twice his size was dragging him off. I got the first two right then. It took a while but I got the big one down by the draw."

"Thank you" was all Dafoe could say. He felt Bayou's heart beating. He knew a tough dog didn't die easily, but Bayou had been chewed up and dragged a long ways.

The sheriff drove Forensia to the hospital, while Dafoe rushed Bayou to the animal clinic. Dr. Pauline Berkley took one look at Bayou and had Dafoe carry him back to a stainless steel examining table.

The tiny vet, who weighed less than the biggest dogs she treated, methodically palpated Bayou nose to tail, paying particular attention to his torn scrotum and bloody eye. She took even more time with his right leg; the fur had been stripped off all the way down to the foot, and the leg looked as raw as a hock in a butcher's case.

"I'll X-ray him, but it'll be a miracle if he doesn't have at least one break in there."

"Coyote dragged him off."

Dr. Berkley was examining his other legs. "Dragged him off?" She shook her head. "He's lucky he's alive."

"Forensia saved him, got her pound of flesh, too: killed three of them."

"Forensia?" The vet glanced at him. "Miss Earth Woman?"

"Yeah, she must have been something fierce. But Bayou's one of her favorite things in the whole world."

"Love brings out the mama bear in all of us. Bayou's lucky she was around. I've had four other dogs and five cats taken by coyotes in the last month. They're getting super aggressive. It's the drought: Everything's drying up from one end of the food chain to the other."

She worked in silence for a few minutes. "Look, Dafoe, this guy's going to lose a testicle, maybe both of them. I think his eye may heal but we won't know for sure for another week or two. But what's going to slow him way down, probably for good, is his leg. Even if it's not broken, he's got torn-up tendons and ligaments and some of his pad is missing. There's no replacing that stuff. Border collies run on a lot of piss and vinegar, but he'll need more than that to ever work again."

"Is this a nice way of asking if I want him put down?"

"It's as delicate as I can be."

"Save him. I don't care what it costs."

"I can't promise you that he'll live. He could get sepsis and—"

"Do it," Dafoe interrupted. "Whatever you can."

Dr. Berkley shouted for her assistant, then turned back to Dafoe. "We've got to get started right now. You should wait outside."

"I'm going over to ER to see Forensia."

A young doctor had just finished putting sixteen stitches into Forensia's left forearm when Dafoe walked in. She had seven more in her leg.

"You okay?" Dafoe asked her.

The physician started to answer. Forensia cut him off: "I'm fine."

When Dafoe heard that she wasn't about to let anyone, including a doctor, speak for her, he figured that she really was doing a lot better.

The physician left them alone.

"Christ, Dafoe, I really went insane when I saw those coyotes ripping up Bayou. I haven't hunted since I turned vegan at fourteen, and there I was gunning them down. The biggest coyote took it personal and tore into me. I had to use your rifle like a club, and when I got him down I really went crazy. Beat him halfway to death before I thought to shoot him and put him out of his misery. It makes me wonder who the hell I really am." She winced and shook her head as she finished, and he knew she needed reassurance.

"The person who saved Bayou's life, that's who. They're operating right now, and he's got a good chance of making it, thanks to you."

Forensia burst into tears of joy and stood up, hugging him. Dafoe held her till she steadied. Then he helped her check out of the hospital, gather up her prescriptions, and get into his pickup.

Tears of rage came hours later, after Sang-mi hiked to a remote meditation cabin with a simple meal for GreenSpirit. She found the Wiccan leader murdered, mutilated, her body drenched in blood.

Sheriff Walker rushed out there as soon as the breathless, hysterical Korean acolyte called 911.

"A ritual murder, that's what we've got," the sheriff later told a large, tightly pressed crowd of journalists who'd raced up from the city. He described the lurid pentagrams that had been carved into GreenSpirit's chest, cheeks, and belly, and promised a "full and complete investigation, no matter where the evidence leads." The comment immediately sparked speculation that GreenSpirit's vicious demise was linked to the one man who might have the most to gain by her silencing: presidential candidate Roger Lilton.

But every witch and Pagan in the region feared that a witch hunt—in the most horrific sense of the words—had begun.

CHAPTER 11

The presidential palace gleamed white as sugar under the glaring sun, a promise of shade and drink amid marble and silk. A mere block away, Rick Birk, seventy-four-year-old investigative reporter, fanned himself furiously as his rickshaw driver made his way through the crowded streets. Despite his discomfort, Birk loved breaking out his tropical-weight safari suits—custom tailored with high collars to hide his sagging neck—for equatorial forays that reminded viewers he was still a dashing, war-torn foreign correspondent.

Decades ago he'd draped his fit young frame in khaki every morning, and he could still wax nostalgic for the years when he wore his bwana garb to cover the Vietnam War for the Associated Press. Especially alluring were his deeply cherished memories of dropping his soft cotton drawers for nights soaked with gin and tonic and sex with a staggering array of Saigonese women. That's if they were women. They were so goddamned teensy that it had been hard to tell in his nightly stupor, so Birk made a point of preserving his upright sense of self by *never* asking their age. Just grab two, three, four of them and go. Break out opium, hash, and Thai sticks, and share the smoke with his newest nubile friends. And then cavort for hours in petite fields of firm flesh. Ah, those *were* the days. *Don't let anybody kid you.* Christ, he was glad to have been alive when you could wet your wick and not get sick. At least not with anything truly ghastly.

His Vietnam reporting earned him a Pulitzer before he jumped the Good Ship Print for the greater fame of television, where he was lauded for possessing the pluck of Morley Safer, the unmitigated gall of Mike Wallace, and the sangfroid of Peter Jennings—all names that meant less and less with the passage of every hour in the fiercely burgeoning multimedia universe of the twenty-first century.

Birk's highest accolades had come decades ago. These days, he was even scorned in his own newsroom. No less than Jenna Withers could hang up on him with outrageous impunity. It helped to know that there had once been a much sweeter time when she would have done penance on her knees for that impropriety—or been out on her ass.

Intimations of his glory days often crept up on Birk when he found himself, as he did this afternoon, on his way for drinks. Or as he preferred to call it, a "briefing from a high government official." In this case, the Maldivian minister of defense.

That these randomly cast, largely forgotten islands should even need a minister of defense would have struck the world as ludicrous, until the second terrorist bombing in a year tore apart a street no more than three blocks from where Birk ambled along . . . *so* slowly that he had to actively resist an urge to slip off his fine alligator belt and flog the little brown bugger hauling him along.

No one but idiots was impressed with his television appearances these days. He ascribed this to the decline of "traditional media," rather than his ravaged looks—the pits and craters from the removal of numerous precancerous skin growths. The relentless sun, not his withered organ, had humbled him most visibly. In bad light, Birk looked pocked with shrapnel, and when he appeared on camera, he layered on more pancake than a drag queen with a five o'clock shadow.

What with the toll of alcohol and the faulty scribes of memory, he honestly couldn't recall the last time he'd been laid; and self-pleasuring—a miserable tonic for the palsied and lame—had been but a limp handshake for as long as he could remember.

In the end, drink became his favorite friend, and the tang not of flesh but of Schweppes and Bombay gin all but came alive on his tongue a half block before he arrived at the palace gate.

Amazing what anticipating a stiff one can do for you, how it can tease with a single imaginary scent. After all, look what poured out of Proust after tasting a simple madeleine. Birk figured the juniper flourish of gin might serve him equally well, if he ever picked up the pen again. He supposed he could give the world of letters a real boost, if he were of such a mind; they were in need of his reserves.

Meanwhile, his driver, sweat spilling off his back in disgustingly swollen streams, brought the rickshaw to Birk's destination. But the man had the ill grace to pant like a cart dog. *A tip, a tip, that's what he wants. Well, fuck me.*

Birk groaned loudly as he lifted his calcium-sapped bones from the thinly padded seat. He paid and even tipped handsomely, leaving the little native smiling. But then all those rickshaw drivers in Saigon had flashed rows of betel-stained teeth before blowing you straight to hell.

"Rick Birk," he announced dramatically in his sonorous voice at the palace gate, giving an imperious flick of his hand to the guard. His name ought to have guaranteed admission. But this slack-skinned brown man wasn't impressed. Almost as bad, he wore what could plausibly have been a bunny suit. The one-piece design seemed more appropriate for toddler wear; it was the color of cheap Easter eggs and had epaulets as large and floppy as rabbit ears. The man raised his hand to keep Birk at bay. Then he entered a gaudily decorated guardhouse with a pink roof, turquoise door, and glass so old and heat-stricken it looked like it would shatter if you sneezed. Birk watched him place a call on a landline. After a few moments he nodded and hung up before returning to send Birk, without escort, to the towering porte cochere where another bunny-suited brown bugger opened the door to the palace's impressively large reception room.

A wonderfully lithe Indian woman in a red sari led the reporter up a winding staircase to the minister's office. The rear view was enticing as the rounded cheeks of her bottom glanced temptingly against the shiny fabric. Never had Birk felt so strongly that youth was wasted on the young. What he wouldn't give to be thirty-five again, with a broad, brilliant smile. Back in the long ago, women like Miss Sari had led him on just such a meandering path to their bedrooms in just such a flirty manner. *Just once more, for God's sake.*

At least she was eye candy. The minister's office lacked all appeal. The walls were white and stark, no more encumbered with style or flourish than the sapped religion they believed in. Wait, he spotted a crescent and a star, and some mumbo-jumbo lettering that might have been Maldivian in origin—or from the moon, for all Birk knew or cared. These Muslims were a boorish lot, positively thirteenth century.

Another look around was a cause for real grief: not a drop of gin. No tonic. Not even a single lonely lime in the minister's office. Water? She offered *him* water? *Whales* shit *in water.*

"The new austerity?" he asked Sari archly, who might have been a secular holdover in her sleek red dress. But she didn't favor him with so much as a smile as she left.

Birk was old school enough to carry a silver flask neatly curved to fit an aging gent's not-so-nimble frame. And as soon as the door shut behind his comely escort, he nipped the elixir that he loved so much.

He'd no sooner felt the gin's first soothing effects when Minister of Defense Hassan Darby entered, a short man with a long beard and the faltering steps of a rickets-stricken midget. His excessively large brown suit didn't help, cuffs overrunning his wrists like starving tribesmen laying siege to the gates of a refugee camp.

"Mr. Birk. So sorry to keep you waiting. It seems we have so many luminaries today that I have only ten minutes for you."

"Luminaries?" It didn't pass Birk unnoticed that he hadn't been included in that breath, but mostly he was gobsmacked that the little brown fucker had the temerity to cut short the forty-five minutes that he'd been promised. Bad enough that he hadn't permitted Birk to bring along a cameraman. "What other luminaries are you expecting today?"

Birk's question appeared to flummox the minister, but briefly: "Surely, you must know about the arrival of the *Dick Cheney.*"

The former vice president? "No, I didn't know. When's he coming?"

"He? No, no." *Ho-ho-ho.*

What an annoying laugh.

"It is the ship the *Dick Cheney.* A giant tanker ship. It is in our Maldivian territorial waters even while we waste Mr. Birk's precious time. Goodness, we are down to six minutes."

The tanker, right. He knew about that. Didn't know it was named the *Dick* fucking *Cheney.* And if the *Dick* fucking *Cheney* was plodding along in local waters, then Senator Gayle Higgens couldn't be far behind. Birk would have to act fast.

"Tell me, Mr. Minister, how serious is your problem with homegrown terrorists?"

"No, Mr. Birk, you must not say . . . what is that word? 'Homegrown'? They all come from far away. No proud Maldivian would ever take the life of his brother or sister. You must get that right in your reports. We insist."

"What about your homegrown jihadists? They're not so proud, are they?"

"Ah, look at this, Mr. Birk." He pointed to his gold Rolie. "Time for you to go. Me, too. A luminary is coming."

Adnan sat in the small fishing boat, squeezed below the gunwale with four jihadists from Waziristan. They'd arrived on his island at dusk last night, minds laden with the schemata of the tanker they planned to hijack, eyes gleaming with paradise. All of them knew death was imminent, either from seizing the vessel or from the detonation of the bomb that Adnan had become.

Last night Parvez had strung a large black Islamic flag between two trees. Then he'd brought out a video camera.

"Adnan, you are a martyr . . ."

Recording Adnan's final statement had always been part of the plan. Even so, when Parvez said those words, Adnan's spirits soared as surely as if he'd been praised by Allah Himself. *Martyr.* The highest honor—and it had been bestowed upon *him*. How great to have lived to hear such praise. The supreme leaders of Islam would know of him, and of Parvez, too, for he was the orchestrator of a martyrdom so great that billions of people would bear witness.

His friend went on: "Do you wish to say anything before you start on your path to martyrdom?"

"I wish to say that I'm doing this, *inshallah,* to make retribution for the Christian and Jewish pigs who are killing my country . . ."

Parvez nodded approval of every word. Then, on cue, the jihadists rushed up from the beach and flanked Adnan for the camera with their guns and heavy cartridge belts and RPGs. Their shoulder-mounted weapons pointed straight to the heavens, and Adnan had been startled to notice for the first time that the rockets were shaped like the minarets of Malé. Surely chance alone could not explain such a blessed coincidence: The unholy who dared to ban the most sacred towers would be answered with minarets of steel and explosives that would claim them in storms of fire and death.

Those weapons now lay hidden beneath layers of netting thick with the rotting smells of the sea. The fisherman who had sailed them past dozens of the country's tiny islands now trailed the *Dick Cheney* and the five Maldivian Coast Guard boats that were escorting it.

Adnan had been approved for duty on the supertanker. Given his experience, training, and seaman's papers, his employment had never been in question. He would be welcomed when he walked onto the wharf, his fully packed vest covered by a layer of clothes.

But disguising his true intentions would get him only as far as the gate to the gangplank. To board would require his fellow jihadists to shoot their way past the Maldivian security forces who would search each sailor. In the past, the security detail often lazed in the sun and performed cursory baggage checks, but Parvez had warned that they would be more alert tomorrow, and that the jihadists must *take* the ship. Adnan's assignment would be to get on board, not to engage in battle. Even so, a Mauser pistol lay under the netting for him. Once on deck, he could hold everyone at bay with the threat of the bomb. He had to buy time, Parvez said, and make them sail the tanker into the ocean. Time to get the attention of Satan's media, east and west and north and south. The unclean everywhere.

The fisherman let his boat drift farther astern of the tanker, and then headed for a beach only three miles from the outskirts of Malé. From there, the greatest journey would begin: to paradise, with the whole world watching.

Rick Birk walked out of the minister's office with as much dignity as he could muster. *Ten minutes.* And to think he'd also been admonished to not even suggest that the Maldives had its own native-born killers. The minister himself had taken a sudden detour to a lavatory, though Birk suspected the man wanted to free himself from the incisive questions of a brilliant veteran correspondent.

Of course, the denial about homegrown jihad was hardly surprising. In his entire career, which now spanned a half century, Birk had run across no more than a handful of leaders in the developing world who had readily accepted that their country's problems lay within their own borders—from a sorry lack of resources and the pervasive futility that poverty inevitably spawned. The rest of the riffraff spewed blame on "outsiders" until, of course, the rude reality exploded with bombs and bloodshed. Then they "got" it—but only in the moments before they fled to Switzerland with their national treasury.

These little brown buggers, however, had a case for finger-pointing: The looming disasters throughout much of Oceania could be laid at the feet of the smokestacked, tailpiped West.

As Birk took the last three steps to the main floor, he spotted Senator Gayle Higgens and her entourage bustling through the main entrance. *Argh,* the sight of her spurred a memory painful as a lesion, a real standout in his fat catalog of sexual misadventures.

She'd been a freshman Texas legislator when they'd met, as foul-mouthed and shameless in private as she was sanctimonious and born-again in public. He'd been young, too, sent to the Oil Patch to cover some long-forgotten hurricane, whose force, even then, couldn't have stood up to Gayle Higgens. She'd rounded Birk up like one of her stray steers and herded him right into her bed. She'd tied him down as if she were a real buckaroo, then laughed bitterly when he couldn't perform.

He'd sworn never to go near Higgens again, and there she was. Christ almighty, aging was pitiless: *Look at her pastry-crust skin; bloated, mashed-potato body; and swollen ankles, shapeless as bread dough.*

She pointed the sharp tip of her pink umbrella at him and bellowed, "Get your rascal self over here, Birk."

He looked around, finding no reprieve.

"What are you doing here?" the senator demanded.

"Scoping out the restless natives," he responded as suavely as he could, wondering why in God's name he was even bothering. But he couldn't help himself: She'd humiliated him almost fifty fucking years ago, yet the moment he saw her he was filled with an unruly desire to reclaim his dignity.

"But you *must* come for the launch of our pilot project. Surely you know about it, you old crow."

Old crow? That's some cheap goddamn booze.

Yeah, surely he did know about her pet project, but the seeding of the ocean with iron oxide held no more interest for him than all the bizarrely shaped sea critters whose names escaped him and whose culinary appeal lay chiefly in their most crushed, pounded, and fully processed, deep-fried forms.

"I'm on the hard news beat, Senator."

She looked at him, openly askance. "*Hard* news?" she laughed. "*You?*" With those few words, and with that sharp inflection, she brought back the single biggest humiliation of his sex life. "We're here to change the world. If you're smart, Ricky, you'll come along."

"I'll be busy."

"Sorry to hear that you'll be *tied up.* I'm at the Four Seasons. Come by for a backgrounder, if you'd like a good one."

Why was everything a double entendre with her? And was that a wink? Had that old sack of nickels actually *winked* at him?

She turned away in the next instant. "Ten o'clock. Down at the port," she said in parting.

He harrumphed. At ten he'd be at the port, all right, but it would be to catch a water taxi to the island of Dhiggaru. He'd found out the name of weather girl's old flame—Rafan Yoosuf—and now knew exactly where he could be found. Wasn't hard. Malé was a small city, and memories were long for beautiful blond girls who scandalized the locals by stealing the heart of one of their sons.

And if Rick Birk understood anything, it was how to trade on resentment to get information. Safe to say that if this Rafan Yoosuf was taking dirt from one island and larding it on another, there would be resentment afloat, never more so than when land meant life.

CHAPTER 12

Blame it on the Barbie Master and Halloween. Jenna could not escape the wardrobe chief's red footwear. First, it was the booty-boosting, toe-crunching high heels that she'd intentionally ruined in the torrential rainstorm. Now it was slippers. It was as if the Master had fetishized the color . . . or her feet. She glanced down. Well, at least these things didn't have those confounded heels. No, these were just ruby-red slippers, but with sequins—replicas of the ones that Dorothy wore so memorably in *The Wizard of Oz.* The slippers formed the foundation, so to speak, of Jenna's costume for the annual "trick or treat" shenanigans on the set of *The Morning Show,* when all but one of the regulars dressed up for viewers. It seemed like a good, even wholesome idea the first year they tried it, but Jenna had noticed that the women's costumes had been getting steadily trashier, shrinking in the hot wash of network competition.

"I've got the sexiest outfit for you," Barbie Master said, looking up from carefully tweezing his dark and narrow eyebrows in a vanity mirror.

Jenna wasn't sure "sexiest" was an adjective that ought to describe any clothes—costumes included—that she wore on morning TV. But as her executive producer and twit extraordinaire Marv Balen put it, "Barbie Master knows best."

The head of wardrobe offered her a blue Dorothy dress so mini that it *might* have provided modest cover for the teenaged—and diminutive—Judy Garland herself. Shamelessly short. "There's no business like show business," Barbie Master sang. Jenna sighed. It could have been worse: He might have dolled her up in a little French maid uniform with black hose, black garters, and more booty-boosting heels. *Wait till next year,* she thought.

Still, Jenna's costume wasn't even the raciest surprise of the morning. That honor fell to Andrea Hanson, who, despite her pregnancy, was posed as a hyper-sexed Daisy Mae from the *Li'l Abner* comic strip. *Her idea, or Barbie Master's?* You never knew with Andrea.

Jenna took a bracing breath and swished onto the set, her stratospheric hemline ogled by virtually every eye in the studio. *Do not bend over a frickin' inch,* she told herself.

Moments later, Andrea greeted viewers, joking about her own "PG-rated" appearance, though considering that the host was in her sixth month, Jenna doubted that many viewers were laughing along. More likely they felt like squirming at the mother-to-be's swollen appearance in Daisy Mae's button-popping, polka-dot blouse.

"Hanson, you are such a hottie," gushed the usually staid Phillip Gates, the show's news anchor—wearing his customary suit. Gates's manner suggested a penis with an untoward regard for expectant mothers. After his breathy appraisal, Gates composed himself and began to deliver the news:

"Halloween took on real horror for Roger Lilton's presidential hopes this morning when a team of FBI agents knocked on the door of his Washington campaign headquarters with a search warrant." Video of dark-suited men appeared. "No trick or treat here as agents arrived only hours after the brutalized body of Pagan leader and self-described witch, GreenSpirit, was found in a remote cabin in upstate New York." A shot of the cabin, taken with a long lens, filled the screen, followed by three-day-old footage of the candidate. "Lilton was once linked romantically to GreenSpirit, and that relationship has become the election season's biggest controversy."

Lilton's press secretary, Jean Mayer, popped up next, calling the FBI raid "a political smear engineered by President Reynolds." Over file footage of FBI chief Martin Aimes testifying before Congress, Gates read Aimes's statement, released that morning, characterizing the visit as "routine," and saying that it did not mean that Lilton was a suspect in the murder.

He didn't rule it out, though, Jenna thought.

Two and a half minutes later, Daisy Mae Hanson turned to Jenna in the Weather Center.

"Here's our own Jenna Withers, eagerly awaiting her unveiling—I think that's the right word—as Dorothy in *The Wizard of Oz.* Jenna, that has to be the shortest Dorothy dress on record. Better hope nobody sneezes in your neighborhood."

Better hope Li'l Abner doesn't demand a blood test, Jenna almost shot back, but she kept her demeanor bright and cheerful, in accord with the unwritten rule of the show that you took Andrea's handoffs with a big smile *no matter what.*

"No twisters or windstorms today, Daisy Mae." Jenna turned to the camera to report the return of sunny skies and the continuation of high temperatures, chatting about how little of the heavy rainfall had been "captured" because the drought-stricken land was so hard and dry, and the storm had been so fierce and fast. "Plus, those high temps evaporated a lot of the moisture before it could trickle into groundwater supplies."

In her earpiece, Nicci said, "Don't get too sciencey," as if the producer knew that "evapotranspiration" was on the tip of Jenna's tongue. But, alas, another unwritten rule of the show was that Jenna should never appear to be a brainiac, and she had to think that this was especially true when she was tramped up like a ten-thousand-dollar-a-night call girl.

At ten of nine, after Jenna finished her last weather report of the day, she held down her hem and bolted to wardrobe, scooting behind the Barbie Master's door. She kicked off the red slippers and pulled off the microdress and white blouse. Quickly, she slipped into a pair of black slacks, a collarless white blouse, and a burgundy jacket with three-quarter-length sleeves. She would have liked to have kept Dorothy's slippers, but the Barbie Master swooped right down on them.

Nicci popped in to remind Jenna that she had a conference call with the presidential task force in one minute. "And there's talk that the White House is about to drop a bombshell on you guys."

Jenna rushed to her office, plugged in an earphone, and patched in to a special White House line. In the seconds of silence that followed, she glanced at a headline in the *Post,* CARNAGE IN THE CATSKILLS, and eyed a front-page picture of the remote cabin.

During their nightly phone call the previous evening, Dafoe had told Jenna that the rain that had flooded parts of the city—harmlessly, in most cases—had apparently proved ruinous to the Sheriff Walker's investigation of GreenSpirit's murder. Walker had announced that he'd called in the New York State Police homicide unit and soon after, the FBI said that it would join the investigation.

In these lazy, waiting moments Dafoe came back to mind, and she found herself thinking how nice it would be to take in an art show with him. Or stroll past the ponds in Central Park. Her reverie snapped when a crisp "Good morning" filled her ear. It was Vice President Andrew Percy's sharp voice. She sat up in her chair as if reprimanded in class.

Forensia, still hobbled by the coyote bite above her knee, limped up a trail with Sang-mi. Both witches carried flowers and candles, planning to build a shrine as close to the murder scene as possible, and to offer prayers to their religious leader.

A half mile from the cabin, yellow police tape cut off their access. Flowers, unlit candles, Egyptian crosses, pentagrams, and a large framed photograph of the murdered woman already rested against the trunk of a dying tree just off the trail. In the photo, the witch's hands were raised, as if imploring the faithful. Forensia looked away, finding it all too easy to imagine the same gesture as a desperate, dying plea in the blood-spattered cabin.

She and Sang-mi added their offerings, leaving their candles unlit, as well; despite the recent rains, not a drop of moisture clung to the desiccated forest.

According to Sheriff Walker, what little evidence they'd found indicated that "a methodical killer murdered that woman. The person who did this had no conscience. None."

Jason, Forensia thought. She didn't buy any of the speculation about Lilton being involved. That's what a lot of cable channels were claiming as they reran clips of Lilton on *The Morning Show,* calling his old girlfriend a "wacko" and saying "I'm addressing that issue head-on."

No, some jerk like Jason had killed her. *No, not* like *Jason,* she corrected herself, *it* was *Jason.* She wondered if he would have the nerve to show his face at the memorial service. It was planned for sundown in the same clearing where he and his teammates had caused so much trouble at the initiation. The prospect of seeing him frightened her: After she'd told the CBS newsman that Jason was always taking money to lead guys to the naked gatherings, the quarterback had sneered at her and said, "You're not gettin' away with this, you fucking bitch."

As soon as she'd heard about GreenSpirit's murder, Forensia left a message for Sheriff Walker, describing the confrontation that had taken place the night of the initiation.

She lifted her eyes and looked around the forest. *Where is Jason, anyway?* She consoled herself with the knowledge that the woods were teeming with detectives and forensics experts, even if she couldn't see them. Then she and Sang-mi kneeled and began to pray silently. But Forensia couldn't stop thinking about the killer.

This is no way to honor GreenSpirit, she chided herself.

"Mr. Vice President, what did you just say?" A female scientist spoke with no attempt to hide her disgust.

Three more members of the task force jumped in, asking Vice President Andrew Percy to repeat himself. Others were groaning in open protest. Jenna cupped her earphone to try to block out any external noise, scarcely believing what she had just heard. A bombshell indeed.

"President Reynolds and I are simply asking you to consider, just *consider,* getting on board with USEI's iron oxide pilot project in the Indian Ocean."

"I thought we were supposed to review geoengineering options, not become a rubber stamp for the energy industry's unilateral actions," Jenna said.

The vice president paused before he replied: "We are, in fact, supposed to review those options, but USEI has taken the initiative to launch a very limited experiment in the Indian Ocean in conjunction with the government of the Maldives. What is so wrong with that?"

"Andrew, you've got to be kidding," said Ben Norris, the balding, freckled, irascible NASA meteorologist. "What's 'wrong with that' is that all kinds of things can go haywire with even a 'very limited experiment' that is targeting the Earth's incredibly sensitive thermostat. The best scientific minds we have should review the protocols—that's science 101. We don't even know if the energy industry conducted any review before shipping half a million tons of iron oxide halfway around the world. Talk about putting random elements into play! Furthermore, Senator Higgens sat here with us just last week and never said word one about this 'pilot project.' Did you know about it then?"

"No, I did not."

Vice President Percy spoke so directly that Jenna suspected that he'd been ill at ease with everything else he'd said up till now.

Norris asked, "When you called us together, did you intend us to rubber-stamp this sort of irresponsible energy industry nonsense?"

"You may not have known what the energy lobby was up to," said Dr. Susan Ornstein, a marine microbiologist at Scripps Institution of Oceanography, "but I'll bet your boss knew. This lets him look decisive on a key issue right before the election. Talk about an October surprise."

"I don't think you're being fair to the president," Percy said.

"And I think that you have no choice but to say that," Norris fired back.

"Five hundred thousand tons of iron oxide doesn't spell 'pilot project' to me," Ornstein interjected irritably.

"No, it certainly does not," Jenna agreed. "It suggests they've already decided what results they're going to get from their 'test.'"

"You watch," Norris said, "a measured cooling of the atmosphere will be announced in a massive ad campaign that's going to tell the world that climate change has been solved. Thanks to the intrepid energy industry, everyone can turn down their air-conditioning and drive all they want. No worries." Norris's voice was venomous. "They're using that supertanker to save the enormous costs of shipping when they start seeding the ocean on a large scale. And to show gullible consumers how 'serious' they are."

"And if we don't 'get on board,' as you put it, Mr. Vice President, we'll look like namby-pamby scientists who are too nervous and scared to ever make such a bold move," said the woman whom Jenna still couldn't identify, but whose contempt she shared.

"But they don't *know* that this is going to work," the environmentalist with the white goatee remonstrated.

"No, they don't. And we don't, either," the vice president said. "But they're being very careful, I think we have to grant them that, and I think we have to take them at their word."

"*Them?* Their word?" Norris snorted. Jenna felt that Norris's thoughts probably mirrored her own memories of the *Exxon Valdez* and *Deepwater Horizon* disasters. "You do know, Andrew," Norris went on, "that there's not one law on the books, here or abroad, that can stop them."

Percy did not respond, but Ornstein plunged back in: "That's absolutely correct. There's nothing to stop them from doing this. This is beyond outrageous."

"I can only relay the president's request that you offer support to this unique—"

"My apologies for interrupting, Andrew," Norris said, "but I can't believe those are your words."

"Well, you're wrong, Ben," the vice president said sharply. "And I think you should consider what this project has to offer. And if you can't lend your support, that's fine. The White House feels that it's on firm scientific footing here, and that the American people will support this bold initiative. There's no need for anyone on this task force to demonize the energy industry over this."

"In other words," the goateed environmentalist said, "the White House already ran focus groups and found that this would look like a splashy move right before election day."

"I know of no such focus group," Percy said.

"Of course not," Norris snapped. "Because then you wouldn't have deniability. Reynolds has got to know that most of us are not going to back this. He's first and foremost a political realist."

"The president and I both trust that you'll consider this a worthy project."

Or, at the very least, keep quiet about it. But even as Jenna thought this, she realized that she wouldn't make any public statements against the "very limited experiment." While she felt professionally insulted by the energy industry's maneuvering, she could not see any harm in the proposed test. It could have real benefits.

But the next instant, Jenna remembered the ominous words of the highly regarded oceanographer, John Martin: "Give me half a tanker of iron oxide and I'll give you an ice age."

They don't have half *a tanker,* Jenna said pointedly to herself. *They have* a full *supertanker—five hundred thousand tons.*

The vice president asked the task force to stay on the line for his chief of staff, Evan Stubb. Then Percy bid them good-bye.

What's Stubb here for? Jenna wondered. She didn't have to wait long for the answer: to do the president and vice president's dirty work.

"I want to remind all of you of the confidentiality pledge that you've signed," Stubb spoke slowly and clearly, "and advise you to keep in mind that we expect you to abide by its legally enforceable provisions."

Half an hour before sunset, the forest clearing grew crowded with Pagans and witches from all over the Eastern seaboard, plus network camera crews and curious onlookers.

Forensia held Sang-mi's hand as they walked toward the gathering. The young Korean had been shaking almost continually since she'd discovered GreenSpirit's mutilated body. Twice she'd said the killing reminded her of the terrible butchery that she'd seen in North Korea.

"What they did to GreenSpirit was so terrible." Sang-mi sounded shattered by fear. "They can do it to anybody."

"No, that won't happen. See, the police are here," Forensia assured her.

"In North"—she meant North Korea—"police do the killing."

"But not here. I promise." Forensia nodded at the New York State Police officers whom Sheriff Walker had requested to protect his villagers. "There's no reason to worry."

Her friend's hand tightened on hers as they wove through the crowd toward Richtor; Forensia's tall, dreadlocked boyfriend stood with other Pagans near a tree-stump podium.

Sheriff Walker was dressed in a jacket and tie. His tiny wife stood by his side, along with their two daughters. The older girl, Suze, looked away when Forensia smiled at her. Two nights ago, Suze had been naked in the moonlight with the rest of the Pagans, only feet away from where she and her fundamentalist Christian family now waited for the service to begin.

Forensia didn't have any more regard for Sheriff Walker's religious beliefs than he probably had for hers, but she greatly appreciated his presence as an officer of the law and as a member of the local community gravely concerned about a horrific killing.

That's how it should be, Forensia thought as daylight dimmed. She was grateful for Sheriff Walker's attendance because it sent a reassuring message to the Pagans and witches that law enforcement would protect them.

Forensia also figured that Sheriff Walker was there to study the crowd. Sometimes a killer really does return to the scene of his crime; that wasn't simply a Hollywood cliché. She scanned the gathering, but didn't see Jason. *Maybe they've already arrested him.*

The witch who'd driven down from Ithaca for Forensia and Sang-mi's initiation stood before the large group of Pagans. A black robe draped her short, fragile-looking frame. Her eyes looked bright, alive—indomitable. Richtor took Forensia's hand as the gray-haired older woman began to read a statement:

"We gather under the most trying and grievous circumstances. We are here to honor the memory of a great witch and a great woman, and to decry the violence that took her from this earthly plane—the hatred and prejudice that murdered our beloved leader to render her message mute. This same ignorance would slay all wisdom, if it could." She paused and looked at the crowd, holding Forensia's gaze for a fraction of a second.

The young woman began to weep as she recalled the details of the crime. According to the sheriff's account, reported in the local newspaper, the murder was committed—slowly—by someone close to her. "This kind of violence," the sheriff added, "is almost always personal."

Sang-mi also cried quietly. She squeezed Forensia's hand harder and pulled her close, whispering urgently, "I have to tell you something. It's very dangerous." Her fear made the words sound like they'd been slashed with the same blade that had tortured and claimed Green-Spirit.

"We'll talk later, okay?" Forensia whispered back.

After the older witch paid homage to GreenSpirit, she said that anyone who wanted to speak in honor of their leader was encouraged to address the crowd. Forensia listened as many of the older witches offered thoughts and remembrances.

When Forensia herself walked forward, she gently patted Dafoe and Jasper Fricke on the arm as she eased past them. Seconds later, Forensia felt the hot camera lights on her back. She turned toward them and squinted, but her words flowed easily:

"I was here with so many of you forty-eight hours ago, when we held a sacred ceremony." When her gaze landed on Suze Walker, the sheriff's daughter again looked away. "We were so honored that Green-Spirit came to conduct our initiation. I will never forget that night. Right there," Forensia pointed to the ground about twenty feet away, "was the circle of power that we shared with her, and with many of you."

Forensia's voice gained force. "She instilled in all of us a powerful sense of possibilities. I can feel that right now, and that's why I know she's with us. But on that night, which should have been wholly and beautifully sacred, she had to stand up to anger and hatred and bullying. And she did stand up to it. She did not back down, and she never would have backed down from her killer. We can take great heart in knowing that we die as we live, and for GreenSpirit that meant she passed with grace and dignity."

Forensia hoped and prayed that she spoke the truth, but the newspaper article once again filled her mind. GreenSpirit's death had been terrible. Who could have faced such torture with grace and dignity?

Dignity? That old witch? He could have spit. *She died like everyone else—crying, screaming, begging me to stop. "Please—please, oh, God, don't do that. Don't." Dignity? A run-over dog has more dignity than her. She didn't have one ounce of it left. I took it all away. It's the first thing that goes, once you get them down.*

He watches Forensia's friends—Sang-mi; that creep, Richtor; the rest of them—listening to everything she says like they're getting paid by the word. If Forensia keeps this up, there's going to be another memorial service real soon. He'll see to that. Just have to wait for the rain to come again. Need it to wash away his tracks. A drought can't last forever.

Rain and blood. You get the two of them together . . . and you can hardly tell them apart.

"Possibilities, that's what GreenSpirit gave us." Forensia took a breath, tried to smile as the last of the light leaked from the sky. "That's what she gave the world. We must let belief in the highest possibilities fill our souls. We have to do everything that we can to make those possibilities real. The best way to honor GreenSpirit is to use everything she taught us to bring out the best that's inside each of us. That's how we creatures of flesh and blood can give GreenSpirit immortality."

After Forensia slipped back to her place beside Sang-mi and Richtor, the first witch to speak stepped up once again and this time asked for a minute of silence. The crowd bowed their heads, then slowly began to disperse.

Sheriff Walker moved over to Forensia, who eased away from her friends. "I'm sorry I didn't get back to you," he said. "We've been very busy, but I want to assure you that we're looking into every lead. Now, all of you," Sheriff Walker's eyes included his daughters, "should know that we can't realistically protect everyone. The person who killed your friend might be living right here in town. He could have been here tonight." Suze shuddered. "I know, it's real creepy, but we just don't know. Or he might be linked to another killing a few months ago far away from here."

"What other killing? Where?" Forensia asked quickly.

"I can't tell you that. It's under investigation. But don't make yourself a target. That's what I'm saying."

Forensia nodded.

"We have a church service in about half an hour," Sheriff Walker said, "so we have to get going, but please, everybody, please be careful."

Forensia watched him gather up his family, turn on a flashlight, and leave. She looked at Sang-mi, took her hand, and glanced around for Richtor. Hard to see in the dark, but she guessed he must have left. Richtor disliked police on principle, and she figured he'd scooted away earlier to avoid Sheriff Walker. She and Sang-mi headed back.

"I can tell you now," the Korean witch said softly.

"Not a good idea," Forensia replied. People were crowding close as they funneled onto the trail. Familiar faces appeared in the light of candles and headlamps, but not many whom Forensia knew well. She wondered if any of the younger guys had been here with Jason two nights earlier, urging him on. Maybe they would report back to him now, or maybe Jason had been skulking somewhere near the back of the crowd. "When we get home," she said to Sang-mi, "we can talk."

The more she talked, the more he loathed her. Before, he'd noticed her tits and those awful witch tattoos, but he could have lived with that. *She* could have lived with that. But every word told him that *he* can't live with *her.* Even when she stopped speaking, his ears were stuffed with her nonsense.

Look at them, crawling back to their holes like they're filled with "in-

spiration." That tall one, she could talk the stink out of a skunk. She talks too damn much for her own damn good.

He knows they live together, her and the Korean. Not many secrets in a town this size. He wonders what they do to each other, the sex they get up to once they lock up. As if that could keep him out.

If there's one thing he knows, it's how to go through a door.

CHAPTER 13

Adnan and the other jihadists slept in the fisherman's house in Malé. Maybe their last night on Earth. Paradise beckoned.

The fisherman told his wife to feed them breakfast. The attractive, dark-haired woman never smiled, and seemed nervous, as she had when he returned early from his trip—even before she'd seen the heavily armed men. She certainly never questioned that he'd brought home no fish.

Her name remained unspoken until they started packing their weapons into the trunk of an old Renault, whose backseat had been ripped out to make room for rifles, ammunition belts, and the RPG with the rockets shaped like minarets.

The fisherman told his wife sharply, "You will stay and speak to no one, Senada."

As he turned to leave, a cell phone rang, filling the immediate silence with a silly pop tune from the West, where godless men made videos of their wives having naked sex with strangers and showed them on the Internet.

Everyone stared at everyone else. None of the jihadists carried a phone, not on a mission where electronic records could destroy many others joined in the holy war against infidels. The fisherman's cell was in his pocket, silent. He looked down, shaking his head.

The ring tone played over and over: "I love you baby, in *every* way. I love you baby, let's go play . . ."

The fisherman followed the trail of pop love to a shelf above the single-burner stove.

"I love you baby, in *every* way . . ."

He smacked aside three brightly painted tin canisters, revealing the device. They crashed to the floor, spilling salt, sugar, flour. A silty fog whitened the fisherman's feet as he grabbed the pretty purple cell phone. He shook it in rage and reared back to throw it at the wall where it had nestled and sung. A hollow-cheeked jihadist pulled the phone from the fisherman's hand. Flipped it open. Handed it back to him.

The fisherman put it to his ear and shouted, "Who is this?" turning his furious gaze on his wife. His enraged voice drew no response.

Senada backed into the arms of one of the strangers. Her husband rushed over, shouting, "Who was that? Who?" When she shouted back, "I don't know," he punched her in the stomach. She doubled over, spittle hanging from her lips. He grabbed her long black hair, yanked up her head, and waved the phone in her face, demanding, "Who gave you this?" He shook her head, yelling, "Tell me!" When she glared at him, he backhanded her face, bloodying her lips. "This is why I have no sons," he screamed.

The Waziristanis didn't speak his language, but they understood a husband's fury and what had been exposed in the syrupy strains of an infidel's song.

They pushed Senada to the floor and stared at her husband expectantly. He kicked her once, then again, waving the phone above his head. He began to stomp her.

Adnan stared. He had never seen such violence. He thought of his mother. No woman should be beaten like this. *No matter what.* But he didn't dare try to stop her husband. These men scared him.

Senada curled into a ball but could not escape her husband's kicks. She cried out at each hammering blow from his bare heels.

The gaunt jihadist who'd ordered the fisherman to answer the phone now threw out his arms and stopped the beating. He shouted at his men and one of them dragged Senada to her knees. When she started to collapse, the minion jerked her upright by her thick hair. He leaned over her shoulder, his long black beard pressing against her back, and spoke rapidly. Adnan didn't understand what the jihadist was saying, and from her lack of response, neither did Senada. The jihadist who was holding her hair forced her to face the man who'd barked the commands.

The leader snapped out more foreign words and his other two men shoved the fisherman to his knees beside his wife. The man's head hung to his chest, moving slightly side to side. He still held the phone. The head jihadist took it from him.

The Waziristani leader grabbed the Mauser pistol from under Adnan's shirt and thrust it into the seaman's hand. He dragged Adnan over to the kneeling couple and forced the barrel of the gun to the back of Senada's head. The jihadist shouted again and pantomimed shooting. Adnan did not move. The other man shouted three more times, spittle landing on Adnan's face.

Adnan shook his head: He was a martyr, not a murderer.

The jihadist jammed the gun into the base of the fisherman's skull, squeezing Adnan's hand painfully. His commands grew piercing.

"No," Adnan said, so softly that he might have been whispering. He slipped his finger from the trigger. The others' eyes grew large. He snatched the gun away and stuck the barrel into Adnan's face, bruising his cheekbone.

Suddenly the room was so quiet that Adnan could hear Senada's quick gasps.

Adnan closed his eyes and accepted his fate, knowing that his regrets would span eternity. What would Parvez think—that his friend had been a coward? That he'd lost his nerve and been shot like a dog?

The fisherman yelled "whore" at his wife. She shouted that she'd never loved him. "Do you understand? Never." Blood dripped down her chin and spilled to the floor. "You're a pig. My father forced me to marry you."

Her defiance needed no translation. The jihadist smacked her head sharply with the steel butt of the gun. The blow made her weep, but she directed her outrage at her husband, spitting in his face and scream-ing, "I love Rafan. Do you hear me? Only Rafan. Not you."

The fisherman lunged for her. She pulled back. A short jihadist stopped him.

A gunshot made Adnan's ears ring. Senada's body crumpled to the floor, eyes open, empty. The fisherman looked at his wife's body, then at her killer, who met his gaze with a flat stare. The jihadist placed the barrel of the gun between the fisherman's eyes and mumbled some-thing. Adnan thought it might be a prayer, since the man raised his eyes to the ceiling as he spoke. Then the Waziristani fired again.

The fisherman's head jerked like a line when the bait has been struck, and his body lay beside that of his slain wife.

Adnan and the four jihadists left the house and squeezed into the Renault. As they neared the harbor, the leader handed the Mauser to Adnan, who stuck it in his pants and carefully arranged his shirt to conceal it.

Adnan felt dizzy and sick to his stomach, but relieved: Martyrdom would still be his.

He prayed to Muhammad . . . *peace be upon Him.*

Crack, crack, crack . . .

Goddamn AK-47s. Rick Birk knew he would never outlive his fear of that rifle. He hadn't heard one since Vietnam, yet he'd identified the weapon the instant the first shot had sounded. The North Vietnamese Army had loved them; back in the day the Russkies gave them away like stuffed cabbages.

Birk ducked behind a pallet of crates stamped with inky Chinese characters, moving so fast that his media laminates, hanging from his neck on a beaded chain, swung up and smacked him in the face. Least of his worries. There were brown buggers in headscarves down the dock to his left, and brown buggers in uniforms down the dock to his right; the ones in uniform were guarding the gangplank to Senator Gayle Higgens's supertanker, the *Dick* fucking *Cheney.*

All the brown buggers had Kalashnikovs. The guys in headscarves looked like Al Qaeda wannabes and were trying to shoot their way onto the tanker. The soldier boys had been searching bags by the gangplank. Duffels had been left open and unattended; Birk assumed their owners had fled. The uniforms had behaved like smart soldiers everywhere and taken cover. Who wants to die for iron oxide? Helluva legacy. But why would anyone kill for it? *This has got to be a first.*

Birk figured this skirmish—they were still firing at one another, mostly blindly—would last about two more minutes, until army reinforcements arrived and picked off the headscarves from behind. The wannabes had no plan, apparently, beyond playing shoot 'em up. Amateurs. They should take some lessons from their brothers-in-arms in Pakistan and Afghanistan. Those guys were ferocious kick-ass fighters. Birk hated their guts but they knew war. Not this piddly shit. *He* could take on these bozos.

One of them had an RPG, and Birk wondered why. If they used rockets, they risked blowing up the gangplank and damaging the boat, which they appeared to want to hijack. *Bring it on,* Birk thought. Rockets made for terrific bang-bang, and show producers adored them. *Where's my cameraman?*

Birk and his photographer had come to the docks to catch the water taxi to Dhiggaru, where Birk intended to flush out Jenna Withers's old boyfriend. Then the shooting had started and the cameraman had bolted. Birk hoped that the chickenshit had holed up somewhere to shoot the entire scene, especially since he was in the middle of it. The "veteran correspondent," the anchors at all the networks would call him. A dashing figure, a stalwart observer caught between opposing forces of evil. Might even save him from the next round of layoffs.

Come on, come on, Birk mumbled impatiently, sweating through his fine Egyptian cotton shirt. *Can we have some sirens? The cavalry? Give me "bang-bang" for the viewers at home. Something, for God's sake.*

He took out his cell and grabbed video of the five jihadists, assuming they had the shortest lease on life. Once the reinforcements arrived, he'd have to try to capture the bloodletting with the phone's crappy little lens. No telling what chickenshit was doing.

He'd no sooner settled back behind the pallet when a fusillade riddled the sweltering air. Birk peeked out in time to see a headscarf rise up dramatically from behind the covering fire and lob a grenade.

Holy fucking shit.

The grenade exploded. Shrapnel tore into soldiers, the gangplank, and the shipping crates. Birk glanced out and saw all five jihadists racing toward the ramp, which appeared intact. The same could not be said for three bodies that, until seconds earlier, had worn the unshredded uniform of this beleaguered nation. The surviving soldiers, seeing themselves about to be overrun, fled right toward Birk, who registered this development with dismay and more profanity. He also noticed that one of the jihadists heading toward the gangplank was armed with only a pistol.

Christ, he's fat.

You didn't see many fatties in the Maldives. But then a suspicion seized Birk and sent waves of fear washing through him: that the fat guy was wearing a suicide belt, or vest. Birk wanted to run, too, but didn't risk any exposure, not with armed men racing toward the crates that he hoped would hide him.

In seconds, Adnan was glad he was lagging behind the other four Islamists: The one with the long beard was mowed down by automatic weapons fire and went sprawling on the pier. Adnan, thirty feet behind him, froze and watched the wiry leader of the Waziristanis open fire on the enemy, who was trying to take cover behind the leg of a massive red crane. The jihadist cut him down, leaving his dead eyes fixed on the steel structure that towered above him.

Adnan ran to the jihadist with the long beard, shaking him. No life. He stuffed the Mauser into his pants and grabbed the other man's Kalashnikov. He'd never shot one of these rifles, but the trigger worked as he imagined. Too well: He shot up one of the jihadists before he realized what he was doing, ripping open his back and head, spraying blood, brains, and headscarf into the air. The man collapsed, facedown. Adnan felt nothing.

Four soldiers ran away, chased by a lone Waziristani.

Adnan sprinted as hard as he could for the ramp. "Nothing else matters," Parvez had told him. "*You* must get on board."

The short jihadist who'd tackled the fisherman raced into view, shooting at the soldiers who'd already been hit by the grenade. The attack appeared unnecessary; the bodies looked barely intact.

Adnan slipped on the blood seeping across the dock. When he dragged himself to his feet, shirt and pants smeared red, he saw the short jihadist stumble; a bullet had ripped through his neck, fired by a wounded soldier who had seemed dead a moment earlier. Blood arced from the jihadist's neck, like water from a garden hose. He clutched his wound, staring wildly at Adnan; then he fell, dropping his rifle.

Adnan turned to shoot the soldier; but his head had fallen to the dock, and his dead eyes saw nothing.

"*You* must get on board."

Alone, Adnan started up the long ramp.

The sounds of the soldiers racing toward Birk grew louder. The jihadist couldn't be far behind. One raggedy-ass headscarf, four soldiers. Why the fuck were *they* running? But Birk knew the answer: The perverse ratio of religious nutbars to political psychos generally favored the former, even when handily outnumbered. Hey, the afterlife promised gardens full of low-hanging fruit and bubbling streams, fine food and drink, and dozens of virgins—good lookers!—swarming over your loins. Even the most rigorous military training couldn't compete with that.

Birk abandoned the idea of trying to race twenty-year-old soldiers being chased by a rabid Islamist. Be worse than Pamplona, where a bull almost gored him in the behind in '73, after Birk had drunk a wee too much courage in his favorite cantina.

The memory had him sucking on his flask, savoring the gin, but he wasn't drinking courage now—just settling his nerves: He decided against trying to run away from the jihadist *and* the soldiers—*all* the brown buggers—after remembering that you never made sudden moves in a firefight that could catch the eyes of jumpy gunmen. For better or worse, the pallet, piled high with heavy-looking crates, provided the only protection, however minimal, on the whole goddamn dock.

All Birk could do was peek out long enough to see the soldiers drawing closer with Mr. Raggedy Ass right on their heels. But the worst part, the fright that made Birk wince and groan and want to stomp his poor fallen arches, was that Raggedy Ass caught his eye.

Oh, fuck a duck.

Birk hadn't prayed in decades, not since the Tet Offensive when the Vietcong pinned him down near the embassy in Saigon. But he prayed now, if profanities interlaced with "Jesus" and "God"—as in "Jesus fucking God"—could be considered, if but for a second only, as a means of petitioning a higher power. (Not a lot of spiritual belief animated Birk, not after all he'd seen of earthly miseries, but self-interest came into play, and he wasn't about to bet against the big bully in the sky, not if he could eke out any kind of edge on the theological constructs that turned other men insanely murderous.)

And there they go. The pounding boots of the soldiers. He watched them pass without ever looking over at him. Their backs quickly grew smaller.

And here comes Mr. Raggedy Ass. Birk saw him rear up and start shooting. *Oh, Christ alfuckingmighty.* All four soldiers fell.

The best Birk could hope for was that the jihadist, having slaughtered the only outright resistance left on the dock, wanted nothing more than to hustle back to whatever nasty business he had planned for the tanker. Or that in the excitement of gunning down four men with a single burst of his dearly beloved Kalashnikov, he'd forgotten about the geezer huddling behind the pallet.

Silence descended, sudden and uneasy. No more bullets, boots, or Raggedy Ass's bare soles. Birk peered out to see if the jihadist had taken to creeping around. No sign of him. Birk looked behind him. No sign there, either. Then Birk heard him—no question—moving along the far side of the pallet.

He clocked the man's every step, and tiptoed away. *Oh, sweet Jesus. Cat and mouse time.*

He had no illusions about which tail-twitching role belonged to him.

Adnan pulled himself up the gangplank to the tanker's main deck, panting heavily and sweating profusely. The deck was deserted. If any seamen or soldiers were on board, they'd retreated.

Following Parvez's instructions, Adnan immediately stripped off his shirt to bare the powerful bomb that circled his torso—bulky packages of C-4 plastic explosives strung together with wires.

"It's important," Parvez had told him, "to show them the bomb right away. Don't worry about them shooting you; they'll never risk setting off anything this powerful."

Adnan hoped Parvez could see him. The first step toward martyrdom had been achieved. If everything else was also going according to plan, his old friend could see him on a computer screen or television, and so could millions of others.

Imagining himself before their eyes, Adnan raised his arms high above his head. A fighter for Muhammad.

A champion.

Birk eased around the pallet, hoping that when Raggedy Ass turned the first corner, he'd see nothing and go on about his homicidal chores like a good jihadist. Maybe he wasn't thinking of the geezer at all. Maybe he'd only slowed down to catch his breath by the only cover on the dock. All that chasing and murdering had to be exhausting.

What was that? Footsteps. But they were getting softer and sounded farther away. *Go, Raggedy Ass. Go-go-go.*

Birk could have howled with joy. Instead, he took a nip from his flask. *You are one savvy son of a bitch,* Birk said to himself. *Pulled another rabbit out of the old hat.*

Birk put away his flask and fished out his phone. He dialed the direct line to the network desk, which was run by a good-looking Brit named

Sheila. A little old for his taste—at least fifty, by now—but not too old for a little friendly phone flirtation. And slim, like Miss Sari.

The septuagenarian correspondent cleared his throat and said, "Sheila, dear, you are not going to believe this, but I'm right smack dab in the middle of a gun battle in Malé." He thought he sounded debonair as ever. "Put me on live."

Oh, baby, it felt *great* to say those four words again: *"Put me on live."* And to deliver them with such well-earned authority. Sounded so good that he repeated them to himself one more time during an odd stretch of dead air; Sheila was generally so perky. That's why it was so easy to imagine spanking her.

"Listen, love . . ." *Getting a little flirty herself with that "love" business. Might have to give her a chance, after all.* ". . . you *are* on live, and if you're really, really smart you'll stop drinking and you won't move when the guy behind you sticks his gun up your arse."

"What?" Birk felt an adrenaline rush that became a tsunami as a gun barrel pressed against his head. Hot fucking steel burned so bad Birk thought he could smell his skin cooking, but he didn't dare move.

"You there, love?" Sheila said. "We're watching you and your friend. Everybody sends their best, I'm sure. Hang in there. No time to panic, old man."

A hand reached over Birk's shoulder, groped for his laminates. Then he was jerked around to face Mr. Raggedy Ass himself, who shouted the universal language of *"Run, asshole, run"* with uncommon force and fluency.

Birk ran, viciously poked and prodded to the gangplank by Raggedy Ass's weapon. He looked around and saw that there was no one to save him; only one barrel poked out from the crack of a metal door, and it was the lens of chickenshit's camera.

Raggedy Ass grabbed the RPG from a dead jihadist and screamed at Birk all the way up to the deck of the *Dick Cheney.* The correspondent had no idea what the jihadist was saying now, but the porker whom Birk had suspected of carrying a suicide bomb was speaking all too clearly of blood and bedlam with his half-naked show-and-tell.

Birk took no comfort in seeing that his deductive powers had remained as sharp as ever. The vest looked like it held enough C-4 to take out the tanker, dock, and anything and anyone else within a half-mile radius.

Raggedy Ass cracked Birk on the shoulder with his rifle stock, collapsing his legs and forcing him to lie down, probably to be executed—and this really hurt—*off* camera.

Birk stretched out facedown on the filthy deck. The metal was so goddamn hot he felt like a boneless breast of chicken slapped on a grill.

Raggedy Ass cuffed his hands behind his back with plastic restraints, tightening them way too much. Birk took this as a good sign: Who cuffs you and *then* shoots you?

Idiots the world over, he answered himself.

Adnan felt sorry for the old man lying on the deck, captured by the surviving Waziristani. The seaman had been hoping that the jihadist would be killed along with the other three, or so seriously wounded that he wouldn't make it aboard. Then Adnan wouldn't have had to worry about the crazy, murderous Waziristanis. He would have ordered the captain to take them out to sea, and after three or four days of world attention, the great martyr would have blown up the tanker so he could have paradise and pomegranates and virgins who would make him want their ridiculous bodies with those silly breasts that shook like rice pudding.

Instead, Adnan eyed the jihadist, who pointed to himself and the ship's bridge. Adnan nodded, and the man ran toward a metal stairway, holding his rifle ready, so he could shoot anyone who got in his way.

That means you, too, Adnan reminded himself.

Birk figured that the laminates had saved his butt. Raggedy Ass must have been smart enough to know the value of his prize.

So they'd use him, and that was fine with Birk. This could resurrect his career, win him a George Polk Award for foreign reporting. Not much competition for it these days because there wasn't much overseas reporting anymore; Americans just didn't give a fig about the rest of the world—focus groups didn't lie—and network executives didn't cram foreign coverage down viewers' throats anymore, not with their corporate overlords constantly carping about the costs of running a global news operation.

So this escapade could turn out to be the pièce de résistance of Birk's career. *Go out in a blaze of glory.* He might win everything— Polk, Emmy, duPont-Columbia, Peabody. And why not? He deserved every one of them, a whole goddamn panoply of prizes. And with any luck at all, he might get to accept them in person, rather than posthumously.

The asshole in the vest had plans, but they weren't imminent or they'd all be dead by now. Birk figured the suicide bomber wanted airtime, and he, Rick Birk, would do everything possible to make that happen. It would keep him alive *and* on camera.

Birk held hostage, day one, he mused. *Look what those Americans in Iran did for Ted Koppel's career, and that poor shmuck looked like Alfred E. Neuman.*

Birk laughed, then stifled his mirth with a mighty effort—*mistake; don't show them you're amused*—but he could feel his whole body shaking. *Maybe that's what an earthquake is,* he thought. *The whole planet trying not to laugh out loud at mankind's latest folly.*

The deck shuddered and Adnan looked up. Moments later he heard automatic weapons fire. Everything according to plan: The jihadist had forced the captain and crew to the bridge. Then the Waziristani had killed them, except for the captain himself.

Parvez had told them to leave the captain alive only till they got out to sea. "He can sail the ship by himself, if he has to."

How did Parvez know all this? Adnan wondered. And in the same moment he realized that Parvez had studied far more than the Koran in Waziristan. He'd studied jihad.

Parvez sat blocks away in an Internet café, watching a computer screen that showed the tanker heading away from Malé. Live video of the hijacking. Parvez had arranged for a jihadist who'd studied with him in Waziristan to set up a camera and provide a feed to an Islamic Web site, which was making this historic event available to the whole world.

The authorities would track down the camera soon enough, but every minute of video would draw more viewers. Even more important, it would attract the attention of world media.

Parvez clicked on the major news Web sites, including Al Jazeera, CNN, and the BBC. All of them were streaming video of the tanker leaving port, noting the decimated bodies in the foreground, and commenting on the "terrorist attack" in barely restrained voices. It was already a huge story. Hundreds of journalists would race to the Maldives, much like the rescuers who'd run to the bombing last week, to try to save the ruined survivors.

And then what happened? Parvez thought with a smile. *The second bomb exploded.*

He lifted his heavy-lidded eyes to the luxurious Golden Crescent Hotel across the street, where every room would soon become home to a foreign journalist.

Kill them all. The most famous faces.

Parvez knew that with each bomb, the story would get bigger, almost as huge as the orange stain that would soon spread across the sea.

Jenna stared stonily at her television, scarcely believing what she was witnessing: Maldivian soldiers blown up and gunned down by jihadists taking over Senator Gayle Higgens's supertanker. That brazen moron. What was she thinking, making that kind of move on her own? And now, thanks to the hijacking, the task force was really in a state of suspended animation. Everything was on hold—except the phone starting to ring beside her. She looked at the digital readout: Marv, the executive producer of *The Morning Show*.

"What's up?" She didn't bother with niceties. Why pretend?

"You watching your old stomping grounds?"

"I am."

"You see Birk getting taken hostage?"

"I did." Birk was unmistakable both in appearance—shock of white unruly hair—and personality, which she declined to consider at any length.

"Elfren wants to see you in the morning. Soon as we're off air."

As in James Elfren, the vice president in charge of correspondents and producers. Smart guy. He didn't waste anyone's time. If he wanted to see her, she was about to take off for the Maldives.

CHAPTER 14

The hijacking of the supertanker trumped every other news story, including the presidential race. As soon as Jenna finished her weather segment, she rushed over to the main set to join host Andrea Hanson and Harold Swenson, a portly, gray-haired senior researcher at the Washington Center for International Terrorism Studies. Swenson immediately sparked an impromptu debate.

"We're looking at a doomsday scenario." The expert sat forward.

"I don't think it's responsible to call it a doomsday scenario," Jenna said. "We don't know that to be the case." She found herself still adjusting to her new role as the network's resident expert not only on geoengineering but also the Maldives. And now a debater to boot.

"How can you *not* see this brazen act of ecoterrorism in those terms?" Swenson demanded. "If they blow up that tanker and release five hundred thousand tons of iron oxide, worldwide temperatures could drop five or six degrees. That's a distinct possibility."

"It is possible," Jenna said, "but—"

"That's a new ice age," Swenson interrupted. "That's doomsday."

"A five- or six-degree drop would be a new ice age," Jenna agreed, "but it's difficult to calibrate the impact of that much iron oxide in the ocean. Yes, it will cause a massive algae bloom; and yes, the algae will absorb carbon dioxide from the atmosphere. But it's more likely that we would see a two-degree drop in temperatures."

Swenson shook his head. "Two degrees? That's no picnic, either. Two degrees would mean massive crop losses in North America, Europe, Russia, and China. We're talking famine. There wouldn't even be summer in many places."

"That's very possible, and that would be horrible," Jenna said, "but we know from the Mount Pinatubo explosion, which did drop temperatures almost two degrees worldwide, that it's not doomsday."

"Can you explain about Mount Pinatubo?" Andrea asked.

"That was a volcanic explosion in the Philippines in 1991 that sent millions of tons of sulfur dioxide into the atmosphere," Jenna said quickly.

"So any drops in temperature in the Maldives would also be felt worldwide?" Andrea followed up.

"That's right," Swenson said, getting back into the discussion. "But Mount Pinatubo wasn't even two degrees. And anything beyond a three-degree drop is the end of the world as we know it."

"Look," Jenna said, "we're sitting here talking about specific drops in temperature when the reality is that we don't know how bad the impact would be."

"Maybe," Swenson said, "but what's very clear now is that suicidal Islamists have taken control of the Earth's thermostat. This," he pointed an accusing finger at Jenna, "is precisely why we can't be soft on terrorists."

"I'm not saying we should be soft on them," Jenna remonstrated. "We should get their hands off the thermostat as fast as we can and make sure that they never get another chance to do something this frightening. But the issue about how much temperatures will drop cannot be resolved here and now, because dumping iron oxide in the ocean is a crude tool, if you want to think of it that way. And dumping five hundred thousand tons is the very definition of chaos theory. That's why scientists insist on small-scale studies."

"And why radical Muslims want to send us into a new ice age."

"Hold that thought," Andrea said to Swenson. "We've got Special Terrorism Correspondent Chris Randall in our Washington Bureau with an important update on the hijacking story."

Jenna shifted her attention to a monitor on the set and watched Randall, a strikingly handsome former Army Ranger, offer Andrea a tight smile. Then he reported that the same Islamic Web site that had released the video of the hijacking had just announced that the jihadists would blow up the tanker—if the industrialized world didn't reduce its carbon emissions by 50 percent in the next five years.

Over video of the supertanker, Randall said, "The jihadists have given the U.S. one week to shut down the country's ten largest coal-fired power plants as a show of good faith."

Randall reappeared on camera, naming a handful of the plants listed by the hijackers.

"Thank you, Chris Randall, special terrorism correspondent." Andrea turned back to Jenna and Harold Swenson. "What do you make of those demands?"

"To be expected," Swenson said. "Al Qaeda's been blaming climate change on the U.S. for the past three years."

"There's no way to get anywhere near a fifty-percent reduction in greenhouse gasses, even in the next fifteen years," Jenna said. "That's a nonstarter."

"I've just been informed," Andrea adjusted her earpiece, "that President Reynolds is calling the hijacking 'Islamo ecoterrorism.' That's a new term."

"I couldn't have put it better," Swenson said. "Maybe Al Qaeda remembers what the oceanographer John Martin once said: 'Give me a half tanker of iron, and I'll give you an ice age.'" Swenson looked pointedly at Jenna.

"I would never go that far," she said.

"Where does this leave us?" Andrea asked.

"On the brink of the abyss," Swenson answered.

"In a dangerous spot," Jenna said, "but—"

"The abyss," Swenson repeated emphatically.

That's how the segment ended. Jenna found it ironic to see herself as the voice of reason after years of being criticized for trying to raise awareness of the dangers of climate change. But her position was nuanced, and she would not join in Swenson's dire prophesying.

Now she was off to see James Elfren. The urgency of the meeting with the news division vice president—scheduled for minutes after *The Morning Show* signed off—signaled its importance, but when Marv hustled to join Jenna on the way to Elfren's office, she knew without question that a pivotal development was in the works.

Elfren's young male assistant jumped from his desk outside his boss's office to escort Jenna and Marv into a spacious corner lair, which was well insulated from the squawking horns, squealing brakes, and piercing sirens of Manhattan traffic. Elfren rose from behind his cherrywood desk and smiled at Jenna. She saw him so rarely—Jenna was not officially in the news division, as Marv was wont to remind her—that Elfren's tall, slope-shouldered stature took her aback. As did his bright hazel eyes and mocha-colored hair. An altogether attractive example of the executive species.

He gestured to a sitting area, and Jenna knew instinctively to take the tufted couch. Marv appeared to weigh the wisdom of claiming the brass tack armchair, before realizing, or perhaps remembering, that that was likely the boss's perch and that it might not behoove him to long so openly for the perquisites of power. Jenna thought Marv looked like a stumpy Ecuadorian general lusting after the presidential palace in the hours before a coup.

Dream on, twit.

"Your outfit was a huge improvement today," Elfren said to her, adjusting his smartly striped tie as he assumed his throne.

As soon as he spoke, Jenna recalled why Elfren had never been a candidate for on-air honors: His voice sounded as if his throat was being continually throttled by a murderous hand. Every high-pitched word sounded panicked.

"Yesterday, you had her looking half undressed out there in that sleazy Dorothy outfit, Marv." Elfren spoke without a smile or any evidence of cheesy, male-bonding humor. To the contrary, this was unadulterated admonishment, Jenna realized, and brought to mind Elfren's other appealing quality: He was a decent guy, a married man with two kids and no reputation for chasing women.

"I'll talk to Jeremy," Marv said.

"You mean you didn't have him clear those outfits with you first?"

Marv looked pained, like he wished more than anything that he could slink back to the fourth floor. "I trusted him."

"I wouldn't," Elfren said in a way that made it clear that Marv shouldn't have, either. "I never want to see that again."

"Numbers were up," Marv peeped.

"So were viewer complaints. Thousands of e-mails have come in. They're still coming, and most of them thought our host looked like a slut. I don't want viewers thinking of Andrea—a mother-to-be—as a slut, Marv. It's *bad* morning television."

Maybe Marv's getting fired. Jenna had never seen a show producer so severely dressed down—*Bad pun,* she told herself. But she loved every moment of it. *Go, Elfren.*

"To the business at hand," Elfren said, to Marv's evident relief. "We've got two stories that I'm concerned about. Let's start with the murder of that GreenSpirit woman. I want you to see what CBS had on just minutes before our show ended."

"I know about it," Marv said.

"I want to go through it with you anyway," Elfren said.

His office had five large, wall-mounted flat-screen TVs. He used a remote to click on the one closest to them. It was cued to the story in question. Video of naked men and women—breasts, bottoms, and pubic areas digitized—opened a report on the killing. The reporter's off-screen voice was filled with gravitas:

"This was the aftermath of an initiation of two witches Saturday night, presided over by GreenSpirit, the self-described witch and Pagan leader who was murdered just hours later. Pagans and witches from a wide region attended the gathering; followers included Suze Walker, a daughter of the Malloy County sheriff, Nate Walker. The young woman wouldn't talk to CBS News," the camera stayed on her as she turned away, "but her father has declared that this high school quarterback, Jason Robb, shown in a recent game, is a 'person of interest' to law enforcement authorities."

"We want to talk to him," Sheriff Walker said to the unseen reporter. "We think he might know something."

"Did you know that your daughter was at the initiation?" the reporter asked.

"Yes, of course I did."

"Are you a Pagan?"

"No, we're Baptists, proud Pentecostals, and so is my daughter. My wife and I don't encourage belief in Paganism but we understand the spiritual curiosity of young people."

"The sheriff's tolerance," the reporter continued over video of the man as he walked away, "may not be shared by everyone in this rural region. People at the gathering say that Jason Robb," the football video reappeared, "the young man the sheriff named a 'person of interest,' threatened some of them, including GreenSpirit, the night before she was murdered."

The reporter then stood before the camera detailing Sheriff Walker's request for help on the homicide investigation from the New York State Police and FBI. The reporter also noted that law enforcement authorities said that the crime scene "appeared to have been compromised," which sounded consistent with the sheriff's own statements the day before.

Elfren clicked off the report. "What did we have on your show, Marv? Biggest story in the New York region, and one of the biggest in the country, and what did you have?"

"There was a screwup on the assignment desk. We've got the Northeast Bureau on their way up there now."

"We had video of downtown Bennel, and aerials from a trip that Jenna took up there last week. And what I'm hearing from you are excuses. First, it's wardrobe's fault that the women on your show look like hookers. Now it's the assignment desk's fault that we're getting skunked. I don't like getting skunked. Do something about it."

"We did, like I said—"

Elfren cut him off by turning to Jenna, who'd noticed that his squeaky voice reached an even higher octave when he was angry. "I want you on the next plane to the Maldives. We've got to take the lead on this story. That's our own guy they've got, and they're probably going to kill him. If I could launch a team of Navy SEALs to grab him back, I would. What I can do is send you to do two things for us: I want you providing expert analysis of the iron oxide threat—you should own that story with your background—and I want you to help the rest of our team with your local knowledge. You game?"

"You bet I'm game."

"I know Birk's very . . . eccentric," Elfren said, "and I'd be shocked if he hasn't insulted you at least once because he's done it to every other woman in the news division, but he's our guy. He's been with us forever, he has his fans, and the old creep's smart."

Jenna laughed. So did Marv. The eight-hundred-pound gorilla in the room had been acknowledged: Birk could be a jerk of the first order.

"What about me being a member of the task force? I thought that would get in the way of any news division duties."

"You'll be going as an analyst, not as a reporter. Give us sound bites. Boil down the science so people know what's at stake. But that does bring up something else that you might be able to help us with, and that's Senator Gayle Higgens. She's going to be besieged by every news organization that shows up on that island, and that basically means everybody. See if you can get her in our corner. We're sending Chris Randall down there with you to do the actual reporting. Do you want Nicole to come?"

"Yes, I do. She's incredibly good on the ground, and—"

"You don't have to convince me," Elfren interrupted. "I hired her. I think you two are a great team, when you're not dressed like you're heading to a *Penthouse* Pets pajama party." He threw yet another steely look at Marv.

Elfren walked over to his desk for Jenna's book, recently reissued with an eye-catching, ecofriendly cover. "I read it last night. I had no idea, I'm sorry to say, that your background was so strong. I knew you'd written a book, but this was very well done."

"Thank you." That he might have read her tome in a single evening was another reason for Elfren's fast-track success: He was a legendarily fast study.

"This is one hell of a story," Elfren said somberly. "Might be the biggest one in my lifetime."

"If they blow up the tanker," Marv asked, "will it look—"

"Orange?" she jumped in. Leave it to Marv to cut to the crassest point. "The video will be unlike anything anyone has ever seen." She would have liked to equivocate, just to stick it to him, but the truth wouldn't let her.

"We're chartering. One o'clock at LaGuardia," Elfren announced.

"Chartering?" She thought those days had ended when the bean counters had executed their coup de grâce on network coffers. Personally, she was glad never to have flown Lears and Gulfstreams: Jets emitted enormous amounts of greenhouse gases, and private jets were the worst offenders by far.

"Look," he tapped her book, "I know about the carbon footprint, but one of our own is on that tanker, and we're going to move as fast as we can to try to help him."

Goddamn brown buggers.

The sun beat down so hard that Rick Birk felt broiled alive in the blinding tropical heat. The skinny jihadist he'd dubbed Raggedy Ass had given him a swig of water but it had been hours since Birk had had a *real* drink. If he'd been dealing with anyone but an Islamist, he'd have offered to split his hooch just to get a few sips for himself. He still had his flask because, interestingly enough, Raggedy Ass and Suicide Sam hadn't patted him down. Everybody—even fucking jihadists—figured he was too old to be a serious threat.

Well, maybe he, Rick Birk, who had survived the Shining Path guerrillas in Peru, the Vietcong, and right-wing death squads in more

Latin American countries than George W. Bush could possibly name, had a gun in an ankle holster and was about to put a stop to all this madness.

Yeah, right. If only . . .

He wondered if he could convince Raggedy Ass that the flask contained very important medicine. He'd always thought about wearing one of those bracelets that lepers and diabetics have for emergencies, only instead of a snake curled around a staff, his would show a cheerful bottle of Bombay gin.

Fuck. Fat lot of good a medical bracelet would do him now. Raggedy Ass was too busy to bother with him anyway. Had more *important* things to do, like dragging dead bodies down to the deck, the back of their heads bounce-bounce-bouncing off every metal step on the stairway, then leaving a big smear all the way over to the railing till they got the old heave-ho. Right in front of Birk. Who *wouldn't* need a drink?

Oh, no, here he comes with number nine. Birk couldn't see Raggedy Ass because the aged correspondent was still lying facedown on the goddamn deck. But he heard the head of number nine—*bumpita-thumpita-bumpita*—and he was keeping track because when he got out of this mess he wanted to be able to report every little detail with absolute accuracy. He could already see the George Polk Award for foreign reporting hanging on the wall of his new *corner* office.

Christ, this one's a moaner. Ah, Jesus fuck, there he is. Not just moaning, but rolling his brilliant blue eyes in crazed panic. Catching Birk's gaze and staring at him while Raggedy Ass hauled him to the railing.

Raggedy Ass paused and stared at the man, whose moans heightened in intensity. Then the jihadist screamed at him. Might have been "Shut up" in whatever bone-in-the-throat language he claimed, but if it was, the tanker crewman paid no attention.

The hijacker lifted the man up and pushed him over. Long way down to Davy Jones. At least fifty, sixty feet just to the water. And the sharks. *Oh, God, the sharks.* Birk's groin tightened. With all the body bait that Raggedy Ass had dumped overboard, Birk figured there had to be a feeding frenzy down there by now. God knows, there were plenty of those deep-blue devils in the Maldives: The country had declared itself a shark sanctuary.

Raggedy Ass wiped his bloody hands on his bloody pants as he walked over to Birk. The correspondent did his best to keep his tone supplicating when he said, "Please, Mr. Raggedy Ass, scum-fuck terrorist, please don't miss my vitals when you shoot me."

Raggedy Ass peered at him suspiciously, as if trying to unlock the secrets of this severely sunburned old wreck.

"That's right, needle dick, blow my brains out proper when it's my turn."

"Dick? Dick?" Raggedy Ass asked.

Oh, sweet Lord. Fucker knows one word of English and it's got to be that one.

Raggedy Ass stared at him, and Birk offered his most craven smile. The jihadist grabbed his shoulder and dragged Birk to his feet. Emaciated, but strong. Raggedy Ass turned him to face the wall, kicked Birk's feet apart as sharply as any NYPD tactical officer, and searched Birk's pockets, finding his cell phone, notebook, pen, a fistful of blank receipts so he could cheat on his expense account, and, finally, Birk's most prized possession.

Raggedy Ass unscrewed the flask, smelled the gin, and pulled his nose away in disgust. Birk looked over his shoulder, watching the jihadist pour out the liquor in a slow, tantalizing stream. The correspondent almost sank to his knees to try to intercept the precious, fragrant flow. But no, he held back and watched the flask empty even as he filled with longing deeper than the sea itself, thinking, *Bastard. Asshole. Shitface. Scum fuck,* and every other deprecation that came to mind.

Raggedy Ass cracked him on the head with the flask, then hurled it into the ocean.

Goddamn him. That flask had more miles on it than a gypsy caravan. *Is nothing sacred anymore?*

Raggedy Ass kicked the backs of Birk's knees, collapsing the old sod into a heap before he walked back up the stairs. Another body to retrieve, no doubt.

How many more before it's my turn?

Birk's eyes dropped to the gin-soaked deck. His tongue followed.

Jenna hurried out of Elfren's office. Marv rushed after her, puffing audibly.

"Lucky break for you, huh?" he said, resentment poorly contained.

"Yeah, too bad for the planet."

Jenna took the stairs rather than endure the elevator with him, guessing correctly that he wouldn't follow her if it entailed any physical effort.

She rushed into her office, giving Nicci a joyful jolt with the news about the Maldives assignment. She stayed in the office only long enough to answer a few e-mails while waiting for her Ford Fusion to be brought around, then sped home. Arriving at her apartment, Jenna was immensely pleased to find Dafoe waiting for her on the sidewalk. After her telephone call from Marv last night, Dafoe was so certain that the network was going to send her overseas that he said he'd "move mountains" to try to see her before she left.

"You made it," she exclaimed, giving him a quick kiss.

"Just got here. You're leaving, aren't you?"

"I am." A distinct stirring bloomed in her belly. "I'm really glad you're here. Was Forensia able to cover for you?" She led him into the lobby.

"With Sang-mi, this time. Those two don't go anywhere without each other these days. In fact, Richtor and three other Pagans are camped in their living room. They figure group living is the first line of defense against whoever killed GreenSpirit."

She nodded. "Makes sense to me."

"How's your time?" he asked with a smile whose meaning was easy—and delightful—to divine.

She glanced at her watch as the elevator doors opened. "I've got a small window." Her driver wouldn't mind a short wait.

The first kiss began as the doors closed and didn't end till they arrived at her floor. *To hell with the security camera,* she thought.

In a minute they were in her apartment, playing another round of bedspring boogaloo. She loved every second of it. He had the richest scent, and tasted *so* good.

But the real intimacy came after their most intense pleasure, when they lay on their sides, facing each other. Her finger trailed the line of his jaw, and then she leaned forward and kissed him softly on the lips. They were so close, inches apart, his look penetrating her much more deeply than even his most eager, aroused exertions. These were the most intensely loving moments that she'd ever known.

She finally had to pry herself away for a fast shower. She dried and dressed quickly, and packed in record time. Jenna was as efficient with her getaways as she was with her weather forecasts.

Together, they headed down to the elevator. Before the doors opened, she gave him one more passionate kiss, knowing it would have to last.

She almost let slip three little words that she hadn't spoken in years. But she feared that "I love you" would only burden such sweet beginnings, though she felt certain that what they shared went well beyond basic chemistry.

So instead of "I love you," she said, "I'll miss you," but she spoke with an unguarded honesty that was as new to her as the power of real intimacy. Even so, in the next instant Jenna wondered whether she should have gone further and stated her feelings with the same robust abandonment that her body had revealed upstairs—with the same intense longing that her heart had felt so palpably when they lay close to each other.

What if you never get a chance to say it?

Dafoe escorted her to the Ford Fusion. The driver took Jenna's bag and she slid into the backseat.

Don't be silly. You'll have plenty of chances. Why wouldn't you?

"Hey." Dafoe motioned for her to lower her window. "Any idea how long you'll be gone?"

"No telling. Could be over before we get there. Could be weeks."

"Do you know where you'll be staying?"

"The Golden Crescent Hotel."

Dafoe bent toward the car window, and Jenna knew he was going to kiss her again, but the driver pulled out and the moment was lost. She waved at her dairy farmer just before she startled at the sight of her own face; it took a second to realize she was looking at a banner ad for *The Morning Show* on the side of a bus.

She sat back, smiling, thrilled by Dafoe, her assignment, and the life she felt privileged to have found.

CHAPTER 15

Parvez snapped his cell phone shut and gave thanks to Allah, the one true God. He walked along the shore, beaming. He had been blessed by Allah with insight and understanding, and with the courage to use both.

Warm surf rushed over his feet, washing away the tracks he left behind. In a moment he would be no more present on the beach than he had been on the phone. In the coded language of Al Qaeda, he'd told them of his plan. And in a reply that both surprised and honored him, his commander had ordered Parvez to return to the café across from the Golden Crescent Hotel at 7:00 P.M. tonight for a rendezvous. They had additional jihadists already in place.

But why should I be surprised by their eagerness? Parvez chided himself gently. *This is the greatest prize since 9/11, and I recognized that. I have great insight and understanding,* he reminded himself. *And courage.*

He looked up and saw another jumbo jet heading for Malé International Airport, and had no doubt that many of the seats were taken by men and women who, upon landing, would soon head to their place of death. With each hour, more of the most powerful media personalities were arriving on the island—and getting whisked straight to its most exclusive hotel.

He cursed the name of the Golden Crescent Hotel as he hurried to his motor launch. Such a blasphemy to use the word "crescent," much less to display crescents and stars like cheap ornaments all over a hotel where liquor is served and women flaunt their sex—where the impious pretend they are important.

We will show them, and they will never forget. They had not forgotten 9/11, had they?

He looked at his watch as he boarded his motor launch and started the outboard motor. Ample time. He headed across the turquoise channel, thinking about the one-two punch that he had in store for the Western world. He knew all about this from his studies in Waziristan. The Koran, yes, he had pored over its sacred words every day. But he had studied the strategies and techniques of jihad just as diligently, and no strategy was more basic or brutal—or deeply blessed—than the one-two punch. The hard fist of Allah for the ugly faces of infidels.

A hotel was the easiest target in the world. You pulled up and the staff invited you right in. Guests were always welcome. Delivery vans came and went, day and night. Busy, busy, busy. Perfect for a bombing.

Adnan's load had lightened considerably. Only two packages of C-4 remained in his suicide vest. He'd put the others exactly where Parvez had told him to. One of these last two would deliver the maximum damage to the most forward part of the hull; four other bombs had been placed aft.

The tanker was much bigger than any ship Adnan had ever sailed on—the length of at least two soccer fields, with many levels. When he'd studied the diagram of the *Dick Cheney* with Parvez, setting up the bombs had looked simple, but everything about the supertanker seemed oversized, even to a seasoned sailor like him. And his job had never entailed rigging a massive ship to blow up and sink.

Finding his way through the warren of hallways, berths, and storage rooms had taken Adnan hours. He'd worried constantly that around every corner he would be ambushed by seamen who'd hidden in the bowels of the tanker. Although only he and the leader of the Waziristanis had survived the assault on the ship, the crew had proved compliant when faced with automatic rifles, the RPG, and a suicide vest. More useful than those had been the short-handled ax that the jihadist had grabbed from a cache of firefighting supplies. While Adnan held an AK-47, the Waziristani had threatened to chop off crewmembers' legs and arms if they didn't tell him where other sailors were hiding. They all swore that everyone was on the bridge but the Islamist had still chopped off the hand of an African, just to make sure no one was lying. Sickened, Adnan had looked away. Later, he'd tripped over the amputated hand on a lower deck; the jihadist had thrown it away. The injured man had screamed and screamed until the Waziristani shot him.

Then the jihadist had killed them all, except for the captain, just as the plan demanded.

Adnan couldn't have committed the Waziristani's gruesome crimes. *This is different,* he reassured himself as he checked the wiring of the last bomb. *You're a martyr,* he thought once more, *not a murderer.*

Studying the diagram of the ship, Adnan had learned a great deal about tankers. The newest ones were designed so that if one part of the hull were compromised, the other holds would not lose their valuable— and often dangerous—cargo. But now that he'd rigged all the bombs to go off in quick succession, the *Dick Cheney* would split apart in sections and dump all the iron oxide it carried.

Then, while billions watched him, he would stand on the main deck and detonate the lone bomb left in his vest. The world would never forget the sinking of the supertanker. Or the martyr from the Maldives.

As he started back up the stairs, Adnan felt as if he were already ascending to heaven in earthly triumph.

Parvez sat in the café at the appointed hour and watched two likely looking men walk in a few minutes later, one much taller and thinner than the other. Without a glance in his direction, they headed straight for his table. They must have been surveilling the café and seen him enter. He should have been as cautious.

Both men were piously bearded and looked serious, and both said their name was Mohammed. Parvez did not believe them, but understood their caution.

The taller man, whose glasses sat below the bridge of his nose, glanced censoriously at a dark-haired Western woman in a short white skirt. The brother looked like he might throttle her. Parvez would not have blamed him if he had. But perhaps she was one of the reporters staying in the hotel. If so, there was no need to hurt her now; soon she would die in flames and rubble. And for those who survived, whose desperate calls for rescue would rise from the ashes, there would be the final knowledge, in the last seconds of their lives, that they had lured even more infidels to their deaths.

Parvez and the Mohammeds shared a pot of tea. They talked about the weather, but even these common words were fraught, as they must be in times teeming with peril.

"There will be sudden storms," the shorter man said, scratching his chin through his beard. "They will arrive out of nowhere." He smiled. "Not even the scientists can see them coming."

"Only Allah," said the taller one. Parvez nodded knowingly.

"A man such as you, living on a small island, he could use help," the shorter man continued. "Is this not so?" He smiled again.

"I am humbled by your offer," Parvez said.

"We must move fast," the taller man added, glancing around. But no one was listening, and the jingly-jangly sound of a CD smothered their softly spoken words. The music annoyed Parvez. Someday music would find its proper place in the Maldives, and it would no longer distract serious men from serious tasks.

They made plans with careful words, and then the tall man bowed his head and said, "We will pray together soon, and our prayers will be heard around the world."

We worship Allah in all kinds of ways, Parvez reminded himself after the men left. Sometimes we pray in the silence of our souls. Sometimes we pray with the shattering screams of the unforgiven.

* * *

Forensia hurried back from the barn to check on Bayou, resting on a blanket in Dafoe's expansive country kitchen. She flipped aside her black braids and bent over to see if she could get him to eat. Poor dog could hardly get around. Not that they wanted him to. "Make him rest," Dr. Berkley had ordered, "even if you have to coop him up in a dog crate."

Thankfully, that wasn't necessary; Dafoe had trained Bayou so well that when Forensia commanded him to "stay," he never moved. Now, she coaxed precious bits of cooked lamb into him.

The border collie loved lamb, but had to labor to swallow the meat. At least he could eat. *And he is recovering,* Forensia assured herself. At times like this, when he gazed at her with his big marbly eyes, she could hardly believe that he'd lived through the coyote attack. Or that her savagery had been the sole instrument of his survival. But she had no regrets: She'd saved him, and no matter how she parsed it, the fact that he lived felt great.

But the torn-up dog, still bandaged and stitched, couldn't herd, so Forensia would have to take over the rest of his chores as well as his master's.

"Let's go," she called to Sang-mi. Her friend was curled up on the couch, looking almost as frightened as she had in the minutes after she'd found GreenSpirit's mutilated body. "I've got to move those cows to pasture and it'll take a while." She knew that the other woman wouldn't want to stay alone in the house for more than a few minutes.

Sang-mi slipped a barrette into her short black hair and almost ran to Forensia, edging past Bayou without so much as a warm glance or word. She didn't care for dogs—a cultural quirk, apparently—but Forensia knew she felt a deep affection for her tall American friend. Last night, they'd sat up talking after Richtor and the others had gone to bed, and Sang-mi had told Forensia about a long-developed North Korean eco-terrorism plot that might dwarf any nightmare in the Maldives.

Forensia was still trying to figure out what to do with this horrifying news, but right now she had to turn her attention back to the more immediate threats they were facing.

She picked up Dafoe's varmint gun and stepped onto the porch, eyeing every tree, shed, and fence post like they were hiding Green-Spirit's murderer.

Forensia missed having Bayou's eyes and ears on full alert out here. There were never surprises with him on duty; he'd even warned her of the attack that had taken him down. Richtor had insisted on loaning her his big lumbering Newfie, but Forensia didn't think the one-hundred-sixty-pound ball of lazy black fur had shifted a single inch since claiming a spread of shade on the porch.

Not an hour went by without Forensia remembering the threat that Jason Robb had shouted at her after the initiation. And she wasn't the only one strongly suspicious of the high school quarterback: This morning she'd glanced at the local news online only long enough to learn that Sheriff Walker had asked anyone with knowledge of Jason's whereabouts to come forward. If the sheriff was making that plea, Forensia figured that Jason's buddies weren't talking; it was widely known that his parents had refused to cooperate with the sheriff, the New York State Police homicide detectives, or the FBI. She did feel sorry for his folks; one son died in Iraq and the other had turned into a killer.

Long as he's not around this place.

Forensia took Sang-mi's hand and headed for the barn.

"My baby kicked me," her friend said.

"Really? Just now?" Forensia asked, still scanning the farm; she never would have offered to help out Dafoe if she'd known how freaked out she was going to be working out here with just Sang-mi for company.

Her friend nodded. "When we started walking, I felt it."

"That's great. First time?" Looking everywhere at once.

"No." Sang-mi smiled slyly. It had been so long since Forensia's friend had brightened that her smile did feel like a first.

Sang-mi had had ample reasons to feel glum. First, her Pagan boyfriend got her pregnant, after insisting that he'd had a vasectomy. Then he promptly took off for three months to "see the sights" in Vietnam, China, and Thailand. A real loser, in Forensia's opinion, though Sang-mi wouldn't hear any criticism of him, saying sternly, "He's my baby's father."

And now it turned out that Sang-mi had been carrying more than a baby. She'd also been bearing the news that she'd divulged to Forensia about North Korea—about a plot that involved her own father.

Sang-mi had told her that the reason the CIA was still debriefing her dad was that he was an expert on North Korean plans to launch thousands of rockets that would release trillions of sulfate particles into the atmosphere. The sulfates would block the sun and send the Earth into a deep freeze that would mean endless winter for most of the planet for many years.

"Dafoe's friend wrote about it," Sang-mi had added, surprising Forensia, who'd known little about Jenna Withers's book, other than its broad subject: climate change.

"What did she say?" Forensia asked.

"She had a section about the North accusing the U.S. and other countries of causing climate change and the famine in the North."

"Is that true?" asked Forensia.

"Who knows," Sang-mi said. "But that's why the North developed this secret plan."

Sang-mi went on to say that the North Koreans had taken an idea advocated by many geoengineering proponents and turned it into a weapon of unprecedented mass destruction. Forensia thought her friend was exaggerating until Sang-mi had explained the worldwide effects of the eruption of Mount Pinatubo in the Philippines in 1991.

"The missiles would be like many Pinatubos," Sang-mi had said, "and the sulfates will make the whole Earth very cold. That's the big reason my father defected, along with me," she patted her belly, "even though he knew that they'd arrest his mother and father and torture them and keep them in prison until they died."

Forensia had been shocked, but Sang-mi had just continued, "They were tortured but we think they are still alive."

"What is the North waiting for?" Forensia had asked.

"For something horrible to happen that they can exploit. That's what the North always does. When the U.S. was busy invading Iraq, the North started sending missiles over Japan, just to let them know that they could reach huge population centers with their bombs. They're always looking for pressure points."

This morning they'd been awakened by a call from Sang-mi's mother, who had been nearly hysterical. Her husband's CIA handler had contacted him right after the jihadists threatened to blow up the tanker. Forty minutes later a helicopter whisked him away. Sang-mi's mother had no idea where he had been taken or when he might return.

Forensia paused in the shade of the barn and turned to Sang-mi. "I don't get something. The CIA took your dad away after the jihadists announced their crazy plans, but what would that have to do with North Korean rockets? That's so weird. There's no connection between them and the Maldives. They have different religions, different cultures, and very different politics."

"The tanker has everything to do with those missiles," Sang-mi replied pointedly. "The sulfates in them and the iron oxide in the tanker both lower temperatures. One works in the ocean and the other in the sky. Both of them together," she shook her head, "would be very, very bad. Not twice as bad—many times as bad. That's the connection.

"The North, they see everybody paying attention to the tanker, and the Supreme Leader," her anger was on rare display, "says to his army, 'Now we can get the whole world's attention.' That's what he wants. And once he gets it, you watch, he'll say 'You think the Maldives is bad? Wait till you see what I've got.'"

"But for what?"

"For everything. They have nothing. They need food, oil, cars, gas, trucks, trains. Anything you can think of. The country is a disaster."

The threat of a double blast of terrorism that targeted the very life of the planet left Forensia stunned. In the seconds that followed, she found herself imagining the blazing sky darkening, and an unkind chill sweeping over the land, frosting the brittle trees and barren stream beds.

She entered the barn and opened stalls, still numbed by the news. The cows often wouldn't budge without Bayou to nip at their heels.

"Go on, move." She had no patience for them this morning. She turned to Sang-mi, who'd followed her inside. "Would the Koreans in charge of the rockets really do that?"

"The president is crazy, and he makes the people crazy. Crazy people do crazy things." Sang-mi's voice was choked. Looking at her, Forensia saw tears pouring from her friend's eyes. Forensia held her close, felt Sang-mi's round belly pressed against her own. The baby kicked. The women stepped apart.

"I felt that," Forensia exclaimed.

"Me, too."

The barn door creaked, and they both spun around. It was a cow, finally leading the herd to pasture.

Forensia nudged the last of the cows out of the barn. Once they were in the parched pasture, she rested the rifle against the fence and closed the gate.

Again, she looked all around them. She was glad to help Dafoe, but she looked forward to having him back later that day. Over the last week, everything had begun to feel unsettled. Anxious. She was sure that her fear had spiked because of what Sang-mi had told her, but she also had the uncanny feeling that invisible eyes were boring holes in her back.

I see them. They're looking all around but they don't see me. I won't let them. Not till it's time. And then all they'll see is me.

He's out in the brush, a good hundred and fifty yards away. The talk in town says this is right where the tall one beat a coyote to death and then shot it. Killed three of them. He wouldn't have figured her for that kind of action. *Maybe she's up to all kinds of fun, especially private stuff with her pregnant friend there. Must get kind of messy in bed when they get going.*

He's kept an eye on her place in town, which is getting downright crowded. First, the Korean moved in, and now a bunch of other Pagans. Supposed to be a tiny two-bedroom. *She must like her fun.*

When the two of them took off early this morning, he figured the Korean was going to help with the farm chores. And if she was going to do that, even being pregnant and all, he figured that the guy who owned this place needed a lot of help. Turned out he wasn't even around. That big-name girlfriend down in the city must be keeping him busy.

He looks through the brush and knows he's got to be careful. Tall one's got a rifle, and everyone knows now that she's handy with a gun. *You can tell just looking at her. She's holding that rifle so easy it might as well be a . . . broomstick.*

He laughs quietly, but tells himself to get serious because there's just no way to get a jump on the two of them out here. *You got to be patient, capital "P." Don't want to be doing anything rash till it rains.*

But he's glad to see they're worried. *You bet they are. Looking all around, heads twisting this way and that, like they're possessed.*

He backs away. Just to be sure. Can't let himself be seen. Then he'd have to take corrective action on the spur of the moment, and that's just not a smart thing to do. *You got to get the jump on them, like you got the jump on the old witch. And you're going to want rain to help you. If it'll come.* He shades his eyes and looks up. Sky looks bleached.

But man, you got to get her, he warns himself. *You can't wait forever because the minute she starts putting two and two together, two and two is going to add up to you.*

Nighttime in North Korea. Satellites from the United States spy on 23 million people, but they capture only darkness blacker than the deepest well. All around the Supreme Leader's nation, lights burn: in China, Japan, and South Korea. They are visible. They are vulnerable. Their lights burn like stars too weak to stay up in the sky.

But we are blackness. We are invisible. Our enemies shudder, thinks Jae-hwa as he enters the Supreme Leader's compound.

Two lines of "pleasure girls" pass him as they exit. They are so young and beautiful, dressed identically in blue jackets and skirts. They lift the burdens of the motherland from the shoulders of the president. And that is for the best, for he is the leader and "We cannot live away from his breast." Jae-hwa repeats this popular slogan to himself solemnly every time he comes to see the great one.

Guards on both sides of Jae-hwa escort him into a vast hall with a ceiling that arches high above him. This marks the beginning of the Supreme Leader's private quarters. At the very end, the most revered one sits at a long table eating rice and vegetables and dark red ostrich meat by himself. Jae-hwa knows the ostrich comes from the president's private farm. So much hunger, but he must eat. He must be strong. Above all others.

The Great One studies Jae-hwa, who wishes that he were shorter so that he could honor the Supreme Leader more by looking up to him with his eyes, as he does with his heart. Then the president smiles and sings. This is a momentous occasion, the highest honor ever accorded Jae-hwa. He beams with pleasure. His son and his son's sons will forever know of the night when the most revered one sang to *him*.

"Our enemies are the American bastards, who are trying to take over our beautiful fatherland. With guns that I make with my own hands, I will shoot them, bang-bang-bang." His voice is so powerful. When he points his finger and fires an imaginary gun, Jae-hwa applauds, beaming, and nods over and over. This is a song all North Koreans know, but none can sing it with such conviction, for none have shown the Supreme Leader's heroism against their brutal foes. Jae-hwa's own son sings this song every day at school, and before he goes to bed. He sleeps soundly because his father works with the Supreme Leader. So much pride in Jae-hwa's home.

Now the president aims his finger at Jae-hwa and pretends to shoot him. Jae-hwa stops smiling. Stops nodding. His hands fall to his sides. *Have I insulted him?* Jae-hwa doesn't know what to do. He thinks of his son: *May you always sleep soundly, even when the guns are real.*

"We have our guns, bang-bang-bang," the Supreme Leader sings again.

The president means the rockets. That's why Jae-hwa is here. For many years the army has loaded thousands of missiles with sulfates. Overseeing the arming of rockets has been Jae-hwa's most important duty since the 1990s, when droughts and floods caused a million people to starve to death. Maybe more, but nobody dares say this.

It was a holocaust of hunger. Mothers ate dirt and fed their babies insects. It was not the fault of the great nation or the Supreme Leader. The extreme weather was due to climate change, spurred by the wastrels in North America and Europe and Japan. The Supreme Leader warned the world that he would not let his people suffer alone. The West ignored him and slandered him. Called him crazy.

They won't ignore the president much longer. The rockets are loaded with enough sulfates to make the whole world share the gnawing hunger of the North.

"The fools in the Maldives know nothing," the president says.

"You are right, Supreme Leader."

"The time is coming to instruct the world. . . ." *This is what the Supreme Leader does so well. He teaches us all,* Jae-hwa thinks. *We are his children.* "The phony election in the United States comes in days. We must act."

"You have been most patient with them," Jae-hwa says.

"Do you think I have been too patient?" the president demands.

"No." Jae-hwa's toes curl up in his boots; he did not intend to offend the most powerful one. "We have waited for your wisdom."

"We must be ready. Are we?"

Jae-hwa tells him that every rocket is loaded. "They will turn the sky black."

The Supreme Leader smiles, and nods at a seat at the long table. A guard rushes to bring Jae-hwa a plate of warm food. Jae-hwa wishes that he could save the ostrich meat for his boy, who has never tasted such a luxury. *Hunger is the burden of heroes.* The Supreme Leader has shared these wise words so many times.

But Jae-hwa would never insult the president by asking to take home food served at his table. To eat with him is a great honor. So Jae-hwa carefully matches the Supreme Leader's every mouthful. Eat when he eats. Chew when he chews. Swallow only when he swallows. Always follow the Great One.

Jae-hwa begins to perspire, and for the first time, notices the heat in the room. If he could, he would bring the heat home to his boy, too. There is no heat for houses in North Korea.

Only frozen blackness. But it protects them. It protects the rockets. The West worries only about nuclear bombs, and cries every time the North launches missiles. The Supreme Leader has been smart to make them worry, because their fear of nuclear war keeps them from seeing the sulfate rockets that will destroy the planet.

And only we will be ready. Only we will survive. Only we have the hard experience of living without light, heat, and the murderous comforts of the West.

CHAPTER 16

A gentle hand shook Jenna's shoulder. A voice spoke, distant as a dream. "Jenna? We'll be landing in about forty minutes, and I want to bring you up to speed so we can hit the ground running."

Nicci? Jenna wondered groggily. She slipped off a black sleep mask and squinted at her producer in the bright tropical sunlight that was spilling into the spacious charter jet. She checked her watch: zonked out for almost nine hours. *Great.* She usually didn't sleep well on planes, but she usually didn't zap herself with zopiclone. Neither did she generally fly on a luxurious Gulfstream with a buttery leather seat that, at the push of a button, converted into one of the plushest beds that Jenna had ever nestled in. Yes, she felt guilty about the outsized carbon footprint of a private jet, but she could not deny, much as she would have liked to, the pleasure of having this kind of transport in a pinch. Now she understood what network old-timers were waxing nostalgic about when they talked about "back in the day." *Old-timers like Rick Birk.*

Jenna groaned, though she recognized that Birk was the reason that she and the rest of the network team weren't flying commercial. If they had been, they would have been refueling back in Dubai about now, instead of arriving at their destination, halfway around the world from their starting point at LaGuardia.

"Want some coffee?" Nicci asked.

Jenna nodded, set aside a soft cotton blanket, and turned her "bed" back into a seat. "Back in a sec," she said.

Returning from the bathroom, she joined Nicci on a full-size couch that was braced against the left side of the jet. The flight attendant, a young man named Anders from the Netherlands, handed Jenna a cup of coffee.

Behind them, Chris Randall, the network's special terrorism correspondent, was waking. In a neighboring seat, his producer, Alicia Gant, was pecking peevishly at her laptop. She was about ten years his senior, and not nearly as warm toward Jenna and Nicci as the former Army Ranger turned correspondent.

"That woman worries me," Nicci said, sotto voce. Randall walked past them toward the front of the plane.

Jenna nodded. Who needed air-conditioning with icy Alicia around? After takeoff, they'd all shared a couple of bottles of Australian Riesling. Jenna had found the two-person camera crew and Chris friendly enough, but Alicia had said very little. Despite her few words, Jenna had sensed the news producer's disapproval of her. She'd thought that maybe Alicia was feeling territorial, so she'd made a point of saying that she and Nicci weren't going to report, only analyze. This had not raised the friendliness quotient one point.

Nicci opened her MacBook. Jenna, after several sips of coffee, was awake enough to notice that her producer had changed into khaki shorts and top.

"You look like a total safari girl," Jenna said.

"I know," Nicci enthused. "I bought this outfit at F. M. Allen two years ago, and I was worried that I'd never get a chance to wear it. I hope I haven't overdone it. I don't want to look silly."

"No, not at all. You look great." Nicci was one of those rare wonders who thrived on five hours of sleep and always looked spritely and freshly scrubbed. But much as the pixyish producer could pass for an ingénue, she preferred her lovers to have long hair, long legs, ruby-red lips, and towering heels. Jenna had often thought the Barbie Master would have been perfect for her—if only he weren't a guy.

"Before we land, you should use a mirror," Nicci said kindly. Part of her role was making sure the "talent"—Jenna—looked her best.

Jenna tugged at her hair, hardly believing that she'd failed to look closely at herself in the bathroom. *I must have really been groggy back there.*

"You want the news about GreenSpirit's murder first, or the Maldives?" Nicci asked. "We've got enough time for both."

"Let's do New York first." A killer might be stalking Dafoe's environs, and that worried her. Jenna realized, uneasily, that her personal and professional lives had become focused not on clouds, rain, or sunshine, but on violence, whose hard hand felt increasingly close. She felt like she'd become the sharp point of an acute triangle—the connection between terrorism in the Maldives and a monstrous murder two hours from home. She wanted to be armed with information on all counts, even if it made her as wary as a Sunday hiker in a forest teeming with dark shadows and the tracks of large carnivores.

"This is a press conference I downloaded a couple of hours ago," Nicci said. She paused the video on a shot of a young man tugging at his shirt collar, evidently uncomfortable in his jacket and tie. "That's the 'person of interest,' a high school senior and football player named Jason Robb. The one next to him in the gray suit is his lawyer. The other two are his parents. They don't say anything the whole time."

Nicci tapped the keyboard, resuming the video. The lawyer was clearing his throat.

"We're here today because Jason is making himself available for questioning in the investigation of GreenSpirit's murder. As soon as we leave here, he'll be talking to police and FBI investigators, but first he wanted to talk to his friends and neighbors through all of you."

"There have been rumors flying around about Jason," the lawyer continued. "Some of them, in our view, have resulted from leaks from law enforcement officials. Today, we'll be asking those agencies to make these leaks stop. A responsible young man like Jason should not be tried and convicted in the court of public opinion. I think that after you hear what he has to say, you'll agree that he's not linked to this heinous crime in any way."

"There's more boilerplate," Nicci said as she moved the time bar button on the bottom of the screen, "but this is where it gets good. The kid's just been asked if he threatened GreenSpirit."

"I didn't threaten her. I did threaten a girl who dumped my brother before he got killed in Baghdad," Robb said. "But I only said that I'd get even with her because she accused me, in front of a whole bunch of people, of taking money from guys to lead them to their naked parties, and that wasn't true."

"What Jason just said can be confirmed with the CBS News crew that was present during the initiation," the attorney interjected. "Of course, no harm has come to the young woman in question, and Jason regrets his outburst."

"Yeah, I'm sorry I said it, but imagine if someone accused you of being a pervert in front of a famous news guy."

"Did CBS pay you to lead them to the ceremony?" asked a woman.

"Yeah, a fat hundred bucks. I wished I'd never run into them."

"It was a consultant's fee," the attorney jumped back in. "That's what CBS News called it when I contacted them to confirm the details."

"So you're a consultant to CBS News," the woman followed up archly.

"I guess so," Robb replied.

"Cronkite must be turning over in his grave," Nicci said.

"The larger issue here is that my client was not involved in any threat against GreenSpirit, and absolutely denies any role in her killing."

"Where have you been, then?" another reporter called out.

"He was scared," the attorney said. "He went to a cabin with his girl-friend. He got in touch with his parents yesterday, and they contacted me." Jason's middle-aged parents nodded. They sat right next to him, dressed in what could have been their Sunday best. "Together, we made immediate arrangements to meet with the FBI and New York State

Police. There's no mystery. That's the story. It's no more complicated than that."

"So the girlfriend's the alibi?" a man bellowed.

"That's correct," the attorney said. "I've questioned her, and I believe—"

"Will Jason take a polygraph?" two reporters interrupted to ask the same question.

"Sure." The young man shrugged, like *Why the heck not?*

"We've told law enforcement that Jason will make himself available for a polygraph exam."

Nicci hit the pause icon. "That's pretty much it."

"I believe that kid," Jenna said. "He's too rough around the edges; his attorney would never have let him take questions if there was any doubt about his innocence."

"My thoughts exactly," Nicci said. "Sounds like you're still catching lots of Court TV," she joked. Jenna's favorite channel after the Weather Channel.

"Not as much as I used to," Jenna responded with a smile.

"Yup, sharing your bed cuts down on all that quality TV time," Nicci said playfully.

"I didn't say anything about anyone in my bed."

"Didn't have to. Last few days you've been lit up like a Christmas tree."

Jenna laughed. "Is it that obvious?"

"As a naked man in Times Square."

Jenna furrowed her brow, returning to the subject at hand. "So who murdered GreenSpirit?"

"No one knows, or if they do, they're not saying," Nicci said. "There have been all kinds of leaks saying the crime scene isn't producing anything useful, which is bizarre because there was blood all over the place. All the attention is back on Lilton or someone associated with him."

"I don't find that credible," Jenna said. "Lilton wouldn't get involved with a freakin' murder. The speculation alone will probably sink his campaign."

Chris Randall came back from the front of the plane and spoke to the TV crew. The rotund cameraman and blue-jeaned soundwoman sprang up and grabbed their gear, which was near at hand. They moved over to the jet's windows as Chris sat next to Jenna.

"I asked if we could get a look at the supertanker before we begin our—"

"If you look out the left side of the plane," the pilot's voice cut off Chris, "you'll see the hijacked tanker, about three miles away."

The glare of light on water was almost blinding, but Jenna could make out the dark shape of the *Dick Cheney*. Beside her, the camera's lens was almost touching the window.

"We can't go any closer because they've got a shoulder-mounted rocket launcher," Chris said.

"Ouch." Jenna smiled.

"Ouch is right," Nicci agreed. "No flybys today."

Chris Randall had a classic, deeply resonant broadcaster's voice and a head full of closely cropped black curls. Jenna thought he bore a resemblance to Barack Obama—a bulked-up younger version with darker skin. Chris looked like kind of a tough guy who'd been tamed, which, given his background as an Army Ranger in Afghanistan and Iraq, probably wasn't far off the mark.

"So I guess we're safe," Chris said, "even if we can't see squat."

"What's that?" Jenna blurted out, pointing to a thin, gray-blue streak bursting out of the glare and rocketing toward the Gulfstream.

"Holy shit," Chris yelled. "That's a—"

Chris was cut off once again as the Gulfstream went into a screaming dive. The correspondent, Jenna, and Nicci tumbled wildly off the couch, rolling toward the closed door of the cockpit. Behind them, the camera crew careered into the wall as gear scattered everywhere. Jenna smashed into Chris's back as the aircraft gained speed and banked hard to the right. The g-forces grew so intense as they plummeted toward the vast Indian Ocean that Jenna couldn't have pried herself off Chris if she'd tried.

Heart-pounding seconds later the plane shuddered like it was about to rip apart, then leveled. The pilot's voice filled the cabin again, so calmly that it was as if nothing of note had taken place: "We were just targeted by a rocket fired from the tanker. We were out of range, but I took evasive action anyway.

"Anders, would you please check on the passengers and come up front," the pilot asked.

Jenna saw the blond flight attendant uncurling from the gold-colored carpet next to her seat, where the sudden maneuver had left him scrunched up like a crumpled ball of paper. The young man got to his feet and asked in a shaky voice if everyone was okay.

"Fine," said Alicia airily, already back to typing. She'd been belted into her seat.

Jenna stood on rubbery legs. "I'm okay," she said. The cameraman grunted that he was all right while he checked his camera. The soundwoman forced a smile. Nicci and Chris appeared to have weathered the tumble, too. The producer dusted herself off, swearing when she saw a big coffee splotch on her khaki shorts.

"Sorry," Jenna said. Her empty cup lay on the gold carpet, which was now marred by a brown splatter pattern.

The weather producer shook her head. "What am I complaining about? Christ, I'm alive."

Chris smiled. "I haven't been fired on like that since Fallujah."

"I've never been fired on," Jenna replied.

Alicia spoke without looking up from her laptop. "Try West Bank, Lebanon, Iraq, Iran, Chechnya, Gaza . . ."—*peck-peck-peck*—". . . Afghanistan, Yemen, El Salvador, and Nicaragua."

Queen of the bang-bang, thought Jenna.

"That rocket couldn't have hit us," the producer continued. "It fell into the ocean at least two miles away. The pilot overreacted."

Maybe, Jenna thought, but she knew that if she'd been in his seat, she would have taken "evasive action," too.

Nicci nudged her. "That tanker looks like it's just sitting there. I don't think it's moving at all."

"Isn't that dangerous?" Jenna asked. "Aren't they more stable when they're in motion?"

"Only in bad weather," Alicia chimed in, then unsnapped her safety belt and stretched out like a diva on the couch across from Jenna and Nicci. Long dark slacks, long dark hair, and dark wraparound glasses. "The forecast is for calm seas," she added.

Jenna bristled inwardly; forecasting was *her* specialty. "Any more demands from the hijackers?"

"It's been pretty quiet," Nicci answered. "Apparently, there are just two of them on board, plus the captain and Birk. All twenty-four crewmembers were killed and tossed overboard."

"One of the jihadists has an AK-47 and the RPG that 'almost killed us,'" Alicia said, as if she were quoting Jenna. *But I never said that,* the meteorologist wanted to protest. "The other one's decked out in a suicide vest," Alicia added. "They came to play." The news producer raised an eyebrow. Jenna had always wished that she could do that. Hers rose together or not at all.

"And they've got Birk," Nicci said.

"I hope he dies," Alicia said blandly, which made her sound icier than ever. Even Jenna, no fan of Rick Birk, thought wishing him dead was over the top: You don't speak ill of the deceased or the soon-to-be-slaughtered. She must have frowned.

"What? That bothers you?" Alicia challenged her. "That asshole once groped me and then threw up on me."

"That would put a damper on things," Chris laughed. His producer, notably, did not.

"Christmas 2003," Alicia said. "Party at Williamson's penthouse." Williamson was the president of the news division. "Then, when I went to try to clean up, the bastard barged in on me, wanting to know if I'd like to 'make it all better' by taking a bath—with him." Alicia stared at Nicci. "He's lucky I didn't cut off his dick and mount it on my wall."

"*Big* ouch," Chris said.

"I doubt it." Alicia let slip her first smile. It looked like daylight seeping through a cracked ceiling.

Jenna noticed that Nicci was staring at the other woman and suddenly realized that her producer's adoring gaze was the cause of Alicia's pleasure. Jenna looked from one to the other. *Oh, no, not her,* was all she could think.

But it made sense: Alicia had long legs, long hair, and brilliantly red lips. Nicci's perfect lover. *I should have seen it coming.*

Jenna looked out the widow. The glare had lessened, and she spotted the tanker's white bridge as easily as she'd seen the gray-blue burst of the rocket. Somewhere, hidden in the length of that enormous vessel, Rick Birk awaited rescue. Or death. And wherever he was, five hundred thousand tons of liquid iron oxide was stored below him.

Get over here, you worthless raghead.

Birk tried to draw Suicide Sam's attention to his laminates by pointing his chin down at his chest. The beaded chain on which they hung was painfully reminiscent of a bright blue noose that he'd seen around the neck of a prominent dissident at a public hanging in Tehran. *Bastards let the poor son of a bitch swing for half an hour.*

The correspondent's liver-spotted hands were bound behind him in plastic cuffs to a three-inch metal pipe that ran along the lower section of a wall in the engine room. He'd been marched there by Raggedy Ass himself. Birk had spent two horrendous hours trying to nap in a seated position, only to be awakened at excruciating intervals by a herniated disc in his lower back. He'd been putting off surgery for years, but at the moment he would have thrown himself on a gurney for the first flight to the body butchers, if only he could.

What he needed far more than surgeons—and what he appeared even less likely to get—was a drink. His mood was as foul and festering as a Superfund site.

Suicide Sam shook his head as if he, a fucking killer, was disgusted by one Rick Birk, one of television's greatest chroniclers of human events of the past half century.

"TV, pee," Birk muttered, thrusting his chin toward his chest for the thousandth time, finding the juxtaposition of words strangely easy on his ears. He hoped the prestige of television would buy him a bathroom break. Maybe even that drink, he found himself thinking once more, yet another delusionary result of his ever-sobering state. But he couldn't just sit here in agony. "T . . . V. *Pee,*" he stressed.

He presumed that Raggedy Ass knew that he worked in television, but Suicide Sam hadn't paid any attention to Birk's laminates, so the correspondent was doing all he could to draw the man's attention to them. He wished he could actually point to the goddamn things—*I look like a fucking bobblehead doll*—but this was not possible. *And what's with the plastic cuffs anyway?* he wondered. Not what he would have expected from jihadists. Bailing wire, maybe. Rope, for sure. But plastic cuffs? Weird. Too Western for these troglodytes, although for all he knew, everything, including plastic handcuffs, had gone global. *Al Qaeda probably buys them by the gross on the Net. Address? Third cave past the bombed Humvee.* Christ, he hated terrorists. Not worth the lice in their straggly-ass beards.

The metal door of the engine room clanged open. Raggedy Ass glanced at him, then eyed Suicide Sam. With a single move of Raggedy Ass's head, Suicide Sam left. Birk figured he was off to keep watch on the captain, who was probably hogtied in the wheelhouse.

Higgens would be right at home here.

Keeping to his soft-spoken strategy, still equal parts desperation and near delirium, Birk looked pleadingly at the top banana jihadist: "Please Mr. Scum-fuck Terrorist, could you rub your two brain cells together just long enough to realize that I'm your greatest asset?"

Hopeless. Raggedy Ass stared at him like he was from Mars. Birk nodded with what he thought was an idiotic grin, trying his damnedest to conform to the jihadist stereotype of a typical American: "CNN. BBC. Pee."

He spoke slowly and loudly, consciously reinforcing the caricature of an American trying to make a foreigner understand him, but this asswipe seemed incapable of even the most basic civilized discourse.

Raggedy Ass walked over to him, shaking his head just like Suicide Sam had.

"Oh, of course, the poor terrorist is all befuddled," Birk baby talked to him.

Raggedy Ass must have picked up on Birk's poorly hidden hostility, because he abruptly kicked apart Birk's legs. The old man became immediately uneasy, having his privates so wantonly vulnerable. Raggedy Ass placed the muzzle of his fifth appendage—the AK-47—right on Birk's balls.

The reporter's spineless smile morphed immediately into a wince, and he rued having alluded to his privates. Then Raggedy Ass exerted serious downward pressure, and Birk was overwhelmed by sickening pain. Turned into a writhing mass of wrinkled, tormented flesh. Even so, Birk managed to keep his gaze pinned to the man's trigger finger.

Oh, God.

"Now you listen to me," Raggedy Ass said in shockingly clear English. Not just English, but English with a thick Southern drawl. *What the fuck?* "You think you're real funny, Rick Birk, but you want to know something?"

That I'm in the deepest shit ever? But outwardly, all Birk could manage—and only barely—was a nod.

"I'd have killed you back in Malé along with the other infidels, if I didn't think you could help us, so stop your blasphemous swearing or I'll send you straight to hell."

"You . . . speak . . . English?" Birk gasped out.

"You're a regular Einstein."

"Who are you?"

"I'm someone who grew up in the Great Satan. I found my true faith nine years ago on a pilgrimage to Mecca." Raggedy Ass's eyes rose briefly to the stained ceiling. "English is my first language. Heard enough? I know I've heard all I want to from you. I've heard every foul word and insult you've spoken." He grabbed a fistful of Birk's white hair, forcing the codger to look up at him at a painful angle. "You're everything I hate. You're everything Allah hates. But I'm going to spare you the horrors of eternal hell for a few more days, as long as you do exactly what I tell you to do."

He pulled out a menacing combat knife, and Birk thought, despite the man's words, that the jihadist was about to slice off his head. Instead, Raggedy Ass cut off the plastic cuffs and dragged the newsman to his feet. Birk's legs almost buckled from a seizure of pain in his lower back, but he ground his teeth and confined evidence of his agony to a single moan.

The jihadist shoved him toward the door. "Out. Walk in front of me. Try to run and I'll shoot you in the spine."

"Where are we going?" Birk couldn't forget what had happened to every member of the crew after Raggedy Ass dragged them to the railing.

"You're going to go 'live.' That's what you want, right?"

Birk staggered from the engine room like he was drunk. Never had he misjudged a man so severely. *Mr. Scum-fuck Terrorist? Is that what you called him? Ai-yi-yi.*

He'd found his own Omar Hammami, whose Syrian immigrant father had married an Alabama belle. They'd given little Omar a small-town upbringing in the heart of Dixie—Bible camp, high school class president, blond girlfriend, drunken Friday night fights—but despite all the advantages that American life could offer, Omar had turned to Islam. And not just any old Islam-in-a-mini-mall-mosque, but Islam in Somalia, where sweet, baby-faced Omar became a leader and spokesman of the Al Shabaab, one of the most brutal Islamist insurgencies.

What's with the South? Birk asked himself in his newborn panic. Could growing up around crackers actually be worse than he'd imagined?

He looked back over his shoulder. "I can help you with your message."

The hometown boy from hell shoved the barrel of the Kalashnikov into Birk's wattled neck. "Shut up. When I tell you to talk, talk. Otherwise, don't say a thing."

Birk had heard those very words before—from an executive producer of *Nightly News,* back when he was still being invited to the set for live tête-à-têtes with the anchor. He'd love to obey, but his rampant and torturous thirst could not be denied.

"Could you spare me a drink, you suppose, from the captain's private reserve? I don't expect he's making much use of it at the moment, and I, for one, work much better when I can wet my whistle."

Raggedy Ass whacked Birk upside the head with his rifle barrel. The correspondent yowled.

"I should kill you now and, *inshallah,* I will when you're no longer needed."

I guess that means no.

CHAPTER 17

Parvez watched the two Al Qaeda operatives drive up to the small stucco house where he had been waiting for twenty minutes. Palm trees towered over the single-story home just three miles from downtown Malé. Parvez peeked out from behind a curtain, smelling meat grilling nearby, perhaps in the small, enclosed courtyard next door. He recalled the veiled words about storms that the short Mohammed had spoken at the café. Storms only Allah could see, the taller one had added. But there would be real storms, too. That was the forecast. Electrical storms to claw the sky. They were a divine sign, coming on this most propitious day. He saw great clouds already forming off the coast.

The two Mohammeds had given him the address of the house and told him to go directly inside, but said nothing about who owned the squat one-bedroom residence. Parvez knew better than to ask about that, or about how they had obtained permission to use it. He still didn't know the men's real names and he doubted he ever would. But whoever they were, they would report to their leaders in Pakistan that the humble cleric in the Maldives had performed bravely.

The jihadists were driving a windowless van. Parvez assumed they had rented it using forged documents and a stolen driver's license. They were smart to have rented a van that looked like a delivery truck.

They backed the van into the driveway, got out, and hurried through the front door. Parvez stepped forward to bless them. But they seemed impatient with his prayers, and the cleric silently forgave them, knowing they were intent on their mission.

Short Mohammed carefully laid aside a pack, the kind university students used the world over, while tall Mohammed headed into the small kitchen and threw open a cabinet. He reached deep inside it, much farther than the space appeared to allow. Parvez heard a metallic sound, like a latch, and watched the man carefully retrieve a cardboard box. When he brought it over, Parvez saw a fuse the color and shape of airline cable. He'd expected to see C-4.

"What are you using for the bomb?" Parvez asked.

"Ammonium nitrate. Nitromethane," the shorter Mohammed said quickly.

Parvez nodded. Now he knew why they needed the van. The ANNM bomb would contain a thousand pounds or more of its murderous ingredients. Parvez smiled when he thought of how the blown-up van would become the principal item of interest in the next few days as investigators combed through the rubble of the Golden Crescent Hotel. An American veteran had used just this kind of bomb in a rental truck to attack his own people in the heart of America. Allah worked in ways as wondrous as they were mysterious.

If they were using a fuse, there would be no martyr for this attack. Parvez told the two Al Qaeda operatives that he regretted that a man would miss this opportunity to become a martyr. He said that he would have blessed the man and recorded his statement, as he had Adnan's, for all the world to see. In his mind, Parvez knew that he would have provided great comfort to the martyr; he had even rehearsed his descriptions of the paradise that awaited the brave jihadist.

Short Mohammed turned around holding a vest. "There will be

a martyr wearing this vest. After the van blows up, there will be rescuers . . ."

Of course, the one-two punch. Parvez almost said so aloud, but decided to let them think they were enlightening him. Sometimes a real leader had to treat men this way to get the most out of them. Look how much he, a simple cleric, had accomplished with his insight, understanding, and courage.

Consumed in his thoughts, Parvez had missed part of short Mohammed's speech.

"I'm sorry, would you please repeat that?"

"When hundreds gather to help," the man said, "you, Parvez, the great cleric of the Maldives . . ."

Parvez beamed with pride.

". . . the Islamist who came up with this great plan, *you* will become the martyr of the Maldives."

What! Parvez wanted to shout. "Tha-tha-that's Adnan's name," was all he managed.

"So there will be *two* great martyrs of the Maldives in paradise. You, too, can become the jihadist of your dreams."

Both Mohammeds smiled at Parvez and nodded enthusiastically.

Parvez smiled, too, but his face felt frozen. *This cannot be,* he said to himself. *Not for a man so wise as me. A man with insight, understanding, and . . . courage.*

Jenna felt flash-fried as soon as she stepped from the Gulfstream, brow and bare arms beading instantly with perspiration from the heat and humidity of the Maldives. Even after drought-stricken New York, the tropical sun felt nasty and brutish on her skin. She couldn't recall ever feeling so hot in the archipelago. The tarmac radiated heat like a backyard grill. But the text she'd just received from Dafoe put a smile on her face: "Hi, Jenna, IMU so MCH. So do d cows! Dafoe." She quickly texted him back: "I ms d cows. O, + U2! Ha-ha."

She pocketed her phone and, exerting as little effort as possible, walked slowly to the private plane terminal. She had no desire to be drenched when she saw Rafan for the first time in ten years. As she approached the entrance, she noticed cumulus clouds forming in the distance. She'd have to keep an eye on them.

Oh, just relax, she told herself. *You've got bigger fish to fry right now.* She took a deep breath, unsure whether Rafan would even be waiting for her. He hadn't responded to e-mails or texts noting her arrival time, and she hadn't reached him by phone. She found his silence puzzling because he'd reinitiated contact with her, but his sister had perished in a ruthless terrorist attack, and Jenna could not fathom how the loss of someone so young and vital might have changed him.

The terminal doors opened automatically, and a rush of refrigerated air welcomed her. As the coolness settled over her moist skin she spotted Rafan. Her heart skipped, and she saw his dark eyes gleaming at the sight of her. He was as slyly attractive as ever, a man whose distinct features matched his mannerisms so seamlessly that she'd been drawn to him as soon as she'd spotted him at a party in Malé, the city to which she had now returned. In the months that had followed their first meeting ten years ago, she'd become even more entranced by his alluring appearance, whether in bed, on a starlit beach, or in the cozy breakfast nook of the condo he owned by the sea.

His beard remained black and closely cropped, and his face and waist were as lean as ever. The decade, despite the loss of his parents and sister, hadn't bowed his back with grief or rounded his square shoulders. But his eyes looked laden, as if they bore all his pain, and when he opened his arms to receive her, she knew that it was he who needed holding.

The rest of her news team might have recognized this, too, because they edged past without a word.

"I'm so sorry," Jenna whispered. "Basheera was an amazing woman." More than once, she'd wondered if Rafan's sister would someday become her sister-in-law. He'd been her first real love, but she was eight years younger than he and had wanted to experience more of life before settling down. His carefully penned letters had trailed her all the way to New York, conveying his passions and desires. Even now, with the memory of their love as alive as the man in her arms, she didn't regret her decision to leave him, but she did rue the pain that Rafan had suffered, and she felt so much more deeply for the agony of his most recent and far greater loss.

"Thank you," he said softly, still holding her and trembling noticeably. "She never forgot you."

He stepped back and took her hands. He spoke softly. "I lost more than Basheera. I lost the woman I loved. Her name was Senada, and she was murdered two days ago."

Without letting go of Jenna's hands, he led her to a couch in the waiting area, moving them away from a long line of Saudis streaming into the terminal from one of the royal family's wide-bodied jets.

"Murdered?" Jenna said with the same disbelief that she'd felt after Dafoe had told her about GreenSpirit's death.

"The police found her shot to death next to her husband. They think Senada was killed by the men who took over the tanker."

Jenna found herself reeling from the news that Rafan had been involved with a married woman. This was the Maldives, not Manhattan. An involvement with a married woman could have gotten *him* killed. "How could what happened to that tanker have anything to do with your friend?"

"Her husband was a fisherman. The police are saying that he helped the jihadists by taking them to Malé on his boat. Then something went wrong," he spoke those last words slowly, "or they killed him to keep him quiet. Her, too."

"Do you think she was involved somehow?"

"No, she never would have helped jihadists. She believed in her faith but she thought the Islamists were insane. She hated what they were doing to Islam in the eyes of the world. And she never would have done it for *him*. It was an arranged marriage. They didn't love each other. They barely spoke to each other." Rafan let go of Jenna's hands. "I might have caused her death. I don't know." He shook his head. "I may never know."

"How could you have been involved in any way?"

"I called her. I'd given her a phone so when he was at sea she could call me and not have to worry about him checking phone bills. Or I could call her. She turned it off whenever he was home, so if it went straight to voice mail I'd know that he was around." Rafan took a chok-ing breath. "Two days ago I called and a man answered. He started yelling 'Who is this?' I think it was her husband. I hung up immediately. A few hours later, I tried again, but there was no answer and Senada never got back in touch. I called the police anonymously."

Rafan's pooling eyes overflowed.

"Had you known her long?"

"Forever, but we didn't really become . . ." He hesitated.

Jenna said, "Romantic?"

Rafan nodded and continued, "Not till a few years ago. She was Basheera's closest friend from the time they started school." He turned away, voice failing. Jenna handed him a tissue.

"I don't know if I can help you much." Rafan's shoulders rose and fell in the weakest of shrugs. "I'm not strong. I wasn't sure I could come out here to see you."

"Rafan, don't worry about us." She reclaimed his hands. They felt cold, chilled by the brute reality of violent death.

"I can't even bury her," he said. "A woman I love, and I can't go near the funeral. 'Why is he here?' her brothers will say. They always had their suspicions. Her oldest brother even threatened to kill her." He sighed. "And now the police are questioning me."

"What?"

"They found Senada's phone and saw the last call that she got. Now her brothers will want my blood. They won't blame the jihadists—they'll blame me for loving her." He groaned. "I had to sneak Senada into the cemetery to say good-bye to my sister. Can you imagine that?" He looked so piercingly at Jenna that it felt like the walls that had sepa-rated them for so many years had burned to cinders in a flash of sor-row. "And now I'll have to sneak into the cemetery to say good-bye to her. I just want to die."

She pulled him close, and when he tried to retreat, she held him tighter.

"No," she said to him. "You can't die. There are people who love you, who will always love you. People like me."

His soft hands—the result of a life spent paging through books and writing densely analytical papers about coral reefs and encroaching tide lines—rose to her face. He held her cheeks in a cool clasp.

"I have to go back to my mosque and talk to God."

Jenna nodded. *It's what we do when we're grieving,* she thought. *We hold on to whatever we can.*

Rafan continued, "I can't let them hijack the faith of my father and mother and sister the way they took that ship, with guns and rockets and murder." His voice staggered under the pressing weight of that final word.

He sounded like the Christians she knew who stood up to the fanatics in their churches—the deniers of science in all its forms, who'd begun by denying evolution, moved on to denying climate change, and would, if left unchecked, denounce the very core of reason itself.

"I will pray," Rafan said, "and maybe I will hear God. But even if I am still deaf to Him, I need to talk to others. Maybe we can stop this madness, one mosque at a time."

Nicci stood a few feet away with a porter and their bags.

"Do you have a car with you, or can we drive you back home?" Jenna asked. "We'll be going close by, to the Golden Crescent."

"Thank you. I can walk home from your hotel."

All of them, including Alicia and Chris and the camera crew, piled into an airport van. They rode in silence.

Parvez felt numb, sitting in the Internet café watching more Westerners climb out of a big, white airport van. He was still reeling from the news that *he,* a humble cleric, a wise man, a great strategist for jihad, had been picked to be a . . . suicide bomber? He could scarcely use the world "martyr." Not for himself. That was for others—pathetic men like Adnan.

The two Mohammeds had told him to continue his surveillance of the hotel and to report back to the squat little house by nightfall. Then he would get all dressed up for the big party in paradise.

Parvez scolded himself for his impiety as he watched the grand entrance to the Golden Crescent. He'd been doing this since noon, and only minutes ago had learned from a jihadist at the reception desk that every room had been booked by reporters and crews. By tonight, the place would be packed. The young man sounded so excited.

Great, Parvez said to himself bitterly.

How could he tell the Mohammeds that using him as a martyr would be a waste, a *supreme* waste. Weren't thousands of poor Pakis lining up to be martyrs? Of course they were: young men, boys even, living miserable lives with so little to look forward to. One of them should have this chance—Parvez would step aside. He'd even be gracious about giving up his place in paradise.

Parvez moaned, almost silently. He knew the Mohammeds would not give him this choice. They wanted him to wear the vest.

He forced himself to return to his task. The Waziristanis' contacts in America had e-mailed Parvez photographs of many network news people. Now the Islamist scrolled through the images and found a picture of the new arrival: Chris Randall, "special terrorism correspondent." *Yes, yes, him. The African-American.*

But who is she? Parvez was staring at a beautiful woman whose hair looked almost white, though it could have been because of the sun's glare. He scrolled through the file once more, but couldn't find her. He could tell she was a star, though—no matter their skin color, their bright, shiny faces made them look like they'd landed from another planet. She'd *never have to be a suicide bomber,* he thought peevishly.

He knew Alicia Gant immediately, having seen her face next to Randall's photo. "The terrorism team," the file said. *They think they know something about terrorism?* Parvez shook his head. *They know nothing. They come like lemmings. Isn't that what they say in the West? Lemmings?* There, he was feeling more like himself again, but then a little voice inside his head said, *What about you, oh great cleric? Are you a lemming, too?* His only answer was another moan.

He saw bellmen unpacking bags from the big passenger van, and he almost shut off the computer because he could not stop thinking of the windowless van that would soon arrive. It would pull right up to the front door, like an ordinary vehicle, and then it would blow up, Parvez would wait until the rescue workers arrived, counting down the last minutes of his life before he'd have to walk into their midst, yell "God is great," or something like that—he was so disheartened he'd forgotten his exit line—and blow them all to hell.

Is God really great? he heard that little voice ask, and that's when he knew Satan was warring for his soul. The Great Satan had made him a target, so he would have to fight back with a bomb.

He buckled down and returned to his task. In a few hours the van would turn the hotel into a huge cloud of dust and smoke, like the towers in New York. On 9/11, jihad had struck the heart of the Western financial world. Soon, Parvez would see the heart of media darkness die. *And you, too, Parvez.*

The holy war for his prized soul was cut short when the man named Rafan stepped from the airport van and hugged the beautiful woman with light hair. *Consorting with Westerners. With media whores. Telling them about this country. As if he could know its true Islamic heart. Only a martyr like me*—Parvez tried on the title for size, and it still didn't fit—*could know such a truth.* Parvez refocused, immediately rebuking himself for his surprise at seeing Rafan betraying his people. Of course he would do all that and much, much worse—a man who would scrape dirt from a sinking island would turn on people of faith in every way possible.

Parvez opened another file and watched the second plane crash into the tower.

The work of martyrs is never done, he told himself. *And now you can join them in paradise.*

He saw the flames and this gave him strength—for about two seconds.

No, this can't be. Me? A martyr? Oh, but it was. He could not avoid the irreducible truth. *Do your job,* he admonished himself. *Wiser men have spoken.*

Wiser than me?

He hardly found *that* credible.

Adnan watched the captain of the *Dick Cheney* struggle to breathe. The Waziristani had duct taped his mouth shut, and the man sounded like a big dog Adnan had once seen snorting horribly on the street.

Adnan had watched helplessly as the animal's chest heaved violently, and then the dog had collapsed in the dust and died.

The captain's complexion looked drained of blood, and he drew his knees toward his chest, like a man huddling over his last breath, protecting it from the greed of his own flesh.

Adnan didn't dare touch him. The Waziristani had killed so many men and chopped off the African's hand. The jihadist was a scary man.

At the sound of footsteps, Adnan looked up and saw the old prisoner being pushed along by the Waziristani, moving past the windows of the wheelhouse. The prisoner leaned against the door, barely able to open it, then stumbled inside. He was filthy, clothes soiled by sweat and dirt from the deck and engine room.

Kneeling, the jihadist tugged gently on the tape across the captain's mouth, tormenting the man with the tantalizing prospect of breath. The captain's eyes grew huge, and his nostrils hollowed from his pained efforts to breathe, cutting off any air. Adnan couldn't help himself; he started to reach down to rip off the tape. The Waziristani looked up at him and shook his head, and Adnan froze.

The captain also stared at Adnan, and his eyes pleaded for help. For life.

What am I afraid of? Adnan asked himself. *I'm ready to die.*

He ripped the tape from the captain's mouth, tearing hair from his beard and mustache. The captain cried out his thanks between suffering gasps. The old man with the white hair watched, shaking so badly that Adnan thought he might collapse.

The Waziristani stood and stared at Adnan, who put his hand on the bomb in his vest. He'd kill all of them before he'd let the jihadist murder him or chop off his hand.

Birk watched Suicide Sam finger the bomb, not knowing if these would be his final seconds.

At least it'll be fast. He hadn't had a drink all goddamn day, and if this shit kept up much longer, he'd rather be dead anyway. He hoped a camera somewhere would catch the big bang.

But the standoff, if that's what it was, ended when Raggedy Ass grabbed his arm and shoved him into what looked like the tanker's large communications room. Screens, computers, radar, sonar, every electronic device Birk had ever heard of lit up the walls and workstations. Diodes blinked all around him.

"I'm going to presume that you know how to operate Skype." Raggedy Ass's Southern drawl turned Skype into a four-syllable word, kind of like what crackers do to "shit": *she-ee-ee-t.*

Birk nodded. "It's pretty easy."

"I want you to set it up so we can talk directly to your network. You called them out on the dock, so you can call them now."

"I'll be glad to." *They're going to love this,* Birk thought.

"This," Raggedy Ass said, pointing to the tiny lens in the middle of the ship's impressive computer center, "is going to be the pool camera."

Pool camera? How the hell does some jihadist know about a goddamn pool camera? Birk wondered if his personal Omar Hammami had worked at a network. *Al Jazeera, maybe.* The fucker was definitely starting to sound like a few of the producers Birk had run through over the years.

"And if your government doesn't agree to start shutting down coal-fired power plants," Raggedy Ass pulled a list of the plants and a pair of blood-encrusted wire cutters from his pocket, "I'll cut off your fingers one by one till they do. Fair enough?"

"Fair enough." What the hell else could Birk say? But Christ, there was no way the United States was going to close down any power plants for Al Qaeda.

Jenna quickly hung up her clothes and put away her bags. Long stay or short, she hated living out of a suitcase.

Before showering, she tried reaching Senator Gayle Higgens through the hotel operator, having learned from Nicci that Higgens had taken one of the suites on the top floor of the Golden Crescent. Jenna's room sat considerably lower than the senator's, in both elevation and price.

Higgens shocked her by answering her own phone. No mistaking that Texas twang.

"It's Jenna Withers from the task force. How are you, Senator?"

"Happy as an old armadillo chowing down on an anthill, but I'm guessing that you're not exactly popping corks on my behalf," Higgens said with what sounded like genuine humor. "I've been getting the nastiest e-mails from some of our fellow task forcers."

"I'm sorry to hear that," Jenna said. The words immediately made Jenna feel like a fraud: in short, a reporter. Total chameleon.

"Sorry? Are you now?" the senator said. "You're one of the greenies, as I recall from my supersecret USEI fact sheet." She was laughing again. "Isn't that right?"

"I would never put it that way, Senator."

"'Course not, 'cause you're trying to ingratiate yourself with me. Well, least you're smart enough to try to lie. But you're terrible at it, gal. You need some practice. Try saying, 'I really admire what you're doing here in the Maldives, Senator.'"

"I'm afraid I can't do that."

"I knew it! You can't say it 'cause you can't lie. You sure you're a reporter?"

"I'm a meteorologist, and I'm just trying to get a handle on what we're looking at with the hijacked tanker."

"I remember now. Well, that explains it. You actually studied something in school other than how to become a professional liar. I might like you 'cause I like people I can see right through. Saves time. You just hold on."

Jenna heard clicks that sounded like they came from a keyboard. The senator still sounded amused when she spoke up again. "You're not one of the scolds, from what I can see. Or at least you got enough brain power to know how to keep your powder dry. You want to hear the truth, gal?" Higgens didn't wait for an answer. "You look totally inoffensive. You are white bread, gal. *White* bread. I've always admired that in a woman, seeing as I've never been able to manage it myself. So you want to know what we're dealing with, do you? Try a sack of snakes at a Sunday school picnic, stuffed with the biggest goddamn diamondbacks you've ever seen. And it's just busted wide open."

"Senator Higgens, I'm just downstairs and—"

"You're here? In the Maldives?"

"Yes. I'm in the same hotel you're in."

"Anyone else from your tribe arrived yet?"

"My producer and—"

"Let's have us a drink. It's five o'clock somewhere."

"Do you want to meet in the lounge downstairs?"

"Hell, no. You get your cute little carcass up here, Miss Stormy Weather. I've got a bar stocked with the finest libations in the world. And this way I don't have to worry about anyone listening in."

"Do you mind if I bring along my producer?"

"No, you bring yourself. No cameras. No producers. No recorders. No nothing on the record. If you're okay with that, I'm okay with you."

"Shall I come up now?"

"Like Jackson and Jimmy said, 'It's five o'clock somewhere.'"

Actually, Jenna glanced at her watch, *it's almost five in New York.* She wondered how Dafoe was doing. As she started to check e-mail, her cell went off: Nicci.

"I'm heading upstairs to see Senator Higgens," Jenna told her.

"You got in? Already? That's great. Alicia and Chris need a sound bite from you about the 'grave threat to the planet.' Their words."

"I'm guessing you mean Alicia's words."

"I'm pretty sure you're guessing right."

"Don't I get to suss it out with the senator first? See what she has to say about the Iron Oxide Express?"

"*Nightly News* goes on in eighty-eight minutes. It's yesterday there today, if you follow me."

"Is the crew ready to go?"

"They're on their way down here."

"How 'on the way' are they?"

"Ah, they're walking in with the gear now."

"We've got to do this fast. The senator sounded overdue for her first drink of the day."

"I doubt that," Nicci said. "She's known for her mimosas."

Jenna ducked into the bathroom and freshened her makeup in sixty seconds flat. She brushed out her hair and touched up her lips just as quickly. Grading herself on the travel curve, she just passed. On *The*

Morning Show curve? Failed miserably. Marv would shout her off the set.

Alicia had commandeered a conference room and set up two chairs facing each other. The camera crew was breathless from racing to get ready.

Chris and Alicia herded Jenna to a corner of the room. "What we need," Alicia said, "is a tough statement about the dangers inherent in this situation. Something like, 'I'm a scientist, and what I've seen has me very worried about the future of the planet. That tanker is full of dangerous chemicals that could change all life as we know it.'"

"You're kidding, right?"

The tall producer said, icily, "You're not debating some think-tank expert on *The Morning Show*. All we need are sound bites." Alicia eyed Nicci as if she expected Jenna's producer to intervene on her behalf. When Nicci didn't, Alicia added, "Just say what they sent you to say. Now let's get moving. Back in New York, they're throwing the piece together and you're wasting time. We'll beat the shit out of every other show, if you'll just do your goddamn job."

"Don't try to script me," Jenna said, temper rising. "I haven't even assessed the situation yet."

"Look," Chris said to Alicia, "let's find out what Jenna is comfortable saying."

Good cop, bad cop, Jenna thought.

"Okay," Alicia said, "what are you *comfortable* saying?"

Jenna ground her molars and took a deep breath, but before she could respond, Alicia's and Chris's phones went off almost simultaneously. They walked off in different directions with their cells to their ears.

"I don't believe it," Alicia bellowed moments later as she slapped her phone down on a long table. She ran to a large, wall-mounted flat screen, turned it on, and flipped rapidly through the channels, flying past Oprah and Ellen and music videos and more before stopping on an image of Rick Birk, who looked haggard and truly scared.

"We're not in the show because of this fuckface." Alicia looked like she might smash the screen.

Birk slowly lifted his hand, revealing a pair of wire cutters clamped around his right thumb, the grips held by a person who remained mostly off camera.

The very first word out of Birk's mouth was "Please," spoken with a tremor. Jenna was shocked—as far as she knew, the correspondent had never uttered the word before. Birk cleared his throat noisily and added, "I need you to listen carefully." He winced, and his eyes darted to his shanghaied thumb. A squiggly line of blood ran from beneath the wire cutters.

CHAPTER 18

A dust storm darkened the horizon, and Dafoe darted from cow to cow, trying to shift them from the pasture into the barn. They didn't want to go, and offered baleful moos. Cows loved routine, and a howling storm at midday was definitely not routine.

"Move," he bellowed, smacking Milquetoast on the hindquarters. He could imagine Bayou's frustration, listening to the herd's ballyhoo while convalescing on his doggie bed. But Dafoe wasn't about to risk his border collie's long-term recovery by putting him to work before he healed fully.

It took another ten minutes of maddening effort for Dafoe to finally drive all but one frisky calf into the barn. The recalcitrant critter kept dashing around and kicking up his hind legs. Between desperate lunges to grab the animal, Dafoe made a fast mental note to sell him. He could tell that this little guy would turn into an ornery bull. The taste of grit suddenly clouded his tongue and he looked up to see the sky darkening directly above him.

The calf suddenly sprinted to the barn. Dafoe followed close behind, finding most of the herd milling outside their stalls and looking dazed. *Hell,* he snorted to himself, *cows looked dazed all the time. They're nature's stoners.*

He got them into their stalls—and just in time. The barn shuddered as the dust storm descended on the farm. The cows raised another chorus.

Dafoe pulled out his cell and saw a text message from Jenna saying she missed the cows, and him, too! Ha-ha. It milked a smile from his frowning face. He called Forensia, who'd headed into the farmhouse an hour ago to pay bills.

"You okay in there?" he asked her.

"We're fine." The "we" meant that Sang-mi was still by her side. "We got all the windows shut before the storm hit. I'm just glad we've still got power."

Dafoe glanced at his milking machines and touched wood. A window near him shook visibly from a gust. The air outside looked as dark as the sky had minutes ago. It was only noon.

"You need to go home and close any hatches?" he asked. Forensia kept a garden and a compost pile, and hung all her laundry on an outdoor line—the country Pagan maiden in every regard.

"We're fine. Where are you?"

"In the barn. I'll be heading over to you in just a moment."

Dafoe snapped his cell shut and looked around, thinking that the gnarly dust storm would have excited Jenna. If a weather front of this magnitude were approaching the city, they'd be breaking into regular programming so she could provide constant updates.

As he eased out of the barn, the cows were still making a hell of a racket, like they could moo away bad weather. Squinting, he bolted to the house. Forensia threw open the door as he reached for the handle. Behind her, Dafoe could see Sang-mi on the couch, seemingly mesmerized by the Weather Channel on TV. For a young woman who'd grown up watching nothing but the numbingly boring speeches of North Korean political leaders, the Weather Channel proved riveting. It even grabbed Dafoe's attention with a report about more than a dozen wildfires eating up Northern California and the Pacific North-west.

"What a day," he said, darting into the bathroom to rinse dust from his face and wash his hands.

"Hey, there's the dust storm," Forensia exclaimed from the living area. Dafoe rushed in as the screen switched to aerial views of a dark cloud blanketing much of central New York. As a farmer, Dafoe couldn't help but consider the wind a sticky-fingered thief for lifting away tons of dry topsoil, like a pickpocket working a county fair.

Dafoe strolled over to his computer. "Billing's all done," Forensia said.

"I'm just checking e-mail."

"Oh, that's right. You've got a big time girlfriend now," Forensia gently teased. "You got to keep up with her."

"I'll never be able to do that," Dafoe laughed. "But she just texted me."

"A good one?" Forensia teased.

"Yes," he said patiently. "A very nice one." His smile vanished quickly when he saw his e-mail security system's warning: UNAUTHORIZED ENTRY ATTEMPT. The bright-red stop sign noted that the attempt had come earlier this morning.

"Forensia, would you come over here?"

She tore her eyes from the TV and casually draped her hand on the back of his chair. "What's up?"

"Look at this."

"Wow. What's that all about?" She sounded genuinely puzzled.

"I'm working on that."

Dafoe had drawn on his considerable experience as a hacker to de-sign his security system. This warning had come up once before, but within hours GreenSpirit's murder had been discovered, and his atten-tion had shifted to other safety concerns. That first attempt had failed, and Dafoe had figured some kid in Singapore or Paris had chanced on the wrong guy and given up when they saw his formidable security.

Once burned, twice cautious, he told himself. He didn't believe that coincidence could explain two attempts to penetrate his e-mail in less than a week. He was a dairy farmer, not the Department of Defense.

"I would never go near your private stuff, Dafoe."

He believed her, and nodded to assure Forensia of this. But his system was telling him that the most recent attempt had taken place just an hour and a half ago, and had originated on his own computer.

When he looked at Sang-mi, she was looking right back at him.

Sheriff Walker marched into his office's only large conference room with an evidence bag more valuable than a dozen of the biggest campaign contributions that he'd received in the last five elections combined. He was a perennial winner, universally popular, and had to know that what he held in his hand could have a huge bearing on the GreenSpirit murder investigation. It might also shock many of his supporters, but his record suggested that ultimately he was an officer who'd rather be viewed as a no-nonsense lawman than a nice guy.

"Gentlemen," Walker announced in a courtly manner as he looked around the room where the law enforcement officers had set up their computers and other investigatory tools. The sheriff appeared to savor the instant attention of the senior homicide detective for the New York State Police, and a serial killer profiler from the FBI, who was examining possible links between GreenSpirit's murder and the savage slaying of a Vermont Pagan. Two agents from the FBI's New York City office also looked up at Walker, who said, "I have found something in the woods that I think will be of great interest." He held up the evidence bag.

"What's in there, Sheriff?" asked Agent Mullins, a mulish-looking man who could have been thirty-five or fifty. Either lucky with aging or cursed by it.

"It's a piece of fabric with what appears to be a bloodstain on it. Looks like it might have come from a bandana; it has part of a paisley pattern, near as I can tell."

Mullins peered through the clear plastic. "Where'd you find it?"

"About three miles from the cabin. I couldn't figure how someone could have gone through all that bramble and dead forest and not left a trace of himself, so I kept looking."

Sheriff Walker might have felt bound to perform such a review because he'd "compromised the crime scene." That was the scorching assessment of the New York State Police homicide team. The review also noted dryly that "The murder is the first one the sheriff has investigated."

"How did we miss it?" Agent Mullins sounded incredulous.

"Don't feel bad, Agent Mullins. I found it on a deer trail that runs down the east side of the mountain. It's tight in there." He held up the bag with the bloody swatch again. "It was stuck to a branch that had broken off a tree. It's not a trail you'd ever take if you could avoid it, but—"

"If you were a panicky killer you might," Mullins finished for him.

"I believe you're right, and I believe this has got mud and blood dried on it," Walker said.

Mullins took the bag from him and stared at the stains. "Hard to tell when it's all dried up like that, but we'll get it to our lab."

The FBI profiler, an older woman named Barb Lassiter, looked up. "The Robb kid had a paisley bandana on in that CBS report. I remember that. I wonder if he's missing a piece of it."

"My thoughts exactly," the sheriff said.

"Let's run DNA on that right away." Lassiter flipped aside her straw-colored hair and eyed the sheriff closely. He thought her smile had "Good work" written all over it.

Mullins was staring at the evidence bag. "Pretty brazen of that kid, or his lawyer, to hold a press conference to proclaim his innocence, if he'd left that kind of evidence behind. Like waving a red flag in our face."

"He passed the polygraph," Lassiter said, still looking at Sheriff Walker.

"He did, indeed," the sheriff agreed.

Mullins held up the bag to the light for another look. "Forensics rules for a reason. If you're a good enough bullshitter, especially if you believe your own lies, you can pass Miss Poly. But we all know that, don't we, Sheriff?"

Walker nodded.

*　　*　　*

Jason Robb ran another passing drill, feeling pretty damn good about his performance—at yesterday's press conference. They'd believed him. *Damn right, mon, 'cause you be righteous.*

Carl Boon hiked the ball through his chunky legs, and Jason back stepped before delivering the pigskin into the hands of Ryan Petress, who dropped the fucker. Petress apologized when he came running back to the line. Jason had noticed that his teammates had become unusually respectful since his return to the team, treating him like a goddamn deity.

The whole experience had been exciting. Even the CBS story a few days ago had turned into a big plus. As soon as Aly Wennerstrom saw him, on the tube in her family's cabin, she got totally horny. She'd pointed to the screen and shouted, "That's you. Oh my God, Jason, you're on TV." "No, Aly," he'd cooed, "I'm right here." And just that fast they'd set off on a hot and steamy bone-down safari. Better than slipping her a roofie. *Fine muff, mon, even with dem rubba boots on.*

She'd told Jason that when they came back to town, she'd had to swear to Jesus—"Really, Jason, I had to put my hand on my tiny gold cross and swear before all of God's angels that every word was true, and now I feel so guilty"—that they'd been "chaste" the whole time. Her mom had believed her; her father said that he still wanted Jason's hide. Hearing Aly's account made Jason realize that he wasn't the only great liar in their relationship.

The Q-back took another hike from Carl, stepped back, and this time drilled it right into Petress's hands—and he held the ball. Yes!

Coach Taverson ended the practice on that high note. Jason felt so good it didn't bother him at all when he spotted two dark-suited guys watching him head to the locker room.

Fuck dem monkeys, mon. You rule.

A powerful impulse seized Jason just before he entered the building. He spun around and flipped them off. Both cops. Both hands. Felt *so* good. Right up there with the bone-down safari in Aly Wennerstrom's sweaty little jungle.

* * *

Forensia peered quizzically at Sang-mi. "What's going on?" she asked. Her friend was staring at Dafoe.

Sang-mi covered her face with her hands and cried, though Forensia could tell that she was weeping only by the shaking of her shoulders. Sang-mi made no sound as she wept.

"Were you trying to get into my e-mail?" Dafoe spoke softly and without any obvious accusation; Sang-mi looked fragile enough to shatter.

From behind her hands, she nodded.

"Why would you do that?" Forensia asked, still puzzled.

"GreenSpirit," Sang-mi said softly. Dafoe asked her to repeat herself, which she did.

"Did GreenSpirit want something from my computer?" he asked. Sang-mi nodded. "What?"

Forensia thought it was strange that anyone would want anything from her boss's computer. Of what possible interest could a dairy farmer be to a typical hacker, much less GreenSpirit?

Sang-mi shook her head and didn't say a word.

"What you did was wrong, Sang-mi," Forensia said, as kindly as she could.

"I'm so sorry," the young woman said.

Forensia squeezed her hand. "Why did you do it? And what did you mean about GreenSpirit?" Forensia recalled the way the murdered witch had talked privately to Sang-mi after the initiation, and how she'd kept the Korean by her side during the circle dance. It pained Forensia to know that the reason these memories were so clear was that she'd felt jealous of the attention that the Pagan leader had bestowed on her friend. Now, Forensia was filled with only the deepest curiosity.

"She wanted to know about my country." Sang-mi looked up, as if that explained everything.

"Okay," Dafoe said carefully, "but what's that got to do with me or my e-mail?"

Sang-mi glanced at him and wiped her eyes. "I told GreenSpirit secrets. The reason we left the North. About the missiles."

"Can someone clue me in here?" Dafoe asked. "What missiles?"

"May I tell him?" Forensia asked.

Sang-mi nodded slowly, and Forensia explained about the rockets tipped with sulfates. "They're the reason that her father is still getting debriefed by the CIA."

"That's astonishing is what that is," Dafoe said. "You're saying that one of the poorest countries in the world is planning to cause a catastrophe that can freeze the whole planet?"

"Korea has many smart people," Sang-mi said indignantly, "and thousands of rockets."

"But that still doesn't explain why you tried to hack into my computer. Please tell me what you were looking for in my e-mail."

"Something from Jenna Withers," she whispered.

"Jenna? Why?"

Sang-mi pointed to an end table where Dafoe had left an inscribed copy of Jenna's book. "Jenna Withers knows about North Korea," Sang-mi said. "It's all in there—the famine and drought, and the Supreme Leader blaming the U.S."

"The missiles, too?" Dafoe sounded like he could scarcely believe that, but Forensia knew her boss hadn't read Jenna's book yet.

"No, not the missiles. That's *secret,*" Sang-mi repeated. "But once I told GreenSpirit about the plans to explode the sulfates, she wanted me to find out if the task force knew anything about the most dangerous geoengineering plan in the history of the world. So I tried to hack into your computer to see if Jenna Withers had said anything to you about the missiles. But now I see that the answer is probably no because you did not know anything about them." Sang-mi shook her head, as if she were disappointed in Dafoe. "Then, this morning, GreenSpirit spoke to me and said that I should try to get into your e-mail again, that it was very important to try one more time."

"She *talked* to you?" Dafoe sounded like he'd been abducted by aliens.

Sang-mi nodded. "Just like you are."

Dafoe glanced at Forensia, who nodded and said, "GreenSpirit is a powerful presence. I sense her all the time."

"But she's dead," Dafoe insisted.

"To you, maybe," Sang-mi said staunchly. "But she says a lot to me. This morning she said that if I found out that Jenna Withers didn't know about the missiles, then I had to tell her about them so that she could tell everyone when she's on TV. That's what GreenSpirit wanted to do—tell everyone. And she said that Jenna Withers will tell the world, once she knows."

"She will, will she?"

Sang-mi nodded patiently. So did Forensia.

"Why don't *you* tell everyone?" Dafoe asked Sang-mi.

"Because no one would believe me. Think about it. A girl from North Korea says there are missiles that will turn the Earth into an ice cube? The daughter of a defector? They would think I was a double agent, or that my father was. Or they would just put me in a hospital for crazy people. But Jenna Withers? People would listen to her. She's on the task force, and she's a star on one of the biggest shows on TV. People will believe her. GreenSpirit said so."

"But your father has told the CIA, right?" Dafoe asked.

"They're making him keep it secret. GreenSpirit said dangerous secrets should be exposed. All of them. And this was the most dangerous secret of all."

Jae-hwa holds a chilly handrail and steps down metal stairs into the heart of a vast missile complex. This is a hallowed place, for it was carved out of the mountain decades ago by men using only picks, shovels, buckets, and the undying courage of their nation.

We have lived in darkness like moles, but we will rule like golden kings, he tells himself.

Dim lightbulbs come alive one by one in row upon row, illuminating three-story-tall missiles mounted on heavy steel rails. Above them, Jae-hwa sees the hatches that will open for the rockets when the diesel generators come to life. Jet fuel for the missiles, diesel for the old railroad engines that move them into place. The past is always slave to a glorious future.

All around Jae-hwa rises a maze of monstrous power. It fills him with the deepest pride to know that the Supreme Leader has engineered the most deadly strategy in the history of humanity—and waited so patiently for the precise moment to strike. Now, with the world's attention on a tanker in the Maldives that could release a massive amount of iron oxide, intense interest has finally been focused on technology that can change the world's climate, just as the Supreme Leader knew it would someday. News people from all over the world are rushing to cover the story. Soon the time will come to tell the American puppet president about the missiles that will make the tanker look like a toy, and the West's nuclear bombs like cheap guns.

Jae-hwa watches soldiers take their stations, then reaches up to rest his hand on the missile next to him. He loves the feel of the smooth metal, the icy cold that numbs his fingers almost instantly, as if the missiles are already spreading their deep chill, even before they explode.

When the Supreme Leader tells the American puppet president what we will do, the West will have to surrender or suffer a terrible fate.

Jae-hwa flicks a toggle switch, and the old generator, a gift from the Soviet Union when that nation was a strong and stalwart ally, shakes the floor.

He orders all the lights off and the hatches opened. Someday, he will tell his son about this historic moment when the missiles started moving into place, drawn by chains that were rusty but still strong. Like the great nation itself.

The night sky appears in the open hatches, a vast blanket of char stippled with the lights of stars and satellites.

We can see you, but you cannot see us. We hold the secrets of a glorious future. You know only the dead secrets of the past.

Diesel fumes thicken the air and a thin smile creases his taut face. Victory, the Supreme Leader says, comes from the might of men with iron in their bones and fire in their blood.

Jae-hwa looks at the steel that points to the stars and his smile broadens. When the Supreme Leader says that the time has come to launch the rockets and draw a dense curtain over the Earth, those lights will vanish.

Time moves slowly when so much is at stake, but now Jae-hwa knows there are only hours to the completion of his mission. Tomorrow, there will be only minutes. And after a few last, furious seconds, Jae-hwa will throw the shiny silver switch that he's waited so many years to touch.

Men of iron. Men of fire.

CHAPTER 19

"I'm being held by Al Qaeda on the supertanker the *Dick Cheney* . . ."

The wire cutters around Birk's thumb had produced a delightfully bright-red line of blood that drooled from beneath the blades. But even as Birk sat there trying not to wince and craving a drink the way a vampire craves blood—he knew that this could well be the best performance of his illustrious career. As long as his fucking thumb remained attached to his hand, he'd be happy to sit there bleeding in front of the teensy computer camera.

"This hijacking has all the earmarks of a well-planned military operation. These men know what they are doing and are well armed. I ask officials of all concerned nations, especially the United States, to listen carefully to their demands . . ."

Birk let his eyes drift to the wire cutters, knowing that in all likelihood he was focusing the attention of millions of viewers on the crimson sideshow. He glanced at the digital time display on the computer screen and knew that if he could yammer for just about one more minute, he'd go live as the lead story on *Nightly News*. As it was, he figured that right this second he was being carried by just about every broadcasting outlet in the world. What a great feeling, everything considered. And when the bewitching hour hit for *Nightly News,* he'd jack up the reporting to a whole new level to try to snag as many minutes of network airtime as possible.

Birk had already noted that every time he made the slightest attempt to pull his thumb away from the wire cutters, Raggedy Ass squeezed a wee bit harder. And voilà! More blood. Birk planned on some serious bleeding as *Nightly News* came on because, as reporters knew the world over, "If it bleeds, it leads."

"The men holding me say that they will start releasing thousands of tons of iron oxide into the ocean if at least one of the ten biggest coal-fired power plants in the U.S. isn't shut down immediately. They're making this demand so that the U.S. can show good faith in the negotiations."

And they were making this demand in no small part because Rick Birk had advised the cracker jihadist to raise the ante incrementally. "Show that the U.S. won't even budge the tiniest bit," Birk said, knowing that if he could stretch out the negotiations, two important things would happen. It would give the newly arrived U.S. military, whose fighter jets and rocket-equipped helicopters were buzzing high above the tanker, more time to stop this terrorist act; and it would get Rick Birk more airtime. Not necessarily in that order.

With all the lethal hardware in the air and on the water, Raggedy Ass had been surprisingly receptive to Birk's counsel, leading the correspondent to conclude that most of the jihadist's planning had gone into the hijacking of the supertanker, and not its actual occupation. *Kind of like the U.S. in Iraq,* Birk thought. As for Suicide Sam, he had a nervous habit of fiddling mindlessly with the different colored wires protruding from his vest, especially when he was staring at the TV screen on the other side of the wheelhouse. Watching the Shopping Network of all goddamn things.

Ye gods, he's doing it again.

Birk forced his gaze back to the tiny computer camera, noting that right this second *Nightly News* was going on the air. He imagined the prissy-boy anchor, Brad Tettle, saying "Good evening" with the far more experienced visage of the great Rick Birk looming over his shoulder.

Timing it as closely as he could from almost fifty years of experience, Birk said "Good evening," and jerked his hand in the grasp of the wire cutters.

Good God almighty. Raggedy Ass squeezed much harder than Birk had expected. The pain was excruciating and the septuagenarian had to fight to keep his composure. Blood washed down the base of his hand and wrist. Very visible. Very good.

"I should start off by saying, Brad," Birk said, assuming an intimacy he didn't have with the young anchor, whom Birk was certain couldn't find his way out of a shoe box, "that I'm sure that you and our viewers"— *Yes, our viewers, not just yours, anchor rot*—"have noticed this minor inconvenience." Birk stared at his thumb. "I've been warned that each of my fingers, starting with this one, will be removed," a nice understated way to allude to the gore, "by these wire cutters if the U.S. doesn't shut down its coal-fired plants."

The best part of this performance—by far—was that Brad couldn't interrupt him with his notoriously insipid questions. For the first time in years, the camera belonged only to the veteran, the one and only Rick Birk.

"But I trust that this painful pressure"—*Wry, Birk, keep it wry,* he advised himself—"will not in any way cloud the clarity of my reporting, live from the heart of the hostage takeover of the *Dick Cheney*."

The whole time Birk talked, he affected an odd and emphatic blinking of his eyes. To any sentient observer, even to brain-fart Brad, it would appear that Birk, in the midst of torture and agony, was cool-headed enough to send coded messages.

That Birk wouldn't have known Morse code from the expiration date on a bottle of mai tai mix mattered not at all because it would appear to the millions watching that he was risking hellacious dismemberment on live TV to send critical messages to America's intelligence agencies. And Birk would have bet a bottle of Bombay gin that the CIA, NSC, and military intelligence were, in fact, scrambling with all their computerized code breaking right this minute to try to decipher his "message," which, as he knew better than anyone, could be reduced to "I'm fucked and so are you."

Since Jenna had arrived more than an hour ago, Higgens had been glaring at the outsize Birk on the huge screen in her luxurious suite and saying very little. Hardly a hint of the outrageous, blustery performance Jenna had witnessed at the White House.

The meteorologist looked at Birk's thumb again; it was hard not to stare. It looked like shark chum, but she had to admire his coolness under fire; she didn't think that she'd fare nearly as well if her fingers were about to be nipped on live TV.

The video clarity from the *Dick Cheney* was surprisingly good, nothing like the crappy Skype experiences that she'd had. But then again, she figured a supertanker had high-end everything. This one sure had high-end drama.

Senator Higgens stirred enough to point to Birk's bloody appendage. "Should have been his dick," she said before quaffing a dry martini like it was a Rodeo Daze Coors Light.

"Excuse me?" Jenna said. She'd left the highly agitated Alicia Gant and Special Terrorism Correspondent Chris Randall lamenting the loss of "their" airtime on the *Nightly News,* only to spend most of her visit watching the senator drink, and then drink some more. Higgens had made one other cryptic remark about Birk—"He's not that hard to tie up"—that Jenna had declined to dignify with a follow-up question, but "Should have been his dick" was just too bizarre to leave alone.

"Did you say—"

"I sure did," Higgens interrupted, "and I speak from experience. His *thing,*" she might have been shooing a fly from the motion of her hand, "would be no great loss to the world."

"I didn't realize you knew him."

The senator's eyes rotated unsteadily to her guest. "Unfortunately, yes, but I suppose anyone who's ever met him considers the experience unfortunate. He's a colleague of yours, right?"

"In a way."

"Count your blessings. He gave *me* a disease."

Jenna didn't know what to say. Wincing visibly, she offered, "I'm sorry to hear that."

"Penicillin did the trick. Long time ago," Higgens added by way of explanation. "I ran into the old turd in the lobby of the presidential palace the other day. Must have been a few hours before they grabbed him." The senator snorted. "Look at him, he's eating it up. He *loves* this."

Jenna thought that Higgens might be right. Birk did appear to be enjoying himself. He'd already cracked a smile or two, and he sounded a lot more sober than her host.

"Senator Higgens, I know seeing Birk like this is a bit distracting, but—"

"Distracting? It's pure pleasure. I just wish they'd get on with it and cut off the damn thing so *he'd* stop having such a good time."

"Okay, be that as it may, I wonder if you could tell me how concerned you are about the possible release of all the iron oxide?"

"It's no big deal. So we'll put on an extra sweater or two."

Or three or four. Maybe skin a polar bear while we're at it. But Jenna confined her comments to another question: "Has USEI considered the liability issues if the iron oxide gets released? The weather impacts alone are likely to—"

"You taking notes, girl?" the senator snapped. Her robust mood on the hotel phone had definitely soured.

"No, not at all."

"Just so you know, we're insured against 'acts of God,' and the last time I checked, these crazies," she stabbed a stubby, heavily ringed finger at the TV, "were doing Allah's bidding."

Birk now appeared to be reading from a prepared statement, recounting the horrors of five hundred thousand tons of iron oxide spilling into the sea. Then he listed the nations most likely to be inundated in the next one hundred years because of climate change. He finished by mentioning the disappearance of an island in the Bay of Bengal that had been claimed by both India and Bangladesh. New More Island, as it was called by the mostly Hindu Indians—or South Talpatti Island, as it was known to the mostly Muslim Bangladeshis—had vanished into the sea, peacefully resolving a potential hotspot through the miracle of immersion.

Jenna felt her phone vibrate in her pocket, and discreetly checked to find that Dafoe had texted her: "cll. import. N. Korea."

What's that about? It was hard to imagine any subject less related to her present concerns than that starving, Stalinist boot camp.

Seconds later Rafan texted, asking if they could meet.

She glanced at Higgens and saw that the senator had fallen asleep. *No, she passed out.* Jenna was never comfortable in the presence of drunks, and now one lay collapsed on the couch, open-mouthed and snoring, while the other stared unseeing from the screen. To be fair to Birk, he did appear coldly sober.

As Jenna crept toward the door, phone in hand to text Dafoe, one of Higgens's young aides came racing up. He took one look at his boss and smacked his forehead. "Not again!" He wheeled on Jenna. "You didn't take any pictures of her, did you?"

"No, of course not."

"What about that?" He pointed accusingly to her cell phone.

"No! What do I look like?"

"A reporter," he sniped.

"I didn't," she insisted, and walked out, recovering quickly enough to text Dafoe that she missed him, "cows 2," and would call later. Nothing felt as urgent right now as attending to the fragile emotional state of her old friend, Rafan.

Jenna met him at a tea shop several blocks from the hotel. He sat facing away from the door, hunched over a newspaper. If she hadn't been looking for Rafan, she wouldn't have recognized him. That was the idea, she discovered.

"I'm worried about Senada's brothers. They buried her today. They couldn't put her in the ground fast enough, like she was an embarrassment to them because she was murdered. Big funerals for men, but for her or for my sister?" Rafan shook his head. "I need to get away." Rafan's eyes shifted furtively, taking in the nearby empty tables.

"Can you do that?"

"No, not now. There's too much work. We're in the middle of a big pilot project." He told her about trying to save an important island by building it up with borrowed dirt.

"Robbing Peter to pay Paul."

"Yes," he smiled for the first time, "you always used to say that."

"About how we're stealing from future generations. That sure hasn't changed. Is your condo safe?" It wasn't like he had building security, or even a doorman, as she did in the city.

"I can't go back there." He shook his head. "I can't even go to the mosque to talk to people about Islamists because her brothers are looking for me."

"Then stay with me at the hotel. I'll have them bring up a portable bed." She took his hand. "Come on, you're staying with me." She hurried him toward the door, but he pulled back, as if he'd seen someone. Jenna turned to look, but spotted only a passing pedicab, and a massive gathering of thunderheads. The cumulonimbus clouds she'd spotted earlier had turned especially nasty looking. She would have loved to have seen the temperature differentials for those clouds and the surface right above the sea. A powerful thunderstorm on the ocean could turn the water into quite a weapon.

"This way," Rafan said, drawing her down side streets to an alley behind the Golden Crescent Hotel. The sky rumbled and they saw lightning over the sea. Jenna remembered darting through the rain with Dafoe; like the sky overhead on that day, the dusky sky above Malé looked ready to burst another seam. It was the stormy season.

"Why are we back here?" she asked Rafan. "We're still going to have to go in the front way." A swirling gust of wind hit them so hard she staggered, and looked up quickly to see the tops of palm trees shaking like raised, angry fists. "My key won't work back here," she added hurriedly. "Why don't you just come with me?"

"Because there are eyes everywhere. I can't walk in the front door with you, go to your room, and then spend the night. It would look terrible for you and for me. But there's a rear door by the pool. You go in the front, then come back through the hotel and open it, and I'll meet you by the big slide and go in the back way."

"You've done this before?" she said to him.

"With you. Don't you remember?"

She paused, then smiled and nodded, recalling their romantic rendezvous after she'd returned from doing research on an outer island.

Jenna headed for a well-lit walkway around the building, smelling salty air as she neared the corner of the hotel. As she turned toward the ocean, the wind pounded her so hard her hair flew straight back behind her, and she realized that she'd been standing in the lee of the hotel.

Hunching down, she bulled her way forward. The last time she'd slipped Rafan into the hotel, the twilight had been much calmer, and she'd been so eager to get him up to her room that she'd run through the lobby to the back door.

Tonight felt very different, and it wasn't just the storm. She had Dafoe in her life, and she felt much more settled, desirous of only him. She'd text him as soon as she got inside.

A wall of rain drenched her.

Startled, Jenna glanced up, horrified to see a waterspout ripping from the shore like a tornado. It tore a path in the sand, ripped smaller palms out by their roots, and headed straight at the hotel—at her!

Get inside! she screeched at herself.

She raced for the entrance, eyes still on the seaborne twister, and plowed into a young Maldivian man jumping from a white van, a look of unbridled panic on his face.

The impact knocked Jenna down. The young, dark-skinned man staggered toward the hotel, oblivious to the fact that his key fob was skittering across the wet concrete. She understood his fear.

A doorman raced over to help her, though Jenna was already on her feet. Together they fled to the lobby; Jenna kept running, anxious to open the rear door and get Rafan to safety. She glanced back to see the fifty-foot-tall spout smash into the hotel. The building shuddered but held; the waterspout had lost power when it moved onto land. The storm was still rocking, though, sending great flashes across the sky.

She sprinted down a hallway, realizing that the young van driver was racing ahead of her. He fled out the rear door. *Into the storm?*

Seconds later, she threw open the door. Rafan was close by and the guy from the van was barely forty feet away and looking back over his shoulder at her. The storm shook every leaf and palm frond in the area, raising a ruckus.

"Get inside!" she shouted at Rafan.

"What's with him?" he asked, jerking his head at the other man. "He almost knocked me over."

"I don't know," Jenna said, ushering Rafan past her and closing the door. "We collided in front of the hotel. The wind sent me flying into him as he was getting out of a van. Then a waterspout almost hit us."

Rafan's expression was curious and bewildered. "But what's he doing?" Rafan asked. "Leaving a van by the entrance and running out the back of the hotel—"

Without another word, Rafan raced toward the lobby, with Jenna close behind. She remembered the Times Square bomber, the naturalized U.S. citizen who'd left an SUV loaded with a bomb in the famous district. By the time she reached the entrance, Rafan was running around the front of the white van. He threw open the sliding side door. When Jenna saw the cargo space, her heart pounded so hard she thought it would beat her to death.

Parvez had moved from the café to a car the two Mohammeds had secured for him. The vest, loaded with C-4, weighed heavily on his shoulders, but his cleric's garb concealed it well. He'd dreaded the arrival of the van, and once it appeared, he waited for the huge explosion like a man facing his execution. No hope. No appeal. Not even from a higher power, for the higher power had sentenced him to death. He found brief promise in the waterspout and the electrical storm, but it had done nothing to stop or delay the bombing. *Nothing.* Parvez could have cried.

Now he watched the traitor named Rafan throw open the van door, revealing sacks of fertilizer and containers of fuel.

Yes, save me, Parvez pleaded involuntarily, realizing his only hope lay with the miserable man who stole dirt.

Do something, traitor. Grab the fuse, you infidel.

* * *

Despite the storm, Jenna detected the smell of flammables. She saw a big stack of what looked like feed sacks in the back of the van, and realized in an instant that the whole cargo area was packed with explosives.

"Run, Jenna!" Rafan shouted, though he wasn't running.

And as much as Jenna wanted to race away, she couldn't, because she saw a barely visible wisp of smoke whipped by the wind. She stepped closer to the van and spied an inch of fuse burning on the carpet, which was marked by a long, dark, trailing scorch mark. Without hesitation, she reached for the fiercely sparking flame. Rafan tried to grab it, too. They jostled each other. Precious seconds lost.

The fuse shrank to a nub, continuing to burn despite the lashing wind and rain. Jenna lunged, grabbed it, and despite the burning pain, she pulled the fuse away and dropped it on the wet pavement. It sizzled and died while she shook her burned index finger and thumb for several seconds. Then she realized that she was shaking and very, very cold.

Rafan's eyes grew huge. He stared at the bomb. Jenna knew he was looking for smoke. Her own stomach was gripped by the fear that a single spark had escaped and that the world would explode.

But there was no more smoke. They'd stopped the bomb.

There would be no one-two punch, Parvez realized. Infidels! *Infidels* had denied him paradise, for surely a man of his deep insight, understanding, and courage would be welcomed there with open arms by seventy-two virgins. But he could not go through with the next part of the plan now that the first punch had been foiled.

True, he could walk over and set off the C-4 in the vest—and that would trigger the bomb in the van. But that was not the plan; a plan that had been devised by wiser men than he. And who was he, a humble cleric from a poor island nation, to question *them*? That the plan had failed—surely that was Allah's will.

Oh, how Parvez rued the loss of his martyrdom as he rushed to slip off the vest. To have been the first martyr of the Maldives. *There, it's off.* Ah, but he would have to leave that honor to Adnan.

He almost dropped the vest on the console next to him. *Be careful. What do you want to do, kill yourself?*

Parvez rested the bomb gently on the passenger seat and drove away quietly, knowing he would live to fight another day. Allah had spared him in the end. Allah the wise. Allah the all-knowing. Why, Allah probably already had His eyes on a poor Paki, a hungry, unclothed boy who needed paradise so much more than Parvez. The cleric, with his deeper spiritual knowledge, could find a way to satisfy himself with so much less here on earth. Parvez's unselfishness flowed to his very fingertips. Yes, it would be only fair to give such a child the keys to paradise.

The wheelhouse stopped shaking as the power of the storm lessened. Birk sat like a supplicant on the floor by Raggedy Ass's smelly fucking feet. His lordship was perched with his AK-47 in the captain's chair, while a few feet away the man who should have been in that seat was bound head to toe and lying on the deck.

The chair looked like heaven to Birk, whose hands, shoulders, back, butt, and sliced-up thumb throbbed, but the chair's occupant, no doubt about it, was the devil incarnate. Raggedy Ass had ended Birk's broadcast after twenty measly minutes. *What's with that?* Birk had wanted the entire half hour. Rare as hen's teeth to have a whole show's worth of face time, but it wasn't every day—hell, it wasn't even every *decade*— that you had a talent of Birk's magnitude reporting from the heart of a Mother Earth smackdown.

"You got diarrhea of the mouth," Raggedy Ass told him in his thick Southern accent. "I could have said all that in five minutes flat."—*flea-a-a-at*—"But no, you got to go on and on. What? You think if you talk-talk-talk it's going to save those fingers of yours?"

The wire cutters were *still* attached to Birk's thumb, the blunt edges of the blades Flex-Cuffed together, like Birk's hands, behind his back. Christ, those fucking blades hurt.

"Next time you're in front of that thing," Raggedy Ass nodded amiably at the teensy camera, "I'm going to make you hold up your thumb— and it's not going to be attached to your hand."

"You're not going to do it live?" The indignity burst out of Birk before he gave himself time to think. *Don't encourage the bastard.* But even after a moment's reflection, he knew that video of his dismemberment would be fucking priceless. How could Raggedy Ass even think of doing it off camera? An insult to injury in every possible way. *What is wrong with these people?*

"That disappoint you?" Raggedy Ass asked.

"No, not at all," Birk lied. He regained his senses enough to think that maybe he could yak his way out of an on-air amputation. "Look, if you start cutting me apart like a roast chicken, I'm going to be useless to you. I'll be in so much pain, you might as well throw me to the sharks."

"*Inshallah,* I will."

"But don't you want me making your case for you? You start cutting through bone, man, I'm done."

Raggedy Ass stared at him so coldly that Birk could almost feel the sharp blades bearing down.

"I can't make idle threats," Raggedy Ass replied matter-of-factly. "I said we'd do it if they didn't start shutting down the plants immediately. That was hours ago, and all we're hearing is how they're not going to shut down a thing, so we have do to it." He shrugged.

Oh, God. The savage climbed down from the chair, reached around Birk, and grabbed the wire cutters. "Please, I beg of you, don't do this," Birk shouted. The pressure only increased. "Give me a drink for God's sake."

His last words before he blacked out.

A doctor finished bandaging Jenna's thumb and index finger in the emergency room at Malé's big public hospital. The care had been first rate, the female Indian doctor kind, but Jenna still found herself shaking every time she remembered how close the fuse came to setting off a bomb that would have taken down the entire hotel, according to the fast assessment of a Maldivian police team.

"You will be okay," the Indian doctor told her. "It is not such a bad burn. But you must keep it clean. You are very lucky."

"I know."

"There are some people in the waiting area who want to see you."

Jenna figured on Nicci, and she was there, but the doctor apparently meant a contingent of U.S. intelligence agents and more Maldivian police. She and Nicci were whisked to a conference room at police headquarters, several blocks away. A Maldivian gentleman in a dark suit told Nicci she would have to wait outside, then asked Jenna if she wanted anything to eat or drink.

"Just coffee," Jenna said, now that her hands no longer shook. "And some water."

The police, and two men from the National Defense Force, had her look through more than a hundred photos, mostly mug shots plus a number of surveillance photos. She did not see the young man from the van. She was asked to describe the man in detail to a young female sketch artist. Alas, none of Jenna and the artist's attempts bore much resemblance to the runaway driver.

Jenna felt herself growing tired, and perhaps the Maldivian in the dark suit noticed, because he had his people step aside so the U.S. intelligence agents could debrief her. That didn't take long. Then a tight-lipped American in his thirties and an older white man of considerable girth led Jenna and Nicci to an SUV. As they drove back to the hotel, the senior of the two told them the bomb had been made from the same materials that Timothy McVeigh had used to blow up the Oklahoma City federal building.

Members of the Maldives National Defense Force, dressed in camouflage uniforms, now ringed the Golden Crescent, which probably made it the safest place in the city.

After thanking Nicci for sticking around, Jenna rushed to her room, flopped on the bed, and speed-dialed Dafoe.

"What a nightmare," Jenna said. "This isn't the country I left ten years ago." She lay back against a cushiony headboard and told Dafoe what she and Rafan had been through.

"You pulled a fuse out of a bomb that filled the back of a van?"

When Dafoe spoke with such astonishment, it hit Jenna for the first time that what she'd done might have been amazing. She'd been in such a pell-mell mode since the attempted bombing, she hadn't slowed to think about it much.

"Yeah, I did," she said, "but Rafan was the one who realized something was up." She added that her old boyfriend had also been taken for debriefing, but since she was done, she expected him back momentarily. "He'll be staying the night, just for safety's sake. I just want you to know that there's nothing romantic going on," she added. "I just don't want him going back to his condo with a mad bomber on the loose, and with Senada's brothers out to get him. At least there are soldiers all around this place."

"I appreciate your telling me, but I always try to trust someone until I can't."

"Me, too, and sometimes it actually works—if they don't work in TV." Jenna laughed. Despite everything that had happened tonight, it felt great to hear Dafoe's voice. It would have been wonderful to have had him by her side. "So what's going on with North Korea? That's the last place I expected to hear about all the way out here."

Dafoe laid out Sang-mi's revelation about the North Korean arsenal of rockets loaded with sulfates.

"I'm sorry to say that what Sang-mi told you makes a lot of sense."

"I take it that that means something to you."

"You bet it does." Jenna jumped up and looked through the big glass doors that led to the balcony. Stars blazed in the tropical night like mica chips splashed across the galaxy. "Blowing up sulfates in the stratosphere in a carefully controlled way is one of the main options that the task force was going to look at. That can block just enough sunlight to cool things down. But what Sang-mi's saying is really scary. Is she sure about what she's hearing from her father?"

"She seems to be."

Jenna walked onto the balcony, looking at the inky ocean that eventually wound its way to the shores of North Korea. "The iron oxide in that tanker is dangerous, but we honestly don't know how dangerous. But there's no question that blowing up millions of tons of sulfates is a doomsday scenario. Volcanoes have done it, so we know that sulfates definitely bring down temperatures. And they do it fast. Huge quantities, like the amounts Sang-mi is talking about, would create winter conditions for years, and that would cripple food production and probably kill billions of people before the sulfates finally dispersed. You can imagine how countries are going to react if their people are starving to death. There would be wars everywhere."

"What kind of mind even comes up with this stuff?"

"The Supreme Leader," Jenna said sardonically, "is a real sicko. But what bothers me most," she went on, "is that the North Koreans are really good at exploiting the worst kinds of fears. They love to wait until world attention is totally fixed on something, and then they up the ante by doing things like launching test missiles or declaring themselves a nuclear power. Or if they suspect that the U.S. is even thinking of any kind of move against them, they remind everybody that they have thousands of rockets trained on Seoul," the capital of South Korea, "and that they'll burn down the city. For an incredibly poor country, they're incredibly good at stirring things up. And you never know when they're bluffing."

"Sang-mi says they're not bluffing," Dafoe said,

"If she's right, and they really do have thousands of rockets packed with sulfates, their timing is perfect because nobody would even want to think about five hundred thousand tons of iron oxide going into the ocean at the same time that millions of tons of sulfates are exploding into the stratosphere. I can say categorically that that would be the end of the world as we know it."

"Well, if that isn't bizarre enough, now I have to take you into the land of the really weird," Dafoe said. "Sang-mi claims that GreenSpirit spoke to her this morning and that she, meaning GreenSpirit, wants you to tell the world about the North Korean rockets."

"Really? They've got the wrong hero, if they think it's me. I'll be talking post haste with the vice president's office about the sulfates, and let the honchos handle this."

"Sorry to even bring it up, but Forensia begged me to ask you to put the message out there. I'll tell her no."

"I think you should." Then: "What do you think?"

"I think it's nuts, you going on the air with something like that."

Whew. "Does Forensia really believe that Sang-mi was talking to GreenSpirit's . . . spirit?"

"She sure does," Dafoe answered.

"She seemed so normal to me."

"Forensia? Normal? Look, Forensia's great, and I love her like a sister, but normal? I'd never say that, and she wouldn't want me to."

"Point taken. If Sang-mi's father is getting debriefed by the CIA, then our side already knows about the rockets. If they're keeping it secret, they might have a good reason."

"*'Might'* is the operative word," Dafoe said. "They also might be keeping it secret because they don't want it to look like the president's been asleep at the wheel. The election's in just a few days."

"Or maybe the left hand doesn't know what the right hand is doing. We saw plenty of that with the FBI and CIA in 2001, and then we had 9/11."

Rafan gazed at the headstones and monuments from behind the twin palms on the south side of the cemetery. The starlight revealed very little, but he knew Senada lay in a freshly dug grave not far from his sister; few spaces remained in the cemetery, so the two friends would be almost as close in death as they had been in life.

He could feel Senada's presence in such a tangible way that he thought perhaps some believers were correct in claiming that the dead guide the living in times of peril. Then he reminded himself that he probably felt that Senada was near because she had stood by these same trees the night she came to say good-bye to Basheera. He ached for both women so acutely that he reached out and touched the air where Senada had stood, willing to accept even a hint of the love that he'd known. But he felt nothing of her. Only the ache. And he would have to enter the cemetery to offer his final farewell without knowing if Senada's brothers were hiding among the graves.

Don't do this, he warned himself. *This is close enough.*

But he had to see her grave, to kneel beside it, to somehow let her know that he would never forget her.

This time he did not pass under the cemetery arch. He moved quietly along the periphery, knowing he would have to scurry in from the shadows on the far side. He had a flashlight, but would use it only if necessary. And he'd brought flowers, which he would lay gently on her grave.

When he stepped from the shadows onto the hallowed ground, he walked slowly, placing his feet as quietly as possible. Row upon row of graves greeted him. He grew numb to their presence, and that, more than anything, explained why Bilal caught him unawares.

"What are you doing here?" Senada's youngest brother demanded, seizing his arm.

Rafan smelled the must of the graveyard, glimpsed crescents and a single cross engraved in stone, and thought that he would soon join the dead who surrounded him. Bilal was a big man in the prime of his youth; a "bruiser," Jenna would have said.

"I have come to pay my respects."

"Don't you know that coming here could get you killed?" Bilal held Rafan in a powerful grip. "I was looking for you."

"That's her grave?" Rafan looked past his accoster at the simple marker with a white crescent.

Bilal nodded. "Yes, and you could—"

"I loved her," Rafan interrupted. "I loved her dearly." His words sounded hollow, eternally empty in the graveyard.

"That was your mistake," Bilal said.

"No, that's not true," Rafan said evenly, as a man might when he feels that all is lost. "Her mistake was *him*."

They both knew whom Rafan meant: the fisherman who'd beaten Senada, and whose jihadist beliefs had led to her murder.

Bilal began to cry, and he released Rafan. The young man sank to his knees and hung his head. Rafan stared at him before crouching and putting his hand on Bilal's back.

"She raised me," Bilal said. "She was like a mother to me. I wanted to kill him so many times. I should have. I should have killed him," he yelled, jumping to his feet.

Rafan looked around. Only the darkest shadows stared back.

"You were her favorite," Rafan said, only because it was true. Senada had spoken kindly of Bilal, unlike his older brothers.

"You may pray for her," Bilal said. "You're safe with me. I'll be back in two days to stand guard. You can come again then. And I'm so sorry about Basheera. Senada loved her so much."

The two men stood together at the grave of a woman they had both loved. Rafan laid his flowers on the freshly turned earth. Both men prayed. And beneath the black night and bright stars, both men wept.

CHAPTER 20

Gruesome. The most sickening thing that Forensia had ever seen. Rick Birk, the old reporter taken hostage, was on TV all the time, and you couldn't miss his thumb. Only it wasn't attached to his hand. *It was pinned to his shirt.* A thumb, just hanging there like a bloody brooch, right below his collar. Forensia almost threw up the first time she saw it.

Birk looked like he was in seven kinds of agony, propping up his bandaged hand with his good one while he spoke, yet he was so brave. Somehow he'd managed to keep talking all day. Even though he sounded weary and hoarse, he still joked about his fingers: "One down, nine to go." But it wasn't funny, and he was shaking so badly that his thumb looked like it had come back to life.

But that wasn't the worst part. *Oh, God no.* She could barely bring herself to look at the worst part. But how could she not? Only one thing poked out of the blood-soaked gauze hiding Birk's hand—his index finger! The terrorists had clamped those awful wire cutters on it;

any second he might clip it off. *Any second.* The tension was unbearable.

All regular programming had been canceled. Every channel was showing Birk, with lots of close-ups of his bloody thumb and those horrid wire cutters. The shows were calling it "The World Held Hostage" and "Doomsday and Dismemberment," crap like that, and they were playing special music and running flashy graphics. You'd think people would get tired of it, but not with the gut-wrenching suspense over whether a terrorist would slip into the picture and snip his pointer right off.

But it wasn't just Birk's suffering. Those terrorists were hell-bent on pouring enough iron oxide into the ocean to freeze the planet. And if people thought that was seriously scary—and Forensia knew they did because there had been huge runs on winter clothing all over the world—wait till they got wind of the North Korean rockets.

Her eyes were drawn quickly back to Birk. It was like she could see all of the world's pain and fear in the face of that poor old guy on the tanker, talking about those awful coal-fired power plants and how they should be shut down or the whole Earth was going to get "colder than a witch's titty." That was another of his bad jokes, which he probably shouldn't have said, and which Forensia couldn't help but find personally offensive. But he really did look and sound kind of delirious. And who couldn't forgive such a brave old-timer with his thumb hanging from his shirt like a piece of rotten—

Rrrrriiiinnngg.

The doorbell interrupted Forensia's thoughts. She tore herself from the TV and opened the screen door for Akina, the frail elderly witch from Ithaca who'd presided over GreenSpirit's memorial service. She'd brought her daughter Magic Margaret, who was as heavy as her mother was light. Sang-mi and Richtor came out of the kitchen to greet them.

They were gathering in Forensia's small house before heading to a sundown séance, where they hoped to make contact with GreenSpirit. With the twin calamities of the tanker takeover in the Maldives and the North Korean rockets, Forensia and Sang-mi felt like they needed GreenSpirit's guidance more than ever.

Their first plan had been to conduct the séance at the cabin where their leader had been murdered, but that idea had been squelched when Richtor reported that the crime scene was still cordoned off. He'd seen as many investigators crawling around the place as there had been on the day that Sang-mi discovered GreenSpirit's mutilated body.

Richtor pushed his lush dreads out of his face and quickly briefed Akina and Magic Margaret on what he'd found.

"Maybe they got a break in the case," Forensia said, "or else they've got nothing and they're desperate."

"Can we shut this off?" Magic Margaret turned in disgust from the TV image of Birk with his bloody thumb.

"No," Forensia blurted out. Then: "Sorry, but I just feel like the least we can do is bear witness to his suffering."

"He's mainstream media," Magic Margaret said. "Who cares?"

"Yeah, really," Richtor groused.

"I care. Okay?" Forensia was genuinely horrified at what she was hearing from her fellow Pagans.

"It would be nice," the elderly witch said, "if they would shut down those power plants, like he's saying."

"Sure, but not because of this cruelty." Forensia was still stunned by Richtor and Magic Margaret's chilling remarks. If you cared about people, then you had to care about all people—even a decrepit old TV reporter. "I'll turn down the sound," Forensia said in the spirit of amelioration. Birk had been on all day and was repeating himself anyway.

She plopped down next to Sang-mi on an old couch. Akina sat across from them in a tattered armchair, elbows on her knees, chin in her hands. Her daughter, who was older than Forensia's mother, settled on a love seat next to Richtor, and said, "The scuttlebutt at work is that they sent more forensics folks down here. They're up to something, I guess." She was a parole officer in Ithaca and had friends in the state police.

Forensia thought Magic Margaret affected an eccentric appearance for someone affiliated with law enforcement. She was an exceedingly large woman with blunt-cut, jet-black bangs and straight white hair. Not charming—weird. The same could have been said for her thick layer of black eyeliner with its even thicker globs of white glitter, lending her the heavy-lidded, piebald look of a basset hound–dalmatian mix.

Magic Margaret's mother, who eschewed all makeup, suggested that they hold the séance where Forensia and Sang-mi had been inducted into the coven. "I can't imagine a more sacred spot."

The Pagans decided that as long as they were going to the clearing, they might as well set up the altar in the circle of white stones to make it as welcoming as possible to GreenSpirit. To that end, they gathered up all their supplies, including the boline, the black-handled knife with the foot-long blade, and the large pentagram of woven animal skin. After the initiation, they'd stored the heavy, rough-hewn altar itself in the nearby forest.

"I'll ride with you," Sang-mi said to Forensia as they were deciding which cars to take.

"Me, too," said Richtor.

After they had been trailing Akina's shiny red Prius for about ten minutes, Forensia noticed her friend freeze. Her dark eyes were focused on the sun visor mirror.

"Don't anybody turn around but there's a car following us. It's been there since we left town. It was back two or three cars, but now it's right behind us."

Forensia glanced in the rearview, which was filled with the reflection of a late model green SUV, but it looked like a smaller sport utility vehicle, like a Honda or Toyota.

"Can you see who's in that thing?" Sang-mi asked.

"No, it's too bright." Late afternoon sun.

"I could reach back behind me," said Richtor, who had gallantly given up the front passenger seat to Sang-mi, "and act like I'm digging for something in my pack. See if I can get a look."

"What do you think, Sang-mi?" Forensia found it odd to defer to her friend, who normally proved so reticent, but Sang-mi had spotted the tail, if that's what it was, and suddenly seemed more adept at this cat-and-mouse business, probably because she'd grown up in a police state.

"Go ahead," Sang-mi said to Richtor.

Both women listened intently as he leaned his long torso over the backseat and rummaged around in his pack.

"They look Asian to me," he said softly, as if he feared being overheard. "Kind of like you, Sang-mi."

"Oh, shit-shit-*shit*."

Those were the first profanities that Forensia had ever heard from her quiet Korean friend. "Don't worry, you're in the U.S. now," Forensia said.

"The North has assassins that go after defectors everywhere," Sang-mi said, alarm bracing every word. "Even their families. They murdered the nephew of one of the Supreme Leader's former wives. Her *nephew*."

"They're really that crazy?" Forensia glanced nervously at the rearview.

"They're crazier than crazy," Sang-mi said. "They have a Web site called *Uriminzokkri,* roughly translated, it means 'Our Nation.' Two days ago they called my father 'human scum,' and showed a photoshopped picture of him with an ax in his face and said, 'You must not forget that traitors have always been slaughtered.'"

"And you think those guys behind us might be assassins?" Richtor asked.

Sang-mi nodded. "From the General Bureau of Surveillance. They are really scary. After their missions, those assassins will commit suicide, anything to avoid capture."

The young Korean defector buried her face in her hands.

Jason had Aly Wennerstrom snuggling by his side in his bright blue 1977 pick-'em-up truck. They'd had to rendezvous by the entrance to the state park because her father hadn't been gulled by his daughter's declarations of Christian chastity, much less by her shrill claim that "I'm still a goddamn virgin, Daddy." But as Aly licked Jason's ear, she allowed that she shouldn't have lost her temper with her papa.

"It's just that I'm such a passionate person," she cooed, pressing closer and running her hand over his thighs and swelling enthusiasm, lingering over the latter for teasing, squeezing seconds. "If I like something,

I can't help myself—I want all of it, and I want it all the time. Jesus would understand, don't you think?"

"Sure, he'd get it," Jason mumbled.

Was she kidding? Jason didn't know, didn't care. But he did love the way that girl could reason her way out of her panties six ways to Sunday. Loved even more the way she unzipped him now and eased *him* out. A monster hard-on, a real barnacle boner. He'd learned in biology only yesterday that those boat-sucking scum had dicks twice as long as their bodies. About the way Jason felt right now with Barnacle Boy in her hot little hull of a hand. *Oh, yeah.* Sweet Aly was moving her fingers up and down and making him so hard. Making it hard to drive, too, but what was a horn dog to do? Stop? Slow down the momentum? Hell no. *Just keep dem rubba on dem road, mon.* He'd drive clear to Buffalo and back as long as Aly was showing her passion. Showing more than passion—sitting sideways and slipping her clingy, baby-blue top over her head. Girl had on one of those see-through bras, and Jason could see everything: her youthful perkiness; her budding excitement; and her hands holding and squeezing herself, doing things he'd like to do.

Now her fingers were working the single clasp in front, where the cups came together in true sartorial inspiration. She paused to caress herself one more time, keeping those doorbells of hers ringing. Jason's eyes were darting back and forth so fast—road to breast, road to other breast—that he might have had money on a Chinese table tennis tournament.

Oh mon, you see dem puppies? She was peeling off that filmy fabric and, *Yes,* he could see dem puppies. When she pressed his hand up against them, *he* could have yelped. Or howled. Or hooted like a screech owl.

"I've got to pull over," he gasped. He thought he'd explode.

But she moved his hand over her breasts, letting him feel both of them, then said, "No-ooo. I like it like this. You do your job behind that big wheel, and I'll do my job with something pretty dang big, too."

She put his hand back on the steering wheel and slipped off her skirt, a short denim number that hadn't hidden much anyway. The girl was killing him. All she had on now was a white thong that he could have flossed with, and she didn't have it on for long. Then she had her hand back on him, pushing her naked, nubby nipples against his arm. "Ever had a BJ," she whispered, "while you drive?"

Time to lie, Jason advised himself. "Nope, never done that."

Without another word, with only another wet kiss to his ear, she disappeared into his lap, and all that thick curly blond hair fell like sprinkles on his legs and belly and balls.

Jason closed his eyes in gratitude, might have said a word or two of prayer, like, "Thank ya, Jesus." Or maybe something along the lines of "Oh, God. Oh, God." Direct and to the point.

Then his pick-'em-up truck flew off the road at sixty miles an hour, and whatever mumbles of appreciation might have been passing from Jason's lips were lost to oblivion, just like the hundreds of millions of tiny sea creatures exploding from Barnacle Boy.

"Jason Robb, you're under arrest." The very first words that Jason heard as he came to, and they hailed directly from Sheriff Walker himself, who had bent all the way over to look in the open driver's side window. To Jason, the sheriff's head looked odd—suspended in space.

Aly was already out of the cab. Jason peered past the sheriff and spotted his honey's feet first, then her legs, and a strange-looking dress that he knew she hadn't been wearing before. No, it was a blanket. Looked like an Army surplus thing. He looked up and saw her face. Kind of banged up—and not the kind of banging they'd been working on.

He kept staring at Aly, who didn't seem pleased to see him, and wondering how the hell they went from having such a good time to this mess. Nothing made sense. Least of all Sheriff Walker: Under arrest? For *what*?

It slowly came to Jason that most likely it was against the law to drive with a naked girl going down on you. Not just any naked girl, either, but a naked underage girl. The next instant, the word "sodomy" came a'calling, chilling him to his . . . bone.

He gradually became alert enough to spot Aly's thong, skirt, and bra on the ceiling, which made no sense whatsoever till he finally realized that he'd flipped his pride and joy upside down. The sheriff's head was starting to make sense, too. It was still hanging there, studying Jason like he was some kind of strange barnyard animal, a five-legged lamb or a two-headed chicken. Something nature spit out and wouldn't take back.

"Anything broke, near as you can tell?" Sheriff Walker asked it like he had to.

Jason grabbed his crotch in raw panic, remembering a fine old movie in which a guy was getting a really cool BJ when his car was rear-ended—and the woman bit off his dick so fast that she might have been a snapping turtle foraging in his lap. But Barnacle Boy was starting to get hard as hickory again. Go figure. *Down, boy, down,* he commanded, to no avail. His dick always did have a mind of his own.

Not only that, Jason's balls ached. How the hell do you still have blue balls after being knocked out? But then he glanced at Aly and recalled her efforts seconds before the crash.

"Why'd I close my eyes?" he mumbled to himself.

"Because you're a murdering sex maniac," Sheriff Walker answered. "Now get out. Unhook that safety belt carefully so you don't die on us before we can fry you. And make yourself decent."

Jason bent Barnacle Boy back into his pants, zipped up, and unsnapped the seat belt, lowering himself to the ceiling of the truck's cab. A few seconds later he crawled out the window.

Walker cuffed him. Then the big dawg read him his rights. But Jason didn't hear much beyond the "Anything you say can and will be used against you" because the words "murdering sex maniac" kept bouncing around his rattled brain.

Much as he could see, Aly was alive and so was everyone else standing around—all the damn cops, EMTs, and firemen with their big red extinguishers just in case his truck burst into flames. So where were all the dead people? Where was even *one* dead person?

The answer came to him with the greatest reluctance, as cold and clear and deadly as black ice. That's when he knew that driving naked, even with an underage honey, would likely prove the least of his worries—and the last sex he'd ever have outside a prison cell.

Forensia eased off the gas when she spotted the highway patrol officer directing traffic into a single lane. Two ambulances and five patrol cars, including Sheriff Walker's old Bronco, lined the side of the road, lights flashing in the setting sun. A pickup truck lay upside down about fifty feet from the shoulder. It had driven through a farm fence; broken slats littered the ground and a post had been sheared off to a ten-inch stub.

"I wonder if anybody's hurt?" Richtor said from the backseat.

Slowing down forced the small green SUV—a RAV4, as it turned out—to within spitting distance of Forensia's car. Akina's shiny red Prius was two cars ahead.

Sang-mi pretended to fix her unflappably straight hair in the sun visor mirror—with her gaze firmly on the vehicle behind them.

"I can see them now. They are definitely Korean." She shrunk into the seat, as if she expected bullets to come flying through the car at any second.

"There are cops here, let's just pull over." Forensia slowed her Subaru.

"No!" Sang-mi shouted. "Don't stop. They don't care about police. Keep moving. I'm not kidding. They will kill us."

Shaken, Forensia kept driving.

"There are thousands, probably tens of thousands of Koreans in New York," Richtor said. "I think they own every other fruit stand in the city. Maybe they're ordinary, innocent people."

Sang-mi shook her head. "Go, go," she said to Forensia.

But they were forced to creep past the accident as a young man crawled out of the driver's window. The RAV4 stayed close.

Forensia kept checking her rearview mirror to keep an eye on the SUV and the road ahead to make sure that *she* didn't drive off the road. As she drew even with the wreck, she glanced over at it, just when the young man turned his head.

"It's Jason," she shouted as the sheriff handcuffed him. Everyone in the car turned to look. An EMT led a young woman in a blanket to one of the ambulances.

"Whoever she is, she looks like she got off lucky," Richtor said.

Sang-mi stayed scrunched down in the seat. A quarter mile later the RAV4 turned onto the highway heading south to the city. The young Korean woman stared silently till the small SUV disappeared under an overpass.

In the White House Situation Room, President Reynolds stared at the supertanker on the TV screen and shook his large head. Bad enough that he had to listen to a washed-up correspondent with a chopped-off thumb mouthing the implacable demands of Al Qaeda, but now the North Koreans had sent him a top secret communiqué that announced they were going to exploit the crisis as much as they could.

Reynolds lowered his eyes to the President's Daily Brief, which summarized all the threats to the United States; the North Korean communiqué was item number one. That dingdong kingdom was ruled by a crazy little bastard in platform shoes who Reynolds long ago had dubbed "the Demon Dwarf." This morning the Dwarf was saying that he would launch thousands of missiles loaded with sulfates that would explode in the stratosphere—releasing billions of sun-blocking particles— if the United States didn't send his country massive shipments of food, grains, seeds, and a full array of high-tech gear for everything from agriculture to nuclear arms. The creepy Dwarf also wanted the top *twenty* U.S. coal-fired plants shut down, no doubt to top Al Qaeda's demand to close ten of them. There was to be no public disclosure of any of this, of course, "including the receipt of this communiqué."

The Dwarf insisted on secrecy in everything. No wonder that was his first condition. But Reynolds hated, *hated* the idea of complying with any of Demon Dwarf's demands. The first concession in any government-to-government negotiation set the tone for every issue to follow. Complying with anything that crazy weasel wanted would send the wrong signal, and it would put the United States on a slippery slope long greased by the blood of his foes. Much better, Reynolds thought, to reveal the Dwarf's threat to the planet so that everyone would know what he'd slipped into his silos. Neutralize the bastard with exposure. But if Reynolds did not keep North Korea's secrets, the madman might very well launch his sun-blocking missiles, spreading SPF 1,000 all over Mother Earth.

The goddamned dictator had boxed him into a corner three days before the election. It was just like the little creep to pull a stunt like this when the last thing Reynolds needed was a crisis of this magnitude seventy-two hours before voting booths opened for business.

What would Lilton and his merry band of destroyers make of this wrinkle if it became public? *Wrinkle? Hell, it's a political San Andreas Fault,* Reynolds warned himself. *Imagine the attack ads. Merciless. Murderous.* "Reynolds let America's most dangerous enemy build thousands of deadly missiles that could destroy the whole world. And now he wants you to give him four more years? Say *no* to Reynolds. Say *no* to North Korean terrorists." Horrible.

If Reynolds made the Korean's demands public, missiles might begin flying. Yet if he stayed mum, it would encourage the man's madness.

Reynolds's cabinet and the directors of the National Security Agency, the FBI, and the CIA were waiting for his response to the Daily Brief. At last Reynolds looked up.

"Before we get started on the subject of secret communiqués, what did we find out about *that* guy," Reynolds nodded at Rick Birk, jawing away on a silent screen, "and his blinking eyeballs? Anything worthwhile?"

The NSC chief said, "Our code breakers have found intriguing links to a little-known drumming pattern of the Lokele tribe in the Congo."

"No kidding?" Reynolds grinned. "Where did that old bugger come up with something like that?"

"That's puzzling and a little troubling," the CIA chief answered from the cheap seats at the far end of the table. "He doesn't appear to ever have had any interest in anything African, other than a liqueur called Amarula."

"Well, what was he saying with his eyes then?" Reynolds asked the NSC director.

"Four words, sir: 'fire mountain' and 'cow curd.'"

"'Cud. Cow *cud,*'" said a bony woman to the NSC director's right.

"Cow cud? Cow curd? What the hell is that supposed to mean?" Reynolds demanded.

No one answered.

Reynolds couldn't believe this shit. "That's it? Fire mountain. Cow curd, or cud?"

An uneasy silence followed before Vice President Andrew Percy said, "It's possible, Mr. President, that he's just jerking their chain."

"Or ours," Reynolds volleyed. *Goddamn code breakers could hear* The Bells of St. Mary's *in a conch shell.*

The president rose to his full height. "Why didn't we know about these sulfates until North Korea decided it was time to tell us?" Reynolds still couldn't get over that.

"Mr. President, we did know about them," said Debra Abrams, the White House national security adviser. She nodded at the CIA chief.

"That's correct, Mr. President," the director concurred. "We've been debriefing a North Korean defector from their U.N. mission."

"Then why am I the last to know what he's been telling us?"

"Verification, sir. We considered the information to be so outlandish that we thought we might be dealing with a double agent. We had to verify everything from sources in situ."

"And have you?"

"Yes, sir. Those rockets are real."

"And they'll really bring on years of winter? Worldwide calamity?"

"That's right, sir," Abrams answered.

Reynolds groaned. He couldn't believe he was enduring this political migraine because of sulfates. *Of all the goddamn things.* Hadn't he played around with them with a kiddy chemistry set when he was nine years old? Here he'd worried for years about the North's nuclear capabilities, and now they were threatening to bring down the planet with stuff that you could buy in toy stores and hobby shops. Like being attacked with a garden hoe, till you found out that the hoe was about to chop down the sky.

"What about a preemptive strike? Is that viable?" he asked.

"We'd lose Tokyo and Seoul immediately," Abrams said. "The Supreme Leader, as he insists on being called, made it clear many times that the instant the North Koreans detect an attack from the U.S. or NATO, they're unloading their silos on those two cities. And if he does that, you can presume that he'll launch those sulfate rockets, too."

Reynolds sat down and massaged his brow. "What about wiggle room? Do we have any?"

"We tell him that we'll give him food aid, that we've always been concerned about the welfare of the North Korean people, and that—"

"The usual palaver," Reynolds cut in. "He's heard that before. Hell, if I had to hear that meaningless claptrap one more time, *I'd* push the button." From the stares he received from around the long table, he realized that he'd better add the standard-issue disclaimer: "I'm joking. Jesus, folks, get real. What are we going to do?"

"We buy time," Abrams said icily.

"What about giving the Dwarf a brownout, or a blackout even? Briefly shut down the plants to send him a signal that we're serious about negotiating. Can we do that?" he asked his energy secretary.

The energy secretary nodded. "We can."

Reynolds liked his direct and satisfying answer. "If we're going to give the Dwarf something in the first round, give him something that feels real. We could think of it as earnest money, a way to say 'We feel your pain.' Domestically, we could blame it on a broken transformer, but tell him privately that it was to show our good faith."

"The problem, Mr. President," Abrams said, "is that Al Qaeda's demanding a shutdown of coal-fired plants, too, and if we have a power outage of any note, *they* will take public credit for it. They'll say it's a sign of how they're already dragging the Great Satan to his knees. They're not going to be quiet."

"Voters would see that as capitulating to Arab terrorists," said Ralph Ebbing, Reynolds's chief of staff, who was leaning against an Oval Office wall a few feet from his boss. "You cannot let that happen."

"So no blackouts then." Reynolds leaned back. "Okay, let's send him a C-17 filled with food. Promise him thousands of tons more."

"You couldn't get a single-engine Cessna with a bushel of wheat to Pyongyang without some aviation geek somewhere Tweeting about it. Sending aid to North Korea? Right before the election?" said the chief of staff incredulously.

Yup, he's right. Reynolds looked around the room and reached out, his hands palms up, like a beggar. "Ideas, anyone? Time is short here."

"We reply that we are looking at any and all ways to satisfy his requests," Abrams said. "And we tell him that we will keep our communications secret, as he's asked."

"Basically, we give the bastard the first round," Reynolds said, "and hope that keeps him happy for a few hours."

"I'm afraid so. It's the best way to buy time and get you reelected. The last thing the world needs right now is a loss of your leadership."

Reynolds harrumphed, but not because of Abrams's toadying. A heretical thought had struck him: After spending more than a billion dollars on this campaign, it wouldn't matter who was president if those missiles went airborne.

"Jason Robb, you are charged with the murder of Linda Pareles, also known as GreenSpirit."

Sheriff Walker spoke formally to Jason in the command post for the joint federal, state, and local investigation into GreenSpirit's killing. The sheriff sounded as if he'd never met the young man before. As if he hadn't watched Jason come of age in this small town. As if the Sheriff's daughters hadn't gone to high school with the boy.

Walker hadn't told the FBI or the New York State Police that he'd planned to arrest Jason. His move came after GreenSpirit's blood had been identified on the scrap of bandana.

None of the agents and state police officers congratulated him. The sheriff's brow wrinkled as he gazed at his colleagues.

"You want to make your call?" Walker asked Jason, like the kid was such an arrest veteran now that the sheriff didn't need to explain that all he got was the one call.

"Sure," Jason said jauntily. "This is bullshit." When he spoke, the kid looked at the FBI agents. He didn't sound remotely disturbed by the murder charge.

The FBI profiler, Barb Lassiter, appeared to study the young man. Not in disgust. Probing—that's what it looked like, as if there were more for her to find out.

She might have suspected she was dealing with a serial killer in her midst. The murder of that Pagan in Vermont and GreenSpirit's killing bore the same "signature," as experts like Lassiter referred to it: eyeballs plucked from the skull and left on a floor in candle wax. And Lassiter had been told by Sheriff Walker that on the night of the Vermont murder Jason Robb hadn't been seen by anyone in town. Not even by his parents. He'd taken off for parts unknown in that old truck of his.

At sundown, the Pagans gathered in the circle of white stones in which GreenSpirit had initiated Forensia and Sang-mi.

They'd set up the altar as she had instructed them only two weeks ago, using the twig broomstick called a besom, iron cauldron, boline, candles, incense, and the animal skin pentagram. Now they sat, hand-in-hand—for this could take all night—and began to chant a secret invocation, asking for GreenSpirit's guidance. The world felt leaden with the worst eventualities. Forensia remembered feeling like this as a young teen, as if an apocalypse were about to rain down from the sky. But this felt worse because now she knew that it could really happen.

Another peculiar sensation swept over her: She felt watched again. She tried to dismiss this by reminding herself that Jason Robb had been arrested. And they were fully clothed.

But still the feeling persisted. It felt so strange that Forensia violated the rule against opening her eyes while trying to summon the dead.

Directly across from her, Sang-mi sat with her eyes open, too, but Sang-mi's eyes were rolled up so that only the bottoms of her irises were visible. They looked like dark crescent moons in a milky sky. Sang-mi began to speak in Korean, beginning in a mumbled monotone, then becoming shrill and desperate sounding.

258 | BILL EVANS

None of the other Pagans knew her language.

Akina whispered softly in the Korean's ear, "Please speak English, Sang-mi. English."

Sang-mi fell immediately silent. But her eyes remained rolled upward, and when she spoke again, seconds later, there was no mistaking her meaning:

"Tell the world. Tell the world."

CHAPTER 21

Jenna watched Rafan sleeping on the portable bed. She'd cracked only a single bamboo blind, but it threw enough morning light into her wide, airy room to allow her to catch his peaceful expression. He looked grateful to have found respite, if only through sleep, from his considerable sorrows.

Late last night, after police had surrounded the hotel, he'd knocked on her door looking thoroughly exhausted. He'd said little as she ushered him in, only that he'd visited Senada's grave and run into Bilal, her youngest brother. "But that was all right," he insisted before pouring himself, completely clothed, onto the twin bed; his long, lanky frame left his sandaled feet dangling over the rose-tinted bloodwood floor. In seconds, he fell asleep.

Jenna saw no reason to wake him now. After performing her morning routine before the mirror, with the added difficulty of a bandage on her right hand, she slipped out the door, eager to have breakfast in the Golden Crescent's open-air, four-star restaurant. Turning a corner, she spotted a Malé policeman by the elevator, relieved that a tight cloak of security still clung to the building. Nobody believed that Al Qaeda's presence in the Maldives had begun and ended with the young man who'd tried to blow up a hotel.

She nodded at the officer, and repeated the gesture when the elevator opened to reveal one of his colleagues at the control panel. More police and members of the National Defense Force were posted at the lobby's entrances and exits. Jenna offered them all her best smile—nothing like a real crisis to make you thankful for law enforcement—and was about to take a table that offered an expansive view of the ocean when she heard a woman call her name. She turned to meet the imperious gaze of Alicia Gant and realized that she could not escape the news producer's company, no matter how unappetizing she might make even the most enticing breakfast soufflé. But what stunned Jenna was when Alicia's companion turned around—and Nicci smiled at her.

They both waved her over. With no concern for pleasantries, or so much as a brisk "Good morning," Alicia said, "We're going to need a live interview with you about last night's attempt to bomb this place to hell and back. If nothing astounding happens with Birk, the network's going back to normal programming and you're the lead story, so we've got to get this done soon."

"I had no idea that we'd have to move this fast," Jenna said.

"Of course not, you're not a journalist."

"Were you going to call me about—"

"I was just about to," Alicia interrupted, "when you waltzed in."

Waltzed?

"Maybe we'll even get lucky," Alicia continued, "and Birk will hurry up and bleed to death. I'm so sick of looking at his face."

Jenna spied a huge flat-screen TV on a lobby wall about forty feet away. "Where is he?" She hadn't thought to check on Birk till now, and she wondered if she'd ever develop strong news instincts.

"He's been off the air since one thirty this morning," Nicci said.

Jenna noticed Alicia slide her hand over to Nicci's. The two women entwined their fingers and Nicci gave Alicia such a warm smile that it shocked Jenna. Not because the producers apparently had spent the night together—though if Jenna could have picked a partner for Nicci it never would have been the acerbic Alicia Gant—but because Malé was Muslim, and only the densest or most naïve sensibility would have failed to read this kind of touching. Jenna looked around protectively; nobody seemed to be staring—yet.

"When should we do the interview?" Jenna asked.

Alicia checked her watch. "I gave the crew an early call so they'd be set up when we finished eating. They're not happy, but tough shit, they're doing it." All spoken in a regal tone that Jenna found irritating; she could just imagine how the crew felt. "We'll do a dry run in twenty minutes. We're on for real in thirty."

"I'll grab a quick bite and run upstairs," Jenna responded.

"No time, and I should probably brief you now. We need you to say—" Alicia stopped as Nicci gripped her hand tightly and shook her head. For a moment, Jenna sensed that Alicia was going to continue issuing edicts, but she said nothing, and the tropical air, thick with frangipani and sudden panic, seemed to settle at once.

Birk woke feeling sick. Just like he'd felt when he was going to sleep. Like he felt all the time now. And his shakes wouldn't stop. A body could take only so much abuse.

His unsteady eyes landed on his bandaged hand, his index finger still sticking out like a chunk of bloody bait from the stained and crusty gauze. At least there were no wire cutters attached right now. Raggedy Ass had dispensed with them so Birk could actually sleep. "I want you getting some shut-eye so you don't blab so much," the cracker jihadist had drawled. Which suggested to Birk that the bearded one really did appreciate the savvy—and always suave—correspondent's premier importance.

It wasn't the first sign that Raggedy Ass had understood that he and his hostage had a confluence of interest, as Birk thought of it. The most telling indication came when his abductor, at the very last moment, realized that cutting apart his prisoner-cum-spokesman like a roast chicken would, indeed, make it tough for Birk to communicate clearly.

If they couldn't torture Birk, there was always the captain. Captain

Moreno had screamed himself hoarse when the jihadist had clamped the cutters down on his thumb. The Waziristani couldn't let the world think that he'd backed down from his very first threat. The captain's thumb, a grisly but convincing imposter, now hung below Birk's collar. The captain continued to bewail his wound.

Birk wished he'd shut up. *What a wuss. He needs to man up. It's just a fucking finger. You don't see* me *blubbering.*

The jihadist eyed his most famous hostage and said, "I'm going to get another finger." He glanced at the captain, whose eyes opened wildly at the unwanted attention. "And I need you sitting still so I can hook it on your shirt while it's nice and fresh."

"Righto," Birk replied, appreciating that Raggedy Ass wanted a proper display; both of them had seen that a finger, especially one hanging severed-side up, leaked a paltry amount of blood.

Birk had come to respect Raggedy Ass's keen understanding of visual content, but that was to be expected because the young man, no doubt, had grown up on *Sesame Street* and had developed a bold sense of color in the broadcast spectrum. Besides, under any set of circumstances, red was always a vibrant consideration.

"I've been thinking about something," Raggedy Ass went on. "Ordinarily, I'd never give a man an alcoholic beverage, but you were shaking so bad yesterday that it was pathetic. It makes us look bad, like we're mistreating you. So how much of this," he held up a bottle of Johnnie Walker Blue Label that he must have unearthed from the captain's private reserve—*Blue Label!!!*—"do you need to stop shaking?"

"Oh, not much. Not much at all. A wee taste should do it—every now and then."

"I don't want you drunk. You start looking or sounding drunk, and I swear to Muhammad, peace and blessings of Allah be upon Him, that I will cut off your head with this." He held up the all-purpose wire cutters.

"No, of course not. I'd never get drunk. I don't even like to get drunk." *Liar, liar, pants on fire.* "I totally understand your concern. It would be unseemly." *Now give 'er here.* "The best way to keep me, let's say, medicated, would be for me to have a few sips every hour." That truly was how Birk had remained functional for decades. The thought of finally being able to sip away after all this misery was a bounty beyond belief. *Thank you, Johnnie Walker, peace and blessings of Allah be upon* him.

Raggedy Ass held out the bottle with two fingers, like it was leprous. Because of the awkwardness of Birk's heavily wrapped hand, the reporter had to clench the cap between his teeth to unscrew it. Still, he performed this feat in a flash. *Ah, the sweetest scent this side of fresh-squeezed pussy.* Birk spit out the cap and took what might well have been the most satisfying swig of his long drinking life. Then a second and a third swig before he saw Raggedy Ass go bug-eyed. Warmth flooded from Birk's belly like the most wonderful glow imaginable, lighting up every cell in his body, even numbing him to the ungodly screams once more rising from the captain.

For chrissakes, shove a sock in his goddamn pie hole.

Alicia had ordered the crew to set up by the hotel entrance, where the van had been. She'd also corralled three members of the National Defense Force to stand in the background in full combat gear. Only feet away was where the waterspout had savaged a garden.

Jenna rushed out of the hotel accompanied by Nicci, who had gushed in a breathy whisper on the elevator that Alicia was "wonderful." Jenna could have done without the effervescence but thought that maybe Alicia needed a little loving to crack her emotional carapace.

If so, it wasn't immediately clear that love had done the deed. The news producer positioned Jenna and Special Terrorism Correspondent Chris Randall facing each other with the sliding glass doors to the lobby behind them. Then she told Jenna that they needed a "strong sound bite. That's not coming from me. That's coming from New York."

"This is the run-through, right?" Jenna asked.

Alicia shook her head, as if in disbelief. "Yes, it's the run-through. Are you ready?"

"Sure," Jenna said.

"I was talking to the crew," the producer said frostily.

What a bitch.

"Can I get an answer?" she demanded of the cameraman, who glared at her and nodded. "Let's go, Chris," Alicia said to the tall correspondent.

He turned to Jenna. "What did you see here last night?"

"I came around the corner of the hotel in the middle of a powerful thunderstorm and saw a van right here by the entrance. I was rushing to get into the hotel, because I'd just seen a waterspout, when a young man jumped out of the van and we knocked into each other, and then he raced off. But a Maldivian friend of mine thought the driver's behavior was suspicious, so he opened the door of the van, and that's when we found the bomb."

"What did you see first?" Chris asked her.

"About a thousand pounds of explosives. Every inch of the van was packed with it. And then I saw smoke from the burning fuse."

"What did you do then?" Chris prompted.

"I pulled the fuse out of the bomb." Jenna raised her bandaged hand. "It wasn't that big a deal, once I saw it, and this is not as bad as it looks. It's just a little burn."

"Hold on," Alicia said to Chris and the crew. "Don't eat humble fucking pie," she scolded Jenna. "You stopped a bombing—"

"No, my friend and I stopped it."

"You pulled the fuse out."

"He tried to, too."

"But *you* did it. Say it! You stopped a bombing that would have been the 9/11 of this part of the world. And skip the crap about it not being a big deal. It's a big deal, so just say it."

"I'm not going to 'just say it.' I *helped* stop a bombing. I didn't do it all by myself." Jenna stepped away from the camera. "The only reason I even saw the fuse was my friend thought right away to check the van."

"What was your friend doing at the hotel at that hour?"

Jenna shrugged, trying to avoid the issue. "That's personal."

"Personal? What is he, married?" Alicia's remark felt sharp as a coral reef.

"I'm not going to get into that."

"Well, then, go get him. He's still up in your room, right? We're going to need him, too, I guess, if you're not going to say what needs to be said."

"I am not getting him. There are people around here who want to kill him and he can't risk being seen publicly."

"I don't care if Dr. Evil is about to put him on a rocket and blast his butt into space, we need him since you're not going to play ball. *Persuade* him. I'll bet you're good at that."

"Go to hell. That's an outrageous suggestion."

"Oh, please. Grow the fuck up." Alicia spun toward Nicci. "Talk some sense into her. We're suppose to do this for real," she glanced at her watch, "in about five minutes."

The weather producer looked clubbed, eyes shifting between Alicia and Jenna.

Jenna returned her gaze and knew that she'd lost her. *To that harridan.* But how do you compete with "wonderful" sex? But Nicci didn't disappoint her.

"What Jenna said was fine, and it'll be fine when we go live." Nicci faced Alicia directly. "And I'm sure it was accurate. She says what she sees. But what you said *was* outrageous. And I think you need to apologize and get a grip."

"Oh, you do, you little twerp. I've got—"

Jenna cut her off: "I'm not taking part in this charade." She stepped away from the camera. "And I'm talking to Elfren about this." Jenna started to walk away. Alicia seized her arm. "Don't you dare touch me," Jenna said. The producer let go.

"Okay, go," Alicia said. "I'll tell New York that you had a hissy fit. I'm sure Elfren will be real impressed when the weather girl says it got a little too stormy for her in the tropics. Me?" Alicia pointed to herself. "I'm talking to Marv right now. I can't believe he puts you on the air. I wouldn't trust you to read a thermometer."

Nicci hooked her arm through Jenna's and towed her back into the Golden Crescent before she could say another word.

Still furious, Jenna pulled out her cell, but not to contact the network.

National security concerns trumped her own anger as she placed her second call in the past eight hours to the man who lived at Number One Observatory Circle in Washington, D.C.

An assistant to Vice President Andrew Percy answered on the first ring. Jenna told the young woman that she needed to speak to him as soon as possible about "a matter of the utmost urgency."

"Vice President Percy is not available at this time, but I'll see that he receives your message."

Jenna could almost see the eye rolling from nine thousand miles away. "That's great, and I appreciate that, but I left my first message a few hours ago and I haven't heard back from him. This is really urgent, and I'm on his task force."

"Which one?"

"On geoengineering."

"All right." The woman sounded bored. "I'll pass this on to his chief of staff."

"May I speak to him now, please. This is really important." In government, Jenna was learning, there was no telling if the left hand knew what the right hand was doing, and she wanted to make sure that the executive branch knew without question that North Korean rockets were on the verge of changing world history.

"I'm afraid that's not possible. I will make sure that your message is heard."

Jenna heard no sense of urgency. It was as if she'd been speaking to an automated message center.

As she and Nicci hurried to the elevator, she tried to think of someone on the task force who *could* get through to the vice president—or higher. She drew blanks. Maybe someone at the Natural Resources Defense Counsel. Stepping off on the third floor, Jenna left a message for the gentleman with the white goatee who'd given her the eye at the first meeting.

As soon as they entered her room, they spotted Rafan walking out of the bathroom with his shaving kit.

He smiled, looking so much better than he had last night. Nicci extended her hand while Jenna fished the room service menu out of a drawer. She handed it to Rafan, saying, "Order something in, please. I don't want you risking a trip downstairs, not with all your 'fans' looking for you. I had to do an interview that turned into a disaster, so I never got to eat. Would you mind ordering me yogurt, fruit, toast, and coffee? I've got another call to make."

"Disaster?" Rafan asked.

"More on that later," Jenna said. "What about you?" she asked Nicci. "You hungry, or did you get enough downstairs?"

"Stop being a mother hen and go call Elfren," Nicci pushed her toward the balcony, "before she does."

But Jenna got no further than Elfren's administrative assistant. As she was leaving a message, Marv called. She picked up expecting the worst.

"You are *not,*" he shouted, "to disrespect our foremost producer of terrorism coverage. You are *not* to leave a run-through for an interview that she's set up about a terrorist bomb until she's satisfied with your answers. You are *not* to unilaterally cancel an interview about a terrorist act. And you are *not* to refuse her reasonable requests to provide sound bites that place you at the center of stopping terrorism."

Four sentences, and each one contained a variant of "terror," Jenna couldn't help noting.

"Marv, shut up." That was one of the great things about having a stellar academic background at a time like this. What was the worst they could do to her? Send her back to an Ivory Tower where she'd teach, oh, maybe two classes a week, and take a sabbatical every six or seven years? "I do *not,*" echoing his emphasis, "have to put up with this kind of abuse. Not from you. Not from her. She was ordering me to say things that weren't remotely accurate. You can ask Nicci, she was there."

"You mean the sex-u-al har-as-ser?" Marv sounded like he was savoring every syllable. "Alicia says that she's filing a sexual harassment complaint against your producer, who didn't like having her aggressive lesbo advances rejected by a married colleague. Nicci's days are numbered."

"Did you say 'lesbo,' Marv? Did you actually use that epithet?"

"So what?"

"For the record, I don't know what Alicia's marital status is, and I don't see that it's even relevant, but I do know that this morning Alicia was the one reaching across the table to hold Nicci's hand. And it was Nicci who told her to bugger off when Alicia tried to bulldog me."

"What are you accusing her of?" Marv shouted. "She's been around longer than you and Nicci combined. You should just shut the fuck up and do your job. Do you hear me?"

"Marv, you stepped way over the line with the very first words you said to me, and now you're totally blowing it. I'm not staying in the Maldives under these circumstances."

"Then leave. *Now.*"

"I've already made that decision on my own, but there's one thing I want to leave you with, while it's still on my mind. I had my recorder hooked to the phone during your diatribe because I'd been doing an interview with Senator Higgens, and everything you just said, you know, 'lesbo,' 'shut the fuck up,' all of it, Marv, is on a neat little disk that I intend to play for James Elfren and anybody else on the eighth floor who's interested in hearing it."

Silence. Then *click*.

Then a smile: Jenna had lied, but how could Marv know? She figured that he had assumed the worst. And why? Because the worst was what *he* would have done, if he'd been in her shoes.

Right then Jenna realized that her reporter's instincts were getting sharper by the second.

Adnan stared at a sapphire ring on the Shopping Channel and turned up the sound. It was the only broadcast he could find that wasn't showing the tanker takeover—and he desperately needed a diversion from the horrors of the wheelhouse. So . . . he locked his eyes on the scantily clad Western women with big breasts and baubles. But what else could a pious Muslim do? The Waziristani had pried open the captain's hand with dire threats to the man's privates—acted out with a shocking *snip-snip* of the wire cutters—and then clipped off his index finger, which took gritty seconds to complete and left the captain screaming and bleeding on the floor. The jihadist had thrown a white towel at

Adnan and gestured with his hands for him to mop up and stanch the wound. Adnan had had to wrestle with the captain, who thrashed around a great deal, which was remarkable, considering that he was still trussed with his hands tied behind his back to his feet. The position left the poor man arched in the shape of a . . . crescent. But eventually Adnan had pressed the towel to the man's swollen, bloody hand.

Bad as all that was, Adnan had just seen the old newsman drink from a bottle of liquor that the Waziristani, a *jihadist,* had given him. Satan's nectar! Surely, Muhammad, peace and blessings of Allah be upon Him, would condemn such a wicked practice. How could a self-professed Islamist commit such a grievous sin? The only explanation possible was that he truly was an American. Maybe even CIA.

Once more, Adnan had to turn away from the old man. His Adam's apple bobbed hideously each time he swallowed from the bottle, and every few minutes he took another big gulp.

Reaching into his vest, Adnan pulled out the two wires that could put an end to this sacrilege. All he needed to do was rip off the plastic caps and bring the wires together.

Booze for Birk. Booze for Birk. The old correspondent could have sung that ditty all day long and added endless lines (*Then he'll work. Then he'll work . . .*). He felt so good he could have danced, too—the tango, mambo, and a tarantella! And romanced the Queen Mother, dead as she was, and her entire entourage while he was at it.

To be finally himself again, slightly tipsy but no longer shaking. To feel every bit as debonair as he believed he looked, despite having not one but two chopped-off fingers hanging from his shirt.

He glanced down, eyes steady, hands steady, delighted to see those free-swinging digits still as a Monday morning belfry. They'd done all the sh-sh-shaking they were going to do. As long as he could control himself and not drink too much, he'd weather this storm. No problem. *The fate of the world, boys. And ol' Birk's got 'er under control. He's just going to have himself another sip or two, that's all, to tide him over, wet the whistle, kiss the sky.* Yes, Birk wanted little more than that nice steady-state incipient inebriation that had served him so well for nigh fifty years now. But damn, hadn't "another sip or two" always done him in, in the end?

At that moment he caught a disconcerting glimpse of his reflection on one of the sonar screens in the wheelhouse. Those fingers from hell pulled down his shirt on one side, which made him look disheveled, shiftless. The sight of his whiskers made him think he'd better shave soon or he'd end up looking like his old acquaintance Yasser Arafat. These Islamists made him nostalgic for that bombastic fart.

The more he looked, the more he realized those fingers looked monstrous and cruel, *insane,* like something Idi Amin might have sported at a Ugandan state dinner—where the meat was always of questionable provenance.

But as Birk's exuberance ebbed, it wasn't the thumb and index finger on his shirt that alarmed him most, and it certainly wasn't his pointer, newly tucked away. It was the finger that Raggedy Ass was smearing with blood right now, and straightening by clamping the wire cutters on it. Leaving it bizarrely erect. Birk dearly wished he hadn't.

"Ah, Birk," Raggedy Ass said with good ol' boy familiarity, "you are something else."

Yeah, I sure am. But when Birk stared at his middle finger, his "fuck you" finger boldly challenging the world, he felt a reinvigorating rush of defiance.

Senator Higgens trundled to the elevator with a throbbing headache. No question, she'd had too much to drink last night, but had she said too much to that persnickety, white bread meteorologist?

Dear God, spare me every last one of your true believers, and deliver me to cynicism, blight, and the most sorely begotten. Amen.

Sheesh, her mood was foul.

In the restaurant, she collapsed into a seat at a table for four. A waiter hurried over with a carafe and poured coffee.

"I look like I need it that bad, huh, bubba?" He didn't reply. Maybe "bubba" was an unknown in these here parts. Maybe her eyes, red as wild roses, were enough to silence him. But enough to keep her quiet? Not with the need she had: "Give me a bloody Mary, too."

Her tired eyes rose to the huge screen on the wall of the lobby, but her grimace quickly turned to a smile wide as the ocean blue when she spied Rick Birk's bloody bandage.

Yes, yes, yes. Another one of his worthless fingers had been chopped off and hung from his shirt. *Whoopee.*

But what made Higgens laugh so hard that she almost sprayed coffee all over the white tablecloth was the finger that hadn't been clipped yet, but that was, deliciously enough, next in line: his middle finger, and it stood straight as an English guard.

Well, fuck you back, Birk, Higgens chortled to herself, mirth overwhelming her once again, along with the realization that no hair of the dog—the bloody Mary had arrived—could ever equal the undistilled spirits of revenge.

"I'm coming home," Jenna told Dafoe. She'd packed her bags after Marv had hung up, then given herself a couple of minutes to catch her breath before calling her guy.

She reclined on a chaise lounge with a creamy iced coffee. In a few minutes she'd have to leave for the airport, and she wanted to use the time to enjoy the view, the brew, and her boyfriend. Nicci already had booked them on a commercial flight. Jenna was fine with that, realizing that her days of chartered Gulfstream jets—and outsize carbon footprints—had likely begun and ended with her trip to the Maldives.

"Today? That's great news," Dafoe said. "It *is* great news, isn't it?" he added tentatively.

"Yes, definitely. I won't numb you with details now, but I don't think I was cut out for the news end of the business, not the way Marv and a certain unmentionable producer do it." Nicci came over, holding up her laptop so Jenna could see an e-mail. "Marv just sent a message saying that Nicci and I have been suspended from *The Morning Show.* Whatever that means. Probably that we're fired."

"The other networks will be bidding for you."

"Maybe for Nicci, but I'm starting to think that I might be better off taking a position at a college. One thing I'll tell you is that I'm not taking this lying down. I've got a call in to Marv's boss."

"I don't care where you end up, as long as it's here a good part of the time."

"So it's okay if I come directly from JFK to your place?"

"Are you kidding? Need a ride?"

"No, you keep your eyes on those cows, and I'll grab a cab to Penn Station and take the train up."

Rafan strolled onto the balcony with a carafe of iced coffee as Jenna hung up. He poured her a refill and perched on the end of the lounge. She caught his smile and remembered why she'd fallen in love with him ten years ago. He looked so exotic and handsome, and when his hand settled on her foot, she felt a familiar tingle, but it was from far away and long ago, and the distance—and Dafoe—had weakened its force.

"Are you going to be okay?" she asked him.

He nodded. "Bilal called this morning. The rest of Senada's brothers are willing to talk to me."

"Is that safe?"

"I trust him. He say it's okay, that they know things are going wrong with our country and Islam. It's crazy. So we'll talk. If I can get them to understand why Senada is dead, I can go to the mosque. Then maybe I can get others to listen, too. We're peaceful people, we don't deserve this violence."

Jenna took his hands. "Rafan, you're so brave. News teams get to take off when the story's done. But you have to stay behind and work out all the disagreements and arguments." She looked at the sea. "There's not a lot of room to get away from people here, is there?"

"No. And it's getting smaller all the time," he laughed.

"Don't joke," she chided him gently. "This is serious."

"I know, and I'm a survivor. I want my people to survive, and we won't if we don't stand up to the Islamists." He looked away and cleared his throat. "I've lost Basheera and Senada, but everybody is going to lose someone if things don't change." He stood up. "I should let you go. I've got to go, too. So little dirt, so little time." He smiled once more, bent over, and kissed her. She smelled the sea air on his skin and felt the tingle move to her lips.

"Be careful," she said.

"Travel well."

Minutes later, as she was also about to leave the balcony, her cell went off.

"Did you really record Marv without his knowledge?" James Elfren asked in his high-pitched voice, not bothering with a greeting of any kind.

"Record him? Of course not. Did he say that? That's bizarre." All's fair in love and network wars. "Why would he say that?"

"I don't know but he did. And he's really upset. Regardless, I take it that you two had quite a row."

"He was screaming at me, if that's what you mean. He was out of control. And he called Nicci a lesbo, which I—"

"I can't mediate this at a distance," Elfren cut in. "But is it correct that you and Alicia are also having difficulties?"

Jenna suddenly felt like the problem child. "That's why Marv called me, because of her. It's not like they're separate issues. She was trying to script me."

"She doesn't see it that way."

"You talked to her?" *Already?*

"Yes. I'm not assigning blame here, but to keep our coverage on track, I do think you and Nicci ought to—"

"We've already made the decision to come back. I would never stay here under these circumstances. We're booked to fly out in a couple of hours. Marv said that the two of us are suspended from the show."

"He might have overreacted."

"Did you tell him that?"

"Jenna, I really can't do this long distance. There's a lot of anger in the air. Come back, call me when you get some sleep, and we'll sort it out."

When he ended the call, Jenna found that Nicci had sidled up to her. "Not good news, I take it," the producer said.

"I don't know. Elfren says Marv might have overreacted with the suspension."

"Might have?" Nicci stomped her foot on the decking.

"And that Alicia's version is very different from mine. Not exactly a bulletin, that. I really wish I had a recording of her."

"I guess we better get ready to do battle when we get back there."

Jenna grabbed her bags and tried to gird herself for what was to come.

But nothing she'd heard from Marv or Elfren, or experienced first-hand with Alicia—and nothing she might have imagined happening on board the supertanker—could possibly have matched the murderous fury that awaited everyone on the other side of the world.

CHAPTER 22

A thick, funereal haze hung over New York City. From Jenna's window seat, she could catch only blurry views of the buildings and bridges below, gloomy glimpses that seemed to mirror the dim prospects of a planet under siege.

Inky waterways appeared as the Airbus descended, and daytime headlights glistened like glittery scales on the snakelike expressways that curled around JFK.

Jenna and Nicci were nearing the end of a full day of travel, sleeping when they weren't keeping abreast of developments in the Maldives. But gruesome as the tanker takeover was, Jenna worried even more about those North Korean rockets. She hadn't received a single call, text, or e-mail from Vice President Andrew Percy's office, despite having left messages twice during a two-hour layover in Dubai.

Nicci, who prided herself on being a "cat napper of the first degree," was shedding her blanket and awakening from her most recent snooze.

"Are you heading straight home?" Jenna asked. Nicci had a one-bedroom apartment in the West Village with more charm than half a dozen high rises in Midtown.

The weather producer nodded and yawned. "I'm planning on at least one day to chill after I call Mikey." Her agent, who looked as boyish as his name suggested, would soon go head-to-head with the suits on the eighth floor. Jenna had already texted her own agent, a former Marine who had issued his opening salvo within minutes of receiving her message.

"Keep your phone handy," Jenna said. "I'll let you know if I hear anything from Elfren or Percy." Though she was increasingly doubtful about the latter. Granted, the vice president was a key player in the cabinet, which had plenty on its plate, but in the IM age what would it take to text her? She was on his frickin' task force, after all. Meantime, the sulfate rockets in North Korea awaited a launch order from a leader widely regarded as a nutbar of the first order.

How does that happen? she asked herself. *How does a total demento get to the point where he can end the world?*

With a seat-jarring *thump* the jet touched down, and an hour later Jenna was in a taxi heading to Penn Station, bypassing her own apartment for a direct trip to Dafoe's arms.

The familiar smells of the city—not entirely unappealing with their kindred associations of home, excitement, and meteorology—greeted her in force as she fled into the station's bustling main concourse. She might not have noticed an Asian man in a black shirt and slacks if he hadn't had his eyes fixed so firmly on her.

Jenna let her vision glide right over him. She'd learned in her first few months on *The Morning Show* that any kind of eye contact could generate the exclamation, "You're Jenna Withers!" Her fans were the nicest people, but once she stopped to say hello, it was practically impossible to get moving again.

But the Asian man didn't look like the others. His gaze felt as sharp as a bone saw.

You're paranoid, she told herself as she stepped onto the down escalator. *Who's going to be tailing you here? They would have had to have been listening to your calls and reading your messages.*

But Jenna had developed a clear sense of how it felt to be watched. It happened everywhere she went. She'd never bemoaned this, but at the same time she'd never felt so baldly observed as she did at this very moment.

As she walked down the platform, she turned and swept her eyes intently over the crowd of afternoon commuters who were making an early getaway.

She boarded the same train that she'd taken on her first trip up to see Dafoe. Today, she anticipated her lover's lair even more keenly, the memory of their frantic lovemaking suddenly as fresh as her feelings of longing.

Lost in reverie, Jenna idly scanned the platform. That's when she spotted the Korean's purposeful gait. She did not look at him directly, but from the corner of her eye she tracked his progress toward her train until he disappeared into the car behind her. She particularly noted how his gaze moved over the windows, including the one that framed her unmistakable face.

She didn't think he'd spotted her. His eyes never lingered, and Jenna had an urge to slip off the train and make a run for it. Or stay and call the NYPD.

And then what? she scolded herself. *Tell them that a Korean caught your eye at Penn Station, and then caught the same train you're on—along with hundreds of other people? That's not even a coincidence. That really is paranoia. How idiotic would that sound on Page Six?*

But the scolding she gave herself didn't ease the eerie sense of eyes boring into the back of her head. In seconds, hairs on the nape of her neck sprang up, a sensation so uneasy that she tried to press them back down, but those pushy little Cassandras would not lie still for long.

Jenna looked back several times, but never saw the Asian man. An hour north of the city, she called Dafoe, catching him at his computer.

She greeted him warmly, then quickly told him what she'd been experiencing. "I feel silly," she added sheepishly.

"Trust your feelings," he responded. "At times like this, that old reptilian brain of ours can protect us from the animals still out there. Sounds like your brain is sending you a warning and then some."

278 | BILL EVANS

Words that brought to mind the almost preternatural awareness that she'd once had of a bear in the Colorado Front Range—confirmed when her group's guide pointed out the critter's unmistakable scat, and seconds later noted a grizzly across a broad glen.

But this creature had left no trace—except for those recalcitrant hairs.

The train pulled into another station. Four more stops and she'd be with Dafoe. "I'll feel a whole lot better just seeing you."

He assured her that he'd be waiting.

She hung up and looked around, then impulsively stepped off the train to see if the Korean followed her, only to find him on the platform, looking quickly away from her.

With a torpedoed stomach, she moved back on board.

"Are you okay?" a conductor asked her.

She nodded before telling herself not to be such a hero. "I think I'm being followed by a Korean man in the car behind us."

"That guy?" The conductor nodded at the man, who was walking away from the train as purposefully as he had hurried to it only an hour ago. She felt so ridiculous that she blushed. "Sorry. That's him and he's clearly got more important things on his mind than me. I'm really sorry."

"Hey, that's fine," the conductor said. "And I like the way you do the weather. Been missing you the last few mornings."

"Thanks. I'm coming back from a long trip and I think I need to get some sleep."

The final leg of the train trip felt interminable. Her worry lightened only when she spotted Dafoe on the platform, looking as scrubbed and cheerful as he'd appeared only a few weeks ago. His appearance reminded her of how disheveled she felt from a full day of travel. But she hugged him unabashedly. Then they embraced, and she didn't care, in their fiercely rekindled passion, that a busybody with a cellphone might be shooting video of her and planning a YouTube entry called "Weather Woman Kisses Up a Storm."

As their lips separated, she realized, astonished, that Dafoe was "the one." She'd never felt that way before, not with Rafan, not with anyone. *But why would you have,* she asked herself, *if he's really "the one"? You had to wait and now he's here.*

He took her suitcase, and as they turned to leave the wooden plat-form, Jenna spotted another Korean man. Like the guy who'd gotten off the train a few stops earlier, he was dressed in black. *Like they've got uniforms.* She squeezed Dafoe's hand in panic.

With a glance of his own, Dafoe took note and led her to his pickup. She slid to the middle seat and buckled up, watching the Korean open the rear passenger door of a black Expedition with smoked windows.

Coincidence? she asked herself, and then Dafoe.

"We'll keep an eye on them. Forensia and Sang-mi *might* have been followed yesterday by Koreans in a RAV4."

"I hate even talking like this." As she spoke, the black SUV pulled away. "And thar she goes," Jenna said. "Okay, that's it, I'm just going to chill." She wrapped her arms around his shoulders and took a great big breath of him, smiling at the faintly sweet scent of hay and sunshine that rose from his skin and clothes.

"You want to hear the latest on the GreenSpirit case, or do you want to take a break from that, too?" Dafoe asked, checking his side view before driving off.

"No, tell me. What's up?"

"They arrested a kid for the murder."

"A kid? Who?"

"A high school senior named Jason Robb. The team quarterback. They got him yesterday."

"Why do they think he did it? Did they say?"

"He threatened Forensia and the other Pagans on the night that she was initiated. Which was the night before GreenSpirit was murdered."

"Do you think he did it?"

"The cops do. The sheriff found a bandana of Jason's with Green-Spirit's blood on it. The FBI lab confirmed it." He rested his hand on Jenna's leg. "I don't mean to alarm you but that car is behind us now, and it left the station before we did."

"Don't go to your place," she said right away. "It's too isolated." She adjusted the rearview mirror, as if she were checking her lipstick or hair, and saw the hulking SUV about six car lengths back. "Let's head to town, and if they follow us, let's go right to the sheriff's office."

Dafoe executed a quick turn on to a narrow country road. "Are they following us?" he asked Jenna, who still had the rearview.

"No, they kept going straight."

"We might be okay."

But Jenna felt jumpy and hoped like hell that Dafoe knew where the tight country lane would take them.

He made a series of turns that led them back to the road to his farm. He reached over and took the mirror, adjusting it and assuring her that he'd keep his eyes open for the Expedition.

Jenna nodded and tried to breathe, but it wasn't easy. Those hairs on the back of her neck were making their prickly presence known again.

Dafoe slowed and entered the long driveway to his house. Seconds later, he said, "They're still here," with no attempt to hide his uneasiness.

"What?" Jenna twisted around, expecting to see the Expedition churning up a tunnel of dust behind them.

"I'm sorry. I meant Forensia and Sang-mi. You thought I meant that black car?"

"No apologies necessary. But you did sound worried."

"Just disappointed," Dafoe said. "They told me that they'd be done with their work and gone so we could have some privacy."

Privacy would have been nice, but at this moment Jenna was happy just to feel safe.

The feeling didn't last long. When they reached the porch, they saw Forensia sitting by the window with Dafoe's rifle in her hands and Sang-mi by her side. Bayou rose gingerly, wagging his tail.

They hurried inside. "What's going on?" Dafoe asked. "And give me that rifle. You're making me nervous."

Forensia handed it over. "You shouldn't be worried about me making you nervous." She spoke with her eyes still on the driveway. "You should be worried about the big, black SUV that was here right after you left. It was idling out on the road when I saw it."

Dafoe and Jenna shared a quick glance. "An Expedition?" Jenna asked.

Forensia shrugged. "I don't know. All I can say is that it was big and had dark windows, and it was the second one in two days."

Dafoe peered at the driveway. "How'd you even see it all the way down on the road?"

"That damn calf we spend half our time chasing got out of the pasture again, and we ended up having to go get him. He got all the way down to those trees near the road. I saw the car when I caught up with the calf."

"Did they see you?"

"Maybe. I grabbed the little pain in the ass and dragged him back before he got out in the open. But they could have seen me; I wasn't thinking about hiding when I went down there. Why? Did you guys see it, too?"

"Yeah, we did," Dafoe said. "At the station. I guess they made you plenty nervous." He glanced at his rifle.

"After being followed yesterday? Yeah, I'm starting to get anxious, you bet."

"The one we saw kept going straight after we turned," Jenna said.

Sang-mi shrieked and pointed. Everyone stared down the long driveway. The Expedition was coming, whipping up dust like a precisely plotted hurricane. Dafoe thrust the rifle into Jenna's hands, raced into the kitchen, and returned with the pistol that he kept stashed in a cabinet.

"This is a pathetic amount of firepower, so let's get out of here *now*," he shouted.

He led them out on the far side of the house, and they raced to a copse about two hundred feet away, Bayou hobbling till Dafoe scooped him up. They heard all four doors of the SUV slam as they stumbled through the patch of forest. Dusk was claiming the land like a looter.

"Assassins," Sang-mi said sharply.

"This way," Dafoe ordered. In less than sixty seconds, he brought them to a dry stream. Jenna had her cell out for a 911 call.

"Tell them to come with sirens, lights, everything," Dafoe said breathlessly.

Jenna spoke in a voice muffled by danger. The 911 operator coolly collected the information. "Please hurry," Jenna pleaded before snapping the cell shut.

Night fell quickly, as it always seemed to after Halloween, when daylight behaves like it's too scared to breathe. The four of them ran through a stand of birch trees, stopping at the edge of an open field.

"Where are they?" whispered Jenna, ears straining beyond the hard exhalations that rose around her. She eyed a spot about fifty yards back, the way she'd once studied brush for grouse and pheasants when she'd been a young girl hunting with her father. She'd always enjoyed the shooting, but the blood and gore of gutting had proved repulsive. And she'd been gunning for game, not people. *Who are chasing you.*

Jenna spotted unmistakable movement behind thick vegetation studded by tall trees—and heard a hard, metallic, snapping sound. Were they trapped by men already creeping around them, closing in from the sides? But if the four of them ran, they'd lose even the spotty cover of narrow-trunked trees. Behind them stood only that clearing.

"We can't go any farther," she whispered.

"I know," Dafoe agreed.

They would make a stand here. *To fight assassins? Isn't that what Sang-mi called them?* Even thinking this made Jenna feel surreal, like she was living somebody else's life.

A loud *crack* froze her thoughts. A bullet snapped a tree limb several feet away and it crashed to the ground. Sang-mi started to bolt. Jenna grabbed her. "No," she whispered. "They're trying to flush us out." Bullets like bird dogs.

Without warning, Bayou barked. Dafoe grabbed his jaw to silence him, but the damage was done and a fusillade exploded. From the muzzle flashes, it looked like half a dozen weapons had unloaded on them.

Bullets ripped into trees or shrieked past. Jenna, crouching, figured that their assailants were shooting blind. Not missing by much, though. *And all we've got is this thing?* She looked at the varmint rifle in her hands. *And a pistol?*

She aimed and waited for another flash, then fired back with the small caliber rifle, knowing that she'd have to pierce a vital organ to bring down an attacker. *At least they know we've got guns,* though from their cautious approach the shooters must have assumed that the four of them were armed.

Dafoe put Bayou on the ground with another command to be quiet, then rose up and aimed into the darkness. When the next shots erupted, he also fired back.

A distant siren reached them, faint at first, but growing steadily louder. The incoming ceased.

Jenna tried to hear whether their assailants were fleeing, but the sirens were so shrill that they blocked any other sound. Then the Expedition's headlights arced across a pasture to their left. The vehicle turned into the field and raced down its gentle slope, speeding past them about a hundred feet away. Jenna and Dafoe both opened fire on it. She guessed that they hit their target, but their light weaponry sure hadn't stopped it.

"Is there a road down there?" Jenna had to shout above the sirens drawing ever nearer.

"Yeah," Dafoe shouted back. "There's an old wooden gate."

Seconds later, they heard the gate shatter. The SUV's headlights rose and fell three times in swift succession as it bounded onto a cattle path.

Dafoe watched and said, "I was hoping they'd lose at least one headlight. Make them easier to track."

They began to work their way back to Dafoe's farmhouse, moving cautiously in case one of the attackers had stayed behind or left them an explosive "gift." Side by side, weapons raised, Jenna and Dafoe took the lead. She found the sirens increasingly distressing because they blocked every other noise.

Only as they inched closer to the house did they find the sheriff's presence helpful. His Bronco's headlights tore a wedge in the night, but revealed little more than cow pies and hoofprints.

Tossing aside caution, they raced toward Sheriff Walker and the New York State Police officer who stood beside him. Everyone started talking at once. The sheriff hushed them with a wave. "One at a time, please," he said, as if they had all night.

Dafoe went first, telling them about the firefight and the escape of the SUV. The sheriff stopped him quickly.

"You engaged in a gunfight with those fools?" He took Dafoe's rifle from Jenna and sniffed it, as if he didn't believe what he'd just heard.

"I'll get out an APB," the state policeman said.

"You do that," Walker replied, amazing Jenna with how much condescension one man could squeeze into three simple words.

"Going to be tough at night to nab anything on the New York State Thruway, assuming that's where they went," the sheriff added. "Anything notable about that vehicle that you can tell me?"

Dafoe replied that it had crashed through a wooden gate. "But both headlights were still working."

"It might have bullet holes on the driver's side," Jenna volunteered.

The sheriff took a detailed report and suggested that they find somewhere else to spend the night.

Where? Jenna wondered. "Can you give us protection?"

"Protection?" he asked, as if she'd made the most absurd suggestion in memory. "My budget's been cut three times in the past three years by the State Assembly. I don't even have a deputy anymore. I can call the feds in the morning and see if they can spare anyone, but I wouldn't hold my breath—I'd find somewhere safe and go there. Give me a ring tomorrow."

Is this what we've come to? Jenna wondered. *We can't even protect our citizens?*

The sheriff and state policeman did pore over the grounds with flashlights, and found where the Expedition had flattened grass in the pasture, but no useful tire tracks turned up until they came across a cow patty with a distinct tread pattern.

After they left, Jenna, Dafoe, Forensia, Sang-mi, and Bayou trooped into Dafoe's house. He locked the door behind them. Jenna looked out a window, worried about other dangers the darkness might hold. Chills climbed her spine. She turned to Sang-mi and Forensia. "Why were they trying to kill us?"

"You have to tell them," Sang-mi said to Jenna.

"Tell who what?" Jenna asked impatiently. "I want to know why they're trying to kill *us*. If they are North Korean agents, you'd think they'd have bigger fish to fry."

"They're trying to kill *you*." Sang-mi stared at Jenna. "That's why they didn't do anything till you got back. They know that you can tell the world about the rockets. GreenSpirit said you will do that."

"I can't tell anyone about anything: I've been suspended from the show. And besides, I'm not about to go on air and start spouting because a dead Pagan witch supposedly said so. That's just—"

"It is true," Sang-mi said. "My father knows about them."

"Then our government also knows about the rockets, right? Because he's being debriefed by the CIA."

"Then why are *we* getting attacked?" Dafoe sounded honestly bewildered. "It could be because of you, Sang-mi. You said that they go after family members, too."

The Korean nodded.

"Maybe because something else is also happening," Forensia said. "That's what GreenSpirit is saying, in a way."

"Oh, please," Jenna said. "Can we at least agree not to quote conversations with the dead?" Her cell phone rang before she could say anything more: UNKNOWN NUMBER appeared on the screen. She answered with a brisk hello.

A voice asked her to hold for Vice President Andrew Percy. Jenna pressed the phone closer to her ear and walked away from her companions, who looked at her curiously but fell silent.

"This is Vice President Percy," she heard a moment later. "I haven't been able to get back to you till now. My apologies."

"That's okay," Jenna said. "I understand. I just wanted to make sure that you knew about the rockets in North Korea that are loaded with sulfates."

Silence.

Jenna soldiered on. "The rockets are designed to explode in the stratosphere. The North Koreans are planning to bring years of winter to the whole planet in retaliation against the U.S. And other countries, too," she added hastily.

"Where did you hear that?" The vice president made no attempt to hide his incredulity.

"From an impeccable source."

"I think you can dismiss your 'impeccable source' out of hand," he replied.

"Why, sir? With all due respect, it's a viable geoengineering technique. One of the simpler ones, in fact."

"Is that why you've been trying to track me down?" His tone turned harsh. Even though he was the vice president of the United States, Jenna bristled when she heard it.

"Yes, sir, that's exactly why I've been leaving messages. I guess you wouldn't mind me bringing it up on the air tomorrow," she said, trusting that he'd heard nothing about her suspension.

"I wouldn't say anything about any rockets," Percy said. "That kind of speculation can be very harmful."

"Not if it's just speculation." His response intrigued her because it didn't add up: If there were no threat from North Korea, telling a TV audience about the rockets would amount to no more than mindless media chatter. But if it were real—

The vice president interrupted her thoughts: "May I confide in you?"

"Yes, sir, by all means." Though Jenna didn't believe for a nanosecond that he would say anything of substance, she played along—and a moment later found out how wrong she could be:

"If you breathe a word about any of this, you're going to end up in a supermax for a long, long time," Percy said.

A heavily fortified federal prison? What's going on? "Why are North Koreans trying to kill me?" she asked.

"Trying to kill you?"

Jenna thought he snorted with derision. She quickly told him what had happened.

"And you've reported this, you say, to the police?"

"That's right."

"Did you say anything about North Korea or rockets to them?"

Curious that he was back to that again. "No, I did not."

"Remember what I said: a supermax." He hung up.

Jenna forced herself to take a big breath before turning to the others, who had listened to her every word.

"The vice president?" Dafoe asked.

She nodded. "And he just threatened me with a long stay in a super-max, if I said a word about the rockets."

"You *have* to tell people," Sang-mi said.

"Stop saying that," Jenna snapped, "and just let me just think." She turned back to Dafoe. "What worries me is I can't stop thinking about bin Laden. For years before 9/11 he threatened the U.S., blamed us for everything. He even had the North Tower bombed in '93. There were people in government trying to get the attention of the White House and the defense agencies, trying to go through all the proper channels, and no one listened until those goddamn planes slammed into the towers and killed three thousand people."

"The Koreans are going to kill the whole world," Forensia said.

Jenna nodded. "North Korea's leader is doing the same thing bin Laden did," she said. "He's blaming the U.S. and threatening us because of his country's droughts and famine, climate change and—"

"He's got a point there," Forensia said.

"No!" Jenna said furiously. "I won't give that bastard even that much. You can't let psychos like him justify *anything* because that becomes a way of their justifying *everything,* even rockets that would end the world."

Jenna sat heavily on Dafoe's couch. "You know what I think? I think Percy just confirmed everything that Sang-mi's been saying." Jenna stared at the young Korean woman, who said nothing, perhaps sensing that the ground had shifted in her favor.

"I remember you saying," Dafoe nodded at Jenna, "that in your book you wrote about how North Korea likes to piggyback on crises whenever they can. You look at the situation in the Maldives, and it's hard to imagine that they'll ever find a bigger crisis to jump on than that tanker."

"There's another reason the North could be moving now," Jenna said. "Because if you're going to be doing something against us, what better time to do it than on election day."

"You're right," Dafoe said.

"You wait till everybody goes to the polls, and then you launch," Jenna added. She pulled out her phone and called Nicci, catching her on the second ring. In a voice as bright and casual as cotton candy, Jenna asked Nicci to meet her at the Shaughn Hotel at five the next morning.

"The Shaughn? Really?" Nicci said.

"I can't go back to my apartment."

"What's up?"

"Can you trust me till then?" Jenna asked.

"You know I can."

"See you. I'll be registered under Dafoe's last name, Tillian."

Jenna looked at Dafoe's rifle and pistol. "Are these all the guns you have?"

"That's it. Up till now, all I've been fighting are coyotes."

"Let's grab whatever ammunition you've got and hope for the best, because I've got a nasty feeling that we're going to be fighting animals a lot more dangerous and devious than coyotes."

"Are you going to tell everyone?" Sang-mi asked.

"If I can get on the air, I'll say plenty. But that's a big 'if' because I've been suspended."

"We may have bigger problems than that," Dafoe said with a telling glance at the dark world outside.

Jenna nodded and grabbed the pistol. "Let's head down to the city. We're sure not spending the night here."

CHAPTER 23

Jenna sat in the front passenger seat of Forensia's rattly, rusty Subaru wagon with the rifle held tightly in her hands. Forensia had gladly surrendered the driving duties to Dafoe; his truck, with a single bench seat, could never have held the four of them. Riding shotgun, Jenna constantly searched their surroundings as Dafoe drove cautiously down a series of country roads before merging onto the New York State Thruway.

Forensia and Sang-mi huddled in the backseat and kept their heads down. They might not have been sure whether the drive south was safer than trying to hide in town, but they'd cast their lot with Jenna and Dafoe, and there was no looking back—except to check if they were being followed.

Dry lightning cleaved the night sky to the west, an atmospheric sideshow that did little to ease the tension in the car, though the threat paled compared to the real danger of a highway shootout. But the trip was unavoidable if they were to get Jenna to the set of *The Morning*

Show early on election day. She held the rifle firmly and her finger never strayed far from the trigger.

Every pair of headlights that overtook the old Subaru felt like a mortal threat, and when a large vehicle raced onto the highway behind them just after they passed a rest area, Jenna could feel everyone stiffen with dread. Dafoe used the mirrors to track the car's rapid approach. Forensia turned around, gasping, "It's a big black SUV," repeating the very words she'd used to describe the black Expedition that she'd first spotted idling by Dafoe's driveway.

But this three-ton behemoth sprinted by so fast that it almost blew their doors off. It had to be doing a hundred and twenty, hardly the low-key profile of a vehicle packed with foreign assassins scouring the thruway for three Americans and the daughter of a North Korean defector.

"Would it bother you if I put on some news?" Jenna asked Dafoe.

"That's fine. Go for it."

"I'm hoping to hear a bulletin that a car full of Asians has just been apprehended."

No such news, but it didn't take long before they heard a headline about the tanker takeover, followed by a reporter's breathless warning about how a world catastrophe could be unleashed "at any second" in the Maldives.

From breathy to boozy—Rick Birk's voice filled the car: "Live from the heart of the hoth-stidge taking over on the than-ker *Dick Cheney*."

Birk sounded drunk to Jenna, though she could hardly imagine that he'd scrounged cocktails from gun-wielding jihadists. Maybe he was exhausted, or frightened half to death. Still, he was definitely slurring his words: "Ther-ists demanding fast, fast action. You hear me? Ther-ists want it fast." Then she heard a loud *bang,* like he'd pounded a table for emphasis.

Christ, he sounds belligerent. Maybe he is wasted.

"How well do you know that guy?" Dafoe asked, keeping his eyes on the road, the rearview, and everywhere else at once, it seemed.

"Not very. He chewed me out the only time I ever talked to him. It was so offensive that I hung up on him. Then he tried to apologize, but I never took his calls. After that, he got taken 'hoth-stidge.'" She giggled, couldn't help herself. "I shouldn't be joking about an old guy who's had three fingers chopped off," although it did feel good, amid all the worry, to experience a few seconds of relief, "but he's a real creep. I haven't met anyone who likes him."

Dafoe listened closely to the radio. "Maybe he's drinking himself to death. He sounds really plastered. If he's found some booze, he'll be lucky if they don't chop off his head next."

Birk could sniff out a purebred teetotaler in less time than it took him to knock back a Manhattan and suck down the damn cherry, and Suicide Sam hadn't *ever* had a drink. *I want his liver,* Birk thought, *when the time comes.*

Raggedy Ass had nodded off, so Birk had tried several times to get Suicide Sam to wrap some tape around the captain's mouth to shut . . . him . . . the . . . fuck . . . up, but this jihadist either didn't understand English or didn't care.

For chrissakes, that weasel's still whining. It's only three fucking fingers, pussy. I should be the one whining, putting up with your bullshit. Your goddamn fingers stink like gefilte fish, and I'm the one stuck with them on my shirt? I'll never get these goddamn stains out. We get out of this jam and you're getting the cleaning bill, buddy.

Birk felt that he had serious grounds to feel so aggrieved. Weasel mouth had tried to bite him—that's right, *bite* him—when Birk stepped over his head on the way to the facilities. That did it. Birk whipped out the old avenger and tried to pee on him—give the sourpuss a serious dose of humiliation—before Raggedy Ass pushed him toward the head.

"Fucker needs a muzzle," Birk said to the cracker jihadist after he'd drained the lizard.

"Tha's lack the pot callin' the ol' kettle black," Raggedy Ass drawled, treating Birk to more of his twisted Southern tongue.

Ye gods, get me away from these people. Birk hadn't been able to stomach crackers in the States—*Why should I, of all people, have to suffer fools gladly?*—and he'd seen no evidence that transplanting them to Muhammad's sacred soil had done anything to improve the bizarre species festering on the murky side of the Mason-Dixon Line.

Birk eyed the captain, knowing that he should be grateful that the fucker hadn't bled to death. Dying, Birk had seen, did nasty things to fingers—curled them up like croissants. Made them goddamn near as crusty, too. *You learn all kinds of shit as a reporter.* That could get Raggedy Ass searching for a new supplier of fingers. Even seeing double, Birk couldn't come up with any potential donors but Suicide Sam and himself. And Sam over there, with his fucking bomb, had a little more clout—in every sense of the word—than Birk.

Speaking of Sam, the bottle of Johnnie Walker was damn near empty, so Birk waved it around to give him a heads-up that the talent needed a new one. But he did it off camera. Least he was pretty sure he'd done it off camera. Maybe not. *Who gives a flying turd? Look at me.* Birk waved the bottle at Sam again and mouthed, *"Go get a goddamn refill, asshole."*

Sam wasn't moving. Birk stared into the tiny computer camera, glanced at Raggedy Ass snoring contentedly on the other side of the wheelhouse, and covered the lens with his bandaged hand.

"Get me another one," he growled at Suicide Sam, *"now."*

Birk swallowed the last of Johnnie Walker's best and threw the bottle at Sam, underhanded. Easy catch, but instead of grabbing the goddamn thing and doing what he was told, Sam jumped aside like it was a bomb. The bottle crashed to the deck and shattered. When the jihadist looked up from the broken glass, Birk made the "hurry-hurry" motion with his unbandaged hand, palm up, fingers waving. A little impatient, perhaps, but given the Job-like challenges Birk was facing, he felt that he'd offered the cretin a pretty forgiving gesture. But goddamn, the "hurry-hurry" didn't move Sam a wee bit, so Birk flipped him off. And when that didn't do the trick, he gave him one more universally understood hand signal: He slid his index finger across his throat.

It never occurred to Birk that threatening to murder a suicide bomber was among the world's most ill-advised acts. And now Raggedy Ass was arising, no doubt shaken from his slumber by the bottle breaking. He glared at Birk.

But Suicide Sam didn't spare the aged eminence so much as a

glance, returning his eyes to the Shopping Channel and a particularly alluring pair of zirconium earrings.

It was almost 5:00 A.M. and still dark when the dilapidated Subaru rattled up to the elegant entrance of the Shaughn Hotel on the city's West Side, which felt marginally safer to Jenna than returning to her apartment. Seeing the dilapidated car, the hotel's doorman started to wave them on—then recognized Jenna climbing out of the front seat. He hurried to open her door. She left the rifle behind.

"We're keeping the keys and leaving the car right there where you can keep an eye on it," Jenna said to the doorman. Nicci would be showing up in an hour and there wasn't a moment to spare.

He shook his head. "Maybe for a few minutes, but no longer. The owner"—real estate magnate Daniel Straub, who was reputed to have pretensions so grand that they trumped Trump's—"is not going to want this thing out here at all."

Jenna strode past him, stuffing a Benjamin into his neatly pressed navy blue jacket. "Take care of that car, and I'll take care of you again on my way out."

After checking into a well-appointed suite, Dafoe went to work on his laptop. She'd never seen him in hacker mode. His fingers flew over the keyboard so fast that he looked like a maestro on a baby grand, and she realized that he must have had a ton of RAM because she'd never seen a laptop with that much speed.

Jenna rushed into the bathroom, spending the next forty-five minutes showering and trying to make herself look professional enough that network security wouldn't bar her from the building.

When she stepped back into the main room, she saw Nicci arriving. Dafoe corralled the weather producer to review a long list of instructions he'd prepared for her. Jenna's phone rang, but she ignored it; let voice mail pick up. She sat next to Sang-mi on the couch.

After carefully going over the list, Dafoe told Nicci, "If you don't hear from us after *The Morning Show* has been on for fifteen minutes, *or* you don't see Jenna on the air talking about those rockets, then do everything on this page just the way you see it. This is critical."

"Don't worry about her," Jenna said, "she'll have us covered."

"What am I going to be hacking into?" Nicci asked.

"Let's just say that it's a widely viewed venue," Dafoe said. "But none of this will be traceable to you. And remember, this is a backup plan. You should do it only if Jenna doesn't make it onto the show."

"Right," Nicci said. "I understand. Now who *might* I be hacking?"

"Tell her," Jenna said. "She has a right to know."

"The White House Web site," Dafoe said.

"Whoa." Nicci smiled. "We're really making history here."

"I wish we didn't have to do this," Dafoe gave his computer a nod, "but if we do, you're right, this one's going to get remembered."

Minutes later, Jenna and Dafoe stepped onto the sidewalk. The Subaru was missing. "Where is it?" she asked the doorman.

"I couldn't stop the tow company. They've got a contract to tow away anything that looks 'unfit.' I tried to tell you. I even called up there but all I got was the message center. Here, this is their card. This is where they're taking it."

Jenna grabbed the business card and swore. Their weapons were on the way to a locked car compound in the Bronx.

"I'm really sorry," the doorman said.

"Jesus Christ, Dafoe. Look." Jenna glanced pointedly down the street. At a well-lit intersection three blocks away, a big black SUV loomed from behind a shiny silver Smart car.

"Cab?" Jenna cried out.

The doorman bolted to the street and blew his whistle loudly, as if to redeem himself.

A yellow cab, waiting at a nearby taxi stand, raced right up. Jenna and Dafoe piled in. She shouted out the address of *The Morning Show*'s studio, looked back, and saw the SUV a half block behind them, close enough to see that it had a dented grill.

She shoved a one hundred dollar bill into the tiny money tray in the Plexiglas shield that separated them from the driver, and shouted, "There's two more of those if you don't stop for anything."

"I take you," he said in deeply accented English, roaring away so fast that Jenna was slammed back into her seat.

"They're almost on top of us," Dafoe said.

Not quite: The Expedition was boxed in by the Smart car and an ancient, pale green Volkswagen Beetle. The SUV looked like Goliath as it rode the bumper of the Smart car. The Bug's bleary-eyed driver appeared oblivious to the aggressive tactics in the lane just to his left.

The cabbie, Korfa Waabberi Samatar, according to his prominently displayed license, raced down the streets like he'd been born in the Big Apple and knew its every rut and pothole, putting some distance between his vehicle and the boxed-in Expedition.

"Where are you from?" Jenna yelled.

"Mogadishu." Somalia. That explained his composure when, in the next few seconds, the Expedition grew wildly reckless.

First, the SUV's horn sounded a long, continuous blast. Then the big, black beast edged up against the Beetle, visibly startling the sleepy driver before ramming his fragile-looking car. The old Bug—a notoriously unstable model under the best of circumstances—flipped and rolled twice, narrowly missed by another hard-charging taxi two lanes over.

"Holy shit," Jenna whispered. She was beginning to feel like she'd landed in the middle of her own *Black Hawk Down*.

Seconds later, as the Expedition raced out from behind the diminutive Smart car, the beret-wearing sport at the wheel changed lanes. Perhaps *Monsieur* Smart car thought he was doing the tailgater a favor, but in a swift and cruel demonstration that no act of kindness goes unpunished, the Expedition plowed right into him without slowing. The Smart car tumbled like a die from the hand of a crazed gambler. Then a Nissan Stanza plowed into the roof of the Smart car, and both of those battered vehicles were smashed by other early morning drivers, resulting in an eleven-car pileup.

Jenna watched, stunned by the unraveling mayhem.

When the SUV was two car lengths back, a bullet shattered the taxi's rear window and glanced off the Plexiglas behind Korfa's gleaming bald head. Jenna and Dafoe dove below the firing line, though bullets ricocheting off the security glass could find them easily.

Jenna inched up, saw the Expedition gaining on them in the left lane.

"They're trying to kill us," she shouted to Korfa.

"No shit," he yelled back.

"Faster," she screamed.

Korfa shocked her by darting into the left lane. The SUV braked and smacked into a series of parked cars on the driver's side. A metallic screech filled the air. Jenna looked back to see the SUV rocking wildly on its wheels. The taxi was racing away at eighty-five miles an hour. *Nice move, Korfa.*

But the Expedition regained its legs quickly and accelerated powerfully. Jenna pulled out her cell. Dafoe stopped her, saying, "If you're calling 911, there are sirens all around us."

Squealing sirens—but no cop cars in sight yet. Their assailants were still roaring toward them. It looked like the Expedition was about to ram the cab. Korfa pressed the pedal to the metal and gained half a car length.

Jenna, fingers flying over the phone's keypad, yelled to Dafoe, "The police should know they're chasing a bunch of North Korean assassins." *They'll kill themselves to kill you. Wasn't that what Sang-mi said?*

"Turn left on Forty-ninth," Jenna shouted to Korfa. "There's an entrance halfway down on your right."

The cab slid sideways as the driver braked, whip tailed as he came out of the sudden turn, then shuddered, straightened, and sped down the street. Jenna finished yelling at the 911 operator and peeked out the passenger side window. She saw that Korfa was about to rip past the studio's entrance. "Stop," she bellowed.

He slammed on the brakes so hard that her face smacked into the Plexiglas. In her adrenaline rush, Jenna barely felt the impact. She jammed two more Benjamins into the tiny tray.

Dafoe dragged her out of the cab and the two of them sprinted toward the entrance. The cab peeled out as the SUV slid sideways to a stop, smashing its mangled grill into the side of a Town Car. An outraged chauffeur jumped out and started shouting at the men pouring out of the Expedition. They shot him twice in the head.

Jenna screamed, "Gunmen! Trying to kill us!" as she raced past the two stunned security guards who patrolled the entrance.

A second later, she heard another round of gunfire. A lot of it, and much closer. Gulping air, she and Dafoe burst through the metal door and careered off the lobby desk where Joe Santoro and Joe English screened all the building's visitors from behind bulletproof glass. She shouted "Killers!" at them, but with gunshots now flying at them from fifty feet away, Jenna's warning proved unnecessary.

The two Joes stepped to the side of the Plexiglas and fired at the darkly clothed men pouring into the lobby.

Jenna heard someone shout and turned to see that Dafoe had been hit in the back. He lay on his side with the wound blooming red.

"Go," he screamed in agony. "Get out of here."

Joe Santoro took a bullet to his shoulder that whipped him around so fast that he might have been dropped into a blender. He smashed into the white marble wall next to him and slid down it, leaving behind a long crimson smear. Dafoe rolled onto his back and his muscles went slack.

"Don't die. *Don't*," Jenna cried.

"Run," Joe English shouted. Then he ducked, and she caught a glimpse of the assassins gunning him down before she threw open a fire exit door and started lunging up the stairs.

Three flights. They rose like Everest before her. Her first steps were scorched by the certainty that she would be murdered any moment. As she made it to the second floor, the door below banged open, and she heard the sound of at least three, maybe four assassins racing up the stairs.

Gunshots crackled and bullets glanced off the concrete stairwell walls. Using the handrails, Jenna hauled herself up the steps as stony chips exploded inches from her head, almost blinding her with edges hard and sharp as shrapnel. She felt wetness on her face; when she swiped her hand across her cheek, it came away pink, and Jenna knew she was bleeding.

She dragged herself up the last flight of stairs. She wanted to get out of the stairwell, but she didn't dare use the second-floor exit. There was only minimal security on that level. One flight up—if she could make it—*The Morning Show* had armed guards. On her way to the city, Jenna had worried that the security detail for the set would keep her away from the cameras; now she hoped those guys would keep her from getting killed.

Her body felt brittle; her arms trembled from the strain of pulling herself up the final flight of stairs. The hours of fear and the long trip were all starting to take their toll. She heard the assassins gaining on her, heavy footfalls that shadowed Jenna with the darkest possibilities. If they gained a few more inches, they'd have a clear shot at her.

She jerked open the door for the third floor, racing through the opening as a shot zinged past her hip with a sizzling sound that fried her nerves. She could tell from her clouded vision that tears were washing down her cheeks, mixing with the streaks of blood from the concrete chips. She bolted directly through another metal door and down the long hallway that was lined with the photographs of network news stars. Gasping, frightened almost senseless, she ran as hard as she could and threw her shoulder into the door on the left that opened to the studio. As she plowed toward the set, she was dimly aware that the theme music for the show had started to play.

Andrea Hanson, who suddenly seemed far more pregnant than Jenna remembered, sat before one of the six precisely positioned studio cameras. She was beaming even more brightly than the lights that lit up her supremely radiant face.

In front of televisions all across the United States, viewers became aware of what was happening at the same moment Andrea did. The commotion drew her attention first, and she turned toward the noise. Viewers saw the shock on the anchor's face as Jenna Withers burst onto the set. What they didn't see were the makeup artists and hair stylists, the stage hands, the lighting and audio techs—more than two dozen people in all—gaping at Jenna's blood-streaked face.

Jenna stumbled in front of the camera that had been trained on Andrea. The startled operator had time to mumble only an incredulous "What?" before the first gunshots tore through the studio and sent everyone scrambling for shelter. The staff of the show had trained for an attack on the set—a dismal sign of the times—but procedures were forgotten in the rocketing terror unleashed by the gun blasts.

Andrea froze. Jenna grabbed her and pushed her toward a hallway. "Get out of here," Jenna shouted above the boiling madness.

Andrea fled, and Jenna turned back as the security team started firing at the North Koreans. She spotted at least four men in black clothes, and realized that with a full-fledged gun battle underway, she had no hope of getting on the air—and maybe even less chance of surviving if she didn't get out of there.

She backed away as fast as she could until she bumped into Marv, who was standing by the side of the set. It looked like he'd rushed down to see what was going on and, having found the horrifying answer, had stepped into a freeze frame. She grabbed her boss and pulled him down before he got himself shot.

"You're going to get killed," she said. "Leave." Which was what she intended to do post haste. But as she started crawling toward the hallway, a fusillade chewed up the floor no more than two feet ahead of her.

Rolling hard and fast back toward the set, she ducked behind the giant, paper-thin flat screen that the weather "map" appeared on. The screen extended from the top of the set to about two feet off the floor.

Jenna hunkered behind the corner where the tranquil climes of Southern California often appeared. Marv slipped under the bottom of the screen seconds later and pressed against her. "Get me out of here," he sputtered. "Get me out of here."

"Shush," she whispered.

Their flimsy refuge couldn't possibly save them; their feet protruded below the map, and Jenna guessed that no one, especially a single-minded assassin, could miss them. But the North Koreans were not the first to discover their hiding place—Geoff Parks was. Kato's handler was gunned down and fell to the floor not five feet from where Jenna and Marv hid. She spotted horrendous wounds to his arm and leg; blood flowed freely from his thigh, like an artery had been severed. He looked tortured by pain, jaw clenched so hard his teeth had to be cracking. Even so, he caught Jenna's eye and valiantly tried to push his gun toward her, though he was unable to move it more than an inch.

Where's Kato? Jenna wondered.

Parks tried to raise himself up with no greater success, then collapsed to the floor with a thud that Jenna heard over the crackling gunfire. She wondered how long the shooting had been going on, but had no idea. Thirty seconds? Three minutes? It seemed an eternity, more so when she saw another security guard taken down from behind by a knife-wielding Korean. Jenna closed her eyes, but not before she saw the blade slice into the man's throat.

She felt like she was awaiting her own execution, and Marv was still whining next to her. "Shut up," she hissed furiously. Then she realized that she could not remain unarmed in a studio rife with murder. She leaped toward Parks's gun and grabbed the semiautomatic, hoping the magazine was full.

Bullets ripped past her, chewing up the weather screen. Holes shattered the surface where Arizona bordered with Mexico, and she heard Marv crying. Jenna detected no pain in his desperate utterances, only panic.

Jenna rose with Parks's weapon gripped firmly in her hands. The corner of her eye caught movement, and she wheeled, ready to fire. A North Korean actually smiled as he turned his revolver from the weather map to her, aiming directly at her head.

But she had the jump on him and pulled the trigger. Nothing—the pistol wouldn't fire: She'd forgot to rack the slide on top of the barrel. The Korean's smile broadened, and she knew she was dead.

Frantically, she reached for the slide. As she did, a blur flashed in front of her—and Kato clamped his powerful jaws down on the assassin's arm so hard that Jenna heard the sound of a bone snapping. The gun discharged anyway. A bullet grazed the side of Jenna's head, burning her severely. She fought the urge to cry out in pain. Millimeters closer and she would have been dead.

She unloaded on her attacker, but Kato's intrepid attack, and her gunfire, had made them targets. The dog yelped piteously as three bullets ripped into his side, slamming the shepherd into the news anchor's desk with such force that he shattered the network logo.

Enraged, Jenna turned her weapon on the man who'd shot the dog, hitting him twice in the neck. Then she saw a wounded Korean hobbling for cover and reaching for his ankle holster. From thirty feet away, she took him out with three shots.

She spun around, as stunned by the sudden lull as much as she had been shocked by the onslaught of killing.

Five New York City Police officers rushed into the studio, weapons drawn. The North Koreans were all on the floor, bleeding and unmoving. One of New York City's finest was on his radio. Another came up beside her.

"Jenna Withers," he said gently, "can you give me your weapon?"

She heard him, knew that he'd requested the gun, but she wasn't giving it up. She simply couldn't, and did not know why. The next instant, Jenna heard whimpering and rushed to Kato, shadowed by the cop who wanted her gun. The dog's long body shook visibly and blood spilled from his mouth, but he wasn't the creature making the sad sound.

When she looked around she spotted a Korean aiming his gun at an officer who had his back to him. Jenna shot the Korean twice—and almost got herself killed in the momentary confusion that followed. Three officers drew their guns on her, but the cop who'd asked for Jenna's weapon jumped in front of her, shouting, "No, don't shoot. Don't shoot." He took her weapon. She did not resist.

As the police stood down, Jenna heard the whimpering again. Disgusted, she walked to the bullet-riddled weather screen and looked behind it, finding a disturbance that felt far more objectionable than any muscle flexing by Mother Nature: Marv.

Jenna looked at him crouched down, and checked her anger. "It's okay, Marv. It's over. You can come out now."

"It's never going to be over. I'm going to have post-traumatic stress disorder the rest of my life because of you."

"Marv, I just saved your life," she managed to say evenly.

"You? You saved *me*?" He stood up. "The only reason you're alive is that I dragged you to safety, and then you almost got me killed when you started freaking out and trying to run away."

Jenna shook her head and turned from him: She had no time for Marv, not with Dafoe shot and possibly dead downstairs. But as she rushed away she did notice that camera one was still on, and a monitor on the studio wall showed a wide shot with Marv clearly visible at its very center. She realized that the gun battle had been broadcast live, every gritty second of it. Every hugely embarrassing second—if you were Marv.

She never stopped in front of the camera to warn the world about the North Korean rockets. Shock was slowly overtaking Jenna, and her thoughts could not escape the fallen. She paused only once before racing downstairs: She knelt by the German shepherd that had saved her life, and checked his pulse. Then she yelled, "Someone call a vet, please." The stalwart heart still beat.

Jenna bolted out of the studio, past officers and emergency medical technicians consumed by the crime and all its gruesome tally. She didn't stop till she found Dafoe lying on his back, eyes open but unseeing. Their emptiness formed a void in Jenna that felt dark and rank and endless.

She dropped to her knees in a puddle of her lover's blood, and with her hands shaking visibly, she controlled herself long enough to check his pulse. He had a heartbeat, but it wasn't strong—and the puddle swelled.

Two EMTs ran up.

"He was hit in the back at least once," Jenna said, moving aside for them.

Now, for the first time, she realized that tears were spilling down her face. She wiped them away, smearing more blood on her cheek. It also dripped to her neck from the bullet that had grazed her head.

Slowly, as she stood, she became aware that news photographers and video camera operators were focusing on her, present like phantoms, silent and surreal.

Jenna never could have known during these grief-filled moments that the photos of her that would appear in seconds on the Web would never be forgotten, or that one of them would earn a Pulitzer for a journalist at the *Times*. His carefully framed shot would reveal a beautiful young meteorologist with a wash of blood in her white blond hair and red streaks painting her face, standing with her hands hanging limply by her side, eyes wide with deepening sorrow.

* * *

Nicci sat in front of Dafoe's laptop carefully—*scrupulously*—executing the keystrokes. No room for error. None. Dafoe had been adamant about that: "Hunt and peck only. I don't care how good you are. Go slowly. One mistake and the whole sequence falls apart, and there's no going back."

The pressure on Nicci was enormous. Jenna hadn't given the world the warning it needed. Nicci had seen it all—Jenna's bloody entrance into the studio followed by a brief disappearance. Then her star had gotten a pistol from somewhere and come up firing. Nicci had guessed that with every passing second, millions of new viewers had tuned into *The Morning Show*. Nothing like this had ever been seen on television—a gun battle in real time, with real death.

And real consequences: Jenna had looked like she was in shock when the shooting stopped. When she'd walked past the camera without pause, Nicci had glimpsed horror on her friend's face, and had understood her muteness: Although Jenna had grown up hunting, and had been handy with both a rifle and pistol since childhood, she'd never shot a person before. When her face had filled the screen for that fleeting second, Nicci had seen not only the horror, not only blood and tears, but sadness so deep that she herself had filled with the ghostly presence of grief. Her own eyes had quickly pooled and spilled.

Two more keystrokes. "Don't fuck up," Nicci admonished herself aloud. Forensia and Sang-mi stared at her, faces wracked by tension.

Nicci finished typing. All she had to do was hit "return." She pointed her index finger, noticed it trembling, and tapped the bar. She breathed like it was the first air she'd taken in a century.

"Let's check," Forensia said immediately.

"You do it." Nicci couldn't sit still a moment longer.

Forensia took her seat, navigated to WhiteHouse.gov, and saw the result of their hacking in all its cyber-glory: A news banner about the North Koreans and the sulfate rockets crawled across the screen beneath a photograph of President Reynolds in the Rose Garden. Nicci guessed that it *might* take thirty seconds for CNN, FOX, and all the other networks, cable channels, and news websites to hijack the banner as effectively as Al Qaeda had taken control of that supertanker.

"You did it," whispered Forensia. The Pagan witch sounded awed.

Sang-mi took Nicci's hand and held it tightly. Then she whispered three simple words: "Thank you, Nicci."

Nine thousand miles away, Adnan stared at the TV in the wheelhouse of the *Dick Cheney,* struck speechless by the shootout in a New York City studio. Even the Shopping Channel could no longer entice him with its bejeweled watches and floral tableware. Adnan had abandoned the consumer paradise for Al Jazeera, which replayed the video of the shootout over and over. He could not look away from the mesmerizing violence.

There they were, all kinds of people getting killed—right *now*—then dying all over again in slow motion. Even a big dog had been shot.

Adnan stared in open wonder, watching each gripping moment unfold, completely unaware of the approach of a Navy SEAL, who tackled him and used a familiar-looking device to snip the wires sticking out of Adnan's suicide vest.

Almost in the same instant, a single bullet killed the Waziristani and ended the hijacking.

Adnan, pinned to the floor with his vest stripped off and his hands cuffed behind his back, heard the old guy who'd been drinking Satan's nectar talking again, speaking a sloppy language that the devout Muslim would never understand.

In a mountain fortress near Pyongyang—long hidden from Western eyes in the sky—Jae-hwa held the old Bakelite phone to his ear with one hand; his other rested on the world's most powerful switch.

All the missile silos were open. All the rockets were ready to launch. Jae-hwa had watched them roll into position, moved by an army proud of its mission, prouder still of its Supreme Leader.

Now Jae-hwa waited to hear the most important words that would ever be spoken on this planet—an order only the Supreme Leader could give.

Jae-hwa's ears soon thrilled to the man's voice. The Supreme Leader spoke gravely, as appropriate for the command that must come. But the loyal soldier, who would have given his own life to spare the Supreme Leader so much as a bee sting or splinter, could scarcely believe what he heard:

"Do not fire the rockets. Every country in the world looks to us for guidance now. I command the world stage. Even men who think they are stronger than us are bowing to me. We do not wish to destroy the world when they know they must give us their full attention—and so much more."

Yes, command the world stage. That is your due, Supreme Leader. Jae-hwa wanted to say this and so much more, but he remained silent until he was sure the Supreme Leader had finished speaking. Then Jae-hwa kept his words simple and humble, as he knew he should, thanking the Supreme Leader for his wisdom, and assuring him that every man, woman, and child would fill with gratitude for his most cherished words.

The Supreme Leader hung up. Jae-hwa took his hand from the shiny silver button, and his thoughts turned to the child in his home, the son who was the treasure of Jae-hwa's life. He felt certain that his boy would sleep tonight—and many more nights to come—in a world no colder than the one he already knew.

EPILOGUE

The funerals came first. The two Joes—Joe Santoro and Joe English—had died trying to stop the North Korean assassins. Jenna attended both services, as did dozens of her fellow network employees. Genuine grief filled the faces of everyone in attendance. The men were well liked and deeply appreciated. Jenna contributed generously to funds for the families of both men.

Geoff Parks had survived. His dog, Kato, hit three times, also pulled through. Master and dog were both healing. Jenna looked forward to seeing the pair patrolling the studio after the first of the year, when they were expected to return to duty.

Jenna did not end up in a supermax, despite the vice president's threats. To her surprise, her efforts to draw attention to the North Korean rockets were credited with sparking a huge surge in voting, which exit polls said proved decisive to President Reynolds's reelection. Roger Lilton conceded the race early and eloquently.

Not only was potential imprisonment never mentioned again but

Jenna, Dafoe, Forensia, and Sang-mi, along with her father, were even feted in a secret White House ceremony. The president cited their "valiant efforts to draw attention to the worst threat the world has ever known."

Jenna also remained on the task force. When the group met again, Senator Higgens gave her a big boozy hug and offered her a substantial stipend to serve on the United States Energy Institute's board of directors.

"But that would compromise my integrity," Jenna said, genuinely aghast at the proposal.

"I tried," Higgens replied with a weighty shrug, reminding Jenna that the energy industry, no matter how great its failings, never allowed itself to become mired in self-doubt, embarrassment, or remorse—not as long as profits flowed thick as crude.

North Korea proved as difficult to deal with as Big Oil and Big Coal. On election day, President Reynolds sent secret messages to the Supreme Leader telling the tyrant that he held him in the highest esteem for his wisdom, wit, and intellect—and by the way, would the Great One please keep the sulfates in the silos in exchange for thousands of tons of food, medicine, and firearms of a distinctly smaller variety, along with luxury items that only a distinguished man with the rarefied taste of the Supreme Leader could truly appreciate?

The pandering went on into the wee hours of the following morning, but Reynolds's willingness to extend the most craven compliments might have saved the world from years of winter, mass starvation, and countless wars.

The president also called on the U.N. to hold a special session to air the grievances of less-developed countries over the impact of climate change. Whether it was simply spin on the president's part remained to be seen, but sometimes spin was a prerequisite to turning around a crisis.

Andrea Hanson took maternity leave the day after the gun battle in the studio. Elfren promptly appointed Jenna as the interim host of *The Morning Show,* and named Nicci as the new executive producer. Eight weeks later Andrea delivered a healthy baby girl, whose photo Jenna displayed the next morning to much rejoicing. Viewers of *The Morning*

Show flooded the network with hundreds of thousands of congratulatory e-mails.

The network had cut Marv loose faster than a trash fish on a tuna charter. While the tabloid press heralded Jenna with lively and largely laudatory headlines such as WEATHER GAL RAINS BANG-BANG ON BAD BOYZ and HURRICANE JENNA STORMS STUDIO, Marv received the less flattering sobriquet of WEATHER MAP WEENIE. The only job he could land was in Boise, Idaho, producing an early morning farm report called *The Spud Spot*.

Marv wasn't the only one caught in a lie on camera. James Elfren received video of Alicia Gant from an anonymous source. The video showed Alicia in front of the entrance to the Golden Crescent Hotel badgering Jenna to say exactly what the producer wanted to hear. Elfren promptly suspended Gant, which proved wise. The same video was leaked to a *Times* reporter, who wrote a scathing story that called into question all twelve of Gant's Emmys, seven of them for reports on terrorism. The next day Elfren fired Gant, saying that the network had conducted a review of her work and found violations of news-gathering principles too egregious to permit her continued employment. She filed suit for wrongful termination. She never formally charged Nicci with sexual harassment, but Nicci showed Jenna a string of annoying e-mails asking her for a "discreet date." Nicci ignored Gant's messages.

Jenna had a pretty good idea where the damning video had come from: the crew that Gant had treated so poorly. Alicia had violated more than common decency in ordering them about like slaves, she'd violated common sense: If you abuse people who can expose your lies, they'll hoop you at the first opportunity.

Jenna's personal life also beamed brightly. Every Friday after work, she abandoned New York City for Dafoe's farm. He'd healed fully from the gunshot wound that had almost taken out a kidney. Bayou also recovered handsomely and greeted her every Friday with as much enthusiasm as his master. Living together on weekends felt like a beta launch for the rest of their lives. As for marriage and children: not yet, Jenna decided. But soon. He was, after all, "the one."

Rick Birk had an altogether rockier experience in the days and weeks after the end of the hijacking. Initially, he was acclaimed for enduring torture, dismemberment, and extreme privation, but almost immediately it was discovered that the captain had been the source of the chopped-off fingers, and that Birk had encouraged the savagery to spare his own hide. Coupled with his drunken appearances on camera before and during the hijacking that were deemed unbecoming of a correspondent, Elfren forced him to retire at the age of seventy-four.

Alas, Birk did not go gently into the night. Rather, he plunged right back into the public eye, proving that in the age of the Internet, there *are* second acts in American life. Birk, like the shootout video, went viral—with the most unlikely companion.

Beaver Falls Glove Company had the squirrelly but intriguing idea to bring together Birk and Captain Moreno for a Web-based ad campaign. Beaver Falls's CEO took a considerable portion of the small firm's earnings for the previous year to pay Birk a fat six figures—the captain half as much—to appear side by side.

Birk, glassy-eyed but not falling-down drunk, sat wearing a pair of Beaver Falls Rick Birk Signature Edition Fingerless Gloves. A large moose head loomed over him from the wall of a hunting lodge. To Birk's left sat a dour-faced Captain Moreno.

"My recent experiences," Birk intoned imperiously, "have taught me the value of fingerless gloves." Birk offered a drinker's generous smile and picked up a tall gin and tonic. "Because, let's face it, sometimes you need all your fingers to handle the finer things in life," said America's most notorious dipsomaniac before draining the drink in a single go.

Moreno glared at him and turned to the camera. Speaking in awkward, recently acquired English, the Spaniard said, "And sometimes you do not need to have gloves with fingers." At this point, he raised his pitiable hand, which had been left with only a pinkie and ring finger to poke out of a red glove. "So why pay for more glove than you really need?" asked the captain, still palpably pissed off.

"That's one thing we can both agree on," Birk said. Then with a glance at the steaming captain, Birk added, "Maybe the only thing."

The captain glared back at Birk, then stared at his miserable hand.

Okay, till now the ad remained marginally within the realm of, well, if not *good* taste, at least reasonable standards, but then Birk snarled, "Oh, stop your goddamn whining. All the time, it's 'What happened to my fingers? What happened to my fingers?' I'll tell you what's happened to your goddamn fingers. I got them. Wore them right off the fucking boat. Here," Birk tossed three bloody fingers at the captain, "let me give you a hand." Then Birk reached behind him. "And here's my shirt. It's got your goddamn blood all over it. Go get it cleaned, it's the least you can do."

The ad ended with a look of shock and outrage on the captain's face.

Later, it came out of course that the entire finale had been staged with the help of "fingers" from a special effects company in L.A., but not before the ad achieved record viewership on YouTube. It also appeared on all the networks and major cable channels, replete with bleeps, where news anchors and show hosts demonstrated indefatigable disgust—even after repeated showings of the entire thirty-second spot.

GreenSpirit's murder was solved, but not as Sheriff Walker had planned. He was charged with the crime, and after dark-suited FBI agents escorted the handcuffed lawman to an unmarked vehicle and drove him away, the special agent in charge of the New York office, Albert Messinger, held a carefully planned press conference. In his prepared statement, he announced that key evidence against Walker had come as a result of "extensive and painstaking" searches over a ten-square-mile area surrounding the cabin in which GreenSpirit had been killed.

"Agents discovered a tiny swatch of clothing containing both Sheriff Walker's DNA and the victim's," Special Agent Messinger said, his blue eyes roving over a phalanx of reporters. "The swatch," which Messinger described as about one inch in diameter, "had been caught on the broken branch of a dead maple tree."

"What about the bloody bandana that the sheriff said *he* found?" fired a short reporter with the bleary, haunted look of too many martinis for too many years. "That had the kid's DNA on it, didn't it?"

"It did, indeed," Messenger replied, evidently warming to the task at hand. "We believe that Jason Robb's DNA was placed on it by the sheriff when he took the young man into custody, which he did by himself despite being part of what was supposed to have been a coordinated state, federal, and local effort. As I'm sure many of you are aware from all the prime-time tutorials on forensics that you can watch almost any night of the week," Messinger smiled, wrinkling his handsomely tanned face, "the sheriff could have lifted Robb's DNA from the bars of his cell, or from Robb directly, without the young man realizing it, and that could have been enough to implicate him. As for GreenSpirit's blood, we believe Walker committed the crime, so he had ample access to that."

"Is that all you've got?" carped a regional reporter who had just written a lengthy story that lionized the sheriff for his "courage, thoroughness, and diligence."

"We think the DNA evidence is sufficient to convict the sheriff of murder, but we also have other compelling evidence against him. Let's start with Sheriff Walker's contention that Robb disappeared the weekend of the murder of the Pagan in Vermont. We now know that that was the weekend that Robb and his girlfriend made their first trip to her family's cabin. The young woman in question would not confirm this detail until she learned that she was pregnant. The timing of conception, while not conclusive, does support her claim, as do paternity tests that were conducted at the Bureau's request. We also now have a credit card receipt placing Robb at a convenience store near the Wennerstroms' cabin two hours before the murder of the Vermont victim, as determined by a medical examiner in that state and confirmed by the FBI's crime lab. It is not possible for Robb to have committed that murder, either."

"Then are you suggesting that Sheriff Walker murdered the Vermont Pagan?" asked a stout, gray-haired female reporter.

"No, we do not believe those crimes were committed by the same killer."

"Then how do you explain the similarities between the two?" bellowed a rugged, well-known New York media figure who sounded highly skeptical.

"An examination of Sheriff Walker's hard drive on his home computer showed that he used his privileged position as a law enforcement officer to request confidential files containing unreported details of the Vermont crime. We believe that he used that information to commit a copycat killing and to implicate Jason Robb in both murders.

"We also found that Walker had personal motives, both for murdering GreenSpirit and for attempting to frame Robb. The sheriff was extremely upset at his daughters' involvement with Paganism, and numerous times expressed those concerns to members of his church, who were forthright in speaking to us. We believe that Walker's anger reached murderous proportions when he learned that his oldest daughter attended a naked initiation ceremony. He found out about this because of a televised report by CBS News in which his daughter could be clearly seen and identified. Jason Robb made no secret of the fact that he directed the news crew to the initiation and gave her name to the press."

"So the sheriff was trying to kill two birds with one stone?" asked a reporter for a Spanish language radio station. "GreenSpirit and Robb?"

"You could say that," Messinger replied.

"Has Robb been released?" the reporter followed up.

"Yes, earlier this morning. He's with his family."

Those who knew the young man couldn't help but ask themselves whether Jason had been chastened by his arrest as a serial killer. The answer was no. Not in the least.

After Aly revealed her pregnancy—and announced that they planned to marry—Jason pulled a Levi Johnston to her Bristol Palin. "No way, dude," was his surly response, delivered with animated hand signs that were vaguely derivative of gang culture, on his Facebook page.

Other mysteries, however, remained unsolved. Forensia and Sangmi, for example, could not contact GreenSpirit again, despite holding five séances. They finally attributed the Pagan leader's ongoing silence to the peace that she'd found since her killer had been arrested. Then they turned their attention to the ongoing drought. A gathering of Pagans, in the familiar clearing where the initiation had taken place, performed a rain-summoning ritual.

Jenna, hearing of this plan, was skeptical. Both she and Dafoe were surprised when, moments after the ritual was scheduled to end, it began to rain. And this was no mere thunderstorm, here today, gone in an hour. The rain held steady for three full days, and when it ended the reservoir where Jenna and Dafoe had met held water for the first time in more than a year—enough to cover the carcasses and skeletons of drought-stricken deer and coyotes.

The last mystery was a murder in the Maldives that proved the final footnote to the tanker hijacking.

Adnan's mother found Parvez's body shifting in the restless tide on the island of Dhiggaru, a bullet wound in the back of his head, a bag of limes with a bomb lying feet away on the beach. The Maldivian media speculated that Khulood had played a lethal role in the murder of her son's oldest friend. She had plenty of reasons for revenge. Adnan had been hauled off to an American prison in Afghanistan and Maldivian authorities had told her that it was doubtful that a man who'd been a would-be suicide bomber would ever be released. Men suspected of far less serious crimes had been held at the prison for years.

But no evidence was found that linked Khulood to Parvez's violent demise, although the bag of limes hinted that perhaps the cleric had wanted Adnan's mother to smuggle the fruit—and the bomb—to diamond island.

In any case, there appeared to be little interest in solving the crime. Khulood did make one public statement. Translated into English it read: "Crime? What crime?" Many in the international community quietly agreed with her concise assessment.

Rafan was not among them, ironically enough. He saw that his beautiful island nation was succumbing to the brutalities that had long afflicted the rest of the world, including the erosion of the rule of law. But he had vowed to try to stop the spread of jihad, and imbued with that spirit he visited Dhiggaru one last time. He walked the shore where Parvez's body had been found, searching for evidence that might have eluded less interested investigators. He found nothing.

His eyes roamed from the ocean to the acres of land that he'd had ravaged for soil, when as minister of dirt he robbed Peter to pay Paul.

Then Rafan looked back to the shoreline creeping ever closer, like ecoterrorism in a world slowly engulfed by the sea.

The warm salty water rushed over his bare feet, and when he stepped away the evidence of his presence vanished as easily as might the protective sky that enveloped the Earth and gave it life.

AUTHOR'S NOTE

Recently I've read a lot about geoengineering and what role scientists might play in finding ways to eliminate or reduce the warming that has been going on around the planet the past twenty years. Is it conceited for mankind to even think it could actually alter the planet's climate, or could this possibly be a reality? After all, we know that for thousands of years volcanoes have put ash and sulfates into the atmosphere and have altered weather patterns around the world, causing changes that have lasted for years.

Take the volcanic eruption at Tambora in 1815 that created "the summer that never was" in the northeastern United States. In 1816 the ash cloud that circled the globe caused so much atmospheric cooling that snow fell during June and July. So it would be only natural for scientists to theorize that sulfates, artificially placed in the atmosphere, would behave like a volcanic ash cloud. The sulfates would reflect the sun's rays back into space, cooling the Earth.

So, could some type of geoengineering be the solution to planetary climate change?

The main contributor to global warming is water vapor from the Earth's oceans. If you could cool the oceans, would that not cool the water vapor, and eventually the planet?

One solution geoengineers have proposed involves the use of iron. Tons of iron oxide dumped into the oceans could significantly lower the Earth's temperature, counterbalancing the heating going on elsewhere in the world. However, these noble intentions could have a great cost, and all geoengineering theories are essentially untried.

That volcanic eruption in Tambora is actually a classic example of what can go wrong. The ash from the volcano caused worldwide cooling and an abrupt drop in temperature. The result was widespread famine in 1815 and 1816 as crops failed due to lack of sunlight and warmth. Livestock, deprived of hay and feed, starved. Hundreds of thousands of people died. Too much cooling could have just the same effect as too much warming—throwing the planet's atmospheric engine out of balance. The right amount of iron poured into the oceans may cure global warming, but is the risk worth the reward?

Recent news reports have detailed no overall rise in global temperatures between 1998 and 2008. News accounts suggest that China's release of sulfates into the atmosphere from coal-burning industrial plants has caused the planet to become cooler.

Iron oxide or sulfates: could they be a geoengineering answer or a planetary nightmare?